D0435706

This special hardcover edition of
The Blood of Ten Chiefs
was published by

**FATHER
TREE
PRESS**

5 Reno Road
Poughkeepsie, NY 12603

The Blood of Ten Chiefs

ELFQUEST®

The Blood of Ten Chiefs

Vol.1

Edited by
**Richard Pini,
Robert Asprin
and
Lynn Abbey**

A TOM DOHERTY ASSOCIATES BOOK

THE BLOOD OF TEN CHIEFS

Copyright © 1986 by WaRP Graphics, Inc.

Elfquest® is a registered trademark of WaRP Graphics, Inc.
Thieves' World® is a registered trademark of Robert Lynn Asprin and Lynn Abbey.

First printing: December 1986

A TOR Book

Published by Tom Doherty Associates, Inc.
49 West 24 Street
New York, N.Y. 10010

Cover art by Wendy Pini

ISBN: 0-812-53041-1
CAN. ED.: 0-812-53042-X

Printed in the United States of America

0   9   8   7   6   5   4   3   2   1

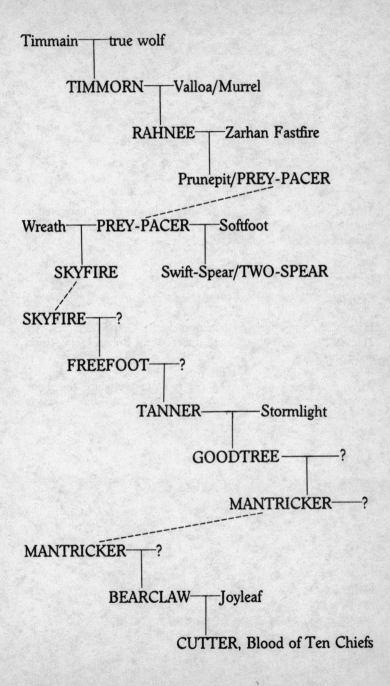

Timmain —┬— true wolf

TIMMORN —┬— Valloa/Murrel

RAHNEE —┬— Zarhan Fastfire

Prunepit/PREY-PACER

Wreath —┬— PREY-PACER —┬— Softfoot

SKYFIRE

Swift-Spear/TWO-SPEAR

SKYFIRE —┬— ?

FREEFOOT —┬— ?

TANNER —┬— Stormlight

GOODTREE —┬— ?

MANTRICKER —— ?

MANTRICKER —┬— ?

BEARCLAW —┬— Joyleaf

CUTTER, Blood of Ten Chiefs

—Introduction and Editor's Note—

by Richard Pini

Riding the train from Poughkeepsie to Grand Central Terminal and back is not one of life's Great Events, even if it does pass near co-editor Lynn Abbey's ancestral home of Peekskill. (I particularly dislike the lemminglike change of trains at Croton-Harmon. How those who make that four-hour-total commute five days a week do so absolutely escapes me; I content myself with the knowledge that Tantalus is not alone in hell.) Even the generally amusing reporting antics of the *New York Post* wear thin after about fifteen minutes, and then it's stare-out-the-grimy-windows time once again.

However, on Thursday, April 17, 1986 I had a reprieve from the usual Metro North ennui, and what a lovely reprieve it was. I got to read, for the first time all collected in one place, the manuscript for this book, volume one in the series collectively called *The Blood of Ten Chiefs*. And a faster four hours I've never spent.

The Blood of Ten Chiefs owes its genesis to two literary parents: one is the very successful series of graphic stories known en masse as Elfquest, created by far-too-talented-for-the-likes-of-me and very patient wife Wendy and myself in 1977; the other is the construct known as the "shared-universe anthology," the creation of which is generally credited to the far-too-talented-etc. team of Robert Asprin and Lynn Abbey with their Thieves' World collections, begun in 1978. (So what is my function among all these far-too-talented people? I exploit. It's an ancient and honorable profession.)

About Elfquest, more in a bit. About Thieves' World and the Asprin-Abbey alliance: We (Wendy and I) have known them (Bob and Lynn) for a bunch of years. We met, more or less, in the bar at a science-fiction convention, which is one of the most open-door inside jokes there is. We got to talking about this and that and books and comics and publishing; I think that it took all of about ten minutes for us to start proposing deals to each other and to come up with ideas for new and progressively more outrageous projects. As it turns out, Bob and I talk the same language. Different accents, but definitely the same language. They were already involved with Thieves' World; we were already involved with Elfquest.

I won't bore anyone with the strange and convoluted intricacies of how a massive project like Thieves' World (and, by extrapolation, all such anthologies) came to be; Bob has written a very entertaining essay on that subject in the first TW volume. Find it, buy it, read it, and be enlightened. However, there is at least one major difference between *The Blood of Ten Chiefs* and Thieves' World—in fact between *TBOTC* and every other shared-universe anthology I know of. And that difference is that while the various characters who inhabit Sanctuary, the central TW city (I must fall back on initials, else I'll go crazy), may roam all over the landscape, they are still rooted solidly in a single time period. One character can stumble across another in an alleyway, for example. But in the world of Elfquest, the history of the ten chiefs of the title spans approximately *ten thousand years*. Since ascendancy to chiefhood is by bloodline succession, chief number one probably doesn't have too much to say to chief number eight. Maybe.

I know. Time out. Just who are these chiefly characters, anyway?

As I mentioned a bit earlier, all of these stories are based on and in the storyworld called Elfquest, which takes place on the physical planet which we've named the World of Two Moons (which name, I hope, needs no explanation). The first chapter of the original quest saga was written and illustrated in 1977; the tale concluded with the publication of chapter twenty in late 1984. Since then, that original story has seen publication in a variety of incarnations: as comics, as handsome collected volumes, as a novelization. All quite successful. The main character was (and is; we're not finished by a long shot!) named Cutter, Blood of Ten Chiefs, and we alluded very briefly in the comics series to the line of Cutter's forebears that stretched back into misty and half-forgotten history. Readers and fans being who they are, bless them, quickly made it known to us that they wanted to know more about these shadowy characters.

By the way, and in case there is any question, Cutter and his kin and tribe-mates are elves.

About elves. There are those creative people out there who will staunchly maintain that they know all about who elves are and what these creatures are supposed to be and act like. These tale-spinners, for the most part, have written stories about elves and maintain that if it doesn't look and act like the beasties they've chronicled, then it ain't elves. Well, I say it's spinach.

Elfquest elves have exactly two things in common with most of the *haute* elves populating much of what passes for fantasy these days: their ears, which are pointed. Other than that, the transplanted (for they are not native to this place) denizens of the World of Two Moons adhere to none of the well-known, well-used conventions concerning the little people. No polysyllabic, tongue-twisting names, no effete mannerisms, no *thee*s and *thou*s, no enchanted swords, stones, gems, or other paraphernalia, and no unicorns. Sensuality, yes—of a most real and earthy nature, for the elves of these stories are primal spirits who know how to love the here and now. Magic, yes—but of a natural kind that comes from within, from the mind and heart rather than the supernatural. The naming of names, yes—but names which are won from the land and the struggle to survive in it, names that carry their weight in blood and pride. And lagniappe: our elves are allied with and ride wolves, because wolves are the most magnificent social animals we know, and what better?

(At this point I would be remiss if I didn't suggest to those folk curious about the original Elfquest saga that they find Books One through Four at fine bookstores everywhere and give them a perusal. The rich story and accompanying background isn't absolutely necessary to the enjoyment of *these* tales, but what's mashed potatoes without gravy?)

So one day, about two years ago, Wendy and I were wondering how we might fulfill the readers' wishes for more information on the ten chiefs, and we came up with the idea of a storybook: ten stories, ten vignettes from each life. We'd write the stories ourselves, and perhaps even publish the book ourselves. We mentioned this to Bob and Lynn, who grinned impishly, and suggested, "Why not do it as a continuing anthology, like Thieves' World, just to pick an example from thin air. We'll even help with the authors and the editing."

I said, "That's a great idea!" Heavyweight writers, I exulted. A major publisher. Respectability.

Stomach butterflies the size of adult pteranodon.

Back to the train ride. I'll be the first to admit, as the fledgling co-editor in the group, that I had my concerns as deadline time drew near. Would the various authors understand characters and a world which had already been created? (This is another difference between *Ten Chiefs* and Thieves' World. The construction of Sanctuary was a joint project from the word go; Hotel Two Moons was by that time up and running—and *furnished!*) Would the background information

Wendy and I'd provided be sufficient? Would the manuscripts come in on time? Would the book be out on time?

Somewhere between Beacon and New Hamburg my fears melted away. For not only did I have a pile of wonderful, exciting, varied, individual stories in my lap, but I could see that a certain synergy, peculiar to shared-universe anthologies, was starting to evolve. That synergy is what happens when one author takes a look at another author's story, says, "Hmmm," and works a tie-in into his or her own piece. It is what takes a bunch of snippets and turns them into a thread. Ten thousand years be damned—we have continuity! And I hear that some of the stories in this volume are actually planned to bridge into the next. What a tangled web. I love it.

To wrap this up, I need to take a cue from a bit of advice that appeared, again, in Thieves' World. (The relationship between Asprin, Abbey, Pini, and Pini truly is not as incestuous as it appears from this introduction—at least, I'll never admit to it.) This sage advice has to do with internal consistency.

The perceptive reader—and particularly that reader who may already be a fan of Elfquest—may come across this or that bit of information (dialogue, exposition, characterization) that seems inconsistent or even at odds with something else read somewhere else. This may produce a certain sensation of cognitive discomfort unless the reader remembers two important rules:

1) There are no inconsistencies.

2) If an inconsistency is discovered, refer to Rule 1.

Seriously, any bending or stretching of what heretofore (or hereafter) might have been considered "reality" is no doubt due to one or more of the following:

First, each writer in this collection has his or her own style, his or her own fascination, his or her own approach, his or her own prejudices, and so on. As long as a writer stays within the (deliberately) flexible boundaries of this world, *vivent les differences!*

Second, the characters in here, major and minor, have their own motivations, memories, needs, and desires no less so than the aforementioned writers. Probably more so. They (the characters) act as they are driven, and while I in my biased way tend to imbue all of them with a certain nobility, in no way should they be considered to be namby-pamby. They act as we might.

Finally, because these characters tend to live a long while (by human standards), and because they tend to think in the present rather than dwell on the past, memories of things get hazy. Lessons learned by one chief may or may not survive the test of time. Cause and effect may become jumbled in the retelling of an event. Apparently, the oral application of dreamberries aids memory, but the potent intoxication that follows may wipe out any benefit thus derived!

(By the way, we do welcome letters of comment; just write to us in care of the publisher.)

The World of Two Moons is a new, fresh, raw place, with many gray areas on the map, and that map will be a long time in the filling. The history of the ten chiefs who lead up to Cutter is likewise peppered with gaps and forgotten tales waiting to be told. And I must say that I look forward with wolfish anticipation to *that* process of mutual discovery.

They had given Whiteclaw back to the forest and the pack that morning. The old wolf had spent his last days in the soft grass beside his elf-friend's den. It had been midnight, or later, when Briar realized the time for mercy had finally arrived and had summoned the healer, Rain, from his root-nest den.

Although the bond between elf-friend and wolf-friend was a special, private thing, the ties between the Wolfriders and the wolf-pack were almost as close. The wolves began their howl before Rain had lifted his hands from Whiteclaw's neck. Those elves who were at the Father Tree made their way to Briar's den to share his sorrow and say farewell to a friend.

There were few among the elves who had not said good-bye to a wolf-friend at least once. One was the chief's young son who had not, as it happened, witnessed such a leave-taking with open, comprehending eyes. He *knew* their wolves, though long-lived for forest animals, could not hope to live as long as a Wolfrider, but he had not *felt* it before. His tongue went as stiff and lifeless as old leather; his fingers refused to touch the somehow-different fur.

With no thoughts except his own despair, Cutter shook off his mother's gentle mindtouch and plunged into the forest at a blind run. He called to Nightrunner, his own wolf-friend. The young wolf, confronted with a choice between his pack and his elf-friend, hesitated only a moment before coming to Cutter's side. He, too, loved the hunt but felt no peace in the presence of death.

They were still together late in the day when Longreach, prompted by a grief he had witnessed many times before, found them. The old elf said nothing at first, just sat where they could see him and feel his compassion. Finally, when the sun began to set, the storyteller spoke.

"The pack and Briar have both chosen, and a fine choice indeed. A yearling so full of wild-water he can only call him Mischief and hope that his den, his clothes and his arrows survive—"

How? The youth's thought rode a wave of emptiness into the old elf's mind. For Cutter, deep in the Now of the wolf-song, there could only be Nightrunner; beyond Nightrunner was an emptiness that made midnight bright by comparison.

"It is part of the Way," Longreach said, laying a hand on both wolf and elf. "It is part of what it means to be a Wolfrider: to dive so deeply into life and love that you lose all sense of yourself and the turning of the seasons; to wake up one morning and find yourself a new person, sometimes full of joy and sometimes pain; and then to dive back in again.

"It has been like this since the beginning. I'll show you—"

Pendulum

by Richard Pini

This time, and for the first time, death bothered Timmorn.

That in itself was very strange, for this twilight hunt seemed little different from any of the others that mingled in the half-elf's memory. Memory itself was mostly an elusive thing for Timmorn, images of recent yesterdays swirling and clouding like muddied water with sensations of long ago— which might be an eight-of-days or many turns of the seasons. But something in this evening, something twisting in his mind as a light snow began to dust the woods, something nibbled at him, something . . .

Certainly it was not, could not be the killing of the prey, the death of the black-neck. That had been a good kill, though Timmorn had participated only little in it. The wolves, the wolves who were his—brothers—no. Yes? His friends, yes, that too. The killing of the prey, the chase, the fluidity of his brother-friends as they ran and harried, the tearing of the throat, the shock and final, reflexive shudder—these were not the source of the irritating itch that Timmorn felt at the back of his mind. All this had happened before.

He paced, restless, tasting his memories of this hunt, sorting by scent and touch this one from the others, seeking a clue. It worried at him, as a burr that he could not reach might. He pulled into clearer focus pleasure at the tang of the hot blood as the buck gave up its life into the ground and to the tongues of the wolf-pack. Pleasure, yes, even though he

9

had not done much to bring down the prey, though he was not really of the pack. Pleasure because blood was strong in the air and on Timmorn's face. Without thinking, he ran his tongue over the sharp teeth that had, after the high wolves had taken their due, helped to break the joints and pull the red muscle from the bones. Yes, it had been a good kill, and promised to be . . .

A promise. The tribe! The fine buck could fill the bellies of the wolves, but Timmorn caught another shred of memory: there would be enough for himself and the ones he had left behind, at the camp. There would be meat for the elves left behind who did not hunt. But the promise was broken, and his stomach was still empty and growled at the blood-taste which promised nothing. There would be no meat. The mad longtooth had seen to that.

Was that it? Timmorn held in his pacing and cocked his head as if to listen more closely to the question in his head. Flakes of snow gathered on his wild hair and pointed ears, and his eyes, his yellow eyes, seemed to glow in the lowering light. Was that it? The pack had only begun to feed when the attack came. Snouts slick and clotted with sweet blood, the wolves did not sense the raging, silvery mass of the rogue longtooth until it was among them, yowling and scattering the smaller beasts in its frenzy. The wolves closest to the carcass had gotten the worst of it, but they had all—all? —escaped the longtooth's fury and tusks. Timmorn held onto the picture in his head: the creature, eyes wild; the wound, ugly and half-healed, that ran along the thing's flank; he remembered the stink of infection. The beast had not come out of its dark place to attack the wolf-pack. No, it had come to feed, to take what the others had brought down, what it no longer could bring down because of its wound and its madness. But that still meant that the pack went hungry now, and that the tribe would go hungry. There would be disappointment, keenly felt, and Timmorn knew even as he thought it that that disappointment would be turned toward him. The longtooth had taken the carcass, and neither Timmorn nor the wolves would follow into the deep forest.

The tall elf, neither wolf nor high one like the ones left behind, glanced back at the spot where the buck had been, where the blanket of pine needles had been thrashed about, where the snow was beginning to cover the blood-soaked earth. The meat was gone, taken. And he saw again, as he had forgotten before, that one wolf was dead.

Timmorn gazed at the torn and ruined body of the wolf. He had known it—it was a young male—as much as he could know any member of the pack that did not know what to do with him. His eyes, so like wolves' eyes, truly luminous now in the glow of the rising moons, narrowed as he tried to catch a thought. It was the wolf that bothered him; why did the wolf's death gnaw at him? he wondered. Then: why did he think on it at all? Then: why . . . ? He growled, soft and deep in his throat, a sound of frustration and confusion. He was losing the wolf in him, not quite gaining the elf.

Timmorn was unique, and sometimes he knew it, though neither with pride nor self-conscience. His mother, he knew, had been Timmain, one of the firstcomers to the world of two moons, many turns of the seasons ago. Timmain, the high one who had made the sacrifice for the sake of all the firstcomers who still lived, and for all who might come after—through Timmorn. She had been the most powerful of those first, the high ones so ill-suited to this world; she alone had retained the ability to change her own form into the one that would give her people a chance at survival. Timmain, mother, wolf as real as smoke. And as she must, and knew it, she mated and birthed Timmorn. Timmorn of the yellow eyes. To the elves, not an elf. To the wolves, not a wolf.

He did not know how old he was. He did not know what old was, or what it felt like, but his muscles were firm and tight, and his blood sang in him when his mind was not clouded, and he himself had sired young ones, cubs. The wolf part of him cared little for time and its passing, although his elfin mind understood the shifting of the seasons and the changes that he saw in the world. The wolf did not much care for thinking either, for thinking went into the past and, with trouble, into the future, and the wolf was *now*.

Timmorn did not remember his mother very well, for she had whelped and weaned him a long time ago and then disappeared. He thought that she must be dead, for she had been a wolf, and wolves did not live as long as the elves of the tribe, or as long as he. He thought of the wolf-pack, and knew the individuals in his mind as well as he could, and he realized that even though there were certain wolves that lived longer than the others, they all seemed to die eventually. Wolves died.

Timmorn had seen many wolves die. He had seen elves die too, for some of his—mother's?—people had succumbed to the harshness of this world. The high ones were frail and needed protection, and not all of them had even tried to put on animal skins and take up crude spears to survive. So some died. And wolves died. But those deaths had been natural, if unfortunate. Because Timmorn ran with the wolves as often as he mingled with the elves, he had seen it when a wolf, old and grizzled and failing, low in the pack, had been set upon by the others and killed. It was the way. It had not bothered him then.

But now, in this night's dark, this wolf's death would not let him go. When the longtooth's attack had come he had scampered back; he knew he was no match for the maddened predator. The wolves had scattered as well, circling, some limping, but staying out of reach of the larger beast. All had fled—all but one. One wolf, a young male, had gotten caught somehow, had not escaped the deadly rush, had been gored and frightened with pain and caught between the longtooth and its food, and Timmorn and all the wolves had watched, just watched, and the young wolf had growled and snapped its teeth and twisted its body and fought and tried and failed, and the longtooth had torn it and thrown it aside and dragged the black-neck buck into the deep forest. And only after a while did the pack go up and nuzzle the dead wolf. That is the way of it, sensed the half-elf, half-wolf, falling back into the timeless *now* of wolf thought.

Except that this time, and for the first time, death bothered Timmorn.

At the encampment, those who were left behind cared as little for time as did Timmorn or the wolf. They did not think of themselves as the "high ones"; that was a name that the others—the wolf-changed ones like Timmorn and his offspring—were starting to call them. If they were anything in their own minds, they were the firstcomers, the exiles. They felt not at all like a tribe. Loss was their kin.

In their minds the accident was still fresh, the betrayal that had thrown them broken and confused to this world, even though it had happened many cycles ago. Because they had learned in their own world, before the tragedy, to do without time, to live outside of time if they wished, memories lived within them eternally. And they tried in this new, harsh place to recreate the gentle timelessness they remembered.

They were doomed, many of them. The world was relentless, and time crowded in upon them, ate at them, made them aware of its uncaring flow. Their bellies complained with hunger, for the physical molds in which they had cast their bodies needed to eat. They shivered and cramped with cold, for their slender and pale forms were suited for a milder, kinder life. As much as they wished it not to be so, life was no longer timeless, but was lived from meal to meal, from fire to windblown fire. Mind and thought could no longer easily exist in that carefree slice of experience that centered between moments-ago and moments-hence. Talking between minds became sluggish and difficult here, and so the firstcomers must string one spoken word after another. Knowledge of other souls became murky; the exiles gave each other and took sounds that were names.

"Seilein?" The voice was soft, by nature and from tiredness. "Seilein, the fire is going."

The speaker was very tall, very slender. He was a firstcomer, and he wore about him a skin that ill-concealed the tattering remnants of otherworldly clothing. His name was Renn; he had so far survived this primitive world, and if he did not die of starvation, disease, violence, cold, heat or other fatal discomfort, he might live forever. But now the fire was guttering inside his windbreak-shelter and he did not know how—he did not want to know how—to keep it alight. He watched dully as the fire keeper brought dried twigs and stirred the wood to bring forth a bit more heat.

"Renn," Seilein said with gentle disapproval, "it's not all that difficult." As she spoke, she removed the fur-lined cap she'd been wearing out in the flurrying snow; she also took off her laboriously stitched gloves and extended her hands toward the fire. The air around her hands shimmered and the flames bloomed for a moment before settling back.

"All you need to do," she went on, "is to place new wood on the coals now and then. I still have a little of the power to start fires, but it's not always necessary." She knew as she spoke that her words were near to useless. Some of the elves, like herself, had managed over time to shake off the lethargy they all had felt in the beginning. She and those who were like her did not simply want barren survival; they wanted to go forward in any direction. But the others, the ones like Renn—there was a part of them that had not landed on this world, that was trapped somewhere in a gray place. The others, Seilein suspected, would never learn to tend fires, or to be even a little comfortable in the few skins that were able to be magically cured, or learn the stirring of pleasure to be found in the touching of bodies, or to eat the food brought by the barely-skilled hunters and the strange wolf allies. . . .

Food. Even Seilein, who among the firstcomers was most determined to fit herself to this world and its time flow, still must catch herself up out of the timeless thought she was so used to. Food. It was dark, and Timmorn, grudgingly, had told the camp that he would bring back food before it was dark.

Seilein knew things about Timmorn that few if any of the others knew, for she had made up her mind to study him. She found him intriguing, and there were the stirrings of other feelings. She knew that he ran with the wolves but did not seem totally at ease with them—or perhaps it was the wolves who had not quite accepted him. She knew that although the wolves chose the dark for their hunts, the elves preferred to move about during the day. Getting Timmorn to appreciate the difference, and then his getting the wolf-pack to compromise its habits, had been the work of many cycles—no, she corrected herself, time here is measured by the turning of the seasons. And that too was new, for the world she'd come from had not seen seasons in eons.

She heard voices muttering in the gloom that was the encampment, musical voices saying harsh, sad things. By now everyone knew that something was not right, that Timmorn, and more importantly the food, was late. Pulling her gloves and cap back on, Seilein went out of the shelter to check the campfires and to overhear and perhaps partake of the conversations she knew she'd find.

"He's forgotten us again. He's too much his mother's shape, not enough of her mind. We can do as well as he can." That would be Valloa, Seilein thought to herself with a faint smile. One who fancied herself a huntress, with her crude spear. To be fair, Valloa was no worse than any of those who tried to supplement the irregular supply of fresh-killed meat brought by Timmorn; by skill or by luck, she had speared her share of small game. And Seilein knew that as many elves as could must learn to hunt, for even when the wolves brought down a big buck or boar, they did not always let Timmorn take a portion back to the camp. But still, she was amused at Valloa's intolerance.

A male voice answered; it was Marrek, who had turned his skills to the making of useful things from the earth and clay of this place. "I still wonder what it was that Timmain thought when she changed. She said that it was for us, for our survival—I even remember the question she asked before she shifted. 'Might it not be better to be wolf?' I still wonder what she meant, but I can't imagine how she intended her son to aid us when he seems out of place with us *and* with the beasts he follows."

"We just don't know him well enough," Seilein said, joining the small group. "There's reason there; there must be. Even though Timmain's gone, her plan must live on in her son."

"You know it's not easy talking to him," said Valloa, "shy and nervous as he is."

Seilein lowered her eyes and spoke softly. "I'll know him. Somehow."

Valloa humphed, and at that moment a commotion erupted in the farther shelters as Timmorn, snarling and biting at the air, loped into the camp. He paced to and fro, his agitation loud, before coming to a kind of rest by one of the fires. Almost immediately tall figures flowed from tents and weatherbreaks.

"What has he brought?"

"He's late."

"I don't see anything."

"It's been too long. The hunger . . ." And the voice trailed off into a low, sad song of times gone.

"He's failed. Why do we harbor him?"

"Because he's still our best hope," Seilein snapped, surprised at her own reaction to the stream of complaints. She knew that there was disappointment, keenly felt, and she knew that Timmorn bore the brunt of it. She could not really blame them for that, but she did resent that they had stopped trying to live. "Besides," she went on, "there's something different—not right—here."

At this, a few of the elves made expressions of surprise or curiosity; the others muttered and turned away, saddened or disgusted, back to the shelters. Seilein moved closer to Timmorn and felt a thrill of—something like excitement as she touched his shoulder. "Tell us," she urged.

Timmorn stared at her for a long moment, his yellow eyes, disturbing and deep, locked with hers. She wondered how he could not feel what she felt. Again, she floated on a ripple, rode a stirring inside her as Timmorn began to relate the events of the hunt, the kill, the maddened snow beast. So lost was she in the new sensation she experienced, which mingled like a strange, dark herb with the guttural sound of Timmorn's voice, that she nearly missed the rise in his tension as he told of the death of the wolf.

"Wrong!" he snarled. "It's *wrong!*" But he could not say why, and would say no more. Shortly, the remaining elves drifted back to their own shelters and fires, and Timmorn was alone. The camp was quiet again, except for the occasional distant cry of some great creature, deep in the forest.

Days passed, and Timmorn did not hunt again with the wolf-pack, for each night he heard the yowling cry of the wounded longtooth, and he refused to go into the woods. Seilein and the others observed that he still ran with the wolves during the day, but when darkness fell, Timmorn was to be found skulking around the camp, worried and irritated. And even though he did not hunt for them, the elves were not much worse off, for those who could still captured what game they could. Still, tempers began to rise, especially in the firstcomers who would not adapt, and who were the most uncomfortable.

Then one night the forest was quiet again with the stillness of snow and cold. The following day was sharp and bright, and Seilein sought out Timmorn as he drank from an ice-crusted stream a little way from the camp. She approached the shaggy half-elf with a mix of feelings: attraction, timidity, resolve. Timmorn greeted her with no more than a throaty rumble, a wolfish grunt.

''We—we've waited to see what you'll do,'' she ventured. ''The ones who can hunt and I are doing what we can, but . . .'' There was no need for her to finish the thought; all knew that the catches had been poor, that the small game was thinning out or getting more clever. Just as all knew that there was a growing resentment against Timmorn.

Seilein took a deep breath before going on. The tightness in her chest, the excitement she felt in her stomach made talking difficult, for the hunt for food was only partly on her mind. She was not just mind now, but body as well, and the voice of her body was loud in her ears. She had set a course of action for herself, and she would see it through.

''There are some of us,'' she said, ''who have been waiting for a long time. Since Timmain. She was as close to being the one who leads as we've ever known.'' As she spoke she moved next to Timmorn and heel-sat next to him, close enough to touch. ''Many of us—of them—looked to you to be the one to lead when Timmain disappeared. They trusted her choice, and thought that you and the wolves would provide.''

Suddenly she made her own decision and reached out to touch him, gently kneading the back of his neck. Again, as she had before, she felt the thrill of contact, of attraction. Timmorn flinched only a little, only once at first touch, and then relaxed, eyes closed, head lolling as her fingers worked.

Seilein wondered if he would touch her, for there were places on her body she enjoyed touching, and she let her imagination wrap itself around Timmorn's fingers.

For several moments, neither spoke. Timmorn, thoroughly enjoying the stroking, suddenly rolled wolflike over onto his back, exposing his belly and groin as if to say, "More." Seilein, lost in her own sensual reverie, was startled, but felt a pleasant warmth in her face. She recalled in a rushing mix the feelings of her sleeping furs against her body; and the time she had tried to touch one of the elf males. He'd been shocked and discomfited, unable to comprehend her innocent experiment. Seilein wondered what Timmorn's furry body might feel like against hers. . . .

Still, though, there was unfinished business, and she shook herself back into the present. "There must be another hunt," she said, her voice low. "Some might die if there's not. The ones who can best hunt will go. I'll go. . . ."

Timmorn sat bolt upright; the reaction shocked them both. "No!" he rasped. "No. The longtooth. There's danger—*you* will be in danger." He leaned toward her, his face almost touching hers. "You must not be in danger. It is wrong." His eyes widened as if he were seeing something beyond her. He almost smiled. "Wrong!"

Seilein collected herself and wondered what had affected Timmorn so. Suddenly he was acting . . . possessive? Protective? Both concepts were nearly alien to her, to all the elves. And yet, in the flush of sensation she was enjoying, neither repelled her. Quite the opposite.

She took his hand in hers. "The beast you spoke of did not cry out last night. You said it was badly wounded; it surely has died. We must go out. Lead us, you and your wolves. You must go to show us the way; *we* must go to learn from you. It's the only way."

Timmorn sat for a long while, not moving. Within him the wolf and the elf whirled, pulling close, scampering away. An ancient feeling tugged at him, one that the firstcomers had long ago forgotten in their timeless immortality. Timmorn tasted the feeling. It tasted of the wolf, and the cub.

"Tonight," he said.

There were five of them, aside from Timmorn and the wolf-pack. Seilein was there, and Valloa, and three males who also showed skill with the spear. The wolves were even less easy than they were when only Timmorn accompanied them, but somehow this night the halfling exerted a will that caused even the high-ranking male wolf to accept the small elfin band.

They hunted, going farther and farther from the camp, deeper and deeper into woods where none of the elves had ever gone. Here they felt more vulnerable, more fragile than they had ever before. Much as they spoke among themselves in the softest voices of the need for a successful hunt, they wondered in minds suddenly made insignificant if they belonged here in this deep darkness, with giant unseen, unknown life all around. They wondered if they would ever belong here.

Seilein watched Timmorn, when she could see him. Though the night was clear and crisp, only one moon shone in partial phase, and its light barely penetrated the needled branches that wove overhead. And Timmorn was like the wolves, a running shadow, a ripple of gray in the deeper gray. The elves followed as they could; they were not without grace themselves, but their own animal beginnings were far in the past. Still, they ran and tried to sniff the night air as Timmorn did, to read the knowledge in a broken twig or tuft of pine needles. Seilein tried to determine in her mind if Timmorn was disturbed this night, or if it was only a reflection of her own subtle fears. Every so often, it seemed, he stopped and cocked his head, as if listening for something just beyond hearing.

One of the male elves had just made the dispirited remark that it seemed that even this hunt was for nothing when there was a yip and the sound of hooves pounding and wolf paws running and a grunting squeal and more yipping and the boar burst from somewhere and ran straight at the elves, who stood there stupidly as if they weren't there, and it was Valloa who acted without thinking and who spun and struck with her spear and the boar screeched and even though it was a clumsy strike it was a lucky one and the boar went down and took Valloa with it and the two rolled across the forest floor and the boar died and covered the elf with its blood.

For long moments, nothing and no one moved. Then Timmorn arrived, followed by several wolves. He took in the scene; his expression of surprise gave way to a toothy grin and low chuckle. The wolves did not quite know what to make of it all; they had not made the kill, so they could not feed in pack order. This had never happened before. They were confused, and Timmorn was enjoying it. Seilein and the other elves joined in with smiles, and good-natured fun poked at Valloa, who sat up and looked herself over and rolled her eyes, and the pleasant anticipation of more meat for a while.

From the deep shadows, the longtooth attacked.

It was thinner, its wound was worse; clearly it was further gone into pain and madness than it had been before. It had tried to hunt and failed; it was close to death. And the elves and the wolves had come back into its dark place and spilled blood for it and there was meat to be had. The dead meat lying on the ground or the live meat next to it covered with gore. The longtooth didn't care.

It charged. Though it showed the ravages of its starvation, it still bulked greater than an elf or a wolf. It bowled into Valloa, its claws raking her leg as its momentum carried it past. The elf screamed; she did not know what pain was and she scrabbled wildly at the air, at her torn leg, at her spear still buried in the boar. Her mind raged blindly.

In an instant there was panic. The wolves scattered; they could do no different. The elves scattered; unassailable fear took them, for they did not know creatures like this, or death like this. Timmorn started to run, wolflike, but in the same instant he stopped and turned to take in the sight of the longtooth turning to charge again, to finish its grisly work on the wounded elf. Memory pounded upon memory, collided with instinct, fought with feelings only recently stirred. He growled, ''Wrong!'' and hurled himself.

He hit the longtooth just as the beast reached Valloa. The impact sent the longtooth careening to one side and sent Timmorn thudding to the ground. He knew the creature was heavier than he, and stronger; even as he snarled and shrieked at the longtooth in defiance he glanced about quickly for something to aid him. He spied Valloa's spear and wrenched it free of the boar's carcass; the elf would not need it now.

The longtooth charged again, the fire in its brain driving it. It leaped at Timmorn, at the meat, at the pain, and flew past as Timmorn caught it in the shoulder joint with the spear tip. It hardly felt the new pain, and spun to attack yet again. It screamed, and leapt, and this time took the spear point squarely in its chest, deep into its heart. The body thumped heavily to the ground and lay there.

Slowly the wolves came back, but Timmorn was already bending over Valloa, gingerly touching at the cruel gashes in her thigh, wincing at the moans that escaped her lips. He could smell her blood over that of the boar and the longtooth— there was something . . . A shock, a tingle, something he'd felt only recently; though not as strongly. Very gently, he touched his tongue to one of the open wounds. Something in the blood.

For just a moment, Valloa seemed to become calmer, despite the pain that beat at her. She opened her eyes. Timmorn bent his shaggy head over her and said gruffly, ''In the blood. Who are you?''

For just a moment a look of puzzlement clouded her face. "You know me—I am Valloa. I'm . . ." Then something deeper passed through and over her, and she said, "But there's another name inside me. I don't know why it is, but I want to say it to you. I am *Murrel*."

Even more slowly the elves returned to the place where two beasts lay dead and Timmorn cradled the wounded huntress. Seilein, still pale with shock but boldest of the little group, went to touch Timmorn, remembering the earlier day's comfort. He turned to her and snarled, showing his teeth, and she drew back in surprise. "Mine," he said, locking eyes with her again, and in that moment Seilein understood what Timmorn meant. She raised an eyebrow as if to say, "We'll see. This may turn out to be most interesting," but what she did say was, "We'll take her back to camp. There are healers there." Then she walked away.

Timmorn turned back to her whom everyone else called Valloa.

Later, Timmorn ran through the darkest part of the night, through the deep woods. His eyes, yellow as twin moons, saw the world swirl mistily by him in the starlight as he ran, his breath and blood singing, the wolf high within him. Somewhere, behind the trees in the deepest shadows, he knew the wolf-pack was with him, though they still ran their own path, black and fluid in the night. Not true elf, not true wolf, Timmorn was both now, instead of neither. That knowledge lived, secure, in his blood.

Back in the camp, the one who had been Valloa slept, her wounds attended by the healer. Among the others, there was some little confusion, for they did not understand why she went by another name now. No matter. The new name, the *Murrel* name whispered in his mind with a voice no one else could hear or share, and it called to him. The two had not joined this night as the voice had gently urged, for she was still weak, but Timmorn knew that matings—and cubs—would come. There was a something, a bond, a feeling he had not experienced before. It was a feeling both fresh and new, and incredibly ancient. It warmed within him.

(And as he ran and turned the new thing over and over in his mind, tasting it, Timmorn also thought of the other one, Seilein. He grinned, wolflike, lips tight over sharp teeth; there would be joinings there too, if he had sensed her own mind and scent correctly. . . .)

It is life, he realized, slowing to a gentle lope. He went in his mind to the place that had been so troubled, to the empty hole that had been gouged there by the death of the wolf days before. The new thoughts filled the hole and soothed it, and they were the shape and color and smell and feel of life.

Timmorn had seen death before, and he knew he would see it again. The world was full of death. But now he could fight it and not scamper aside from its fangs and claws like a frightened wolf who only knew self, and not others.

He did not yet know if the new feeling meant much or little to the others, the ones who slept and tried and succeeded or failed, but at that moment, in the now that filled him up, it meant all.

The young elf-woman's face showed the effects of an eight-of-days spent eating poorly and sleeping worse. Dark bruises clouded her green-and-gold eyes, and her gestures, as she slid down the tree trunk to sit amid its roots, were weariness personified. Even her hair, normally full of sunlight and curls, fell limp around her face.

I don't know what to do, she sent to the elf hidden in the branches above her. **Could it be Recognition?**

The leaves rustled and Longreach leaped to the ground, agile for all that Bearclaw was his fifth chief. "If you have to ask, it isn't Recognition," he said with a sly smile.

"Then what is it? Finding my soulname was nothing compared to this. No matter what I do there's an ache somewhere inside. I wake up from a sound sleep knowing that I've dreamt something awful but not being able to remember it. Sometimes I just go to the tall grasses and run until I collapse. Not even my wolf-friend can help me."

Longreach loosened the laces of his tunic and produced a small, lumpy pouch from which he removed a handful of wrinkled berries. He offered them to Nightfall, then poured them into her hand when she refused to take them.

"A story? I don't see how a story can help me."

"There are many stories you've never heard, little one." The storyteller leaned against the tree as a farseeing look came over his face. Longreach no longer needed the berries

25

to find the treasure trove of Wolfrider memories. "Some stories, I think, wait for generations until the right pair of ears is born to hear it."

"I don't want to hear how Darkwater quested for two turns of the season before she found the secret of setting the feathers in an arrow's tail," the adolescent warned. "I want my answer *now*."

Longreach frowned in feigned offense. "I wasn't even thinking of that one. And anyway, she was looking for something while you've been found by it."

Nightfall relaxed. They all came to the storyteller, sooner or later, when there was no one else who would understand. And his wisdom was already soothing her thoughts; she'd been thinking something was missing instead of noticing something had been added.

"The high ones' blood runs strong in you, child. Your mother's mother had almost no wolf-blood in her. But Timmorn's blood runs strong too; you get that from your father who would have been chief if Mantricker had died before Bearclaw found his name. You mustn't be surprised when the bloods rest uneasily against each other. It's a hand of generations or more for the rest of us, but for you it is as it was near the beginning of the Wolfriders.

"I'll tell you about Rahnee the She-Wolf, and why she'd understand how you feel."

Coming of Age

— *by Lynn Abbey* —

The spear flew from her fingers as the great stag rose
on its hind feet, ready to leap from the quiet clearing. The
sharp stone tip struck deep, but not in heart-flesh where
it would have dropped the stag in its tracks. Hidden in the
bushes, the silver-haired huntress heaved a bitter sigh and
took up the chase again.

Cursing inwardly, she followed the wounded beast deeper
into the forest, tracking it by the smell of its fresh-shed
blood. She need not keep it in sight nor exhaust herself in
matching its early pace; its wound would kill it soon enough—
though it was not her way to let her prey die of blood-death
and exhaustion.

Burdened by the height and breadth of his antlers, the stag
kept to well-cleared trails, not like smaller game which went
to ground in briars or swamps and, like as not, became a
meal for scavengers rather than hunters. No, the danger now
was that the blood would draw other hunters who would
reach the dying stag first and who did not need shaped stone
to make their kills. She should have called her brothers and
sisters to her aid, but they would have seen the poorly placed
spear and mocked her skill as a hunter.

She pressed on, beyond the hunt's boundary, head held
high and her mind tingling with the scent of blood. There
were sounds on her left and a breeze brought wolf-smell
mingling with the blood—true-wolves, whose friendship could
not be relied upon. Without breaking stride the hunter brushed
her hand along her thigh and felt the knife that rested there,
slung down from her waist. A *metal* knife, ancient beyond

27

belief, with an edge sharper than any wolf's tooth or cat's claw, and her most prized possession.

She howled as well—a warble that would tell any wolf or other predator that this prey was claimed. The one running beside her held tongue and kept pace. A loner, then, who answered no pack and would attack her as soon as the stag. Gulping air, she ran faster and shed her pride to send an image of the trail into the minds of her huntmates.

Perhaps the lone one caught her image. It happened that way, sometimes, when the hunt had blood in its nostrils and the true-wolves were close by. Whatever, it dropped back and she ran alone, setting the images in her mind so she could find her way back when it was over.

Her breath was fire, but it was worse for the stag. She heard it crash into the underbrush and found the strength to sprint the last distance. Knife drawn, the huntress threw herself across the fallen, gasping beast and ended its agony. It had begun to cool before her breath came easily again and she levered herself up to her elbows.

And into her father's yellow-blazing stare.

Who are you? he asked with mind alone.

Not that he didn't know, in a general way, that she was one of his. All the hunt was his; what wasn't *other*, elfin, was his one way or another. The hunt was his children, his grandchildren and beyond—down to those who neither spoke nor sent but were long and sharp of tooth.

"She-wolf," she replied, daring to sit on her haunches as the fire in his eyes ebbed back.

She was not the highest among his children—and the hunt reminded her of it. Names were for the ones who mattered; the ones who had earned them. And of late there had been very few of Timmorn's first-born like herself with names.

The hunt had mated within itself and back to their yellow-eyed ancestors. They'd become peerless killers and regarded the first-born as failures. Strength and success were what counted within the hunt, and it did not matter that their offspring were often misborn and did not survive their milk-days.

The crossbred hunters lived longer than the true-wolves and scorned the others with whom they shared space and food. And the others, the elves, had grown wary, seeming content to take only what the hunt wished to give. But she was first-born; her mother was one of the others. It showed in her eyes, in her hands and in her teeth, but mostly it showed in her loneliness: neither hunt nor *other*.

How are you known to your mother?

The silver hair shook and fell over her face, hiding her shame. "Murrel?" she whispered her mother's name and dared to meet those topaz eyes. "I am she-wolf to her as well. They do not love us, father," his she-wolf daughter told him, challenging him as no one in the hunt or elsewhere did. "They need us, but they do not love us. They would rather have the true-wolves for pets than listen to our songs."

Timmorn squatted down beside her, as close as he'd ever been to this particular child of his. She noticed the white hairs of age mingled through the coarse, tawny fur that covered far more than his scalp. So, he felt it too—the pull of the wolf-blood that made the hunt forever from the others who, though they were mortal and often died, did not *need* to die.

It has gone wrong. His hand closed over hers, making the mind images stronger and filled with sadness. **Timmain's sacrifice—my mother's sacrifice—is being lost.**

Timmain. That was a name that could draw the hunt and the others closer together in the moonlight. Or it had, once—not in her short lifetime. There were too many of the hunt now whose thoughts were closed to memory and several of the others who did not care to be reminded. The others said, or more exactly *thought*, among themselves that there was a bit of Timmain in her. Not that she'd know. She'd seen herself reflected off still water, but Timmain, the legend who had saved the others by going to the true-wolves, had never returned to her elfin shape.

She's spoken to me, came her father's thoughts—as if he'd known hers. **I've done what I could do. It's time for me to leave—**

Her eyes widened and she tried to pull away. Timmorn Yellow-Eyes was all that bound the hunt and the others together and secured a small, uncomfortable world for the first-born who did not fit with either group.

—And time for you to find your real name.

He let her pull away and turned his attention to the stag which they would have to haul back to the common camp. She helped him, using her metal knife to make swift, straight cuts through hide and muscle, but kept her frantic thoughts carefully to herself.

Names were important to the hunters; given more often than found, they were what separated the ignored ones, like herself, from the powerful ones like her father, Yellow-Eyes, or Threetoe—who bulked as much as Yellow-Eyes, had never spoken a word in his life, and whose mind images sent her scurrying for the shadows. Names were important to the others, too, but the elves were born with their names and never changed them.

Once, as her milk-days were ending, she'd asked Murrel about her name, but the tall, beautiful woman had only turned aside and closed her eyes. She'd given her the metal knife, but a knife wasn't a name. So she remained a she-wolf, as simple and unremarkable as that. And if she made her lair at the edge of the camp and had little cause to talk or send to anyone else—well, at least she didn't have to deal with challenges from the hunt or the unending weaving and mending that filled the days and nights of the nonhunting elves.

They bled the stag and buried the offal—a waste of delicacies, but there were only the two of them to carry the carcass, slung from her spear, back to the camp. Even Timmorn, for all that he was the most ferocious hunter these forests had seen, did not want to guard their prize through a moonless night.

By sundown, Yellow-Eyes reminded her, though the images contained in the thought were more complex and carried his confidence that the stag, which she had brought down herself, would raise her status in both groups at the camp.

They smelled the lone wolf again, the one that had paced the huntress during the chase. She gathered images to send it away, but Timmorn forbade it. The wolf, his thoughts proclaimed, was their protector as they slowly brought their burden through other beasts' territories. But there were other things hidden in his images; shadows of awe and respect that she could not understand and did not dare to question.

The sun was the color of the leaves of the sugar-bushes when they came to the stream-border of the camp they had used since she was born. Most of the hunt rose to greet them, nostrils flared to read the nuances of their scent. There were no fresh hides stretched between spear-poles to dry; whatever the hunt had brought back was small and already eaten. Threetoe pushed to the front of the hunt, looking uncomfortable as he stretched up to his full height. The look he gave them was not at all friendly.

Murrel and the others were more open with their welcome calls, though perhaps no more sincere. The hunt usually ate first, the unquestioned right of the hunter, and when the kill was sparse the others made do with berries, roots, and gristle. A stag, Timmorn's stag, would see their bellies full for once. They were already starting a fire in the pit when Yellow-Eyes and his daughter splashed out of the stream.

Timmorn struck the antlers loose from the stag's skull and

Selnac, lately his favorite among the others, stepped forward to receive the prize. He thrust them instead into his daughter's limp hands and proclaimed, with a sending more triumphant than it should properly have been, that *she* had brought the stag down with one spear, alone.

She could have proclaimed herself Stagslayer or Lonehunter or something similar in the moments after her father's powerful images. Instead, with the bloody antlers scratching her arms and legs as she ran, she escaped to her tree-branch lair beyond the clearing, beyond the eyes of the hunt and the elves.

Embarrassment and unfamiliarity robbed her of triumph and left her with bitter resentment. If *he* hadn't been there— If the hunt instead of her father had answered her call she would have simply given the stag to Threetoe. The dark- and shag-haired hunter would have kept the antlers to himself and let everyone know that the kill had been his, but for a while, at least, she'd have eaten a bit better.

The hunt understood. Status should be changed slowly; too much attention brought challenges or worse.

Daughter who calls herself she-wolf!

Timmorn's thoughts burned upward from the base of her tree. He did not climb and did not have to. His images carried a commanding power that would have brought even Threetoe belly-crawling through the leaves.

"Yes, father?"

The hunter must attend her feast.

She followed him, then, to the fire pit, sat atop the fur-draped stone seat of honor, and felt utterly miserable with the eyes of the hunt glaring at her. The others smiled; she was first-born, after all, and more like them than many in the hunt. Perhaps they thought the first-born, having half their blood from their elfin mothers, *should* be the better hunters. They had never seen Threetoe hurl his spear.

Threetoe threw so hard that bones and flint shattered more often than not. The others feared him—and so did the hunt.

The feast drew to a close as the fire died back to embers. Samael, an elf, brought forth a deep wooden bowl filled with sun-wizened berries. Everyone, hunt and other, took a handful. The dreamberries still held their fragile group together, though whether the young, silent members of the hunt actually shared images and memories with the ancient elves was a question no one ventured to answer.

When the bowl returned to Samael, that green-eyed elf arose and prepared himself for the night's story. But flickering, outstretched arms of shadow fell across his face: Timmorn would have their attention. Samael sat down, plucking another handful of berries from the bowl as he did.

**I have led you all for many twists of moons and seasons. Many, elf and hunt alike, do not recall the times before when Timmain made her sacrifice and went to dwell among the true-wolves. She went to save her people, to bring the strength and cunning of the true-wolves to those whose memories held only gentleness.

She could do nothing for those already born; she meant her sacrifice to benefit their children. She sent me, her child, to teach her people to hunt, to move them safely from the land of long winters, and to insure that her sacrifice was given to the children.

The gathering around the fire pit grew edgy. With the dreamberries in their bellies they heard and felt Timmorn's thoughts in painful intensity. But they felt Timmain too, even the sharp-toothed silent ones and especially the anxious firstborn who'd wrapped herself in the honor-seat furs.

I have failed, Yellow-Eyes howled, filled with his mother's despair. **Her people do not hunt and do not have children. *My* children see only each other and chafe to be free of their weaker, elfin kin—and I grow old. I can no longer hold my family together, so I shall let it fall asunder and pass my spear to the strongest of my first-born.**

No one had marked the spear beside him until he flung it

across the fire pit into the ground at his silver-haired daughter's feet. They all gasped, but none more loudly than she did herself, recoiling from the stout wood as if it were a venom-snake looming over her in the night.

Find your name, kitling, he sent to her alone.

She didn't, though she did take up the spear and hold it firmly through Threetoe's menacing glower. The dark hunter looked away. He sent no thoughts or images to her. He didn't need to; his posture said everything: how long can you hold it, *first-born*—if Yellow-Eyes truly leaves.

They watched her, her father most of all. She felt the stirring of leadership deep within her but it could not rise far enough to reach her thoughts and actions. Shivers of anxiety radiated out from her spine. The wolf-song told her to surrender Timmorn's spear to Threetoe and become his favorite, but, as little as she was prepared to succeed her father, she was even less inclined to turn her neck to Threetoe. There were murmurings, sent and spoken, as she marched out of the firelight, but no one stood to challenge her.

Timmorn's speech had shocked them but not as much as their realization, shortly after dawn the next morning, that he had made good his promise. The hunt, led by Threetoe, spread into the forest, searching for Timmorn's scent. They returned at high-sun. He had vanished without a trace. His trail entered the stream at the edge of the camp and had not emerged either at the rocks which marked its source or the downstream waterfall.

The hunt had been equally ineffective at flushing up any game. None of them were hungry, but the knowledge that they had nothing to eat—except for the gleanings of the timid others—weighed heavily in everyone's mind.

Timmorn's nameless daughter had followed the hunt after sunrise, fully aware that they'd find no trace of her father. He had come to her in the dead of the night, scaring her half out of her wits, and demanded her assistance. She had carried him around the waterfall and taken him to a glade where, he promised, he'd remain until the two moons were both above the treetops. He was not gentle with her as he told her what he expected her to do.

In the frosty time before dawn, as she scurried back to her lair, she'd almost decided on a name. One of the fancy words that the others used when they didn't want the hunt to understand: Starcrossed. It fit her mood.

And there was no doubt that she needed a name now. Eyes followed her every move—or the movement of Timmorn's spear, which she kept at her side. Timmorn's Daughter, Spearbearer, Firstchosen—those were the more complimentary names she heard whispered from mind to ear. The hunt had other names, names that would remain with her if she lost the spear.

The tense air exploded after sundown when the hunt, which scorned the others' glean-foods as always, used their own failure as an excuse to make a challenge.

We'll starve with you as our leader, Threetoe snarled from the darkness on the opposite side of the cold fire pit. **We're starving already.**

Her fingers grew cold and clammy on the smooth wood of the spear. "Food was set before you—to share *equally* with the others." Her heart pounded but it sent no strength to her trembling legs or to her frantic mind. Timmorn had said she'd find leadership within her; at the moment she didn't think she could find her way back to her lair.

"Roots and leaves," another voice—Rustruff, Threetoe's lairmate and the dominant female of the hunt. "What are we? Forest pigs? The blood of true-wolves, not pigs, moves within us—or have you forgotten?"

"The blood of the high ones moves within us as well—or have *you* forgotten?" Timmorn's daughter replied, knowing she was losing the contest for dominance with each word she uttered.

Threetoe strode to the edge of the pit. Starlight caught his eyes and turned them feral silver. **Timmain gave herself to the true-wolves and never came back. Wolf-blood is strongest. Wolf-ways are best—the right of the strongest to lead—**

It was blasphemy to turn Timmain's sacrifice around like that. The elves drew a collective breath of shock and the first-born, including Timmorn's daughter, felt their hearts go cold.

"The true-wolves are animals," an unfamiliar elfin voice proclaimed. "Animals no different from the forest pigs. Timmain chose true-wolves because she could touch their minds and take their shapes. The forest pigs had migrated from the land of snows already; she could not use *them*."

Zarhan, whom the hunt called Fastfire because of his hair, which was the color of the setting sun, and his magic, which made flames come to the fire pit, edged in front of the other elves. Like Timmorn's daughter he was just leaving his adolescence, but unlike her it had taken him several hundred full turns of the seasons to reach that age and in the eyes of the hunt he was as ancient as the rest of the others. He was no hunter, but, because of the fire pit, he held the hunt's respect.

Momentarily nonplussed, Threetoe faltered. His shoulders fell, his back slumped, and he lost his edge of dominance even within the hunt. It took Rustruff, whose position of privilege absolutely depended on Threetoe's continuing stature, to set him on the track again.

"The pack is not led by nameless she-wolves!"

A snarl of assent passed through the hunt. They took up the refrain with their minds, assaulting Timmorn's daughter with the taunt of **she-wolf, she-wolf,** reminding her of her lowly, nameless status. They would have succeeded had their target been a true-wolf or if she had not already felt so alienated from the more atavistic of Yellow-Eye's children. Instead, by driving her from them, Rustruff and the hunt pushed her further into her mother's heritage. She found the strength her father had seen from the beginning.

"As Timmain *became* a she-wolf to save her people," she both said and sent. "So I *am* the She-Wolf and I will make her people whole again!"

She took her father's spear, spun it under her wrist, and slammed its flint head into the ground. The butt, which some elf long ago had carved into the likeness of a growling wolf, bared its teeth across the fire pit. Then, so fast and subtle that the just-named She-Wolf had no time to flinch in surprise, the carved head began to glow. The eyes and teeth showed a seething red that spread to include the entire ominous wooden skull before the whole butt burst into flames.

The She-Wolf pulled her hand back; she trusted fire no more than Threetoe. But she kept her advantage.

"Take it if you dare," she screamed at him and watched in triumph as he broke away from her stare.

The hunt drifted away from the fire pit, their thoughts as quiet as their tongues. Most of the elves retreated too; displays of such sheer dominance were alien to them. **Like father, like daughter** their thoughts echoed as they accepted her leadership. The first-born, a group of no more than a half-dozen, lingered longer. Their thoughts were confused—wondering if any of them could have done what she had done, or could have done it better, or sooner. The She-Wolf outwaited them.

Only Zarhan remained, watching the flaming spear-butt rather than her.

You? she asked in a narrow thought for his mind alone.

He smiled and shrugged and faded into the darkness.

She stayed by the spear throughout the night, falling asleep in the endless time before dawn when the spear had been reduced to glowing ashes. She dreamt of her father, which did not surprise her, and of her grandmother, which did.

Timmorn, in her dream, towered protectively over the members of the hunt. They were born of his wolf-spirit, he told her. Their elfin nature was deeply buried but no more lost than her own leadership skills had been. They needed time to understand themselves just as the elves and the first-born needed time. She should forgive them, Timmorn asked, and wait for them.

She-Wolf nodded. Yellow-Eyes gathered his children in his arms and disappeared into the brilliance at the edge of her dream.

She recognized Timmain and saw the truth behind the whispers. Timmain had been a high one—an elf from the place beyond the sky; there was no real resemblance between them but the She-Wolf felt that they were true kin to each other.

Care for my children, the unspeakably beautiful vision told her. **Love them. Make them part of yourself.**

It was the same command Timmain had left in her son's mind, but it opened different doors in the She-Wolf's memory. The high one smiled and vanished through one of the open doors.

The spear was gone when the dawnlight awoke her; the ashes scattered on a sharp-edged wind. The hunt was gone as well, every last one of them save the other first-born. The elves, misreading the signs, thought they had gone searching for game worthy of a great celebration and began, in their naive way, to anticipate the feast. Zarhan knew better—She-Wolf saw that in his eyes—and the first-born, who'd seen at once that the hunt had taken its few treasures as well as its weapons.

"How will you tell them?" the first-born who now called himself Treewalker asked. "They're expecting a feast."

She-Wolf looked up from the fire-scarred spearhead she fondled in her hands. The elves—should she start thinking of them as the true-elves just as the four-footed wolves had been true-wolves?—were busy with their berries and bits of leather and fur. Gift-making—the offerings they gave the hunt after special meals; the clothing that would keep them warm through the bitter winter she could smell on the wind.

Words formed in her mind—and the anxious, fearful reactions they would provoke. She could not tell the elves that the hunt had abandoned them. Besides, everyone deserved a feast. No one had eaten well the previous day, and if the ascendance of a new chief did not call for a feast, then nothing ever would again.

"They'll get a feast," she said to Treewalker. "*We'll* get it for them. Gather the first-born by the stream."

"We're not hunters—not like you."

"You're exactly like me." She grabbed his shoulder, shaking him hard for emphasis. "And don't you ever forget it!"

Treewalker staggered back, stunned that she had done what neither Yellow-Eyes or Threetoe would have dared: laid hands upon him. She-Wolf knew it too, though touching and discipline were common enough between a mother and her children. But then, she thought of them as her children— even though she'd never had children of her own before. Breaking away from her stare, Treewalker shook himself straight and went off to find the remaining first-born.

They gathered at the upstream drinking pool, proclaiming the names they had chosen for themselves since dawn: Treewalker; Mosshunter—the smallest among them and the most daring jokester; Laststar—the She-Wolf's older, full sister; Glowstone—who wore his name from a thong around his neck; Frost—who carried a javelin and shed her fear like a snake sheds its skin; Sharpears—whose talent the hunt had recognized if not named and, to everyone's surprise, Zarhan Fastfire.

"Elves hunted once—before the sacrifice," he explained a bit self-consciously.

They had hunted, but they had not hunted well, the She-Wolf thought to herself, or Timmain's sacrifice would not have been necessary. This blending of elf-blood and wolf-blood, which left the first-born in constant doubt of who or what they were, would never have occurred if the elves had been able to take care of themselves in this world. She might feel better when the hunt had receded into the morass Timmorn's mixed heritage made of deep memory for his children—but perhaps the hunt, by giving into the wolf-blood completely, had the right of it. Perhaps *she* was the one leading the failures and outcasts, not Threetoe.

Or perhaps it was Zarhan himself. Threetoe she had understood and her fear of him went through every layer of her mind unchallenged. Not Zarhan. His eyes filled her with the smell of lightning as if she, like Yellow-Eye's spear, might burst into flames.

She should have sent him back. She was chief now and Timmorn wasn't around to see that she kept her promises. The first-born would stand with her. They were eager to hunt together and almost as discomforted by the true-elf's presence as she was. But the promise weighed too heavily in her mind, and she could only hope that he would discourage himself.

"Come on then."

In any other season Zarhan's unnaturally brilliant cloud of hair would have been a liability. Come winter, when the forest was reduced to a world of grays, browns and deepest evergreen, it would definitely need to be concealed from any color-sensitive prey, but now, in autumn, he was no more conspicuous than any of the sugar-bushes.

And about as useful, although the She-Wolf knew it was unfair to blame all their missed opportunities on their least experienced hunter. Twice Frost threw her javelin too soon, panicking their quarry and sending it to cover. Treewalker and Sharpears almost came to blows over the former's tendency to sing while he stalked. Even the She-Wolf was finding her mind too filled with other thoughts to fling her weapon accurately. Zarhan, who used his spear like a walking stick but kept his mouth shut, was about the least of their problems.

At last, well after midday, they came upon a flock of wattle-necks intently devouring a small glade of wild spelt. The fair-sized, slow-flying birds took no notice of the hunters as they fanned out around the glade.

All together . . . now! the She-Wolf sent as she sprang into the glade, spear high and ready for the kill.

The birds squawked, flapped their wings in the dust, and defended themselves with beaks and wickedly sharp claws. Still, when the commotion settled, they had killed five and could fairly taste the juicy meat in their mouths. Seven hunters, five wattle-necks; they had a long way to go and much to learn but they weren't going to starve just yet.

No . . . wait. Only six hunters. Zarhan was missing.

The She-Wolf gathered her energy to send his name in every direction before she heard thrashing in brush beyond the glade.

Zarhan! She let the energy loose, knowing full well that at such a short distance it would echo between his ears.

The brush froze, then emitted a wattle-neck and a sending-staggered elf. He'd trapped the bird, but he couldn't bring himself to strike it. The spear went wide each time he thrust, then it would swing in a swift arc and bat the bird back to the ground. The She-Wolf raised her own spear to end the spectacle.

Another hand fell gently over hers. **It's his—if he can. If not—it lives.** Sharpears reminded her of the hunt laws by which she, herself, had lived.

She relaxed and let the frantic duo return to the glade. The true-elf's face was nearly as red as his hair when, as much by accident as design, his spear struck home.

"I killed it," he muttered, sinking down beside the still-twitching body. "I killed a living creature. . . ."

Laughter stuck in the throats of the first-born. Fastfire had no wolf-blood singing in his heart to tell him that hunting and killing were the ways of the predator, but he had elf-blood that let him share his stunned emotions with all those who could feel. There was little that passed for consciousness in the wattle-neck's brain, but it had known terror and it had felt death.

Never in jest or the lust of the hunt, the She-Wolf told them, making her first laws. **Never with cruelty or mean-ness. And never a mother with young if there's another choice to be made.**

They voiced their accord as the hunt had always voiced it—with heads thrown back and a wolf-howl wrapped around their tongues. Zarhan Fastfire tried, choked and fell over backward. The suppressed laughter made its escape.

Zarhan looked around, his mind that dark swirl of hidden thought which told all of Timmorn's children when their elders were angry, disappointed, or worse. With equal parts of distaste and determination he got the bird through the carry-noose of his borrowed spear and put his back to them.

The true-elves were inexperienced and disinclined, but they weren't incompetent. Zarhan strode out of the glade in the proper direction; the first-born hurriedly gathered their own kills and raced to catch up with him.

"Talk to him," Laststar advised as they jogged through leaves the same color as Zarhan's hair.

"Why," her silver-haired sister replied.

"They are the elves—Timmain's blood. Their anger hurts."

"They are as arrogant as Threetoe and even more danger-ous."

The She-Wolf glowered at Laststar until the other female looked away.

"It will get worse, She-Wolf," the elder sister said, and there was an image under her words that had nothing to do with hunting.

It did get worse, though not in ways any of the first-born had anticipated. Their entire group had shrunk to less than a third of its summer size. They needed less meat, but in actuality there were fewer hunters to provide it. The first-born, with Zarhan, Talen, and others of the younger, hardier elves, braved the snow-covered forest every day. On more than one bitter occasion they returned to the camp with little more than sacks of fist-sized rodents, which even the first-born preferred cooked and disguised within the elders' root stews.

Nature itself seemed against the She-Wolf and her inexperienced hunters. The snows had come early, before the last leaves had fallen, and they'd come heavy. Small game was around in some quantity. They could smell and they could hear it scampering through tunnels beneath the snow. The true-wolves were thriving and the more atavistic of the hunt could have followed the ravvits and mask-eyes back to their teeming dens. But not the first-born.

The cold, dry winds came early, too, putting a thick crust on the snow that held their weight—sometimes. The deer were starving, and the hunting was better for a while—though they'd pay the price, eventually, for each weakened doe whose misery they ended. Then the deer staggered south. The first-born hunted vermin again and listened while the elders clicked their tongues over the stewpots.

"Timmain's sacrifice! Timmorn's cunning! That's all I ever hear any more!" the She-Wolf muttered as she struck the flint with her chipper-stone. Too hard. Too deep. The would-be arrowhead shattered, and black splinters shot into her fingers.

Glowstone sniffed the air and set his own stones aside. "If Timmorn were here they'd howl a different song," he added darkly.

"No they wouldn't," Talen told them, not looking up from his lopsided spearpoint. "They do this every winter."

"That's not true," Zarhan injected.

"Yes it is—well, maybe it's a bit worse this year. But the hunt never heard any of it. They laired together outside, and we stayed here in the cave. We didn't exchange hardly a word or thought with them until the spring thaw."

Zarhan grunted noncommittally and went back to whatever mystery he was perpetrating with the ribs of one of their last big kills. The She-Wolf stopped sucking on her bleeding finger and tried to remember the previous winters. Had the hunt laired together—apart from the others? Apart from the first-born as well, she guessed; she couldn't remember being with either group. Alone. Yes, alone; by herself almost the whole time and, yes, eating rodents. That was how she'd known where to find them.

Memory played tricks on the first-born. There were things you remembered in your nose and eyes as if they'd just happened. Then there were the gaps. The She-Wolf shivered involuntarily. Whole years were gone—more than years, she suspected—vanished into the wolf-blood and the wolf-song. It had been worse for the hunt; they never knew the time was gone except through the dreamberries.

The berries had held them together. They had shared things on the nights when Samael brought out his bowl. They saw Timmain through the elders' eyes and images older than that: a marvelous mountain rising out of the forest, full of light and music. It was more than sharing, though; they became individuals, too, with their whole past opened up and the wolf-song reduced to a faint throbbing.

Sometimes it was better when the berries had worn off and the emptiness had gone back to its hiding place.

"Well, I wish they'd do some work, too," Treewalker exclaimed, putting a welcome end to the She-Wolf's unseen wanderings.

Zarhan Fastfire examined the bent, delicate, sharp-pointed thing he'd made from the bone a moment before speaking. "Everyone does what they can, Treewalker," he explained.

Hooks—that's what he called his little pointed things. He said they were far better at catching fish than a spear though none of the first-born could imagine how he was going to throw it or how it was supposed to kill the fish. Certainly he was the only one who *could* make them, and he was worse with the chipper-stones than Talen so no one complained.

He put the hook with the others, then turned back to Treewalker. "Who made your boots? Who made the double-hat that keeps your ears warm?"

Treewalker looked away. "Murrel," he admitted after a long pause.

The elders made all their clothes. They knew how to scrape the bloody hides, then wash and stretch them, then work strange-smelling magic on them that sometimes made the hair fall out and always made them soft and supple. The first-born didn't know how; they'd have been naked or stinking if the process had been left to them.

If the elders weren't busy it was because there was nothing for them to do: no fresh pelts to scrape and freeze; no more reeds to be worked into baskets; no more leather to be turned into clothing. All they had were piles of flint and Zarhan's pile of bones. The She-Wolf stole a guilty glance at her mother, who was napping beneath a mound of furs, then took up another piece of flint.

"They're always cold. They're always hungry. Timmain's sacrifice didn't help them at all. They can't get smaller or learn to hunt."

It seemed to be Fastfire's day to contradict and lecture. "I don't think that's what the sacrifice was for," he mused aloud, setting his bone-carving implements aside. Unlike everything else he'd said so far, his thoughts about Timmain were ideas he'd never put into words before and he had the first-born's undivided attention.

"If it had been just that the high ones were too big and ate too much, or because they weren't good hunters, she wouldn't have needed to make the sacrifice. Look at me—sure I'm taller than all of you, but I'm *shorter* than everybody else. Everybody's been smaller than their parents. Everybody—Talen, Rellah, me, Chanfur, even Feslin would have been shorter if she'd lived. Timmorn Yellow-Eyes towered over me like an oak tree. I remember Murrel's father; he was taller than Timmain!

"And we're hardier; that started almost from the first, too. Smaller, stronger, more resistant to the cold. But way before the sacrifice the high ones were the hunters, not their children. They hunted in their own ways—with magic—and the oldest were the best."

The first-born, except for the She-Wolf, shook their heads. Samael—tall, stately, and ancient—would not even *touch* a weapon and would only eat meat that had been boiled beyond recognition. It was impossible to imagine him, or anyone like him, beating the bushes for game. Only the She-Wolf had been listening closely enough to suspect that the elders hadn't used spears, bows, or rocks to make their kills.

"What kind of magic?" she asked slowly, her dreams about Timmorn and his mother bubbling to the forefront of her mind.

Zarhan smiled—she was the one he'd really been talking to, the only one whose understanding and acceptance he craved. "Many kinds. Some of them could paralyze prey with their sendings. My grandfather could make anything burn—*anything*—even things that shouldn't burn like water and rocks. They would drive a herd of black-neck deer with his fire until the whole herd collapsed with exhaustion or stampeded into a rock chasm—"

"A whole herd of black-necks?" Glowstone shuddered with a different sort of amazement. "Didn't they know that was wrong? The weakest, the slowest—a few at a time—but never the whole herd. No wonder their magic stopped working for them. I'm just as glad we have wolf-ways instead of magic."

"You're right!" Zarhan danced over the flint-pile to give a surprised Glowstone a hearty embrace. "The key to the sacrifice. The old ones didn't belong here! They used the magic they had from the sky-mountain to survive here, but the world here rejected them. Their magic got smaller along with everything else. I can only make fire where it could properly be; my father's magic was somewhere in between.

"Timmain's sacrifice: she gave her magic to this world to create Timmorn. You, Timmorn's children, are truly a part of this world. It won't reject you or your magic."

Sharpears tightened his lips, exposing teeth that weren't lupine but did have the strength and edge to tear through raw meat. "We have no magic," he declared, locking eyes with the elf.

It was challenge as practiced and perfected by the hunt. The flame-haired youth felt a savagery rip through him that threatened to leave him numb and senseless. He'd seen this in the hunt; seen the weaker hunter turn his head and offer his neck in submission. He fought to keep the cords of his neck from twisting around. "Are you wolves or elves?" he croaked.

Sharpears was trembling as well. Challenge seldom lasted more than a few heartbeats. That was its virtue—it established order without harming either side. He had had the strength. Fastfire knew he was beaten, but the ignorant elf hadn't known how to quit, and now Sharpears was himself strained past his limit.

"We're both," the She-Wolf snapped, placing herself between them.

Zarhan thumped to the floor behind her.

"Challenge right!" Sharpears gasped. "My right! Submit or dominate—you had no right to interfere."

"Challenge me instead."

Sharpears simply looked away. His heart and mind would burst if he met her icy eyes. The She-Wolf kept him twisted before her while she contemplated the audacity of her gesture. Yellow-Eyes had never interfered in the challenge squabbles within the hunt; Threetoe didn't even notice them unless he was, himself, involved; but she had leaped in to stop one from reaching its ordained climax.

Why? she asked herself, blinking and letting the other first-born come erect again. Because it was one thing to have a leader but something less to have everyone arrayed in rigidly descending order. Because her father had told her to bring the halves together again. Because she wasn't sure which of them was right and didn't think hunt-challenge was the way to learn.

Grabbing her spear from the stack at the cave entrance she stomped out into the bright, cold sunlight. She marched past her old, solitary lair, past the faint boundary of the camp and into the forest. A straight track that stumbled over fallen logs and flinched as branches snagged and snapped.

Zarhan.

He destroyed her peace; twisted her leadership without ever challenging it. Worse, he put ideas in her mind that the wolf-song could not swallow. They were both wolf and elf, she and her brothers and sisters, not some part elf and the other part wolf but two complete, ever-shifting natures. Natures that were, for the moment, at war within her.

Though the hunt had its order of dominance it had never so completely emulated the true-wolves that only the supreme male, Threetoe, and his mate, Rustruff, had offspring. Each year had seen the pack grow slightly in size as more were born and survived than died. Laststar's children had departed with Threetoe, but the She-Wolf had no such emptiness in her heart.

Everything had changed since the cold had driven them all into the elves' cave. The wolf-song trilled a burning chorus and so did her elfin self. Sharpears had emerged as their best hunter. His tracking and stalking skills were superb; he was almost always the first to make his kill, and the She-Wolf's dreams were filled with musky thoughts of him. She had only to nod and smile in a certain way to bring them together— then he would become the leader, not she. But that was the way of wolf-song.

She understood the wolf-song, accepted it and knew how to resist it. The storm that pushed her toward Zarhan Fastfire was less easily grasped. He had magic and he did not hear the wolf-song. He had wisdom and courage but he was no leader. He was clever with his fishhooks and traps and he learned things in a quicker, subtler way than any of the first-born could. His name echoed through her thoughts.

"I do not want either of them!" she shouted to the uncaring trees as tears froze on her cheeks.

What she wanted, the images of Zarhan and Sharpears said together, had nothing to do with it. She slumped down against a tree trunk and buried her face in her hands.

Yellow-Eyes! Timmorn! Father! Set me free!

He could have heard her if he'd been within a day's journeying, but she knew he wouldn't come. Choices never bothered Yellow-Eyes; he never made them. He embraced whatever his dominant self—wolf or elf—had pointed him toward. He'd left the consequences to his daughter.

I don't want to bring the halves together!

She was deep in self-pity when the nearby juniper rustled and startled her back to awareness. With her spear half-ready she rose to a crouch and waited. A wolfish head thrust through the evergreen: full-grown but small, probably a lone female. She lowered the spear slightly.

It isn't just me, is it? she sent to the wolf—not that she actually expected an answer. **The first-born always stayed apart from everyone, even each other. Now we're together and with the elves as well. The whole cave is crowded and edgy.**

The wolf whined and took a hesitant half step toward her. The first-born female brought her spear back up. Timmorn could communicate with the true-wolves as could some members of the hunt. Her own abilities were limited, unreliable, and particularly confused by this wolf. She lowered her spear only after the wolf squatted down.

We have no children. There were always children in the winter and everyone fussed over them—even the wolflings that wouldn't live until spring. We'll have to have our own children now. The wolf-song leads me to Sharpears. How do the elves know?

Something startled the wolf. It rose and, staring at her, emitted a plaintive song. Timmorn's daughter sniffed empty air, but the wolf would sense danger long before she did. She'd been gone long enough. The cold had seeped past the layers of fur and straw lining her boots. If danger was coming, she'd best get back to the cave.

Nothing dangerous appeared on that day or on any of the next days—only more of winter's harshness. They were gaunt and had scoured the nearby forest of game when the snow-pack finally began to melt. Even then the winds stayed cool, moist, and out of the north; the ground remained boggy and the deer, upon which their survival depended, did not return from their southern ranges.

Samael and the dreamberries reminded them of the years-without-a-summer, which had precipitated Timmain's sacrifice. The stream at the edge of their camp flooded beyond its banks. The icy waters did not recede. Their camp became a bit smaller, though, without the hunt, no one really noticed.

And no one talked about the slivers of odd-colored ice which rode through the torrent.

Fish throve in the flesh-numbing water. Zarhan tied lengths of flexible gut to his bone hooks and showed everyone how to make them dance in the currents. Fish chowder became the taste and aroma of springtime and everyone got thinner beneath the winter furs they still wore.

"Where are the deer?" Sharpears said to the sky and the forest as he stood beside the She-Wolf above one of the empty grass valleys.

"South. Where the ice has left the air."

"Do we go south after them?" His asking was a sending as well, filled with the dreamberry memories of the treks Timmorn Yellow-Eyes had led.

The She-Wolf sent rather than replied—a flash of long-dead memory: the high ones sprawled in their own blood. **You know what we'll find,** the memory chided.

A shiver that owed nothing to the raw wind passed between Sharpears' shoulders. The memories were powerful for all that they were short-focus and unconnected: *Those* had killed Timmain's people; *Those* had sent the high ones into the clutch of the long winters; *Those* were fear, fright, nightmare and death. Wolf-song taught each of them to distrust the tall, five-fingered hunters more than any other beast in the forest, and the dreamberry memories from the high ones told them why.

"It is better to be hungry," Frost agreed, having felt the sending as she joined them.

But that was a lie. The She-Wolf knew it even if the other first-born and the elves did not. They would have to go south to the edge of the five-fingers' range because it would be better to fight with outsiders than with each other.

The chieftess had actually made up her mind the last time the moons had crossed above the treetops. The changeable crescents were catching up to each other again but she had yet to tell anyone else. Each day that she delayed their departure was another day of slowly ebbing strength; the knowledge that she was weakening the tribe rasped painfully within her. Each day she contrived to steal into the forest alone to send a plea to her father, whose death she had not felt, and the hunt, which surely must have survived the winter. There was never any answer.

She could not leave so long as Timmorn lingered in her perceptions of the wolf-song and they needed the hunt as they had never needed them before.

Selnac's time had come. Swollen and irritable, Timmorn's last favorite among the elves was ready to deliver herself of his cub. The young She-Wolf ached with inadequacy: Timmorn had always judged his cubs. He'd taken each newborn into his arms and known its nature. He knew if it was hunt or first-born—or if it could survive at all. It was a judgment the She-Wolf knew she could not make. Her forest sendings approached the intensity of a prayer and the desperation of a curse.

The moment came on a day when the She-Wolf could not escape the cave. The rain had gone cold and hard, covering everything with a treacherous glaze of ice. Trees rattled with the wind and painfully shed their branches while, as deep in the cave as possible, Selnac whimpered and called Timmorn's name.

Hidden within dreamberry languor or the recollections of the eldest, who had known Timmain before she became a wolf, lay the knowledge that she had been something else before the high ones had been stranded on this magic-desert world. Something that never worried about strength, stamina, death or the agonies of giving birth for the beautiful shape they had chosen—and were forced to pass along to their unexpected children—was poorly adapted to the rigors of ordinary life.

The She-Wolf felt the newborn's first gasp, as did everyone in the cave. They were so few in number, so bound by blood that they could not help but be aware of each other. Holding her breath, the She-Wolf approached the fur-mound on legs that seemed no longer her own.

How would she know? What should she look for? What if the cub was hunt—now that the hunt was gone?

They cleared a path for their chieftess, letting her watch as Murrel gently wrapped the newborn in a patch of the softest suede the elves' art could create. Its hair was a soft nut brown and was already drying into a lavish halo around its face—but, then, it was Timmorn's child and that, at least, was always his legacy. The child twisted its dark pink face into a burping little cry and thrust a tiny fist beyond the suede. Life—and time—stood still as the fingers uncurled, one by one.

Four or five? Elf or Wolf? Life or death? One, two, three . . . four—and the last stuck out at an arrogant angle to the rest.

The She-Wolf went dizzy with relief as pent-up air and anxiety escaped her. Something—her father, or maybe the part in her that might yet become a mother—suggested she take the infant in her hands and raise it high over her head for all to see, as Timmorn had done; but she fought that impulse and watched in silence as Selnac was propped up with fragrant pillows.

Selnac radiated more fear than love as she took her child in her arms for the first time. She offered it to her breast and curled around it, her midnight black hair hiding her own face and the child from view. When she uncurled there were tears in her eyes.

"She has no name," the mother said in a strangled voice. "Empty. Empty. *Empty!*"

Murrel fell to her knees, embracing them both, absorbing whatever other words and despair Selnac needed to share. The other elves, even Zarhan, pressed tight together, closing out the first-born and emanating a sense of pure mourning.

What? Treewalker asked the rest of Timmorn's children.

No name, the She-Wolf repeated. **We aren't born with our names—they are.**

It was just as well they were sending not talking. She couldn't breathe through the pounding of her heart, and her tongue was as dry and useless as old leather. She had known all along that elves always had names, while Timmorn's children only had names if they had the brazen courage to take them, but she had never thought about it. The gulf between her and her mother, like the one between Selnac and the newborn child, was wider and deeper than anything which separated true-wolves from first-born for all that the differences could not be so easily seen.

Her feet were taking her backward, out of the cave. Her hands took up her spear because they always did when she left. But her eyes did not truly see and her mind echoed with screams and howls. Her feet went out from under her not two steps beyond the cave entrance; she careened down the wet, icy slope toward the stream.

Survival instincts that were well-rooted in all parts of the She-Wolf's nature struggled to protect her. She flung the spear far to one side and contrived to make a tucked-in hedgehog of herself. Her efforts came too late. She met the boulders at the stream's edge with an extended arm that twisted and shot numbing pain straight to the back of her neck. In shock and suddenly unable to move either arms or legs, the She-Wolf came to a stop with her face only a hands-breadth from the water.

She heard them calling from the cave—asking if she was all right. It was in her thoughts to tell them that she was; that she could not have so thoroughly disgraced and embarrassed herself by falling from the cave all the way to the stream. But, though nothing hurt, nothing would move. She could not even send her thoughts.

*   *   *

Zarhan reached her first, having found outlet for his fire-magic through the soles of his feet. His hands were strong and gentle as they sought her injuries and gathered her out of the slick mud. They trembled, too, but not from the cold. His sendings struck her like lightning but they carried no images nor even words; they were empty—as empty as Selnac's child.

She found the strength to turn away from him and to ward her eyes from his with her hand, but movement banished the numbness. The She-Wolf, unwilling and occasionally unwitting chieftess of elves and first-born, knew nothing of the care with which Zarhan carried her back up that slope. She roused a moment when they laid her on a fur-mound and removed the sleeve-laces from her tunic.

"Selnac cannot help her," someone said—probably an elf, probably Samael.

"Her arm is broken—see how the wrist is turned back. Selnac's *got* to help her." That from one of the first-born, no doubt.

"She will have to wait, or heal herself." An elf again.

The She-Wolf sighed. If she had been a wolf it would have been easier. She would have crawled to her lair, lain down, and packed dirt around the injury and then waited. If the bone healed before she starved, then she would walk and hunt again. If it healed wrong, then she would, in turn, be hunted. It was all the same to the true-wolves: no questions, no doubts, no worry about right or wrong—just do what you did and, maybe, survive.

She threw herself into the wolf-song but not far enough. The cave was dark and sleeping when the top-fur was drawn back. The She-Wolf felt warm fingers work their way along the bone toward the fracture.

Zarhan? The thought flashed and faded, unsent and unspoken. She knew those hands, though she had not felt them for many long years.

"Murrel?" she whispered.

"I am not Selnac," the elf-woman apologized. "The healing gift does not run strong in me; does not run at all. But memory does, and I cannot let you lie here. I cannot heal you, chieftess, but I can make the bones meet straight so you can heal yourself."

Eight fingers went rigid. Even through the sheet of pain the She-Wolf had a thought to marvel that an elf could be so strong. Then the pain passed, replaced by a vague throbbing, the fingers relaxed and began to pull away.

"Mother? Don't go."

It was dark in the cave: charcoal silhouettes against black stone. The She-Wolf couldn't see the expression in her mother's eyes, but she felt the same defeat she had seen in Selnac's eyes make Murrel's hands rest heavy on her arm.

What do the names mean? the younger woman sent.

Murrel sighed. "First there is the name—always the name. Your own name, your lover's name, your child's name. When our people—Timmain's first people, the ones who came from high in the stars—were where they belonged, they knew each other by their names because their shapes changed with their moods. Names passed instantly from one mind to another and when the names joined, sometimes, a new name was created. I don't understand how—Timmain couldn't ever explain—but it wasn't like this.

"I think that all *we* have left from the high ones is our names."

The emphasis was not lost on the She-Wolf. "And *we* do not?"

"I do not understand, daughter. Timmorn had *his*. He was born with it even though Timmain had lost hers somewhere in your wolf-song. I heard his name more than once, filling my mind day and night until the world was shaped for the two of us alone. And there would be a child; and my heart would ask its name—and it could not tell me. Not you nor any of your brothers and sisters.

"And we *never* hear you, not the way we hear each other or heard Timmorn. I know what he told you, before he left, and it can never be unless we hear your names."

A drop of warm liquid splashed against the She-Wolf's arm, then disappeared into the fur. She reached for her mother's hand. There was movement in her fingers, but no strength and Murrel began to pull away.

"Zarhan, mother."

The pulling away stopped.

"I hear his name, and Sharpears' name. Sharpears I understand, but not Zarhan Fastfire."

Despite the darkness the She-Wolf saw the smile spread across her mother's face. The elf-woman quickly wrapped her daughter's arm in stiff leather and tucked it beneath the top fur. "There's hope then," she whispered more than once. "If anyone can find a name it will be Enlet's son."

The She-Wolf's arm healed more slowly than she would have liked—more slowly than it would have had Selnac not needed all her healing energies for herself and her child—but it did give every indication of healing properly. The nameless child, the last of the first-born, clung to life with a tenacity that kept much of the cave awake at night and grumbling in the morning. But neither the child nor her mother could be said to be thriving and, though the ice had melted, the cold deerless spring was giving every sign of becoming a cool and equally deerless summer.

The She-Wolf learned one of leadership's hidden lessons: the leader is the one in front when the pack starts moving. Mosshunter, the most atavistic of the first-born, challenged her while her arm was still bound in stiff leather and the stench of boiled, smoked or stewed fish had penetrated the very walls of their cave.

"We need meat," the diminutive hunter snarled, hurling his half-empty bowl into the stream. "Meat with red blood in it! We follow the deer the way the wolves do!" His eyes and thoughts locked onto hers.

He hadn't meant to challenge; he was only the most outspoken, not the strongest. She turned him aside with little more than the focus of her thoughts against his, but his outburst sparked others less easily controlled.

"You haven't hunted since you fell," Sharpears stated, his stance suggesting that he was more than ready to take over her duties.

"We can't make leather from fish scales," Samael added.

Treewalker set his bowl aside and joined Sharpears by the wall where the spears were kept. "The forests around here are empty. There's nothing to hunt worth eating. It's time we moved on."

The She-Wolf glanced toward Zarhan, almost without thinking about it, and then immediately regretted it. The flame-haired elf looked away from her—not because he would not challenge her, but because he would not help her. She pushed herself to her feet, studying the firm-set faces as if she had not seen them for a long time.

Healing had pushed her deep within the wolf-song and she had not, in fact, taken note of the growing discontent. Nor, more importantly, had she noticed the shifting alliances among the first-born. Sharpears wasn't waiting for her anymore; Laststar stood close beside him. Likewise Treewalker and Frost had paired.

The birth of Selnac's daughter had forced a resolution to the mating tensions that had been slowly building since the hunt's departure. The first-born had made their choices and the elves—if Talen and Selnac's closeness meant anything, or Samael and Chanfur, standing hand-in-hand. The patterns her father had left to break were being perpetuated, and she had missed it all, lost in the timelessness of the wolf-song.

"All right, we'll move, then." She shook her arm free of the sling that held it motionless above her waist. "We'll go south, where the deer are—and the five-fingered hunters who killed so many of the high ones." She turned to Samael, giving him a hard, commanding look. **It's time to remember,** she sent.

Tension snapped and re-formed itself. Mention of the savage five-fingered hunters brought the first-born out of wolf-song. They did not want to remember what had happened at the sky-mountain; the elves dreaded reliving it. But Samael found his trove of winter-dried fruits and counted them carefully into a basket. He glanced at the She-Wolf, hoping she'd reconsider her command, but her eyes remained hard and he took the first three berries.

They remembered the slaughter, the terror, and the years of panicked running that had taken them far from the sky-mountain and cast them adrift in this world with only Timmain's now-lost wisdom to guide them. To be sure, Timmorn had led them back to the forest from the frozen flatlands farther north, but he had stopped among the trees that remained ever green and refused to go closer to the five-fingers' territories.

Then, when the remembering was over but the power of the berries yet remained, the She-Wolf challenged her tribe. She thrust the dangers of their journey deep into the wolf-song itself. Here in the ever green forest they were the most canny hunters, but there, where the deer had gone, they would live in five-fingered shadows.

The elves would have abandoned the idea; they would have accepted starvation or an eternity of fish-and-vermin chowder. The first-born writhed inwardly with their refreshed memories but the wolf-song *did* demand red meat and *did not* cower away from danger.

"We will leave," the She-Wolf told them all, "when we

have smoked enough fish to last us eight days' walking.'' Then, her arm throbbing, she returned to her fur-mound and went to sleep.

They left after four smoke-filled days of preparation. The She-Wolf spent much of that time sending her thoughts deep into the forest. It was a futile quest and the wolf-song, she knew, would absorb any guilt or ill-feelings she might have over leaving Timmorn and the hunt behind, but so long as the deliberate activity of breaking up the camp kept the wolf-song submerged she had to keep trying.

She should have told them to prepare a month's worth of food—or none at all. Their supposed eight-day supply was gone when the cave was only four days behind them. No one, not even the She-Wolf herself, had imagined how hungry they would be after a day of walking weighted down with furs, baskets, bowls, and weapons. They shed their belongings each night and left a few behind each dawn when they started up again. In Timmorn's day their migrations had been undertaken with the help of the hunt's strong shoulders. None of the elves could carry their fair share of the burden and soon, not more than eight days' wandering from the cave, even the first-born were carrying little more than their best weapons and furs.

The forest changed slowly, a few more of the spreading, leaf-dropping trees mixed in with the evergreens for each day they marched south. But the hunting remained hard. The tall paths, which in other seasons had guided the deer from meadows to streams, were encroached by berry-vines and the stream-banks were marked only with the restless tracks of predators like themselves. When, as often happened now, the She-Wolf called a halt that lasted several days, the unfamiliar terrain proved as empty as hunted-out forest around the cave.

The elves were too tired to complain; the first-born sought refuge in the wolf-song which lowered horizons and made deprivation bearable. Hunt, sleep, walk—a daily cycle broken by eating only if the hunting had been good. The She-Wolf did not notice when Selnac gave her daughter, whom they had taken to calling Journey, to Laststar; the wolf-song *saw* and sang the changes into timelessness until it took conscious effort to recall that anything had ever been different.

Nor could she ever reconstruct the moment when Murrel started calling herself New-Wolf and used Glowstone's second-best spear as a walking stick. That it had happened was somehow important and she fought to the edge of the wolf-song to ask the elf about it. But the smiling answer: **We found his name beyond your wolf-song** made no sense and was swiftly forgotten.

Only one discord sounded within her wolf-song: Zarhan Fastfire. He lurked at the edge of her vision and the edge of her thoughts. Like all the elves he had withered during the journey. His eyes were hollow and ringed with smoke that would not wash away. He staggered more than walked and his name crept into her dreams like a wounded animal. His agonies became her agonies; she drove his name away but kept the pain and brought it with her deep inside the wolf-song.

The elves knew how many days it had been—and could have told the first-born, had Timmorn's children been able to ask the question. The tall, slightly-built elders sent prayers to their ancestors begging that the journey might end soon, but they dared not fall behind the relentless She-Wolf who pulled them farther south.

Their silver-haired leader, grown more distant and wolflike with each passing day, rejected each likely lair with a toothy snarl and a sending that contained few, if any, elfin words. Deer—the image was burned into her narrowly-focused mind—if her tribe wanted deer, then she would lead them until the deer were plentiful again.

The end came at dawn—the seventy-second dawn, Talen was heard to remark—at the shore of a broad, shallow lake.

Countless split hooves had churned the soft dirt into mud, and out amid the reeds was the largest deerlike creature elves or first-born had ever seen. Mosshunter could have curled up comfortably between the tips of the beast's spreading antlers. Samael, the tallest of the elves, could not have seen over its shoulder.

A collective sigh of awe rose from elves and first-born alike as they considered the bounty nature had at last set before them. A second sigh rose from the first-born: would their flint-tipped spears bring the beast down?

Fire, Zarhan advised them, with images of his grandfather's methods.

Relays, TreeWalker replied. None of the first-born would carry fire in their hands as Zarhan's images suggested.

Their first hunt was futile, though Frost stumbled, literally, into a den of mask-eyes, and Glowstone said that he'd noticed a rocky ledge that might serve as a base camp. Their second, a few days later, was worse. They brought the beast to bay before it was truly exhausted. It charged, swinging its murderous antlers, and flung Mosshunter head-over-heels into the brush before making its escape.

No good, the She-Wolf seethed as they bore Mosshunter's broken, barely breathing body back to the rock ledge. **No good. We leave.**

She told them to retie their bundles, and Selnac challenged her.

He can't be moved, the elfin healer sent white-hot words into the She-Wolf's mind. **Go yourself. We remain.**

The She-Wolf learned there *was* another way to break a challenge—and more about the qualities of leadership. She admitted she was wrong without bending her neck but insisted, successfully, that they not hunt the branch-horned beast with spears again. She thought time and temptation denied would bring them around to her opinions, but she hadn't noticed the changes that had settled around the elves.

Rest and an abundance of small game had lifted the weariness from those narrow shoulders but their limbs remained lank and sinewy. Chanfur called herself Changefur; Samael named himself Dreamkeeper and so on until only a few of the elves kept their birth names exclusively. They still couldn't hunt, but those agile fingers that turned reeds into baskets were busy turning vines into huge creations that Zarhan said were nets.

Their audacity enraged the She-Wolf. These beasts weren't deer—and they had said they wanted *deer*. She turned on Fastfire when he brought her his new ideas for hunting the branch-horn by driving the beast under a tree from which waiting elves would drop the net, which would keep it from charging. If he had challenged, she would have broken him utterly; but he was Zarhan. He slipped through her anger with a smile.

She remained behind with the frailest of the elves, Selnac, Mosshunter, and little Journey, who giggled as she toddled after the pacing chieftess. It went against the blood to wish them ill, but she could not wish them well either, and she slipped into the darkest parts of the wolf-song when an exultant sending proclaimed to the whole forest that the hunt had been successful.

Zarhan led the procession that brought the prize back to the rock ledge, holding one end of the three spears they needed to carry it. His excitement and satisfaction transcended words or sendings—and the She-Wolf met it with a look that was pure ice.

Challenge me, damn you.

Her sending should have rocked him. Narrowed focus as it was, it had the power to turn the other elves and first-born with him pale. But if he showed any reaction at all it was nothing more than a slight slump to his shoulders and a darkening of his eyes.

No, he replied, and he looked away—ignoring her rather than submitting.

She stormed away from the ledge, noticing but not caring that she left Journey crying behind her. The wolf-song was a dark rage within her; she understood Threetoe at his worst now. Stripping the bark off a luckless sapling, the She-Wolf gave way to immutable, primitive rhythms of the wolf-song: a distrust of invention and cleverness; the hatred of change; and the fear of it. She was a she-wolf again, nameless and feral, when Zarhan Fastfire dared to place his hands on her shoulders and sent an empty brilliance into her mind.

Timmain's lost magic rose within her. The snarling creature who whirled around to face her tormentor glowed with the power to *become* a wolf forever. Had she succeeded in her lunge for his throat she would have been a wolf the moment his blood passed through her lips, but he met shifting with fire and forced her into a challenge.

Now—if it's the only way.

His fire faded; he could not bring himself to hurt her. He fell backward, borne down by her weight and ferocity. His physical strength was simply not enough to protect him. He closed his eyes and put all his effort into one last, radiant sending.

Rahnee!

The sound thundered and echoed in her mind. She hesitated just long enough for him to throw her to one side.

Rahnee!

It stunned her; left her gasping in her own saliva. She gagged, coughed, and fell limp as the latent magic ebbed away.

"Rahnee," Zarhan whispered, lifting her head into his lap and wondering if he had lost her after all.

He was asleep with his arms still around her, his spine propped against a tree trunk, when the nightmare ended and she opened her eyes. Her lip was swollen and lifeless where she'd bitten through it; there wasn't a muscle in her body that felt strong enough to move. It was just as well. Had she been able to slip away from him in shame, she might never have returned. Instead, trapped there in the moonlight, she had the time to make peace between the wolf-song and the newly-illuminated corners of her elfin-self. It would never be easy to have two complete natures; at least now they both had names.

No, only one name: Rahnee the She-Wolf, just as he was Zarhan Fastfire.

How long did you know? she wondered, believing he was still asleep.

I heard your name long before you were born. I did not know, for certain, it was you until just now.

Love did not grow quickly between them, but then, Recognition cared nothing for the parents—only for the children. They were luckier than some of the others. Samael never came to terms with the passion that drove him to Frost and, for her part, Frost would never reveal the name she found on the other side of the wolf-song. Rellah would bear Sharpears' child—and her dislike of him grew faster than her belly.

Like a songbird caught in a storm, Selnac fluttered from one first-born male to another. Recognition drove her to a frenzy and her healer's soul, which knew Journey had been her last child, could do nothing to alleviate the pain. They found her one early winter morning, floating facedown by the lake shore. Their relief that her suffering had ended was as real as their mourning that she was gone.

By spring a new generation was appearing. Rahnee and Zarhan called their first son Brighteyes, knowing that in time he'd claim one of the many names they heard between them. He was one of a double-hand of imps who ran circles around their elders and taxed the ingenuity of the hunters to provide enough food for them all.

The tribe rarely had more than six able hunters at a time. One of the giant deer fed them for three days, but they dared not bring down more than one of the beasts between cycles of the moons. Fish chowder made an unheralded return to their diet, and Rahnee began to dread the coming of cold weather.

She was the unquestioned leader—unchallenged since she had found her elfin name. Zarhan was the clever one who turned their ledge into a hide-roofed lodge and showed them how to turn the sticky clay by the lake shore into watertight pots and bowls. He hunted regularly and successfully, but he had no magic solution to their looming problem.

"Bring back Threetoe," he whispered in jest one late autumn night when Rahnee's anxiety kept her awake in his arms.

She froze and shook free of him. The wolf-song still stood between them, pulling shadows across her memories. Their interests never matched perfectly; their jokes often fell on thorny ground. She had forgotten Threetoe, the hunt, and her father. The dreamberries could bring back the memories without pain, but Zarhan's casual recollections were the root of many of their quarrels.

"I didn't mean it," he said softly, not yet daring to touch her again.

Rahnee reached back in the darkness and held his hands tightly. **I've got to leave,** and shared with him the dream-image of Timmorn and the hunt. **I forgot. He's waiting for me.**

Privately Zarhan Fastfire judged it unlikely that Timmorn or the hunt remembered much of anything after almost two years of utterly feral existence, but he knew better than to say anything about it. He even accepted the burden of leadership in her absence, knowing that he'd share it with Sharpears. The first-born were calmer now, but the wolf-song ran deep and passed beyond an elf's understanding. A part of his life went with her when she headed back north, but she didn't notice it.

The snow was deep when she returned to the cave. Their home of many dimly remembered years had been taken over by a bear who chased her back into the forest. The scent of elves and wolves was long vanished; the wolf-song that had guided the She-Wolf came to an abrupt end.

Muttering curses as she went, Rahnee blundered from one half-remembered glade to the next. Late in the afternoon she caught the tang of the true-wolves but nothing of her father or the hunt. All the maturity and wisdom she had pieced together with Zarhan evaporated as she hurled her spear at a tree and watched, dumbfounded, as the spearhead shattered into eights of pieces.

Father! Timmorn! Yellow-Eyes!

She howled until the sun had slipped below the trees and her throat was raw from the unaccustomed exercise. Chewing on the tip of an uncured pelt she wore draped over one shoulder, Rahnee climbed into the tree that had broken her spear.

She-Wolf.

The summons startled her out of a dreamless sleep. Rahnee grabbed at the nearest branch and barely saved herself from falling; she wasn't used to sleeping in trees anymore.

Daughter.

She scrambled down the trunk, falling the last eight feet and not minding at all. Timmorn was there, majestic, glowing a soft warm gold and a little bit frightening in the moonlight. She'd forgotten what he really looked like, how much he was a wolf who walked on two legs. Or perhaps he'd changed. His sendings were different than anything she could remember: raw, as if it hurt him to send as it had once hurt him to talk.

She-Wolf?

Nodding, Rahnee took a cautious step toward him. "Father, I've come to find the hunt. To bring them home."

They burst out of the shadows. Eights of them—not the

hunt and yet not true-wolves either, though she was not certain how she knew that since they were true-wolves in every way her eyes could see. They leaped at her, and she saw death waiting for her even after she'd begun to understand. She locked her fingers behind the ears of the nearest animal and stared deep into the silver-ice eyes.

Not elf, not hunt, yet not quite wolf, it stared back offering its strength, loyalty, and timeless love. All it wanted was a name.

Silver-Ice. You're Silver-Ice.

It whined and pressed against her with an exuberance that reached deep into the wolf-song. The rest of its pack milled about, impatiently waiting their turns.

Only one, she told them, not knowing if or how they would understand her.

Silver-Ice retreated enough to let her stand up and shake the snow off her clothes. He thrust his nose against her bare wrist: **Go** and **Now** filtered through the wolf-song—the only way Silver-Ice could communicate with her.

"Timmorn? Father?" She peered beyond the glade-edge and tried to push the wolf away.

Gone. Go. Now.

The wolves felt her sadness without understanding it and shared its burden with her. They howled and dried her tears with their fur and, in the morning, followed her south.

The cord of finely-woven gut snapped taut with a splash. Longreach was on his feet almost as fast, keeping the cord tight and hoping the now-bowed fishing-pole wouldn't snap from the strain. He'd found the notion of fish-hooks in an old story back when Bearclaw was a cub. Now he felt, and with no small amount of pride as he gave the pole a quick jerk and brought the rainbow fish onto the bank beside him, that not even Zarhan Fastfire knew as much about the art of catching and cooking fish as he did.

To a man, woman, and cub, the Wolfriders had yet to develop a taste for cooked fish, though, as in the past, they were grateful enough for it when the hunting got lean. They indulged him because he was the oldest of the Wolfriders, dutifully sharing his meals, pretending the taste didn't make their noses wrinkle. In many ways they were all like cubs to him these days.

Of course there had been a time when he'd firmly believed there was only one way to hunt and that was full speed with the scent of blood in your nose and a spear held steady beside your ear. Most of them still did. It took age or crisis to make the Wolfriders change their ways—and even then it didn't always last.

Longreach paused in his thoughts and took a knife to the fish. After expertly wrapping the fish in moist leaves he set it with several others in a little pit and opened the kindle-box Rain had helped him make.

Fire was one of the main things that came and went for the Wolfriders. Bearclaw's crop, now they liked a gentle light in their bowers but no flames dancing before their eyes. Longreach had to smolder his fish, and Rain, who made the tallow for their lamps, only lit his rendering fires once or twice in a turning of the seasons. It hadn't always been that way.

The elves—the full-blooded ones who had none of Timmorn's blood—they liked fire, liked it about as much as the five-fingered humans did. Maybe more, because some of them could make fire with their minds alone. But then the high ones were always a bit like humans. Perhaps that was why Two-Spear—

Longreach shrugged his shoulders and cleared *that* story from his head. It was too fine a day for such a dark tale. No, if he was going to let his thoughts wander while his fish smoldered, let them wander through a tale when fire saved the Wolfriders—

Plague of Allos

—————————— *by Piers Anthony* ——————————

The great *wolf* lay as if asleep, so that even when a random leaf tumbled across his nose no whisker twitched. His fur was as brown as blown sand, his paws as gray as weathered stones; when he lay still, as now, he tended to fade into the landscape. Instead it was his elf-friend Prunepit who moved, and rather clumsily too. There seemed to be no chance for a successful ravvit stalk. Yet the elf seemed confident; his sling was poised, a solid pit in the pouch.

His arm moved. The pit flung forward to strike in a thick patch of grass. Sure enough: a fat ravvit leaped out, startled by the near miss.

The elf jumped to the prey's right, herding it toward the still wolf. The ravvit veered left.

Now! the elf cried in thought, sending not so much a word as a target region: a spot in the air not far to the side of the wolf's nose.

The wolf leaped, biting at that spot. Simultaneously the ravvit leaped, coming to that spot just as the wolf's jaws closed.

In a moment it was over; the prey hung from the wolf's mouth, dead. Another hunt had been concluded successfully.

"Let's go home, Halfhowl," Prunepit said, satisfied. "There isn't another suitable animal in the vicinity." He sent another spot location, and leaped at it; the wolf made a swift dive, putting his back just beneath that spot as the elf arrived. Prunepit was mounted so efficiently that it seemed as though they had rehearsed that maneuver many times. Actually they had not; the elf's sending made rehearsal unnecessary.

Prunepit was the son of Rahnee the She-Wolf, but there was no evidence of this in his aspect. He was neither handsome nor large, and his brown hair fell down across his eyes in chronic tangles. His skill with his chosen weapon was mediocre; he normally missed his target, as he had just now. He had to carry a good supply of ammunition because of this. Prune pits were lighter than stones, and their regular shapes made it easier for him, but still it was evident that he lacked the physical coordination ever to be truly effective. Worse, his sending was defective; he could not properly tune into other elves, and consequently was forever getting things garbled. He was not simpleminded, but sometimes seemed so. The other elves of the tribe were of course circumspect about their attitude, but it was true that if any member of the tribe could be said to be held in contempt, that member was Prunepit. Rahnee had never expressed disappointment in him, but surely she had felt it.

Yet it was also true that in this time of the hunting drought, he alone had maintained his ratio of kills. This was because his telepathy was attuned to animals rather than to his own kind. Halfhowl had been the first wolf to recognize this, and had chosen Prunepit to be his elf-friend. Theirs was the closest bond between elf and wolf, and this was part of the reason their hunts were almost inevitably successful. Halfhowl never had to listen for Prunepit's directive, either physical or verbal; he knew it as fast as the elf did. He was always there when the elf wanted him, and there was no subservience in this; it was as though the desire to be there had originated with the wolf. Often that might be true; it did not matter. What mattered was that the two never miskeyed; they always acted with such perfect coordination that the other elves and wolves could only watch with muted envy.

The other part of the reason for success was Prunepit's identification with the prey. He could tell the prey's next move at the same time as the prey did, for animals did not think ahead in the way elves did. From a distance this made no difference; there was no catching the prey anyway. But in close action, the prey's specific dodge became critical. In the hunt just completed, Prunepit had in effect linked the minds of ravvit and wolf, allowing the two bodies to coincide.

The others of the tribe had chosen to believe that Prunepit was mostly lucky; it was hard for them to accept the notion that this elf who could hardly send to his own kind could be superior with other kinds. Thus Prunepit's status was higher among the wolves than among the elves. It seemed likely that he would in time turn to animal-healing as his life's work.

There was a commotion as they drew near the holt. Something had happened—and Prunepit felt a surge of dread.

Another elf would have known instantly what the problem was, but the vague dread was all that Prunepit could receive. It involved his mother, known as the She-Wolf.

Rahnee had led a party out to explore the nature of the allos, the big saurians who seemed to be swarming into this region. The allos were huge, vicious reptiles, not as efficient predators as the wolves, but their increasing numbers were making them a nuisance. When the horde swept through a region, hardly any other species of creature survived. The allos were normally solitary hunters, and their relative clumsiness enabled them to prey mainly on the old, the infirm, and the unlucky. Now, their numbers increased perhaps a hundredfold, they required no subtlety of approach; they saturated the range, snapping up everything that moved. Migratory prey had all but disappeared, if its migration took it through the infested regions.

It was obvious that blind, ravening hunger would bring the allos to the region of the Wolfriders, for here the hunting had until recently been good. Now it was not—because of the depredations of the allos—and it was likely to get much worse. What would the reptiles hunt, after the last legitimate prey was gone? The answer just might be: elves.

So Rahnee had gone out to assess the menace—and now there was a commotion, and no sign of her wolf, Silvertooth.

Softfoot hurried out to intercept Prunepit. "Your mother—" she cried. "Silvertooth is terribly injured, and—"

Then he knew. Rahnee was dead, and the tribe was without its chief.

It was worse than that. Rahnee's party had included the best hunters of the tribe—and most of them were dead too. There was no obvious prospect for new leadership. Rahnee's lifemate Zarhan was loyal and good, but he had no interest in taking her place. Prunepit, her son, seemed to follow his father's temperament. He had never imagined challenging her for leadership, and would have felt disloyal to try for it now that she was dead. Even had he not felt this way, he would have known that no elf would follow a leader who was defective in sending; how could the tribe coordinate in times of crisis? He did not grieve for Rahnee as a son might, for they had not been really close after he grew up. But her loss was tragic for the tribe, and he wanted to steal no part of her glory. Still, there had to be a leader, for the dread allos were swarming closer, and in a few days would be here.

In the confusion of the horror of the disaster, one voice emerged with clarity. This was Wreath, the loveliest of the younger female elves, the object of much male interest. She was brave, beautiful, and cold; her fair hair framed her face like a lattice of snow. It was said that her heart was formed of extremely pretty ice. She had never, to Prunepit's knowledge, done anything for anyone other than because of calculated self-interest. She was a fine huntress, adept with the bow, but had no pretensions toward leadership; it seemed that that would have been too much work to suit her. When she encountered a male routinely, her inclination was to inhale, smile, and give her magnificent cloud of hair a careful toss, causing him to catch his breath and lick his lips while his heart accelerated. Her own heart never fluttered, however. In short, she was a flirt, not a leader. She had been looking for some time for a companion, but had wanted to be absolutely sure she had the best match. That meant Recognition—and it hadn't come. Perhaps, Prunepit thought, that was just as well.

"Why don't we choose as chief the one who can stop the menace of the allos?" she inquired brightly. "Because if we don't stop them, soon they will wipe out all the prey in our forest, and then we'll starve."

This made so much sense that the others were amazed. Why hadn't any of them thought of it? There was a murmur of agreement.

"So who knows how to stop the allos?" Wreath inquired.

That was where it went sour. No one had any notion. The allos, according to the description of the survivors of the party who had straggled home, were big, vicious, and numerous. No single Wolfrider could stand against an allo in combat, and indeed, their best hunters had been savaged as a group. The elves were simply outmatched.

"If we don't get a leader," Wreath pointed out, "we shall have to flee our holt."

But no elf stepped forward. If the She-Wolf had been unable to stop the menace, how could any of them?

The tribe spent a glum night. Softfoot stayed up late, talking with Prunepit. "There has to be a way!" she kept saying. She was a warm, understanding person, lovely in her personality rather than her appearance. Her hair was like a fuzzy, dark blanket. Her feet had seemed malformed in her childhood; they had in time grown normally, but she was not swift on them and was a much better rider than runner. She was good with the spear when on her wolf. She alone of the tribe had appreciated Prunepit's strength and had not perceived him as mentally stunted. It had not been hard for him to love her, and he had never regretted their association.

Reluctantly, Prunepit spoke. "I think there might be—but if I'm wrong, it would be even worse than now."

She virtually pounced on him. "A way! What way?"

"You know how I hunt by relating to the prey," he said, "and by putting it in touch with Halfhowl."

"Yes, of course; you have never received proper credit for your skill."

"Well, if I could relate to an allo, then we could hunt allos. That would give us and our wolves suitable prey, and help reduce the numbers of the reptiles, until the normal ratios of animals returned."

Softfoot shook her head. "You couldn't hunt an allo, Prunepit! They say that a single allo killed Rahnee and two other hunters and two wolves, and it wasn't even the largest allo! Those monsters have horny scales that make them almost invulnerable to our weapons, and their teeth are horrendous. We can't even recover Rahnee's body from them.''

"They are like snakes," he said doggedly, suppressing the thought of his mother's body; there was indeed nothing the elves could do about that. "That means they are slow to move in the cool morning, and not too smart. They can't have armor on their eyes. If we knew how to avoid their teeth and claws, we should be able to score on a weak point. And I do know.''

She began to be swayed. "You aren't afraid? An allo is no ravvit, you know; it's a predator.''

Prunepit's mouth was dry. "I'm terrified. But we have to find a way to fight allos, and I think I can.''

"Sleep now," Softfoot decided. "If you still think the same in the morning, we'll talk with someone.'' This was her way: to consider something, then sleep, and reconsider. It seemed to work well enough. She had done it when they had become lifemates, taking time to be certain. Prunepit was glad to have her doing it now. If she concluded that his notion was viable, in the morning, then perhaps it was. He had spoken forthrightly enough, but the thought of hunting an allo made his body cold.

"I think we should test it," Softfoot announced in the morning. "But not on an allo.''

Prunepit hadn't thought of that. He liked the notion. "What can we test it on? There isn't any prey near.''

"On mock-prey," she said. "One of the wolves, maybe. If you can catch a bit of leather the wolf holds between his teeth, when he knows you are trying to do it and doesn't want you to—''

Prunepit considered. He had never tried that on a wolf; his effort had always been to cooperate with Halfhowl. Yet

Softfoot's reasoning seemed valid: if he could do it with an alert wolf, he could probably do it with an allo. "But what wolf? We need to integrate with our own wolf-friends; that's the key to this. I won't attack an allo alone; I need to coordinate an attack by a hunting party."

"Maybe a volunteer," she suggested.

Prunepit called to Halfhowl with his mind. As always, he did not send coherent instructions; it was more of a single thought, the concept of a wolf agreeing to do something special. In a moment Halfhowl tuned out; he was inquiring among his kind.

Prunepit and Softfoot walked out through the forest, waiting to meet with the wolves. The dew was bright on the leaves, and things seemed peaceful. Yet they knew that the ravening horde of allos was moving closer; peace was illusory.

Three wolves cut through the trees toward them. They were Halfhowl, Hardfoot, and Silvertooth. The first two were Prunepit and Softfoot's wolf-friends, both tawny and somewhat shaggy. But the third—

"You are the volunteer, Silvertooth?" Softfoot inquired, astonished. "But your injuries—"

Silvertooth was Rahnee's wolf-friend, and had dragged herself back to help give the warning after the disaster. She was silver in more than the tooth; her fur was like the light of the moons, seeming almost to glow despite her advanced age. She was limping now, and moved slowly, for she had lost blood. She should have been lying in her den, recovering what strength she could.

Prunepit touched her mind, and understood. "She feels she has no better use than this, now," he reported, translating the feeling to human terms. "She could not save her elf-friend, and may die herself, but she can help the rest of us oppose this menace."

"That is very generous of her," Softfoot agreed. "Then we can do it now."

But another wolf approached, this one with a rider. "Do what?" Wreath asked. "Why is Silvertooth out here?" Her wolf, Curlfur, stopped, and she dismounted. She was, as always, a splendid figure of a woman, even bundled as she was for the morning. "I saw the wolves coming here, and so I followed."

"Prunepit has a way to stop the allos," Softfoot said. "We're about to test it."

"Oh? What is it?" Wreath turned to Prunepit, gazing directly into his face for the first time.

As their eyes met, something happened. Prunepit had always known that Wreath was beautiful; now her beauty seemed to intensify like the sunrise, striking through to his heart. He stared at her, almost unblinking. "Aiyse," he said, awed. It was her soulname, a thing she had never told another person.

"No," she whispered, horrified, staring back at him. "Not this!"

"What's the matter?" Softfoot asked, perplexed.

"It's Recognition," Wreath said, never breaking off her gaze into Prunepit's face. "I know your soulname. Owm. I know its meaning. But I never sought this!"

"Neither did I," Prunepit said. She had, indeed, read his soulname: that concept-sound that defined his essence. The thing that distinguished him from all other elves. His ability to relate telepathically to animals was defined by that name. "I love Softfoot."

"It can't be!" Softfoot cried with dismay. "This—we have other business!"

"Not anymore," Wreath said. Then she wrenched her gaze away. "Oh, why did this have to happen now?"

"Maybe we can fight it," Prunepit said without conviction.

Softfoot regrouped. "Fight it? Easier to fight the allos!" she said angrily. "Recognition is absolute." Then she realized what she was saying, and tears stifled her. Her relationship with Prunepit had been based on understanding and acceptance and respect, not Recognition. Recognition was the involuntary mating of particular elves, seeming to be a mechanism of the species to ensure offspring that bred true.

"It must be a mistake," Prunepit said. "I don't love Wreath."

"And I don't love you," Wreath said. "I never had any interest in you! I don't have any interest now!" For the first time, he was seeing her expressing genuine emotion—and of course it was negative.

"Let's be practical," Softfoot said. "Recognition doesn't care whether two people love each other, or even whether they like each other. It's just a mating urge. We all agree we don't want a—a longer relationship. Could we perhaps hide it?"

"From whom?" Prunepit asked. "It's all I can do to keep my hands off her!"

"Try to manage it, though," Wreath said grimly.

"From the others," Softfoot said.

"To what point?" Wreath asked. It was obvious that this was a phenomenal nuisance to her, despite its validity.

"To the point of getting the mating over with the least disruption of our lives," Softfoot said with difficulty. She would have given anything to have been the one to Recognize Prunepit, and now had to accept its manifestation in one who didn't want it or him. "Since Recognition can't be resisted, the only way to make it go away is to complete it."

"Complete it?" Prunepit said with horror.

"I know you love me," Softfoot said. "Why don't you do what you have to do with her, and when it's done, turn your back on it and be with me? I confess it's not my favorite situation, but it does seem the best way through."

Prunepit looked at Wreath. "And never tell the others," he said, finally understanding what Softfoot was offering.

"And never tell the others," Wreath said, brightening. Her cold nature seemed unaffected by the Recognition; she was eager to minimize its inconvenience. "Maybe that would work. Except that when the baby comes—"

"Any elf would be glad to think he made it—with you," Softfoot pointed out. "Who would suspect Prunepit?"

"I have not *been* with any elf!" Wreath protested.

"They won't believe that," Softfoot said. "They'll assume you have a secret lovemate."

"Meanwhile, we can try to stop the allos," Prunepit said, uncomfortable with this dialogue.

Wreath looked at Softfoot. She was quick enough to recognize the proffered convenience. "When?"

Softfoot shrugged. "Now, if you want."

"I *don't* want! But if it's medicine I must take, the sooner the better, so I can forget it."

"We were going to run our test," Prunepit said with an edge.

"Let's find a good place for it," Softfoot suggested. Prunepit was unable to read her exact meaning, but evidently Wreath did.

They mounted and rode their wolves to a sparse section of the forest, well clear of the elves' usual haunts. They drew up at a large thicket of brush through which animal paths threaded. "There," Softfoot said brusquely. "I will scout about with the wolves."

"Now, wait—" Prunepit protested as she rode off. But Wreath took him by the hand. "The faster we get this over with, the better," she said. "If we're lucky, one time will do it. I assure you this is no fun for me."

"Oh." He followed her into the brush. He never would have believed that he could anticipate such an act with such a lovely creature with so little enthusiasm. Wreath had no concern at all for his feelings, or for Softfoot's. If she could have gotten bred without being physically present, she certainly would have done it.

But when she opened her leather tunic and smiled at him,

he found it impossible not to react despite his awareness of the calculated nature of her actions. Her bosom did not look as if it contained ice; indeed, she was warm all over. Perhaps the Recognition changed her nature, for this one occasion. All the elfin conjectures about the loveliness of her body when naked were emphatically confirmed.

"Turn your face away," she said, reminding him abruptly of reality.

He did so, trying to imagine that it was Softfoot he held, but it was no good. He knew it was Wreath, and that she was facilitating this chore so that it would take the very minimum time. Such was the compulsion of the Recognition that it made no difference.

Softfoot rode Hardfoot, circling around the thicket. The wolf had been named for his thick claws and heavily callused pads. His tough feet were exactly what she needed, and she had always appreciated this. Perhaps that was why Hardfoot had come to her, to be her wolf-friend. The terrain was ragged, but no more so than her thoughts. She knew she had done something foolish: she had made a decision that could affect the rest of her life, and had not slept on it. If it turned out wrong, it would be because of that carelessness.

Yet how could it turn out wrong? Recognition could not be opposed. She was no strong telepath, but she had picked up enough to know that what had passed between Prunepit and Wreath was valid. She also believed them both when they said they had neither sought nor wanted it. Recognition did not require its chosen to seek it; it chose on its own basis, trampling under any other concerns. If she had fought it, encouraging her lifemate to flee it, he would have sickened, and his love for her would have suffered. From the moment the Recognition occurred, Prunepit and Wreath were destined to mate. There was nothing else Softfoot *could* do except accept it.

Then where was her error? As she mulled it over, she

knew what it was. She had ignored Wreath's motives. Oh, of course Wreath had no more choice than did Prunepit; Recognition accepted no motive but its own, as it went single-mindedly after the best combinations for the breed. But Wreath had always wanted to better her status, in whatever manner status existed among the elves. If she could have fascinated a chief, so as to be the lifemate of the most influential member of the tribe, she would have. But there had been no male chief of her generation.

Now, however, Prunepit might become chief, if his idea for hunting allos worked. If he became chief, he would be suitable material for Wreath's interest. Her interest, once aroused, was apt to be devastating. She would, quite simply, take him for her lifemate. Prunepit had settled for Softfoot partly because it had never occurred to him that a woman like Wreath would be interested in him. Indeed, she had not been, and would never have been, but for the Recognition. But what was planned as a strictly temporary tryst was in danger of becoming more than that, and Softfoot could do nothing to prevent it. Wreath's beauty, and her total self-interest, and the Recognition, made that clear.

Yet what could Softfoot have done? She was sure she had made a mistake, but she could not see how she could have avoided it. Maybe if she had slept on it she would have found a way. Now she was stuck; she loved Prunepit, and would always love him, but perhaps would lose him.

She laid her head against Hardfoot's furry shoulder and let the tears flow. The wolf ran on, completing the scouting without her direct guidance. He was aware of her misery, but did not fathom its source, so he let it be.

Prunepit and Wreath emerged and mounted their wolves. Physically, they seemed unaffected; it was as if nothing had happened. But mentally everything had changed; the compelling hunger of the Recognition had abated.

Another woman had made love to Softfoot's lifemate, and had done it better than Softfoot had ever been capable of. Cold as Wreath was, she was always good at what she put her mind to, and Recognition made it easy. No, there was no way Softfoot could compete—if Wreath decided on more than mere mating.

Prunepit joined Silvertooth, setting his hand on the great wolf's head for the strongest contact, explaining the role required of her. The wolf understood: she would run and dodge and feint, never truly attacking, and her actions would be scored as attacks. She was weak, but this she could do. She accepted a piece of leather; this she would protect with her mock-life.

Now Prunepit conferred with the others. "You must not try to guide your wolves," he told the two women. "You must use your weapons only as the opportunity arises; it will seem like chance, for you will not know how your wolves will move."

"I don't like that," Wreath said. "It will be like riding a strange wolf."

"I know. But my plan is to link the minds of the wolves to the mind of the prey, so that they can maneuver as fast as it thinks. No wolf—and no rider—will be in danger as long as that is the case. Then the riders will be able to strike at will."

"If they don't fall off their mounts!" Wreath exclaimed. "I'm glad this isn't a real allo!" She could readily have added that she would have been even happier if she hadn't had to undertake a real mating.

Now they started the test. The three riders on their wolves surrounded the mock-allo, who growled and snapped convincingly, but never let go of the banner. But when Silvertooth lunged, the wolf before her dodged away, while the two others moved in closer. She snapped to the side, but again the target was moving at the same time she did, avoiding her without effort.

Then Prunepit reached forward just as Silvertooth hesitated, and caught away the banner. It had been almost too easy; it seemed like sheer chance. Had the prey reacted differently—

"Let me be the allo," Wreath said, dismounting. "Anything I tag is dead." She took the banner from his hand and held it aloft.

"No, we could not take it from you, without suffering losses," Prunepit said. "I cannot relate well enough to elfin minds, only to animals. But the allos are animals."

Wreath nodded. "I think it will work," she said. "We must try it with the rest of the tribe."

Prunepit grimaced. "They will resist the notion. No one likes to have any other person between him and his wolf."

"Not if six of the finest young elves show how well it works," she said confidently. "Then the women will believe, too."

"Six young men?"

"I will ask them," she said. "They will not refuse."

They did not refuse. No male elf refused anything Wreath truly wanted, however crazy it might seem. Not even this. The elves were openly skeptical, but the demonstration worked.

"Now we must go and tackle an allo," Prunepit said. "Only when we have proven that we can kill allos without taking losses, will we know that we can handle this crisis." For the numbers of the elves were not great, and had been depleted by the recent disaster; they could not spare any more lives without throwing the viability of the tribe into question.

They rode out the next day, a party of their best remaining hunters. They did not have far to go, for the allos had forged steadily toward the holt. All too soon they encountered the first one.

It was a giant of a reptile. Its hide was knobby rather than scaly, but tougher than any ordinary leather. Its color was faintly reddish, as if heated by the sun. But this was morning; the sun's full heat had not yet come, and the trees shaded the ground. The creature moved somewhat lethargically. Even so, its huge claws and teeth made it formidable. It outmassed the elfin party, and it had no fear.

Prunepit stared at the monster, daunted. The thing was so big, so ugly, so sure of itself! It did not flee them; instead it came purposefully toward them, taking them to be prey. It did not move as fast as the wolves, but no elf afoot would be safe.

Would his system of mind-linkage work on such a monster? Prunepit quelled his doubt. It had to work!

"Remember," he called. "Let the wolves guide themselves."

The elves nodded. They had seen it work in the rehearsal; they did not feel easy with it, but they knew what to do.

The group of them spread out to surround the allo. Prunepit reached for the reptile's mind—and was appalled. The thing was a nest of sting-tails, concerned with nothing but hatred and hunger. Hatred for all other creatures, and hunger for their flesh. This was simply an attack entity, with no concern for danger, indeed hardly any awareness of it. Charge, bite, tear, swallow—that was its desire.

The allo leaped for a wolf—but the wolf was already moving out of the way, while three on the other side moved in close, their riders lifting their weapons. A spear plunged toward the monster's ear region, and an arrow winged toward its eye.

The spear slid off; the ear was armored, and the point was unable to penetrate. The arrow seemed about to make a perfect strike—but the monster's heavily ridged brow squinted, and the arrow bounced off and was lost.

The head whipped back to snap at the three attackers. As before, the three were moving before the head did, retreating, so that the great teeth closed on air. Simultaneously, the wolves on the far side moved in close, and their riders attacked.

A spear sought the monster's nose. But this too was armored, and the teeth caught the spear and crunched it to splinters. The allo bit at anything it could reach, whether flesh or wood. If it ever caught any part of a wolf or elf, that would be the end of that creature.

The allo lurched this way and that, thinking to snap up its tormentors, but they were impossibly elusive. Prunepit had linked the minds of the wolves to the mind of the reptile, and the wolves had better minds. They reacted more swiftly to the allo's thoughts than it did itself, so that any action it tried was useless. The system was working!

Or was it? The attacks and counters continued, but the allo was taking no significant injuries, and the longer the action proceeded, the more alert the reptile was becoming. It was really a standoff, with neither side able to harm the other. Prunepit had assumed that once they nullified the reptile's attack, it would be only a matter of time before they killed it. Now he saw that this was not the case.

What good was it to harass the allo if they couldn't hurt it?

There was a growl from the side. A second allo was coming!

"Withdraw!" Prunepit cried.

The elves resumed contact with their wolves. The group fled from the allos, outdistancing them. But the field of battle belonged to the reptiles.

They drew up in a glade. The wolves were panting; they had been working hard. The elves were in good order, but they had lost a number of spears and arrows.

Prunepit was dejected. "The thing is too tough," he said. "Our weapons won't dent it!"

"But it couldn't touch us!" Softfoot exclaimed. "We were like ghosts to it!"

"Ghosts can't hurt real folk," he reminded her. As a general rule, elves did not believe in ghosts; a dead elf was dead, with no apologies. But the five-fingers believed, and so the concept was known, if not respected.

"We just have to find its weak spot," Softfoot said. "If we strike there, then we'll have it!"

The discussion lapsed. There had been no evidence of any weak spot. The allo was protected at every point.

There was a crashing in the brush. Another allo was coming! Hastily the elves mounted, and the wolves fled the glade. If there had been any doubt who controlled the terrain, this removed it. It was becoming increasingly evident why the allos had defeated Rahnee; the elves had never before encountered so tough an enemy.

Prunepit found himself riding next to Wreath. She beckoned him closer. Did she want another mating? This was hardly the time, even if the Recognition was developing its imperative again.

But she had another matter on her mind for the moment. "I think the allo must be soft inside," she said as Prunepit's ear came close.

He laughed bitterly. "I do not care to go inside it!"

"But if we could attack it from inside—"

"How? Without first encountering its teeth?"

"By getting something inside it," she said. "I notice that it bites at anything it reaches. Suppose it bit a burning ball of tar?"

Prunepit's mouth dropped open. "The tar pit's not far from here!"

"Yes. Why don't you tell the others?"

"But it's your idea!" he protested. "You should have the credit for it!"

"I want you to have the credit."

"Why?"

"Because if it works, you will be chief."

"Yes! So you could be—"

"I am no leader," she said. "You know that. But you could be."

Prunepit was not at all certain that she lacked qualities of leadership. Wreath had fought well and kept her poise throughout, and now she had an idea that well might turn the tide of battle.

She was also infernally beautiful, and his Recognized.

Her wolf veered away. The dialogue was over.

Prunepit shrugged. Of course Wreath did not want to be seen with him. They had agreed that no one would know of their Recognition. Still, she could have given her notion to another hunter. Why had she wanted him to have the best chance to be chief? He was sure that she had a selfish reason, and it bothered him to be the beneficiary of a gift whose motive he did not understand. Still, Wreath was Dreamkeeper's grandchild and she remembered things even Zarhan had forgotten.

Softfoot rode close. She did not speak; she just glanced at him. He knew she had observed his dialogue with Wreath. Surely she misunderstood its nature!

He beckoned her. "She has a notion!" he called as she came closer.

Softfoot made a moue.

"Not *that* one!" he exclaimed. "She—"

But Softfoot's wolf diverged, and he could not finish. He had hurt her, without meaning to. If only he could send to his own kind as well as he could to animals!

Well, perhaps his action would clarify it. "To the tar pit!" he cried, gesturing in its direction.

At the tar pit they drew up again. There were no allos here, yet.

"If we gather tarballs, and light them, and feed them to the allos, that should kill them," Prunepit said.

The elves considered. "How can we feed the monster a

tarball?'' Dampstar asked. He had come by his name when traveling at night, seeing a star reflected in the river.

''With an arrow,'' Prunepit said. He picked up a stick, dipped it in the thick tar, and got a blob on the end. ''We must have the tar-arrows ready, and light them when we approach the allos, then shoot them in when the time is right.''

''But only the wolves know when the time is right,'' Softfoot pointed out. ''We cannot connect to the mind of the reptile.''

''I might do it, if Curlfur warns me,'' Wreath said. She was an excellent shot with her bow. ''But I will need some help in setting up my arrows.''

Several male elves volunteered immediately to help. Prunepit was left alone for a moment with Softfoot.

''It was a good notion,'' she said. ''I'm sorry for what I thought.''

''But I don't understand why she gave it to me,'' he said. ''She said it was because she could not be chief, but I could. Does that make sense?''

''She wants her child to be the offspring of a chief,'' Softfoot said, biting her lip.

''But if no one knows the father—''

''The blood knows.''

He looked at her. ''You know I could not resist the Recognition. But my feeling for you—''

She turned away.

''It's *your* child I want to have!'' he cried.

''I cannot give you what she can.''

''How do we know that? Breeding is not limited to Recognition! Maybe—''

She faced him. ''I have not denied you,'' she said. ''I would have your child if I could. But it may not be possible. That may be why the Recognition struck. *It* knows.''

"If only—" he began. But then the elves returned with Wreath's arrows, each dipped in tar.

"We must have a firepot, too," Wreath said.

They filled a container with the tar, and the elf who had the fire-talent struck flame, lighting it. The tar burned with guttering vigor, throwing up thick smoke. The wolves shied away from it, apprehensive about the fire, but Prunepit touched their minds and showed how this fire was their friend. Curlfur even consented to carry the firepot, smoking in its harness, so that Wreath could have it ready without delay.

It was now midday. Prunepit hesitated. Was it wise to tackle the allos again now, when they would be most vigorous? Yet if they waited another day, the reptiles could be almost at their lodge. It would be better to do it here, where there was still room to retreat.

They rode slowly back to intercept the allos. It did not take long; the horde was in full motion, on its search for what little prey remained.

"We must strike quickly, and retreat," Prunepit warned them. "We don't know how long it will take the tar to do the job. It doesn't have to be fast, just sure. Now turn over your wolves to me."

The elves did so with better grace than before; though they had not succeeded in killing the allo, they had appreciated the perfect coordination of the wolves, and had understood its necessity.

They rode up to meet the first allo. This one was larger than the one they had tackled in the morning, and faster, because of the heat of day. It screamed and charged them with appalling ferocity, its jaws gaping.

Wreath stood her ground. Calmly she touched an arrow to the firepot, waiting for its gooey tip to blaze up. Then she fitted it to her bow and took aim.

Prunepit saw that Wreath was going to be overrun, but he couldn't even yell; he had to keep the wolves connected.

Wreath fired her arrow. The aim was perfect; the missile shot right into the throat of the monster.

Then Curlfur moved, almost slowly, for Wreath was not holding on. He carried her just that minimum required to avoid the charge of the reptile, while wolves to either side crowded close, harassing the creature.

But the allo had abruptly lost interest in the wolves. Smoke was issuing from its nostrils, making it look like a beast from a sky-mountain nightmare. It swallowed—then screamed, as the burning material coursed down its throat.

The agony hit Prunepit like a savage storm. The allo was burning inside! Quickly he broke his mind free—and suddenly the wolves were on their own, the connection broken.

But the job had been done. The allo whipped about, trying to free itself of the pain. It rolled on the ground, its tail thrashing wildly.

The commotion alerted another allo. It charged in, intent on the first. Without hesitation it bit, needing no inducement other than helplessness. The elves watched, horrified yet fascinated by the savagery.

"Kill one, distract one," Softfoot murmured.

"But we have no meat for our wolves," an elf pointed out. "We need a kill we can butcher."

"We'll get it," Prunepit said. "Now we know how to kill the allos."

They closed on the feeding reptile. It growled, warning them off, but did not stop feeding. Wreath readied another arrow.

Prunepit linked the minds of the wolves with that of the second allo. They circled close. The allo growled again and made a feint, opening its mouth wide—and Wreath dipped her arrow and fired it.

She scored on the inside of the mouth. Now the allo roared, trying to spit out the fiery barb but only burned its tongue. The tar was stuck in its mouth, blazing.

Unfortunately, this new commotion attracted several other allos. They came in a monstrous wave, big ones and small ones, smelling the blood. The elves had to flee.

"There are so many!" Softfoot exclaimed. "Every time we kill one, more come!"

Prunepit nodded. This problem was so much more complicated than he had supposed it could be! He had thought that when they killed one allo, that would be the turning point. Instead, the problem had grown with each success.

Wreath rode close again. "You know why you're having so much trouble?" she asked. "It's because you're not thinking like a chief."

"I'm *not* a chief!" he replied.

"You showed how to deal with the allos," she reminded him. "That makes you chief. But it will never work unless you believe it yourself."

"But I can't just declare myself chief!" he protested.

"Why not?"

"They would laugh!"

"If you don't, they will die, as the allos overrun our holt."

He was very much afraid she was right. He had taken on this mission because of the need; he had not thought beyond it. Now he appreciated the greater need: for a continuing leadership that could handle problems as they came, whatever they might be.

Still, he did not feel competent because he couldn't solve the problem of the numbers of allos. What good was it to slay one, or two, or three, or eight, if more always came?

He mulled that over as they rode, outdistancing the reptiles. He felt ashamed because so much of his thinking had been done for him by the woman who didn't want to share his life, Wreath. A chief didn't let others do his thinking! For that matter, what chief had a name like Prunepit?

Then he suffered a major realization.

Stop at the next good resting place, he thought to the wolves. That was the elfin version; the actual message was simply a vision of a nice spot, with wolves relaxing.

When they stopped, Prunepit called out to them to gather around. "We agreed that whoever solved the problem of the allos would be chief," he said. "I have shown how to solve it, so I am declaring myself chief. I admit that the problem is not over yet, but I will dedicate myself to dealing with it. I am the only one who can unify the minds of the wolves with the mind of the prey, and that is what we need to do this job."

He paused, but there was no reaction. They were waiting to hear him out before drawing their conclusions.

"To signify this determination, I am taking a new name," he said. "I enable the wolves to link with the prey, to pace it, moving before it can move. Therefore I will call myself Prey-Pacer, and that will be my name as long as I am chief."

Still they did not speak. He hoped he was not making himself ludicrous. The key element of his assumption was coming up.

"But I do not know all the answers to all the problems. I never expected to be chief, before my mother died, and have had no practice in it. I know I will make mistakes if I try to decide everything myself. So my decision is—to make no significant decision without first getting the best advice I can. For example, I don't know how to stop the allos from taking the meat of whichever ones we kill. Does anyone here know?"

They considered. "Why don't we kill one and butcher it quickly and haul it up into a tree where they can't reach it?" Dampstar asked.

"That sounds good to me," Prey-Pacer said. "Does anyone have an objection?"

"Yes," Wreath said. "Those beasts track by the smell of blood as much as anything else. They could collect under that tree and never leave."

"But then we have a way to stop them!" Softfoot pointed out. "We can hang flesh in several trees, and the whole horde will stop right there."

The elves pursed their lips, thinking about that.

"Well, either they'll stay by the tree, or they won't," Prey-Pacer said. "If they stay, they won't bother us elsewhere. If not, we have a cache we can return to. I think it's an excellent suggestion, and I'll do it if a better one doesn't come along. Thank you, Dampstar."

Dampstar grinned with pride, just as if a real chief had complimented him.

Wreath nodded, gazing at Prey-Pacer with new appraisal. He was making it work.

But Softfoot was looking at Wreath. What was passing through her mind? She must be suspicious that Wreath was reconsidering about keeping the secret, and might decide after all to be the lifemate of a chief. Prey-Pacer was suspicious of that too—and knew that as much as he loved Softfoot, he would not be able to deny Wreath if she decided to take him. That single mating with her—already he felt the yearning returning. Perhaps it was only the Recognition, asserting its hunger to generate the baby it had chosen. But perhaps it was his own fickle male nature, vulnerable to beauty no matter what his mind said.

There was a roar. Another allo had come across them, and was charging in.

The elves leaped for their wolves. But Wreath reached for an arrow first, dipping it to the firepot. She took aim at the monster bearing down on her.

Prey-Pacer, astride Halfhowl, looked back, abruptly realizing that Wreath had not mounted. He had never witnessed an act of greater courage! But it was foolish courage, because she had no way to escape the reptile in time. Already the allo's huge head was orienting on her, sweeping down as the terrible jaws opened. Curlfur remained close to her, but could not make her mount before she was ready.

Wreath fired into that open mouth. The flaming arrow went right into the throat. The allo choked, but its momentum was such that even as it stumbled, it was coming down to crush the elf-woman. It was far too late for Prey-Pacer to do anything, even if he had been able to act.

Then a shape shot by, passing almost under the falling monster. It was a wolf and rider, leaping to intercept Wreath. The rider launched from the wolf, pushing off to tackle Wreath and shove her out of the way as the allo's head and neck whomped down at her.

The monster struck the ground. Wreath stumbled clear, safe by the narrowest margin. But her rescuer had not made it; her legs were pinned under the fallen allo.

Then Prey-Pacer realized who it was. Softfoot lay there, unconscious.

Prey-Pacer was the first to reach them. "Why did she do it?" he gasped, horrified.

Wreath swallowed. She was not so cold as to overlook the narrowness of her escape. "Because she loves you," she said, awed.

"But you are her rival!"

"And she was protecting your child—whoever carried it," Wreath added. "I think I could not have done that."

Softfoot groaned. "She's alive!" Prey-Pacer exclaimed.

"But will be lame, I fear," Wreath said. "She never was apt on her feet, and now will be worse. She will need a lot of attention." She gazed down at Softfoot, and a tear rolled down her cheek. It seemed that her cold heart had at last been touched. Then, as the other Wolfriders arrived, she raised her voice. "Get sticks! Lever this monster off the chief's lifemate! She saved my life!"

Then Prey-Pacer knew that no matter who bore his child, no one would try to separate him from Softfoot. One woman had acted with measureless courage and brought down an allo single-handed. The other had acted with similar courage, and with measureless generosity, and won the respect and gratitude of two who would not forget.

Prey-Pacer was indeed chief, and was known as the most superlative of elfin hunters despite his seeming inadequacies of weapon and of sending. It took time, but he succeeded in abating the menace of the allos, and they retreated to their former obscurity. He sired several children. Among them was Wreath's daughter, to be named Skyfire, inheriting the beauty and nerve of her mother. Another was Softfoot's son, to be named Swift-Spear, trained in his mother's weapon. But for a long time, only Softfoot's cubs were known as Prey-Pacer's offspring, until the secret no longer mattered.

It had happened again as it had happened so many times before. A hunting human and a hunting Wolfrider had unwittingly crossed paths not a good run's distance from the Father Tree itself. And, of course, the Wolfrider would have to have been Moonshade. Not that the black-haired elf had been harmed; by all the retellings Longreach had heard, elf and human had both panicked and run in opposite directions, but Moonshade was Strongbow's lifemate and Strongbow rarely needed encouragement to inflame his hatred of the five-fingered hunters.

Bearclaw himself was little better. He'd just come back from one of his hand-of-days wanderings and was in no mood for Strongbow's challenges. Longreach was one of the few who knew where Bearclaw wandered and, though he'd never say it aloud and certainly not at a tense howl like this, he suspected the red-eyed chief of drinking a bit more of his dreamberry wine than was wise.

Piss-pot cowards, all of you, Strongbow's sending roared into all of their minds. **They're coming closer all the time. Will you wait until they burn the Father Tree around us?**

"Piss-pot yourself. They've been *there* and we've been here a long time. It's just that *we* know where 'there' is and *they* wouldn't know 'here' if they were standing where I'm standing right now."

97

Fog-brained idiot. You'll wait until they *are* here before you do anything.

"I've done something. We're watching; we're being careful—a lot more careful than you'd be, thundering up to their stink-breath caves."

If it had just been the two males posturing and snarling as they so often did, Longreach would have simply headed back to his own den. But Moonshade's encounter had been closer to the holt than any similar event in recent memory. And if it was one thing the Wolfriders had learned as the seasons turned it was that humankind was the most dangerous, unpredictable hunter in the forest.

Worse, the other Wolfriders were starting to take sides as bitterness took root in honest fear. There had always been those who wanted to run as far as possible, to live where you never saw the mark of a five-fingered hand; and there were always those who wanted to carry the hunt to humanity as if it were possible to purge the world of two moons of their presence.

At the moment, though, neither Strongbow nor Bearclaw had the least notion of the effect their loud, private quarrel was having. Longreach sighed and, completely unnoticed, got to his feet. It was going to be necessary to sober them both.

"Enough!" he said in a voice that had carried through more howls than these two had seen between them. "You're thinking with your mouths. The worst that can happen to a Wolfrider isn't meeting a human—it's becoming so lost in his anger, his hatred, and his fear that he loses the Way. Without the Way it doesn't matter what you do, or why you do it—you've already lost yourself.

"And it can happen to the best of us—"

Swift-Spear

by Mark C. Perry & C. J. Cherryh

The wolf Blackmane heard them moving through the woods, but he was not frightened. These new humans were a soft breed; they ran from elf and wolf alike. Besides, he was not done with his meal yet. . . .

The men moved closer through the undergrowth, their sweat staining the summer air with the scent of their fear. They knew this was one of the werewolves that the forest demons rode. But their fear was overridden by hot anger. The calf the wolf had stolen was the fifth that these dark ones had killed in the two months since the tribe had come here. They could not afford such loss.

"Are we cowards?" their leader, Kerthan, had cried when the wolf had taken the calf. He had stood in the middle of the village holding his magic spear aloft. "Must we hide in fear whenever the demons' wolves are hungry? How long before they kill full-grown animals? How long before they get a taste for our children's flesh? The gods have promised! The world is ours! We must cast the demons out or lose favor in the gods' eyes forever!"

Kerthan's head resounded with his speech as he inched closer to the great wolf that fed in the clearing. It was he, Kerthan, who had led the people to this territory, he who had made the first stone hut in the plain below the woods and dared to declare the land his own. He grasped the spear tightly. He must kill the wolf, or the people would turn on him and leave. He must kill the wolf. . . .

Blackmane sniffed the air and moved from his prey, growling as he saw one of the men creep from the woods' cool shadows and stand upright, staring at him. Blackmane growled again, warning off the scrawny man-things—it was his kill, and these were none of the pack—but the man did not retreat or advance; he held a spear-fang and pointed it at him, and the acrid, strange smell of the weapon coming faintly against the wind made Blackmane's short hairs bristle. He had never smelled this cold thing before in his short life; it burned with the scent of anger and fear, seared the air about him. . . . The human pack moved on either side of him, to drive him from his prey in his own hunting-range.

He snarled, indecisive, measuring the man with the harsh smell; then backed a step away, misliking the situation, almost ready to run and leave his prey. He had hunted alone. He was apart from his pack. They were in theirs. Danger. Danger in this, and they outnumbered him.

Then the scent wafting on a wind-shift behind him set the hair bristling up again and flattened his ears to his skull. . . . The human pack had closed behind him, surrounding him; and the man-leader held the spear-fang, muscles tensed—that meant—attack!

With a howl he charged straight at the man. . . .

Kerthan's spear flashed in the sun, driving deep into the wolf's thick shoulder. The force of the blow spilled the beast to the ground.

The humans behind him cried with one voice and surrounded the struggling animal. "Kill it," Kerthan cried, and did not cease to jab at the wolf with the keen-edged spear while the hunters with him hit it with clubs and sticks and fell at last to gashing it with knives, wounding each other in their frenzy.

Swift-Spear raced between the trees, his heart light with the freedom of his strength . . . freedom for the moment from the demands of the chieftainship his father Prey-Pacer had bequeathed him. He ran beneath the summer leaves, leaped up the gray rock outcrop that rose on the margin of the stream, and looked back grinning and panting at the elf-woman who ran behind him, at Willowgreen, whose hair flew and whose bare feet skipped lightly enough over the forest mold—but not the match for his speed, or his long stride. Tall herself, with the high ones' blood in her—she had their languor too; she was fair and pale and breathed now with great gasps while she laughed. . . . " 'Show me a sight,' " she breathed as she climbed after him. " 'Show me a sight,' indeed! What is there to see here?"

He had the answer ready, his mouth opened.

And stumbled to the ground, grabbing his head. There were men and there was the smell of metal. He saw the hunters. He heard a cry inside, first of anger, then of terror and of pain. He felt the tear of flesh.

"Blackmane!" he shouted aloud, even as his mind sought his friend. He felt a brief flicker reach to him, then gray emptiness. Swift-Spear fell to his knees.

"Ayooooo!" he cried in agony. He knew that Blackmane was dead.

In moments the wolf lay battered and chopped beyond recognition. The men laughed and danced, spotted with the wolf's blood, and Kerthan cut off the still warm ears as a trophy.

"They can be killed!" Kerthan said, his voice loud and strong in victory. "No longer must we fear them." He shook his spear, hot drops of blood from it spattering them all. "Kerthan will protect you with his spear! This is our land and no one will take it from us!"

"Swift-Spear!" Willowgreen cried, and shook him with both her hands as he sat crouched atop the rocks. There was no response. The elf sat with his hands clasped between his knees, his brown eyes wide and shocked. She took his face between her hands and peered into those eyes in search of sense, but there was no reaction at all, not in the eyes, not in the mouth, which remained slack; his skin was chilled and he did not shiver; and there was no contact with his mind, none that she dared seek. *Blood*, she got. And, *metal*. And after that she leapt up and went flying down from the rocks, panting as she ran the winding forest trails—

—past the marks the elves knew, past the familiar rocks, and over the fallen log, and through and through the trees with constantly a shriek in her mind: **Help, help—**

Wolves cried out in the forest. None were hers. She was too tall, too fair, too strange for them, and they always distrusted her. **Help,** she called out to them, and did not know whether they heard her or understood. The pain was sharp in her side, and branches raked her hair. She stumbled and caught herself on the old ash, and ran and ran, all but mindless with the pain and the terror as she skidded down a hillside and through the thicket.

And crashed full into the arms of a presence she had not felt, hands that seized her by her arms, and eyes yellow and terrible as any wolf's, a face narrow and hard and familiar to her.

Willowgreen, the mindtouch came to her, and the grip held her and shook at her till the thoughts came spilling out, the things she had seen, the fact that Swift-Spear was left helpless because she knew nothing of weapons and nothing of what had brought Swift-Spear down, and only ran, ran, ran, for help.

The elf's hands released her, pushing her away. He was less than her height; he was small and slight and his hair was not elf—it was black-tipped and strange, strange as the mind which could stalk so silently and insinuate itself unfelt. "Fool," Graywolf said. "Helpless fool!"

Which stung worse than the thorns, for he was Swift-

Spear's cousin, and had never loved her, never thought her of any worth.

"Go tell the tribe," he said; and said with his mind as he left: **Quickly!** with such force and anger that she stopped in her tracks and did not follow him. **Quickly!**

She fled, in motion before she had decided; she flung up her arms to shield her from the branches, and ran, breathless and aching.

There was still that quiet, that most profound quiet that had held Swift-Spear motionless. No one could hear that silence and move. And yet, he thought in that dim, remote center where he was, yet if he could move, and break that quiet, then none of it would be true, and that silence would not exist, and the world would be whole again.

He tried, desperately. He felt with his mind wider and wider after that essence which eluded him.

He felt a presence finally, and sought after it. It was wolfish and familiar. For a moment he hoped he had found what he sought . . . but it grew and grew until he knew it was something else; it filled the space about him, driving other things away. In that presence were yellow eyes, and a voice in his mind that was like a wolf's, which had the essence of a wolf but an elvish mind all the same.

No, he said with his thoughts, forcing it away. But it was too late, the presence he had wanted was gone, and this one had made it impossible to recover it. "No!" he howled aloud and struggled in a hard-handed grip that closed upon his arms. He flung himself up and struck at the intruder, knowing as he struck who it was, and seeing with the return of his vision the wolf-mane of hair, the narrow, elvish face, and yellow eyes. He raged and shoved away, but Graywolf was as quick on the rocks, and prevented him with a grip on his arms and a touch at his mind: **Blackmane?**

He had not wanted to think the thought. But the question

had its answer. *Dead, dead, dead*. So it became true. So he knew he could not get back to that place where he had been, deep inside, where a motion might disturb the dead. He had admitted that thought and therefore the other thought was beyond recall.

Therefore he slumped down with Graywolf's small brown hands clenched on his wrists; he sat on the rock and he looked his friend in the eyes. . . . More than Graywolf had come. There was the wolf-friend, prowling below the rocks, hump-shouldered, ears flat to the skull—Moonfinder was his name. Not Blackmane. Moonfinder, second in the pack—till now. Till Blackmane was dead and Graywolf's friend came to sudden primacy.

"Where?" Graywolf asked, jolting him. "Where dead? How?"

"Humans," Swift-Spear muttered, and shoved off the grip that hampered him, thrust himself over the side of the rock on which he sat and landed on the next and the next, so that Moonfinder shied away and flattened his ears.

He paid no heed to this hostility. He cared nothing that Graywolf and his wolf-friend followed him, or that all the woods were roused, the call going through the forest in wolf-howl and the rising of birds. He had his spear in hand. He ran without sight in the present, searching out of his memory all the detail of the place where Blackmane's mind had stopped.

Trees, growing in such a pattern, of such a type, a broken branch, a thicket. It was like all other places. There was only one such specific place. He ran and he racked his memory of the forest on the borders of men. He listened to the sounds of the wolves and the cries of the birds. He heard his own harsh breathing and heard the steps which coursed like a whisper behind him.

He ran, for all that, alone. His friend, a wolf he knew. None of these were help to him. The pack-leader was dead,

Blackmane was dead; humans had intruded into the woods, the humans who had encroached closer and closer to the tribe with their strange stone buildings and their diggings and hewings and making of things. They had brought death with them. But when did they not?

It was the forest edge. That much he knew. He knew the way the light had fallen. Knew the size of the clearing. Knew the prey Blackmane had taken. It was all burned into his mind. He gave these things to Graywolf, as he gave them to the forest, to anything which would listen—he knew that Graywolf and Moonfinder searched with their own understanding; and Graywolf was half a wolf himself, not the shapeshifting kind, but wolf by disposition, wolf by senses and by instincts, elf by mind and by a curious blend of elvish and wolfish cunning.

And it was Moonfinder, or it was Graywolf, who first smelled the blood. He was not sure. It came from both minds at once, and into his own, so that he changed his direction on a pivot of his foot and followed the scent of blood and of men. But both scents were cold.

Memory of trees and reality of the forest began to merge. Birds flew up and screamed warnings; but only selfish ones: the enemy was gone, the chance of revenge was fled, like the warmth in the blood.

The tribe is coming. He caught that thought from Graywolf's mind. He did not care. He plunged ahead, fought his way through the underbrush, and at the last, having caught the scent of the place (or his companions had, and he knew it) he did not run. He had no wish to find what he had now to find, what, his senses told him, was screened from him by the brush.

Willowgreen came with the hunters. Her skin was torn and her feet were bleeding, and worst of all was the pain in her side; but she followed as best she could. She had no weapon.

She had her little magic, which could heal the worst of her cuts if she had had leisure, but she took none and only bit her lips and followed at what speed she could the swift-coursing Wolfriders, limping heavily at the last, after even the wolves were winded.

She came hindmost into the clearing, among Wolfriders who gathered and stared numbly as Swift-Spear cradled the bloody corpse.

They all waited. The silence went on and on.

"Graywolf." Swift-Spear's sudden voice was harsh. Graywolf looked up, a small figure, fey and furtive, by Moonfinder's side. And Swift-Spear rose and turned to the others, his slim form covered with his wolf-friend's blood. "Graywolf goes with me. The rest of you go back to the tribe, move them farther into the woods."

"What will you do?" someone asked.

Swift-Spear turned and looked down at the mutilated corpse. "I go to get his ears back." He looked up again, his eyes dark with emotion. "I go to get myself a new spear." He licked the blood off his hands. "A man-hunting spear."

The hunters lingered a moment in shock. Then they began to move. But Willowgreen limped forward, one pace and two.

"Get back to the tribe!" Swift-Spear snarled at her. And with his thought came resentments that she was what she was, that she had hurt herself and that she was helpless to heal even that. **Take care of yourself,** the thought came. **Or can you do that much?**

It struck her to the heart. She stood there with her hands held out to offer sympathy, and then she did not know what to do except to let them fall, and turn and walk away after the others, with no strength left—he had said it—even to heal herself.

But Swift-Spear set out with that tireless run that meant distance, and Graywolf ran behind him, afoot, with Moonfinder coursing along the game trails. There was blood on the trail. It was not that hard to follow. And that Swift-Spear had no haste to follow it was indication that he had no haste for his revenge.

Graywolf marked this. And marked the thoughts that strayed to him from Swift-Spear's mind—wordless thoughts, like pain and rage that did not care what it wounded, like a wolf in its extremity snapping even at a familiar hand. He kept silence himself and did not invade this privacy, which leaked resentments of him, whose Moonfinder had the primacy now. They were very secret thoughts he intercepted—*Follow me because you could be chief, you with your wolf-friend that bowed only to Blackmane—do you want what he wants? Follow because you expect I may fall, and you will come back bringing the dead—to challenge my sister, is that it, cousin?*

Thoughts like that fell like blood, scant and seldom, smothered in anguish and self-reproach: *Graywolf, my friend*—which was the way with wounds, which tried to seal themselves; and Graywolf, whose mind could go silent to his prey, still as deep waters, heard things of private nature. It was his gift, and his curse, to live with too much honesty.

Like now, that he had sense as Willowgreen had not, to put these things away and to remember them for what they were—private fears, the things in-spite-of-which. They made Graywolf wise. Like knowledge of his own—*I hate you, my friend, I hate myself that I hate you, I hate the fair, the bright elves that hate the sight of me, of which you are chief, and kindest, giving me no enemy. Fool, do you think they would ever follow me?*

If we die we will only please our enemies in the tribe, mine and yours, cousin.

But, my fair, my bright, tall friend—temper is your privilege. I have had to master mine, or go mad. So I follow you, and indulge yours.

But all the latter was quiet in that still depth where Graywolf stored things and mulled them over, and where he made his choices.

In this case the choice was already clear.

And in Swift-Spear's another kind of thought that shot like lightning through the moiling anger: a chief's thinking, a cold, clear reason that sought to use the anger for its own ends. *Revenge can serve two purposes. There are always two purposes. The tribe would not approve this. But if I win they will; and after that, they will approve anything.* And he knew he was right, for it was his gift to know such things. He had the magic of the born leader, the empathy for others' dreams and wishes, and the strength to stave off the corruption such power always brought.

It was that kind of thinking that daunted Graywolf, the kind of thoughts anyone had, but that came to Swift-Spear most surely in his hottest rages and his coldest passions. It was that faculty for planning that surpassed any of Graywolf's own capacity that made him doubt, deep in that secret well of opinions, whether he, Graywolf, was not indeed the lesser, born deficient in elf-blood and with too much wolf in him to be capable of such calculation. So he was doomed to be pack-second, deservedly—and perhaps . . . in his blackest self-despair, he wondered whether other elves also had some mental attributes he lacked, secret things, like his own inner secretiveness, that let no thoughts out to betray what proceeded there. In that sense he was deaf and helpless, not knowing whether he was greater or lesser than other elves; but knowing that he was helpless to think Swift-Spear's thoughts, or do other than run behind him, following, because they neither one could be free of the other.

The trail ran to forest edge. It ran onto the downslope, which led out under sunlight and into the valley where humans lived. And the humans in their foolishness and their bravado—or was it knowledge of the wolves?—did not take any pains to hide their trail through the grass, to seek the rocks or the hillsides to throw off pursuit.

Moonfinder was nearby, keeping to the undergrowth as long as he could. **Come,** Graywolf said to him. And the wolf defied instinct and joined them in their course, which was not like the foolish humans—straight to the goal.

They were Wolfriders, stalkers and hunters. They did not trust an easy trail leading to an easy target. No, not that simple to trap such as they. Graywolf was not surprised at all when Swift-Spear left the track and sought the rocky hillside, where there was vantage and where the prevailing wind brought them information.

The human camp lay spread across a small hill. It was full of straight lines and built-things that confused the two Wolfriders.

"There are so many," Graywolf hissed between fanged teeth. Swift-Spear did not answer. Even in his pain and rage a clear voice still spoke to him.

Here are things you have never seen before. . . .

The humans all lived close together in their strange stone tents, as no other men ever had, all of them seeming in constant motion, going from one place to another. What did they do? Why did they build such homes? What did they know that he and the other elves did not?

Graywolf's strong hand grabbed his shoulder and shook him from his wonder.

"Swift-Spear." The elf pointed down at the humans. "That—uh—those trees. They are dead, yet they stand upright. Even wolves could never jump that."

Swift-Spear stared at the high fence for a moment. *Why this? Ah. Of course. These men are smart, very smart. . . .*

It is a barricade, he sent to Graywolf, **to keep enemies out, to keep the world out!** Behind them Moonfinder whined at the scent that came up from the village.

"So many. Which one killed Blackmane?" Graywolf's

harsh voice hurt the chief's ears, hurt him with its reminder of why he was here, what he had come to do. Swift-Spear searched the details of the distant figures below them. Many of the elves claimed they could not tell one human from another, but Swift-Spear had taught himself on his lone spying missions to see the differences. He looked for the tall, bearded one. The black eyes and scarred body he had seen last through the dying eyes of his wolf-friend.

Swift-Spear's vision blurred and his breath stung him, coming in short gasps. He dug callused palms into his eyes. The memory was too fresh! Red blood, wolf-friend's blood, sound of flesh ripping, scents of fear, of death. Eyes going dim . . . pain, pain! Cold numbness as strong heart stops, lungs collapse . . .

Graywolf shuddered at his friend's thoughts. Swift-Spear was reliving Blackmane's death as if it happened now—again. *He* was the wolf, *he* was dying. . . . There was something wrong and Graywolf could not understand it. A moment ago his chief had forgotten his anguish, losing it in those bright, strange thoughts that Graywolf knew he could never understand. Lost in that *why?* that always tore the two of them apart.

Moonfinder, belly to the ground, bumped his head into Graywolf's side, seeking comfort. The elf hugged his wolf-brother to him, biting the wolf's nose to calm him. The thoughts leaking from Swift-Spear affected them both, and Graywolf struggled to find his elf-blood and not to join the wolf in his animal whine of confusion.

"Silence," Swift-Spear said aloud. The two bowed their heads and stared back with yellow eyes. "That one." The chief pointed to one human striding through the village surrounded by other men. "He is their chief." The sun reflected off the man's spearhead. "He will give me Blackmane's ears. He will give me his spear. And"—the Wolfrider stood up—"I will *take* his life!"

"How?"

"Chief to chief, as it has always been. The challenge. One against one, but this time the loser dies!"

Graywolf said nothing. It was right, even if the tribe was not here. Neither of them had any conception of warfare. This was their only choice. This was their path to vengeance.

Swift-Spear strode boldly down the hillside, leaving the other two to wait. The stink of the human camp was bitter. Why would they live with their own waste? Even the wolves would not soil their own dens. He could see now that outside the great barrier there were plants in straight rows growing at the same pace. Among them women worked, pulling up the bitter weeds, digging up more ground. Like Willowgreen's herb garden, but he knew enough about humans to know that they grew these not for healing, but for food. And now that he understood the barricade, he knew why. This way they would not have to leave, this way they would not have to follow the trails of the beasts. They could stay and build their things, could do things in their days that elves never had time or thought to do. Not even the high ones. . . .

Kerthan heard cries and reached the front gate as the women streamed through it, all pointing behind them and shouting inarticulately. He and five of the hunters went out to find what the uproar was all about.

Outside the walls he saw, walking across the fields, one of the forest demons. It was taller than most he had seen, and well-muscled. Its hair was light brown and dangled in two side braids. It wore some pelt about its loins and carried a stone-tipped spear. Twenty paces away from Kerthan it stopped.

"Chief," it said in the people's tongue. It shook its spear at him and pointed to the wolf's ears pinned to the top of the outward-opening gate. "My!" It hit its chest. "My!" It pointed at him again. "Chief!" And shook its spear once more.

Kerthan felt the people crowding behind the gate, knew their fear of the demon. He watched the creature for a moment, trying to decipher its strange actions. He looked up at the wolf ears, the flies buzzing about them now, then looked back at the demon, staring at its sharp-pointed ears. "My," it said; it must mean "mine." *Those are his ears? No. His wolf.* Everyone knew that the demons paired unnaturally with the werewolves. So it was his wolf and he wanted the ears back.

And looking into those strange eyes at this range, Kerthan knew the demon came for more than the trophy. It came for him.

"Leave us, demon!" he cried aloud. "Leave us or die as your cursed monster died—by this!" He lifted up the magic spear he had found so many years before.

The demon's eyes narrowed at the sight of the weapon, its head lowered between hunched, broad shoulders.

"Chief, chief!" it cried, making stabbing motions with its spear.

Then Kerthan knew. It meant to fight him, to take blood vengeance for the death of the werewolf. He looked it over. He had killed the wolf . . . but a demon! That was different, even with the magic spear.

"Kill it!" he yelled at the others behind him. "Kill it! It means to curse us with its black magic!"

The men turned to one another, some still spotted with the dead wolf's blood. Finally Creth, Kerthan's youngest cousin, took a hesitant step toward the demon. The creature ignored him, staring at Kerthan with hot eyes. Creth took another step, and, lifting his spear, threw it at the monster.

It was badly cast and Swift-Spear saw it coming and dodged easily aside. He cursed himself for not learning more of the human language, but he knew that their chief understood him, knew that the man knew why he had come here. Why did the human not fight?

Another man threw a club at him, nearly hitting him. Swift-Spear danced away. Why were the others attacking him? *What madness is this?*

"Chief! Chief!" he cried as more of the humans moved toward him. Their leader was yelling incomprehensible words at them as he stepped back into the line of the crowd. Now ten human hunters faced Swift-Spear and a thrown club hit him in the chest, knocking him down. As he fell, the humans stopped for a moment and a sigh went through their ranks. Then with a great cry they charged him.

Swift-Spear rolled to his feet and braced himself—earned his name again as he dodged amongst his enemy, every thrust of his stone weapon drawing blood. But he was unused to this kind of fighting, and the humans surrounded and outnumbered him. Even as he killed, he, like Blackmane before him, was being killed.

Graywolf could not understand the men's actions any better than his chief, but now, too late, he recalled the tales of the high ones, about their long-ago first meeting with the humans. He leapt on Moonfinder and the two raced toward the battle. **I am coming, brother,** he sent ahead.

But no answer came back.

"Ayoooooo!" Graywolf and Moonfinder cried together as they charged into the enemy. They flashed through the men, spear and fang taking a dreadful toll. Graywolf leaned down to grasp Swift-Spear, pulling him up and atop the wolf's shoulders as it sped on toward the waiting forest. Swift-Spear was covered with blood, hanging as a heavy weight in Graywolf's arms, his mind for once closed to his cousin as the pain of his wounds wiped clean any coherent thought.

Swift-Spear spoke in the human language over and over. "Chief . . . chief . . ."

*   *   *

The ride was a nightmare for Graywolf. He struggled with all his imagination, trying to decipher exactly what had happened. Had the humans misunderstood Swift-Spear's challenge? Or had they in their guile simply pretended ignorance in order to trap the elf and make sure of a kill?

He urged Moonfinder to greater speed, Swift-Spear's blood hot and wet across his chest.

He sent ahead to the tribe, but his thoughts were so chaotic all they could understand was that in some way their chief was hurt. Graywolf followed their thought-patterns deeper into the woods. His mind and heart were in turmoil, which was worse, the gaping wounds in his friend, a friend and cousin he now realized was more precious to him than anyone or anything; or the lack of direction, the void of comprehension that now haunted him. He *needed* his curse/gift, needed to feel Swift-Spear's pain-thoughts, needed to hear his chief's inner voice—or how else was he supposed to understand anything? How was he supposed to feel, with Swift-Spear lying in his arms, bleeding, bleeding to death? And why did his own warm tears join the cooling blood of his friend?

They waited for him in a shadowy glade far from the old holt. The elves moved out of Moonfinder's way as he rushed through them and toward the center of the camp where a huge fire burned, where Willowgreen waited for her lover.

Graywolf slid off the wolf with his chief in his arms, and laid the bloodied form in a bower already prepared. And with tears in her eyes Willowgreen the healer started to tend the sorely wounded elf.

Two high ones approached: Talen and Rellah. Graywolf rose and gave them a look of undisguised loathing.

"Humans did this," Graywolf hissed. Aloud. He never mind-sent to the high ones.

"Yes. Humans." Rellah's voice was hard. "Your message was garbled, wolf-boy, but we were able to untangle it enough to understand." She towered over the Wolfrider, her golden hair reaching to the ground. "He was a fool to go there. What do you expect from humans?" Her eyes were filled with scorn. "You wild ones will be the death of all the tribe. Have you learned nothing from our wisdom?"

"Enough, Rellah." Talen's male voice was sharp. "Leave the boy alone!"

Graywolf only snarled. He wished to stay by Swift-Spear's side, but Rellah's contempt, hurled with a high one's force, was too much for him to bear. He walked away from the crowd watching the healing, his mind trying desperately to shut out all the stray thoughts that battered him.

He will die.

He never should have gone.

The humans will pay!

They are evil. . . .

What will happen to us?

The high ones are right. That fool halfling will get us all killed one day. This last thought from Swift-Spear's sister Skyfire. Graywolf pushed his way through the crowd, Moonfinder padding behind. It was too much, too much. . . .

Forgive me for leaving your side, my brother, but if I stay I will kill one of these tame dogs who have no time for your pain. And surely it would be your own sister my fangs would seek first!

Swift-Spear struggled to wake up, his mind treading strange paths of nightmare that neither Talen nor Willowgreen could follow or understand. Even as the elf-woman's power knitted the terrible wounds together, she looked for something else, something not found in flesh alone. She searched for his name, his secret name, the one he held from all others.

Concentrate on the healing, girl, Talen sent to her, breaking off her futile search. Even now, near death, Swift-Spear kept his true self from her.

Tears of exhaustion blinded her. She was so tired, she only wanted to sleep, to curl up somewhere in soft warmth, she had not strength enough—

Rellah bent and touched her shoulder, only that, and it was like a wash of wind and rain, cold and clear. Strength went through her and a mind went through her mind, sorted through the thoughts, discarded the doubts with a disregard of her weaknesses so thorough that she felt dismissed and insignificant.

But Swift-Spear himself did not accept the high one. It was Willowgreen he reached for with his mind, it was her he would not let go. His powerful spirit, trying to help her heal his battered body, moved within her magic, wild and passionate, like the rolling of thunder before a terrible storm. He was strong, the strongest of all the elves. She shuddered at an unbidden memory of those powerful arms about her. He would not die, but he would—as he seemed destined constantly to do—change; and with him, change all of them.

And he rejected the high one, a rejection so strong it was Talen who retreated; it was Rellah who gave back, frowning, and left Willowgreen clasping Swift-Spear's hand to herself with all her strength.

"It is done," Talen said to the crowd of waiting elves. Willowgreen could feel their relief, a warm current riding the sweet summer air; and Rellah's anger like a cold wind. And another: Skyfire pushed her way to the fore and Willowgreen, still wrapped in her healing magic, perceived her lover's sister as a thick cloud of dank and foul smoke.

"We must go! The humans will come after *us* now!" Skyfire brandished the spear she always carried even though she was not yet one of the hunters.

Peace, Talen sent. Aloud, he continued: "The humans will not dare to come so deep into the forest, not for a while, anyway. And your chief must rest."

"When he is better, we must leave, go far away," Skyfire insisted.

"That is for the chief to decide." Willowgreen, still holding Swift-Spear's hand, looked up at the young elf, struggling with exhaustion and with anger. "He has lost his wolf-friend. What have you lost?"

"And what would you know of wolf-friends, healer?" Skyfire shot back.

"I know he loved Blackmane as he loved nothing else." Willowgreen rose to tower over the elf-woman. "And I know if it was you who had been hurt he would be more concerned with your pain than with any fear of the humans."

Skyfire said nothing to that. She just turned her back and walked away.

"She is hot for her womanhood." Talen touched Willowgreen with a pale, thin hand. "She is jealous of your stature in the tribe, that is all. She will come around."

"She is hot for the chieftainship," Willowgreen muttered. "She disagrees with everything Swift-Spear does. It is a pretext, an excuse."

"Perhaps this time," said Talen, "it would have been right to disagree. It was so foolish of him to think the humans would fight him fair."

Willowgreen said nothing as she stared at Skyfire's retreating back. She reached up and wiped the tears from her eyes. And from Rellah there was only cold comfort.

Go, Talen's thought came, soothing and quiet. **Go, my child. There is nothing more you can do here.**

Willowgreen looked down at the sleeping form of Swift-Spear, watching silently as Talen knelt down to take up a gourd of water, a handful of moss, to wash away the dried blood from the Wolfrider's chest. She knelt down too and took Swift-Spear's head in her lap.

"My place is here," she said, "with him." **And *I*, I will protect him from anything that dares try to hurt him, human or elf. . . .**

*   *   *

Graywolf slid down from Moonfinder's shoulders and kept a firm grip on the brindled fur—tugged at it slightly to focus the wolf's attention on the place below them in the twilight.

Now was the wolf-time. Moonfinder lowered his head and turned and nosed Graywolf's arm, quick, anxious gesture. And in the way of wolves another of the pack came ghosting through the brush, a loner who disdained the elves; No-name was all he answered to, and he was grudging and suspicious, living on the fringes and showing up unpredictably. Moonfinder bristled up when he came up onto the rocks and slunk into shadow, high-shouldered, flat-eared silhouette in the fading light above the human camp.

No-name was scarred with battles, more than a little crazy. He was a disease in the pack, one that Blackmane had not tolerated—but he would not leave them alone, refusing to leave the pack, refusing to accept the pack's allegiance to unwolves. No-name was a wilder thing, and more than once taunted Blackmane himself, knowing that the pack-leader, being elf-ensorceled, would not execute him. Too much peace. Too much soft living, perhaps. Graywolf knew this one, read his attitude in that surly slink into the fading light as he caught the ghostly, wordless thoughts of a hostile wolfish mind. Joy that Blackmane was dead. Satisfaction. And Moonfinder, second-leader, supporting the dead pack-leader with a tenuous hold on the pack as yet unchallenged, felt a fear that no human ever put into him; he bristled, and bared teeth, and growled his uncertain displeasure, so that No-name slunk a little less and let his tongue loll.

He infected the air itself with unreason; and Graywolf licked at his own not-quite-elvish teeth, and the hairs lifted at his nape and his smooth hand knotted on Moonfinder's fur to prevent him from violence. **No.** Now was not the time for challenges, least of all challenge when his own chief lay wounded and diminished in his authority. They were alike, he and Moonfinder, two pack-seconds equally desperate in their attempt on a situation that had defeated their chiefs; and *this* came, this hateful killer, radiating satisfaction in the prospect of bloodshed. That was what brought the loner: a project to No-name's liking—No-name was eager to help, would take pack-second's orders; that was in the wolf-thoughts.

Moonfinder growled and snapped at No-name's closest approach; and the loner skittered aside and slunk back again, bristled all down his lank shoulders; but when Moonfinder started to go farther, Graywolf clamped his hand down on the wolf's muzzle, hard, dodged teeth and held him a second time till Moonfinder gave him the throat, a little twisting of his head to be free: *Peace,* that meant, *my leader*. But not too much humility; and not too much of standing still; that was against the wolf-nature. And the twilight was coming down in which wolves and a halfling elf saw very well indeed.

Come, Graywolf said, and slid down among the rocks, hardly more conspicuous in taking that line of half-lit shadow than the two wolves which skirted the rocks, one on a side. He did not ride, now. He would not tire his wolf-friend for a retreat which might well be in desperate haste. Now it was stealth he wanted; and he had as lief be without No-name, but no thrown rock would shake that shadow, Graywolf knew that from experience; not even Moonfinder's teeth might drive him farther than around the hill and a few moments back—he knew No-name's tactics. So he tolerated the loner himself, who trotted along the hillside like a trick of the eye for any human watching from that place below.

Beside him, Moonfinder glided—not easy at all to spot a wolf in deep dusk, in the scattered scrub and rock of the slope that led down to the stone camp. Less easy to spot an elf with a wolf's instincts and a mind that thought in past and future.

Wolf-boy, the high one had called him, and driven him away with a force of mind that he could not put a name to nor describe nor even remember. That was the way of the high ones: subtleties so tissue-thin that one could never catch them on the wind or smell or taste them, or accuse them in words. They just *were,* and that was the trouble with them, they *were,* all in the past and the power that they never used on enemies—

—only on their own kind, a force that had made the hair stand up at his nape; and the animal had risen up in him and shamed him and driven him from his friend and from the council.

Therefore he went to redeem himself—and Swift-Spear. It had been no fool's act to challenge the humans. It had only given the humans too much credit. And wolf-blood and wolf-instinct hated that mewling retreat of the tribe, that milling in confusion once the chief was down. Wolf-blood understood it very well; and knew what to do about it—

But there were the high ones, whose power sapped the will out of the tribe, and left only the confusion apt to their kind of guidance, which was chaos, and leaderless.

To which Skyfire and her little band ascribed—only Skyfire had her own motives, like No-name, the loner on the fringes. It was power for which Skyfire had her appetite, and if it took her brother, if it took the tribe, if it demanded ducking the head and mewling soft answers to the high ones who might disavow her brother in her favor—to all these things she was apt.

Graywolf chose his own allies. He aimed to prove the humans vulnerable, as Swift-Spear had said. And most of all he meant to do what wanted most doing, so that Swift-Spear would not have to do it—because he knew his cousin, that he could not rest or forget or delay for his healing. What had broken in him was too profound and too close to the spirit, and lying defeated and within the high ones' nebulous disapproval—no, Swift-Spear would not bear that. He would go against the humans again. And Swift-Spear, having less wolf and more of high blood in him, would dwell too much on immaterial things like pride and honor. Graywolf's intentions were simple and direct: do the deed and nip the flanks of the intruders and tell them they were fools to stay near the woods and greater fools to enter another's hunting range, greatest fools of all to make their tents under the sun, of stone that could not be moved.

Then a cold doubt came not to wolf-mind, but to the elf in Graywolf. *Could not be moved.* Wolf-fights were skirmishes, ending in retreat for one, territory for the other; elves fought sharply and keenly, and retreated when it was time for retreat, carrying all they had, in this age when elves, like wolves, had no possession which could not be moved.

But this, Graywolf thought, frightened, halted for a heartbeat where the gardens began, before the tall wooden walls, over which the tops of stone huts showed; and human stink wafted on the wind, mingled with the smell of grease and smoke and water. *They cannot carry away the stone, can they? Or their food-gardens. They expect to win all their fights. They do not think of moving.*

Dim light and the whisper of trees. Swift-Spear blinked, unable to reconcile this with the dirt and the flash of weapons and the ring of human faces where he had, he thought, died. **Blackmane,** he sent hopefully, in the thought that if that were not true, then perhaps the other were not—it was that hard to give up his friend.

But when he moved in the next moment and felt the twinge of healing wounds, and when he turned his head and saw Willowgreen bending down to kneel with a cup in her hand, when he saw how wan and worn she was and felt the pain everywhere, then he knew that the time was after and not before the fight at the wooden wall; and that somehow he had lived—

Graywolf, he thought. He had not come alone to the human camp. He had only gone alone to the challenge.

"Graywolf is alive," Willowgreen said, having caught that fear spilling from his mind; and lifting his head into her lap she gave him the cup to drink and showed him in that quick way of a weary and powerful mind how Graywolf had come riding in with him, how she had healed him.

There were other impressions, quickly snatched away, but not quickly enough: the memory of Skyfire with her spear. The two high ones, Rellah and Talen, his own face through Willowgreen's eyes, bloody and pale and senseless as he lay in her lap, her hands pouring strength into him, the great fear— And anger then, indignation, as the high ones dealt with Graywolf, as Graywolf walked away, head bowed, shoulders tense with anger—

I tried to tell them— she began.

Tried. Tried. His heart ached. There was pain behind his eyes and in his throat. **Tell him I want to see him.**

But the figure in Willowgreen's eyes only walked away into the woods, began to run, and he knew that direction, he knew the dread in Willowgreen's heart, though no one else would have seen and no one had noticed or turned his head: it was Graywolf's talent, such a silence—only he could not trick the eyes.

"He has gone back," Swift-Spear murmured, and sought to get his arm under him. He thrust himself up to sit, and flung off Willowgreen's protesting hand. "Ah!" The pain surprised him.

"Lie down, be still!" **Do not think of going after him; he is no fool, he will not—**

Unfortunate word. *I ache; could she do no more? Do not think of going after him? Fool. Maybe she is right and I am that; but better a fool in courage than wise in cowardice.* But she had tried to hide her fear for him: that and her fierce protectiveness warmed his heart—nor could he forget the power in her healing. In her own way, he realized, she had strength like his; and she would never betray him.

He gained his feet. She stared at him in shock, thinking first that he was her chief and then that he was her lover and that she never mattered to him half what he mattered to her.

That she separated herself from the high ones and their tutelage, that she tried to be Wolfrider and was not—did he never understand, had he nothing better than resentments, was there for her nowhere to call hers? And because he was who and what he was, he did not see her turmoil—and even if he had seen, being who he was, he would not say the things she needed most to hear.

But Swift-Spear went on his two feet, grabbed up his spear where it leaned against the woven wood of the bower, and used it as he went, to keep his steps straight. The pain he smothered. She felt it keenly, and knew if she followed her heart and followed him he would rail on her and tell her she was no help at all.

The only service she could do him was silence, and she clenched her hands in her lap and kept that silence; she wove it all about him, with an effort that beaded her brow with sweat and left her trembling and unable to rise from where she sat.

By then he had vanished into the woods, no elf having seen him pass, and there was no more that she could do. She did not see the gentle smile he gave in answer to her gift.

The stench of smoke and human was very strong now on the wind, and Graywolf moved carefully, keeping his hand on Moonfinder's shoulders, his own black-tipped hair bristled up like a crest and his elvish ears atwitch. He wanted to sneeze. Surely so small a sound would not be heard in the evening noises of the camp. He smothered it, and Moonfinder jumped and ducked his head.

Faugh, yes, Here. There was the blood-smell, wolf-blood and corruption amid the filth, there was death and a human smell thick as wolf-smell in a den, and every instinct warned Graywolf that it was foolhardy as venturing a cave, out of which such smells came. The sky overhead was a lie; this open place was not safety but a trap; and the cruelty that made humans mutilate as well as kill, that made them fight in packs and respect a leader they had to defend from challenge— all these things advised Graywolf what he could look for if he made the least error.

But he wrapped his thoughts about himself very tightly, went into that silence in which he could move unfelt, and laid hands on the dead trees that made up the wall, that part of the wall that had moved and shut him out. He pushed at it and it did not move; he was wary, for it might be human magic which had made it stay, and he worked delicately, not to disturb anything which might alarm the magic-worker, if there were such.

He peered through the cracks, seeing stone tents and one fat human waddling along with a gourd in hand. He heard voices; he saw the stain of fire on walls; and of a sudden a drum began a slow pulse, a drum of a strange, high tenor. Even their music was strange; and alien voices rose in weird, harsh laughter that sent shivers down his back.

No, the wall would not give to any effort. But he was elf, and the dead trees, their branches roughly lopped, their trunks bound together with twists of fiber, left irregular crevices between, which were no difficult matter for elvish hands and feet. He laid a cautioning hand on Moonfinder, who sniffed at the binding ropes and insinuated his nose between the cracks.

Then he set his knife between his teeth and stepped up onto those ropes, his small, four-fingered hands finding a grip here, a crevice in which a clenched fist became an anchor while he pressed himself close to the wall and one foot sought through empty air—up, and up, and up, till he had an arm over the gate.

Over the sharpened logs, then, carefully, silently, arms

taking the strain as he let the other leg over, his ribs between the two sharp points while he hung there and glanced down past his arm and the inside of his knee to see the place where the human monsters had fastened Blackmane's ears. Death stink was thick here. He sweated and drew air carefully past teeth clenched on the blade as he spidered his way over the wall one log at a time. His limbs were trembling now. Sweat was stinging his eyes.

Now, now, he had reached the place. He held with one hand and seized the blood-stiffened, stinking remnant of a friend, and pulled with all his strength. It came free; he stuffed it in his belt while his clenched fist, wedged tight in a crevice between logs, grew numb and his legs shook with the unnatural angle.

Then he swung his body flat against the wall and began to climb again.

"Hey!" a shout rang out, shocking him to greater effort. Tumult broke behind him, below him. He sought handhold after handhold, and a weapon hit the logs beside his face, another on the other side below his waist. He flung an arm over the top of the wall, between the sharpened logs, as a third and a fourth weapon hit about him and a fifth scored his side. That last was goad enough to launch him over, reckless of the scoring the points of the logs gave his leg and his ribs, or the height of the drop below him. **Moonfinder!** he cried out with his mind, and hung and dropped and hit the ground with a force greater than he had planned, which buckled his legs and sprawled him flat and stunned as his head hit the earth.

Moonfinder!

He was still moving. He was blind with the blow to his head. He had lost his knife in the shock when he landed; he could not tell which was the way to the wall and which the way of escape as he reeled to his feet and braced his legs, but the sounds of pursuit told him, a howling of many voices that were elflike enough to be terrible, not so deep as trolls, but something halfway— *Kill him,* they would say, *catch him, take his ears—*

He did not know what more they would do. He heard the thump of wood behind the wall as a heavy, wolfish body shouldered him—as Moonfinder's scent came about him and his vision cleared in spots and patches of twilight and chaos. He felt after the prize he had come for, that was in his belt, and in dazed habit he wondered where his knife had gotten to, scanning with his eyes even as he realized his balance was deserting him and the world had gone unclear and sounds echoing—he was falling, and the wall was opening, and he made one frantic snatch at Moonfinder's fur, deathgrip hard as the wolf lurched into a run in the mistaken trust his rider was with him. Graywolf heard a wild growl and snarling and human shrieks—felt No-name's presence, and clung with all his strength to that one grip as Moonfinder dragged him on, scraping him along the ground and bruising him with rocks, then cutting him with the leaves of the row-plants as they took out through the garden.

His grip was sliding. He felt it go and sprawled in a tangle of limbs, got to his knees and staggered to his feet and tried to run, reeling from this to that as the din of human voices pursued him through the tall row-plants. **Moonfinder!** he cried. Shrieks broke out behind him; and wolfish snarling. **Moonfinder!**

Moonfinder came back for him. He grasped the shoulder-fur and slung himself onto his belly on Moonfinder's back as a sharp yelp and a shout reported No-name's location. The row-plants crashed and tore as human shapes began to come through the wall of foliage and stalks, and he had no need to tell Moonfinder to run—the wolf gathered himself and hurtled down rows of leaves that cut like knives.

It was rout then. Until No-name, crafty in his crazed way, circled round to the flank, and darted within the stone camp and savaged the first humans he came to before hurled stones and weapons drove him elsewhere. But he came to a flock of sheep and took his escape right through the fold, crippling and killing as he went, so that some died under his fangs and some smothered as they attempted to climb each other's backs against the wooden wall.

No-name doubled and stretched in an all-out run then, a gray streak in the night through the open gate, past terrified humans, with missiles pelting after him. His tongue lolled as he ran. There was the taste of blood in his mind, and wolfish laughter at which Graywolf shivered, where pursuit had turned in confusion and he and Moonfinder, at forest limits, drew breath and waited for the crazy one.

But more than that was coming. There was hate. There was desperation and fear down in that valley; and if humans had retreated for the moment, if No-name passed small and scattered bands of humans that fell back in terror of him, it was because it was night and because it was the wolves' time.

"Fall back, fall back!" Kerthan cried, waving a torch. "Do not follow them now!" Of which Graywolf, hearing, understood not a word, but he understood the terrible thought that came to him, of humans in numbers invading the woods, of noise and hammerings and shouts, and fire leaping up in piles of brush. Thoughts not of burning the forest, but of scouring it and taming it to use. Of a terrible enmity between the stone-place and growing things.

He shivered, and seized on Moonfinder's fur with sweating hands. **Come, come,** he urged the wolf, and flung himself onto Moonfinder's back as all the world spun crazily with a stink of blood and fire—but that was No-name, trotting along by them, his coat singed and reeking of sheep and human blood and heat.

He had done something of which he could not see the end, that was what Graywolf knew. He felt after the scrap of

stiffened wolf-hide which still rode safe within his belt and
felt a dim, dazed sense of things far beyond his control; of
things for which his chief might blame him, and even kill
him, and Swift-Spear would be right—he was too much wolf,
and his thoughts did not run far until it was too late; then the
elf in him could see the consequences, terrible, irremediable
consequences; he wished that he had died there at the wooden
wall—but that, too, Swift-Spear would have avenged, and
nothing would be different.

And then Swift-Spear was there, staring down at the battered Wolfrider. Swift-Spear's too-pale flesh glowed in the
night, his eyes burned a hard silver. Unconsciously Graywolf
slid down and bowed his head, went to his knees and sent to
his chief—sent him the passion and pain of his acts; and waited
for payment. . . .

Swift-Spear made no answer, only held out his hand, and
there Graywolf placed the grisly trophy of a wolf-friend.
Swift-Spear felt the stiffness of the skin in his palm, but this
time he fought off the memories, if not the emotions. Looking down at Graywolf and Moonfinder, he felt something
change, something twist and turn till it broke. This was not
his way. He was more than this, his people would be more
than this—more than wolf, more than elf, more than man.

"Stand up," he said, his voice gentle. "Stand up, my
brave elf." Reaching down, he grasped Graywolf's shoulders, gripping them hard. "None shall bow, no elf shall bow
head to another, not even to a chief, not even to me."

With that he turned, knowing that Graywolf and Moonfinder
would follow—even the renegade No-name; and knowing that
Graywolf would not take it kindly if he should notice
Graywolf's wounds; and knowing that things between them
had changed. . . .

Graywolf followed, the pain of his hurts forgotten, the
bizarre bloodlust of No-name thrust to the back of his mind, the
same as he ignored Moonfinder's confusion. What was this,

what were these new thoughts leaking from his chief's mind? He felt sure of Swift-Spear's care for him; and under that the boiling anger that Graywolf thought a match for any human evil. And there was this new thought—this blood thought, this word *war*.

They waited for him, the whole tribe, Wolfriders, high ones, and those trapped between. They stood in the clearing, watching. Even No-name could not resist Swift-Spear's call. As the chief walked into the midst of the gathering, Graywolf stood back: he, too, waited.

Swift-Spear measured them all with his newfound vision, his hard eyes. The eyes of a chief.

"You all know what has happened!" He spoke aloud. He would not send; he, too, knew the high ones' tricks, and this day his strength would not be blunted. "You know of Blackmane's death, of my challenge to the humans, and you know the humans' answer."

Rellah stood forward. "We know of this one's answer," she said, pointing at Graywolf. "Stupidity! Now the humans will come for us!"

"Yes, they will." Swift-Spear smiled. "They will come."

"We must flee!" Skyfire pushed her way to the front of the crowd. "We must flee this disaster you—*you!*—have put on us!"

Others nodded, but Swift-Spear blocked out all sendings. "We will not flee," he said; and the elves all looked at one another. Before anyone else could voice dissent, Swift-Spear moved to stand in front of Skyfire. He looked down at her hand, which clutched a hunting spear. *This I must take care of first*, he thought; and aloud: "Put the spear away, sister."

She went pale and took a step back.

"You have not earned it," he said. "You have no right. Put the spear away."

Skyfire turned to search out the faces of her followers, but they melted backward in the crowd; they were young, and Swift-Spear was chief.

"Or would you challenge me?" Swift-Spear put out his hand, watching her, watching her stance, her muscles. Would she dare? "Give me the spear, little one, your time will come." His voice was gentle, but his clenched teeth made his jaw muscles stand out in high relief.

And she handed the weapon to him as she must. This was not the time or place and he could defeat her easily, perhaps then banish her from the tribe.

He turned his back on her, the spear in his hand, and she moved away, her pride hot. This day she would not forget.

"What—?" Rellah began.

"Enough." Swift-Spear dared meet those blue eyes, dared for the first time to meet the high one's wrath, and he felt it heatless compared to the fire burning in him. "I will speak," he said; and the whole tribe watched as the high one stepped back, her face taut. But she said no words, sent no thoughts.

Graywolf understood all this. He smiled, squatting down to hug Moonfinder, who watched it all. He took it in, learning from this chief, this pack-leader who ruled them all.

"The humans will come, as they have always done." Swift-Spear hefted the spear, not thinking, not questioning the words that rose in him. He trusted them. He trusted his heart and mind to work as one, and to do and say the right thing. "But this time we will not run away. —Rockarm—" He looked suddenly at an older, scarred Wolfrider. "What would you do—if humans caught your pretty Sunflame?"

The elf looked down at his daughter, his mouth hard. "I would go and get her back." Rockarm's dark eyes glittered in the starlight.

"And—" Swift-Spear moved within inches of Rockarm, feeling the elder elf's hot breath on his skin. "—What would you do if, as you were about to free her, the humans thrust her through''—he jabbed with Skyfire's weapon—''with a spear, and killed her?''

Rockarm looked about him, unsure. But his chief's eyes demanded truth.

''I would kill them,'' Rockarm said, his voice harsh.

''If they catch her, if we run now and they do catch her, they will kill her, Rockarm, as they will kill us all.'' Swift-Spear turned away, paced the circle, catching each elf's eyes. ''It has ever been the way of humans.'' He spun about suddenly. ''Is that not right, Talen?''

The others moved away from the high one as Talen tried to answer the chief. ''Well, they have, I—''

''They have killed, Talen. Did they not kill our people when first we came to this world?''

''Yes, they did, we all know that, I mean . . .'' Talen could not grasp Swift-Spear's mind, could not find his thoughts. The chief was closed to his probing: his mind, if not his emotions, was closed about in metal.

''And have they not killed us ever since; have they not always killed?''

Talen just nodded. Swift-Spear felt the power, the aching power of his words.

''I will tell you something,'' Swift-Spear spoke quietly, once again pacing the circuit of the crowd. ''I thought that we could learn from the men. We had become too much wolf.'' No one reacted to this. ''I thought—*this is their world, they were here first, they will know how to live, how to build the right way.*'' He stopped and planted the spear in front of him. ''Since Timmorn's day, we have learned from our wolf-brothers. They have taught us to survive. But I want more than that, much more!'' He pointed at the stars. ''We came from there, did we not, Rellah?''

She just shook her head once, slowly, her mind confused and lost. She could not see his path.

"Did any of you—" Swift-Spear gritted his teeth. "Did any of you ever think of going back?"

"Of course. But it's impossible. We don't know the way. The sky-mountain is lost, destroyed," Rellah answered him absently, her mind still trying to decipher the puzzle that was Swift-Spear.

"Destroyed." Swift-Spear shook his head. "What do the humans do if one of their stone tents is destroyed?" He did not wait for an answer. "They rebuild!"

"Swift-Spear," Talen interrupted him. "We cannot *rebuild* the sky-mountain, boy, it was not something that was *built* as the humans build with stone."

"Now!" the chief shouted at him, "now, no, we can't rebuild, but we *could*, if we quit running, if we built instead of hiding."

"That is not the way!" Skyfire could keep quiet no longer. "We hunt, we dance, we love, each day we move, like—"

"—like *wolves*," Graywolf added. His yellow eyes gleamed in the moonlight. *O Swift-Spear, my cousin, oh, you dream such dreams.*

"We are not wolves, we are not men, and—" Swift-Spear withdrew the spear from the earth, gazing at it, rolling the head in his hands. "We are not elves, not, at least, what elves once were. We are more—or less—depending on what choice we make."

"What sort of choice?" someone shouted out.

"Not to run. To build—if we wish. Perhaps we will not build with stones and clay as men do, but perhaps with mind and magic as once the elves did." He looked up. "I, we, we have learned nothing. We have learned to fight, we have learned that we *must* fight, for food, or warmth—fight other animals, fight the weather, fight the land itself. And now we must finally learn how to fight men!" He crouched over, ignoring his newly-healed wounds, bunching his muscles to feel the thrill of their strength. He walked in a circle, stalking like a hunter.

"I will fight," he chanted in a monotone. "I will fight the men as they choose to fight, not chief to chief, but tribe to tribe. I will wait for them when they come to the forest. I will wait with wolf cunning and wolf strength, and I will trap them with elf mind and elf magic. I will kill them, drive them from the forest. I will burn their stone tents as they would burn our woods!" He stood up and turned to Graywolf, smiling at his cousin. "I will get a new spear, a man-hunting spear." With that, he cast Skyfire's weapon into the night air. It flew straight and true, seeming to pierce the stars themselves. "Then, one day, I will follow that spear!" He stood, waiting.

"I will fight with you, my chief." Graywolf strode out, and he, too, turned to stare at the high ones.

"And I," said Rockarm.

"And I, and I . . ." other voices added.

Swift-Spear smiled. It was change, hard change, but life was hard.

He turned to the eager faces. "We must plan," he said, and walked away.

The high ones stood together, undecided, unsure what this meant, or what to do about it. Skyfire watched as one by one her followers walked after Swift-Spear. She turned on her heel. This was not right, this was not the way.

And Willowgreen watched them all, with stinging, silent tears falling on the ground at her feet.

The men came. They moved into the woods as silently as they knew how, their eyes wary and their weapons sharp.

The forest waited for them, cool in the shadows, a breeze making the limbs sway, arms waving them on, deeper, deeper into its waiting grasp, and into the hands of its children.

The men were hunters now, but they could not match the

Wolfriders, who had not only intelligence and cunning, but animal senses. And so, unwillingly, their chief led them, along the false trail the elves had laid to show the men their path to death.

Kerthan grasped his spear tighter. It was darker here amongst the trees than he had thought it would be. The forest had long been man's enemy, and he knew that somewhere in it the demons waited. But the fight at the village had proved that, fierce and savage though the devils were, they could be killed; and though he remembered well the strength of the demon chief's arms, he was sure that his own men, so much larger than the demons, were more than a match for their enemy. Besides, it was daytime. *Man's* time.

He waved two young hunters to the front. The trail was well hidden, but his men could follow it. The demons were overconfident, trusting in the forest to protect them. *Huh,* he thought, *we will find their camp, we will burn them out, we will slay every one of them, and their werewolves! Then the forest will be ours!*

He looked over at the shaman. The old man was walking quietly as any of the hunters, his thin lips moving silently, his withered hands clutching the human-skin drums with whitening knuckles.

I must keep my eyes on that one, Kerthan thought. Ever and again the old man had quarreled with Kerthan's plans, but the clan's need for vengeance burned hotter than any senile warnings. The demons had left two families sonless, and one fatherless. Vengeance and blood-call lent strength to men's arms, Kerthan knew that—lent a strength that would overwhelm any of the demons' black magic.

He grinned, showing white teeth. His mind was full of plans and satisfaction as he led his men down the path prepared for them.

*   *   *

A bird call trilled above the humans' heads, and Swift-Spear smiled to hear that sound. The humans were walking right into his trap, open-eyed and smug in their arrogance. He shifted in the mud in which he knelt. It had taken all Nightdancer's power to call enough moisture from the air, mixed with what water the others could bring, to turn this spot into a mudhole. That, combined with the fact that here the trees grew so close together that the men would be separated one from the other, made this a perfect battleground—for the heavy men would find this muddy footing much more treacherous than would his nimble Wolfriders. It would have been easier, much easier, if the high ones had lent their magic to the fighting, but maybe it was better this way. Now everyone in the tribe would have to admit that it was he and the Wolfriders who had done what no others had done before: fight the humans, and win.

Two young humans broke through the foliage in front of Swift-Spear, but he let them go. He wanted no alarm to warn the enemy. Besides, they would be taken care of, another stone's-throw down the trail. He waited, breathing slowly and evenly. He could feel the presence of his elves and wolves all about him, their thoughts and emotions tightly leashed, waiting to explode and drive through the humans as the human weapons had driven through Blackmane's sleek hide.

He bit his lip at that thought and that name. Blackmane, who should be here by him, his soft fur and warm breath present to comfort him, here to wait with him as he had waited so many times before.

Swift-Spear shook off those memories. Now was not the time. He needed no thoughts of his dead wolf-friend to kindle his anger, or his hate.

Kerthan slipped in a patch of mud, swearing under his breath. He looked about him. His men had had to separate from one another to pass here. This was no good. If the demons attacked them now . . .

"Hoy!" he shouted. "We must—"

But a cry cut through his words. To his left a man stared unseeing, unmoving, then dropped his weapons and covered his eyes with a piercing shriek of agony. Kerthan added his cry as the afflicted man fell to his knees and tried to tear out his own eyes, to blind himself to whatever vision assailed him.

"To me, to me!" Kerthan yelled as behind him the shaman's drums began a mad beating. A wolf's howl shook the air about the chief, and in seconds all the men within his sight were fighting for their lives as wolf and demon appeared from nowhere to attack.

"Kill them!" Swift-Spear cried. He burst from his cover looking for an enemy to slay. A man fell to the ground in front of him, wrapped in a net his elves had cast from the trees. Swift-Spear drove his spear deep into the helpless man's chest. "Ayooah, brothers!" he howled in bloodlust. *And today,* he finished in his mind, *we have vengeance for the first meeting of man and elf.*

Graywolf plunged into the battle, Moonfinder at his side, both of them eager to find their prey. The first man they came to was smashing through the brush with his club, his mouth open in an unvoiced cry. Graywolf's spear went through the human's neck, the blood geysering to cover the elf and his wolf-friend.

Graywolf twisted the spear once, watching as the man collapsed, probably completely unaware of his own death. Almost, the young Wolfrider felt pity. He kicked the corpse as he turned to find new prey. "Ayooah!" he cried. *Almost,* he thought.

The humans were caught in a deathtrap, and they all knew it. Though the elfin magic was small and could delude only a handful of men at one time, one by one those enspelled were butchered by the Wolfriders. The humans had nothing to offset the magic, and on the slippery and boggy ground they were proving no match for the elves and their wolves.

Kerthan smashed his fist into an elf's face. Quickly he shifted his spear to a two-handed grip and skewered the bleeding demon. But there was no exhilaration in this kill. He could see only a handful of his men still standing, and the shaman's magic was doing no good. Had the gods deserted him? Were they punishing him for his pride? He bit through his lip. There was no chance. Even the bark of the trees was wet. The cleansing flame he had depended on would do him no good.

"Back," he cried. "Back to the village!"

But if any of his men heard him above the battle, they were too busy fighting to heed him.

Suddenly the drums stopped and Kerthan turned to see a wolf ripping open the shaman's throat. His men began to break, and those who could threw down their weapons and ran for their lives; but behind each raced a wolf or an elf in hot pursuit. Kerthan started to run, but the wolf who had killed the shaman leapt up to block his way. The chief held his spear tightly, trying to meet the crazed eyes of this monster.

No-name, Swift-Spear sent, **this one is mine!**

The wolf stared up at the elf who was covered in man's blood. For a moment he thought of disobeying, but there was something in this elf, something which burned behind those strange eyes. And for the first time in his life, the mad wolf bowed to another's will, presenting a bared throat. He went to his belly and waited, his limited mind struggling with what this new submissiveness betokened, and where it came from.

Swift-Spear ignored the sound and the smell of the fight around him. No humans would leave this grove alive, especially not this human! He glared up at his tall enemy and raised his stone-tipped spear.

"Chief," he hissed at the human. The human nodded understanding. This time he would not run, for they both knew that there was nowhere for him to go.

Kerthan noted the bruises on his enemy's body, but he knew it would be no advantage to him this day. He had seen the terrible damage his people had done to this demon, and he knew by all rights it should be dead and not fighting. Kerthan's eyes strayed to the point of his metal spear and he felt strength and hope in that sight. Here was the magic spear, the first weapon ever to kill a werewolf! Its magic would be powerful enough to kill this demon that refused to die! And with this monster's death, the other demons would flee from his wrath! He, Kerthan, Chief of the People, would prove once and for all that this was man's world; and men would do as they pleased, with no one to say them nay.

The bright spear darted out, and barely in time the elf dodged its deadly edge. He countered with a vicious slash that forced the man to jump back. The human skidded. Quickly Swift-Spear was on him, and the two antagonists crashed into each other with a roar of outrage.

Kerthan fell to his back, the shock of the fall knocking the air from his lungs. He kneed at the demon, but the monster caught the blow on his thigh and retaliated with an elbow slammed to the ribs.

Kerthan grunted, shifting his weight to throw his enemy off, but the demon hung on. The two rolled in the mud, howling their mutual hatred to the indifferent sky.

The man bit Swift-Spear's hand, and the pain made the elf let go of his own spear. Quickly the elf chief grasped the terrible weapon with both his hands, and the two wrestled for it with all their great strength.

But for all the man's power, the elf chief knew that this day, this fate was in his hands; and though the human was strong—was not Swift-Spear the strongest of all the tribe?

And this was the day he would prove strongest of all, both men and elves. . . .

With a sharp twist he ripped the metal spear from his enemy's grasp and sprang back. As the man tried to rise, Swift-Spear cracked the butt of the weapon under Kerthan's chin. Quick as thought, the elf chief reversed the spear and thrust it through his enemy's heart.

Swift-Spear retreated then from the corpse that lay pinned in the mud by the spear. The man's blood was hot on his skin. That was it? It was over so soon? The man had been a good fighter: Swift-Spear knew few others of the human tribe would have had a chance against him in fair fight, but still . . . so quick? So easy to kill your nightmares? One thrust and the fear that haunted the elfin-kind for so long is ended? He sighed as he withdrew the spear. *Not so quick, really*, he thought. *Not so easy*.

There would be the tribe's own dead and wounded. And though he had avenged Blackmane, it didn't really seem to matter all that much.

The elves came to the village at midday, Swift-Spear leading them, the mad No-name pacing quietly by his side. The humans closed the gates against them, but they knew it would do no good. Kerthan had taken all the hunters with him. There were only old men and boys to defend the village now. The elves stood outside the front gate, and the humans looked over the barrier, staring in fear at their demonic conquerors.

Then a tall one, tall as a man, walked out from the fierce band.

"Humans of this village," Talen said—for he alone of the elves knew the human tongue. "Your men are dead."

A few sobs answered this, but none were really shocked. After all, many of them had expected this outcome. The bravest just wanted to die with some dignity.

"Our chief"—Talen waved a hand at Swift-Spear—"has decreed that your village is an evil place, and it must be destroyed." Now crying could be heard from inside the walls. "However," Talen continued, "you will be allowed to leave in peace."

The people within the walls stood shocked, a few whispering among themselves. Could this be? Was this a trap? They moved closer to the wall to hear the tall demon's words.

"On one condition," Talen concluded.

So here it comes. Many of the villagers nodded their heads in perverse satisfaction.

"He does not know if you have honor, but some things must be sacred to you. He says if you will pledge by these things never to come here again, and to make no more war upon his people, you may go free, with whatever you can carry. Or," Talen added in a harsh voice, "you can die. I suggest you waste no time making your decision."

The humans marched off into the west in a long line, shocking the elves with how many things they wished to take with them. One old male talked quietly with Talen and Swift-Spear beside the front gate as the people of the village filed past, sneaking last looks at their lost homes.

The man bowed once to Talen, then to Swift-Spear. His mouth was tight and his eyes were hard.

"We will keep our pledge. The tribe will never come to these lands again." He drew himself to his full height. "I am glad you have explained this to me. I am glad you have given us our lives. But do not expect me to love you for it." Talen translated this for Swift-Spear, who responded quietly in the faintly musical language of the elves.

"My chief says," Talen answered the human, "we do not want your love, nor do we want your hate. What is important to you is not important to us. You have painted your destiny in blood, and you have paid the price. Remember that always. Go in peace.''

The man bowed, but he heard the words that Talen murmured under his breath:

''I would that we could have been friends.''

The old human just nodded his shaggy head once and followed his people into exile.

The night was lit by the burning village. Wavering fires made Swift-Spear's shadow dance at his feet as he stood to face the tribe.

''We have done as we had to do. We fought and won, not for love of fighting, but for justice. No longer will we hide from any threat, but we will face it boldly, and in this world to which we have always been strangers, we shall make a true home, and a new life.'' He raised his left hand which held his stone-tipped spear. ''I shall carry this spear in the hunt, I shall carry it to remember what *has* been.'' He held out his right hand, which grasped the metal spear of Kerthan. ''And I shall carry this spear, to remind me of what *can* be, what *will* be if we have the courage to find it!''

He stood tall and bold, the homes of his enemy burning behind him. He felt the warmth of the flames playing across the muscles of his back. *Alive! I am alive!*

And he knew his people rejoiced with him.

''No longer shall I be called Swift-Spear.'' He shook his weapons at the tribe. ''But Two-Spear!''

''Two-Spear!'' they shouted back, and even the high ones joined that cry.

''Two-Spear.'' He met their eyes and gloried in what he saw there. ''I shall weld the old and the new ways together, and I shall lead you down a path that no elves before us have dared to dream of!''

And with that he cast both spears into the air, one and the other, as if he really believed that they could pierce the stars.

They came as they always did after the howl had filled their memories with Two-Spear. They came like the first stars at dusk; Longreach saw Scouter arrive at his brookside bower and when he looked up again there were eight Wolfriders silently choosing their places on the rocks and grass. They loved the recklessness that characterized Prey-Pacer's son but, like too much honey, they could not always digest what they'd swallowed.

"He was mad, wasn't he," Scouter said, more a statement than a question, "like a sick wolf."

Longreach shook his head. For all their vividness and detail, the memories and stories of Two-Spear were the hardest to hold in the mind. He knew Timmorn better than he'd known the ill-fated chief.

"But Huntress Skyfire had to drive him away. He moved against the Way so he lost his wolf-friend and his place with the Wolfriders." That was Clearbrook, but she was speaking her own hope and imagination, not from the treasure of memory. "He would have destroyed the Wolfriders with his madness."

The storyteller unslung his pouch of dreamberries. "No," he said as he handed the soft leather bag to Scouter. "Two-Spear was the only chief who ever made the five-fingered ones leave once they'd made their stone-piles. And Huntress Skyfire didn't set the Way until after he'd gone. But he *was* mad, and that made him leave the Wolfriders when they would no longer follow him.''

Cutter pushed the wheat-pale hair from his eyes and stared at Longreach. "Not follow their chief?" His interest was clearly personal.

"It has happened at other times. Zarhan Fastfire left before Prey-Pacer tied his hair in the chief's knot, and that was madness, too. Though his was a grief that could not swallow his lifemate's death. He left alone, but there have been others, by themselves or in small groups, who have gone and never come back.''

They vanished from the Wolfrider memory, the treasure of which Longreach was the guardian. There had been a few who had not vanished from his own long memory, and there might be more if the feud between Strongbow and Bearclaw flared instead of smoldered.

"But never a chief, excepting Two-Spear?" Bearclaw's son demanded.

"Only Two-Spear and an eight or so of his followers.''

The youth seemed satisfied, but not his slightly older friend. "It always seemed that he'd gone alone," Skywise mused, spitting his second dreamberry pit into the brook. "But now I can *feel* that some would have gone with him and believed that he, and not Huntress Skyfire, knew the Wolfriders' Way best.''

There was no question that the silver-maned Wolfrider ran deep—too deep to be the guardian of the dreamberry memories, though that truth cut Longreach's heart like one of Bearclaw's cold, metal knives.

"I wonder where they went?" Skywise asked the treetops.

A shiver ran down Longreach's spine. Dreamberries were for remembering and sharing memories—not for asking unanswerable questions. He could see that Skywise had caught the others. Their eyes were glazing over and the youth's mouth was open as if he could answer his own question.

"We are the Wolfriders," Longreach intoned, wrenching control of the howl away from the unsuspecting dreamer. "We are Huntress Skyfire's children. She knew the Way, she lived it, and she taught it to us—"

Tale of the Snowbeast
—by Janny Wurts—

That year, the season of white cold was worse than any elf in the holt could remember. The storage nooks were empty of the last nuts and dried fruit; and still the wind blew screaming through bare branches while snow winnowed deep into drifts in the brush and the hollows between trees. Huddled beneath the weight of a fur-lined tunic, Huntress Skyfire paused and leaned on her bow.

"Hurry up! It's well after daylight, past time we were back to the holt."

A soft whine answered her.

Chilled, famished, and tired of foraging on game trails that showed no tracks, Skyfire turned and looked back. Her companion wolf, Woodbiter, hunched with his tail to the wind, gnawing at the ice which crusted the fur between his pads.

"Oh, owl pellets, again?" But Skyfire's tone reflected chagrin rather than annoyance. She laid aside her bow, stripped off her gloves, and knelt to help the wolf. "You're an unbelievable nuisance, you know that?"

Woodbiter sneezed, snow flying from his muzzle.

"This is the second night we come back empty-handed." Skyfire blew on reddened hands, then worked her fingers back into chilled gloves. Woodbiter whined again as she rose, but did not bound ahead. Neither did he hunt up a stick to play games; instead he trotted down the trail, his bushy tail hung low behind. Hunger was wearing even his high spirits down. Skyfire retrieved her bow in frustration. The tribe needed game, desperately; the Wolfriders were all too thin, and though the cubs were spared the largest portions, lately the youngest had grown sickly. Tonight, Skyfire decided, she would range farther afield, for plainly the forest surrounding the holt was hunted out.

A gust raked the branches, tossing snow like powder over Skyfire's head. She tugged her leather cap over her ears, then froze, for something had moved in the brush. Woodbiter stopped with his tail lifted and his nose held low to the ground; by his stance Skyfire knew he scented game, probably a predator which had left its warm den to forage for mice in a stand of saplings. Skyfire slipped an arrow by slow inches from her quiver. She nocked it to her bowstring and waited, still as only an elf could be.

The shadow moved, a forest cat half-glimpsed through blown snow. Skyfire released a shot so sure that even another elf might envy her skill; and by Woodbiter's eager whine knew that he scented blood. Her arrow had flown true.

But unlike the usual kill, her companion wolf did not rush joyfully to share the fruits of their hunting. Woodbiter obediently held back, for in times of intense hardship, game must be returned to the holt for all of the tribe to share. Skyfire elbowed her way through the saplings, grumbling a little as snow showered off the branches and spilled down her neck. She picked up the carcass and felt the bones press sharply through the thick fur of its coat. Half-starved itself, the cat was a pathetic bundle of sinew; it would scarcely fill the belly of the youngest of the cubs. Skyfire sighed and worked her arrow free. She permitted Woodbiter to lick the blood from the shaft. Then, as wind chased the snow into patterns

under her boots, she pushed her catch into her game bag
and resumed her trek to the holt.

She arrived exhausted from pushing through the heavy
drifts. Breathless, chilled, and wanting nothing more than to
curl up in her hollow and sleep, she unslung her game bag.
Shadows speared across the packed snow beneath the trees
that sheltered the holt; but the tribe did not sleep, as Skyfire
expected. Elves and wolves clustered around the blond-haired
form of Two-Spear, who was chief. Closest to him were his
tight cadre of friends, including Graywolf, Willowgreen, and
sour-tempered Stonethrower.

Skyfire frowned. Why should Two-Spear call council at
this hour, if not to take advantage of her absence? The chief
might be her sibling, but to a sister who liked her hunts direct
and her kills clean, Two-Spear's motives sometimes seemed
dark and murky, as a pool that had stood too long in shadow.
And his policies were dangerous. Elves had died for his hot-
headed raids upon the humans in the past, and the chance he
might even now be hatching another such reckless solution
for the hunger which currently beset the tribe made Skyfire
forget her weariness. Woodbiter sensed the mood of his
companion. He pressed against her hip, whining softly as she
pitched her game bag into the snow.

A younger elf on the fringes turned at the sound. Called
Sapling for her slim build, her face lit up in welcome.
"You're late," she said, cheerful despite the fact that hunger
had transformed her slender grace to gauntness.

It was unfair, thought Skyfire, that lean times should fall
hardest upon the young. She pushed the game bag with her
toe, trying to lighten her own mood. "I'm late because of
this." Then, as Sapling's thin face showed more hope than a
single, underfed forest cat warranted, she forced herself to
add, "Which was hardly worth the risk."

Sapling paused, her hand on the strap of the game bag, and
a wordless interval passed. Dangerous though it was for an

elf to fare alone during daylight, when men were abroad and chances of capture increased, the game in the bag was too sorely needed to be spurned. "The other hunters made no kills at all," Sapling pointed out.

The admiration in her tone embarrassed; brusquely, Skyfire said, "Is that why Two-Spear called council?"

Sapling hefted the game bag. "He plans to send a hunting party deeper into the forest than elves have ever gone, to look for stag."

Which was wise, Skyfire reflected; except that all too frequently Two-Spear's intentions resulted in discord and chaos. Frowning, she pulled off her cap, freeing the red-gold hair which had earned her name. "I think I had better go along," she said softly. And leaving the game with Woodbiter and Sapling, she stepped boldly toward the clustered members of the tribe.

Her approach was obscured by the taller forms of the few high ones whose blood had not mixed with the wolves, yet Two-Spear saw her. He stopped speaking, and other heads turned to follow his glance. "Skyfire!" said her brother. "We were just wondering where you were."

Skyfire endured the bite of sarcasm in his tone. She looked to Willowgreen, and received a faint shake of the head in reply; no. Two-Spear was not in one of his rages. But at his side, the half-wild eyes of Graywolf warned her to speak with care. "I wish to go with the hunting party, brother."

"You went with the hunting party last night," Two-Spear said acidly. He tossed back fair hair and shrugged. "Yet again, you returned alone. In strange territory, that habit could endanger us."

Skyfire bridled, but returned no malice; the carcass in her game bag was too scrawny as a boast to prove her success on the trail. Instead she sought a reply that might ease the rivalry that seemed almost daily to widen the breach between herself and this brother who was chief; above anything she did not want to provoke a challenge. The white cold made difficulties enough without elf contending against elf within the tribe. Still her thoughts did not move fast enough.

Sapling came hotly to her defense, calling from the edge of the council. "The Huntress brought us game! She was the only Wolfrider to return with any meat."

Skyfire gritted her teeth, embarrassed afresh as hungry, eager pairs of eyes all focused past her. Jostled as tribe-mates pushed by to crowd around Sapling and the pathetic bundle in the game bag, she hid her discomfort by pressing her hair back into her cap. Aware only of Two-Spear's sharp laugh, she missed seeing Graywolf part the drawstrings. The bloody, bone-skinny cat was held aloft, a trophy of her prowess for all the tribe to see.

Yet hunger robbed the mockery of insult; and even the tribe elder who had taught her dared not mock her affinity for the hunt. When the vote was cast, Skyfire found her name included in the party of seven that would seek new territory to forage. That satisfied her, though the choice of Two-Spear's henchman, Stonethrower, as leader of the foray pleased her not at all.

The kill was skinned, then divided among the youngest cubs. Emulating Skyfire, Sapling tried to refuse her portion, until the focus of her admiration sternly instructed her to eat. At last, bone-weary, the finest huntress in the tribe since Prey-Pacer retired to her hollow and curled deep in her furs. The only things she noticed before she fell asleep were the dizzy lassitude of extreme hunger, and the snarls of the wolf-pack as they fought over the forest cat's entrails. The sound gave rise to discordant dreams, in which she faced her brother over the honed points of the twin spears he carried always at his side. . . .

"Get up, sister."

Skyfire opened her eyes as the fair head of her brother

tilted through the entrance to her hollow beneath the upper
fork of the central tree. His eyes were blue, and too bright,
like sky reflected in ice. "You promised to hunt down the
grandfather of all stags, remember? Stonethrower is waiting
for you."

Stung by the fact that this was the first time since she had
been a cub that her brother had succeeded in catching her
asleep, Skyfire peeled aside her sleeping furs. She reached
for laces and stag fleece to bind her legs against the cold.
"Tell Stonethrower to sharpen that old flint knife he carries.
I'll be ready before he's finished." But her retort fell use-
lessly upon emptiness; Two-Spear had already departed.

The worse ignominy struck when she emerged, arrows and
quiver hooked awkwardly over one arm while she struggled
to lace her jerkin. Her other hand strove and failed to contain
the brindled fur of her storm cape. She hooked a toe in the
trailing hem and nearly fell out of the great tree before she
realized that sunset still stained a sky framed by buttresses of
black branches; the cleared ground beneath was empty of all
but the presence of her brother. In all likelihood, Stonethrower
was still in the arms of his lifemate.

Hunger made it difficult for Skyfire to control her annoyance. With forced deliberation, she sat on the nearest tree
limb and began to retie the bindings that haste had caused her
to lace too tightly. She pulled the chilly weight of the cloak
over her shoulders and hung her quiver and bow. Then,
hearing Stonethrower shout from below, she rose and grimly
climbed down. By the time her feet sank into the snowdrifts
beneath, her temper had entirely dissolved. Woodbiter had
bounded up to nose at her hand, and her thoughts turned
toward game, and thrill of the coming hunt.

The hunters gathered quickly after that. But unlike more
prosperous times, as the afterglow faded and twilight deepened over the forest, they did not laugh or chatter. Their
wolves did not whine with eagerness, but stood steady as

riders mounted. Then, Graywolf with his unnaturally silent tread breaking the trail, seven elves departed with hopes of finding meat for a starving tribe.

Night deepened, and the cold bit fiercely through gloves and furs. Fingers ached and toes grew slowly numb. Yet the elves made no complaint. Generations of survival in the wilds had made them hardy and resilient as the wolf-pack that shared their existence. Beasts and riders traveled silently through the dark while the wind hissed and slashed snow against their legs. The weather was changing. Though stars gleamed like pinpricks through velvet, the air had a bite that warned of storm.

Skyfire did not travel at the fore, as was her wont; on foot, to spare Woodbiter the stress of carrying her when his ribs pressed through his coat, she hung back toward the rear of the line. These woods were barren of game, and she preferred to contain her eagerness until the holt lay well behind.

Yet even starvation could not entirely curb Woodbiter's high spirits. He cavorted like a cub through the snow drifts, snapping at twigs to show off his strong jaws. Skyfire smiled at his antics, but did not join his play. She dreamed instead of green leaves, and the fat, juicy haunch of a freshly killed stag.

Clouds rolled in before dawn, flat and leaden with the threat of snow. In the hush that preceded the storm, Skyfire sensed movement behind her on the trail. She paused, a shadow among the snow-draped boles of the trees. The other elves passed on out of sight ahead. Skyfire held her ground, and again the faintest scrape of leather on bark reached her ears; someone followed. Not a human; the tracker moved too skillfully to be anything but an elf. Tense, and troubled, and wondering whether Two-Spear's madness had progressed to the point of setting spies after his own hunting parties, Skyfire bided her time.

After a short wait, an elf emerged between the trees,

thickly muffled in furs, and moving with the stealth of a stalker. Huntress Skyfire did not wait to identify, but sprang at once on the unsuspecting follower. Her victim squealed sharply in surprise. Then momentum bore both of them down into a snowdrift. The tussle which followed was savage and sharp, brought to an end when Skyfire pinned the other elf's neck firmly beneath the shaft of her bow. Her cap was knocked askew; enough snow had fallen down her collar to put fire in her temper as she shook the hair free of her eyes to view her catch.

A merry face with tousled dark curls grinned up from a pillow of snow.

"Sapling!" Skyfire raised her bow, angry now for a different reason. Two-Spear's recklessness had provoked the humans to boldness; often now they set snares for unwary Wolfriders. And Sapling was still almost a cub, having yet to shed her child-name for the one she would earn as an adult. "What are you doing following the hunters?"

Sapling sat up, the hollows carved by famine accentuated in the growing light. "I wanted to be with you."

Skyfire turned her back, arms folded, and her cap still crooked upon her head. "You're lucky the humans didn't catch you instead." She spun then, and glared at her young admirer. "You know they caught Thornbranch. They burned him. You're not too young to remember."

Sapling scuffed at snow with her toes. She seemed more embarrassed than cowed by the reprimand. Tall, now, as her mentor, Skyfire was forced to realize that little remained of the cub who had once tugged at her tunic. Sapling had nearly grown up. If she had tracked this far without drawing notice, she would not disturb the game, and she would be safer with the hunters than on a return trek to the holt.

"All right." Skyfire set her cap straight with a hard look at her junior. "If you dare to track your elders, then you can act like one."

Sapling's face lighted up. "I can stay?"

"That's for Stonethrower to decide." Skyfire hooked her bow over her shoulder. "Now, come on."

Dawn brightened steadily as the two elves followed the trail of the others. Clouds lowered over the blown tops of the trees, and the air smelled of storm. Wisely, the Wolfriders had chosen to sleep out the day in a hollow by a frozen waterfall. By the time Skyfire and her companion found them, an enterprising elder had broken the ice to hunt for fish. The others had rolled in their furs, pressed close to the wolves for warmth, except for Stonethrower.

"You dallied, but not to hunt game this time," he commented as Skyfire appeared with Sapling in tow.

Yet his sarcasm was wasted on Huntress Skyfire. Woodbiter had not answered her call, and a swift review of the pack revealed the fact that he was not present. *Owl pellets,* she thought; with Sapling now under her care, the last thing she needed was that wolf getting into another scrape. Feeling the cold, the hunger, and all the weariness of the night's march, she met Stonethrower's dark glance. "Woodbiter's not with the pack."

The older elf shrugged. "He ran off ahead of the others. Like you so often will."

Skyfire bit back a retort. Instead, she closed her eyes and *sent*, seeking that pattern of awareness that was uniquely Woodbiter's. She found nothing. Alarmed, she put urgency into her call; and the wolf-consciousness that answered showed a thicket of briar and hazel, shot through with fear and the terrible, burning pain of a pinched leg.

"Woodbiter's in trouble!" Skyfire freed her bow. She tensed like a wild thing, ready to run and aid her wolf.

But Stonethrower stepped squarely in her path. "There's a storm coming. You gave Two-Spear your word that you wouldn't be going off alone."

At this, Skyfire felt a soft nudge from Sapling. Warmed suddenly by the presence of a friend, she smiled. "But I won't be alone. Sapling will come with me."

Stonethrower narrowed his eyes, and sent, **She doesn't belong here.**

I know, Skyfire returned. **What are you going to do about it?**

Stonethrower considered the young elf at the Huntress's side; he also thought upon other instructions that Two-Spear had given concerning the sister who always found ways to evade the will of her chief. "I'll go with you," he said at last.

In other circumstances, Skyfire would surely have argued against taking her brother's henchman long. But Woodbiter was in pain; for that she would brook no delay. She sprang into the forest, Sapling a shadow at her heels, even as Stonethrower moved to gather his weapons. He had to run to catch up. Though day was fully come, the wood seemed dim, gray with the threat of a gathering storm.

Gusts rattled the branches like bones overhead, and the first flakes whirled and stung the faces of the elves who hastened to Woodbiter's aid. Soon the snow fell more thickly, the surrounding trees veiled in white; even Stonethrower appreciated the forest instincts for which Huntress Skyfire was renowned. She led her companions without error through a tortuous maze of ravines. Once her keen ears caught the chuckle of current beneath an ice-covered stream; and only swift reflex saved Sapling from a dunking. Although Stonethrower questioned the wisdom of continuing with the weather against them, a glance at Skyfire's face forestalled any comment. The green of her eyes shone with a clear, fierce anger that elves who hunted with her had seen only once before, and that the time Woodbiter's mate had been killed by a human hunter.

For by now they had come far enough that the wolf's

sending became clear enough to interpret. Skyfire gripped her bow until her knuckles whitened and said, "He is caught in a trap, the sort that humans set to break the legs of foxes." She paused, and as an afterthought added, "We have not far to go."

Skyfire drew ahead, then, despite the efforts of Sapling and Stonethrower to keep up. They followed breathlessly, twisting past trees gray and scabbed with ice, through hollows where the wind howled like a mad thing, and over snowdrifts spread like snares for unwary feet. Sooner than either elf thought possible, they came upon the Huntress, bent upon one knee in a depression between a steep bank and the roots of a twisted tree.

"Look," she said without turning.

Stonethrower and Sapling crowded closer, and saw the track of a huge beast, oval-shaped, with evidence of a pointy claw at one end. The snow fell less thickly in the shelter of the draw; the track, though not fresh, was plainly discernible as something not made by chance.

"What is it?" asked Sapling, more than a little scared. The track was wider than four handspans, and half as long as her spear.

Skyfire frowned, and Stonethrower knuckled his beard, a habit he had when something distressed him. No Wolfrider had ever seen anything like such tracks, and quick sending among them established understanding they were troubled. A beast that size was bound to be dangerous.

Stonethrower quietly suggested they turn back.

Frightened herself, but driven by loyalty to Woodbiter, Skyfire regarded him with the contempt she usually reserved for humans. "Why should we? Are you afraid to go on?"

Swirling snow and the wail of wind through the draw filled a tense interval. Then, without speaking, Skyfire whirled and continued on. Sapling accompanied her. Left an untenable implication, Stonethrower followed after; but under his breath he muttered that Skyfire's belief that Two-Spear's reckless ways would eventually lead the tribe to ruin was an unbalanced accusation at best. In the opinion of the older elf, the sister was as stubborn as the brother, which was precisely why the two were continually at odds.

The draw deepened, narrowing into a defile where snow fell thinly, and then only when driven by odd eddies of wind. The prints of the strange beast showed plainly upon the faces of the drifts. Skyfire followed, nervous, but insistent the place of Woodbiter's captivity lay very near at hand. The elves labored through deeper and deeper drifts, sometimes sinking to their waists. The terrible tracks kept pace with them, even when the cleft of the gully widened and they found the wolf, crouched in the open and chewing at his bloody right hind pad.

No one rushed forward with joy. The tracks here were many, and thickest, and plainly associated with the snare. Perhaps they were made by monstrous, splayfooted humans, or bears with terrible cunning. But Skyfire refused to be cowed. She scouted the area with a thoroughness even Stonethrower respected. Then, borrowing Sapling's spear, she advanced into the clearing and bent at the side of the injured wolf.

Steady, she sent. Woodbiter whined, but he stopped struggling as his companion knelt at his side. Gently she scraped away the snow, felt through wet and matted hair to assess the injuries to her friend. The trap which held him was primitive. Green, springy sticks of sharpened wood had clamped his leg just above the first joint, strong enough to tear the skin and confine, but not to break bones. Angry enough to kill, Skyfire steadied Woodbiter's leg in one strong hand. Then, using Sapling's spear as a lever, she forced the sticks apart.

Woodbiter jerked free with a yelp. Trembling from his ordeal, he leaned against Skyfire, nosing her hair and ears in appreciation. Yet his friend did not respond with scolding for his carelessness, as she might have done another time. Instead, leaning on Sapling's spear, she stared at the perfect, reddened paw prints pressed into new snow by Woodbiter's limping steps. She ran her tongue over her teeth. With her wolf safe, now was the prudent time to start back to the stream where the other hunters had camped. But something too deep to deny rejected the safety of retreat.

Stonethrower arrived at her shoulder. Though impatient to be off, he did not intrude upon Skyfire's mood; instead he knelt beside her and with the flint knife he had once stolen from a camp of humans, began methodically to hack the water-hardened thongs which bound a collection of green branches into a deadly snare for the forest-born.

Skyfire spoke as the last bent bough whipped straight, then snapped between Stonethrower's thick fists. Her tone was cold as the wind that hammered snow through the branches beyond the shelter of the draw where they stood. "I'm going after them."

Stonethrower cast away a snarl of severed thongs. "That's folly. You saw the tracks. Whatever creature set this snare is large, and clever, too much for an elf."

Skyfire curled her lip. "Larger, yes, but not so fierce, I think. Only cowardly beings like humans ever set traps for animals."

"But Two-Spear said—" began Stonethrower, only to be cut off.

"Two-Spear isn't here. *His* wolf did not lie bloody in a trap for half a night." Skyfire jabbed the spear into the ground hard enough that ice scattered from the butt. "Are you stopping me?"

Stonethrower met her angry eyes, his hand tightened on the haft of his flint knife. "I should." But he made no move to do so as Skyfire spun away and continued down the gully.

Woodbiter whined and followed, and Sapling did likewise, too young to know any better.

Stonethrower went along as well, out of duty to his chief, but he regretted that decision almost immediately. The wind bit like the hatred of the humans, and the tracks, half-obscured by blown snow, were soon joined by a second set, and then a third; the new prints were twice the size of the first ones.

Skyfire stopped to test the tension of her bowstring, and Sapling wordlessly took back her spear. Stonethrower tried to resume his argument, then waited, as he realized that the Huntress herself was deaf to any spoken word. Deep in communion with her wolf, she waited while Woodbiter applied his keen nose to the frightening tracks in the snow.

The effort was a vain one; freezing wind had long since scoured any scent from the trail. On nearby twigs the wolf detected faint traces of resin, but the smell was unfamiliar to his experience, and to the elves as well. Unable to imagine this beast as anything but huge and dangerous, even the boldest of the four companions hesitated while the snow whirled and stung their exposed faces.

"We should go back," Stonethrower repeated. "The others should be warned that this part of the forest is unsafe for elves."

Skyfire stood poised, her hand less than steady on her bow. Then, suddenly resolved, she said, "No. Danger to us is danger to the holt. And the snow makes good cover. I say we follow these tracks and find out what sort of beast sets traps that snare wolves."

Her tone would brook no compromise. And unlike her brother, who was chief, Skyfire was not susceptible to counter-argument, or cajoling, or flattery. Once she made up her mind, she stuck to her purpose like flint. Stonethrower had a scar to remind him, for when she had been a cub, he had once scooped her off some sharp rocks in a streambed when

the current had swept her young legs out from beneath her.
He remembered how she had sulked because he had refused
to let her attempt another crossing at the same site. If anything, her determination had grown with her years, and
Woodbiter's limp made her angry and dangerous to cross.
Quite likely Huntress Skyfire herself was fiercer than the
great beast she tracked, the older elf concluded as the others
set off once more. But his attempt at humor failed as snow
chased itself in eddies down his collar, and his fingers numbed
on the flint haft of his knife.

The gully narrowed and widened, then opened into a
frozen expanse of marsh. Wind rattled through ranks of frost-
killed reeds, the tracks now showing through a swath of
crushed stalks. Here and there a softened patch of bog had
frozen the imprints intact. Woodbiter sniffed and snarled, and
favored his hurt leg. Only Skyfire and Sapling seemed unaffected by the bleakness of the landscape, the former warmed
by her desire for redress, and the latter, by the thrill of being
away from the holt on her very first adventure. Stonethrower
endured in dour silence, and almost rammed into the thong-
laced tip of Skyfire's bow as she stopped without warning
and pointed.

"Do you see that?"

Stonethrower looked where she indicated and felt his heart
miss a beat. The snow had slowed, almost stopped, and
rising above the ridge he saw blown smudges of smoke;
where there are fires, the old adage ran, *there are always
humans.* Worse, the fearsome tracks led off in the same
direction.

Sapling jabbed her spear-butt ringingly into the ground.
Skyfire tested the points on her darts, each one with singu-
lar care. This once Stonethrower did not argue when the
sister of the chief suggested they scout out the size of the
camp on the ridge. Though the site lay outside the Wolfriders'
usual hunting ground, no humans had inhabited this portion

in past memory. The fact that giant, splayfooted ones did
now might threaten the entire holt.

Grimly, three elves and one companion wolf started forward. The bare ice of the marsh offered little concealment,
which obliged them to go carefully. Only the wolf spoke,
soft, high whines of uneasiness at the scent of the humans on
the wind. The elves moved in silence, absorbed in their own
thoughts. Skyfire squinted often at the fire-smoke and wondered what game the humans might have caught in their traps
besides the unfortunate Woodbiter. Sapling tagged at her
heels, excited to be included, but wary and nervous. Over
and over she tried to imagine what sort of creature had
walked over the snow to lead them here. The tracks were
fearsomely large, yet they crossed the deepest drifts seemingly without miring; that humans might use strange beasts
to tend their traplines seemed dangerous and cruel to an elf
brought up to love the thrill of the live hunt.

Stonethrower did not think of men or fearsome beasts.
Instead he considered Two-Spear, whose dark, fierce temper
did not run to temperance. He believed all humans existed to
be battled, and likely this camp would merit no exception. A
message must be sent back to the holt, and at the soonest
opportunity, the older elf decided. Yet he mentioned nothing
of this as he set foot in Skyfire's boot tracks and began his
ascent of the ridge.

The elves climbed, buffeted by gusts that were barbed with
ice driven off the flatlands below. Even the least experienced, Sapling, blended invisibly with rocks, hummocks,
and tree boles. Soon the three lay flat on their bellies at the
crest of the rise, the white puffs of their breaths mingling
with the last, thinning veils of snow.

The air smelled of smoke. Woodbiter growled low, almost
soundlessly, while the others gazed upon tents of laced hides,
and fires beyond counting. Noisy packs of humans trod the
snow to mire in between, more humans than the elves of

Two-Spear's holt could have imagined existed in the whole of the world of two moons. The men carried weapons, spears, and flint axes and shields of hide-covered wood. Their cloaks were shiny with grease, and their cheeks dark hollows of starvation. No game roasted over the fires, but small children huddled close to them for warmth, too starved and dispirited to cry.

Huntress Skyfire pushed herself back from the crest and rolled on her back. Her green eyes stared sightlessly at sky. "They, too, lack game. No doubt that's why they're on the move."

Stonethrower offered no comment.

But Sapling said, "I saw no beasts among them, not one in the entire camp."

Skyfire rolled onto one elbow and eyed her keenly. "That's true." She smiled, more with relief than humor. "I don't think beasts made such tracks. Come look."

The two of them wormed back toward the crest, noses all but buried in the snow. Silently, Skyfire pointed, and Sapling saw large, wooden frames with sinew laces interwoven between. The middles had lacings; and a moment later, when a band of human scouts entered the camp from the east, they wore the same devices strapped to their feet. Sapling stifled a giggle. Obviously, the heavier humans needed such clumsy things to keep from miring in the snowdrifts, inconvenient though they would be for walking or running with any speed or stealth.

"No wonder they catch no game," she whispered to Skyfire, then turned, only to discover the Huntress had retreated back down the slope and was engaged in a subdued, but heated argument with Stonethrower.

"Two-Spear must not be told!" she whispered emphatically. "I agree the humans offer threat, but we cannot fight so many and hope to survive. Better the entire holt moves to another part of the forest than have everyone killed in a war."

"Now look who's talking of running!" Stonethrower glared at the redheaded sister who was so like, and yet so different from the brother who held his loyalty.

Uneasy to be holding a confrontation so near an encampment of humans, Skyfire tilted her head to one side in a way that never failed to endear. "At least wait until nightfall before starting back to inform the other hunters," she pleaded. "Woodbiter's lame, and all of us could use a few hours of rest."

Stonethrower grunted through clenched teeth, but offered no further argument as the three descended the slope. The snowfall thickened again as the Wolfriders crossed the marsh, icy flakes rattling among the dead stalks of the reeds and whispering across bare ice. Finding a sheltered place to spread sleeping furs took longer than any of them anticipated. Weary, and weakened still more from hunger, Skyfire and Sapling fell immediately asleep. Neither was aware that Stonethrower sat brooding and awake. By the time he rose and slipped soundlessly into the storm, not even Woodbiter noticed, dreaming as he was of game, with his nose tucked under his brush, and his injured paw curled carefully beneath.

Sundown came with snow still falling, and the light failed swiftly, turning the forest the gray on gray of winter twilight. Skyfire dreamed the dry crack of snapping bones as humans decimated the holt of the Wolfriders. She jerked awake. Snow flurried from her furs, and she took a moment to orient. Sapling still slept, but the snap of the bones was real enough; not handspans past her still form stretched Woodbiter, the rich scent of blood on his muzzle.

"Where did you get that?" demanded Skyfire, eyeing the meat between his paws with an envy impossible to hide.

Woodbiter blinked, a flash of triumph in his light eyes. He sent a confused flurry of images, and through them Skyfire gathered that he had learned the secret of the humans' traps;

this kill, or at least this portion, had been stolen from one of them.

"You rogue!" Skyfire's merry laugh caused Sapling to stir from her furs. "If that's a haunch of stag, the least you can do is share."

Woodbiter rose with the grace of a sated predator, a grace that bordered upon disdain for the rag of meat he had spared for his companions. Still smiling, Skyfire shook Sapling's shoulder and said, "Look, we have something to eat before we must go into the cold and dodge humans."

Sapling sat up and stretched. "Where's Stonethrower?" she said, and came swiftly alert as Skyfire's green eyes narrowed to slits. The hollow where they camped was empty, but for the two of them and the one wolf. Stonethrower was gone.

"He'll be running to fetch Two-Spear, like an owl after mice." Skyfire slung on her bow and quiver, anger infused in her very motions. "That means you and I have to think very fast, and find a way to send these humans packing out of this section of forest!"

"What about Woodbiter's catch?" demanded Sapling.

The reply came brisk as Skyfire shook snow from her cap and jammed it over her hair. "We'll eat on the move. Come on!"

The elves slipped out into the bracing twilight chill, the wolf a shadow at their heels. They stole from tree trunk to thicket to thornbrake, wary of leaving tracks for humans to find. Once they had to duck into cover as a party of hunters passed by, returning to camp after checking their traps. The humans walked unaware they were watched from cover, or that the devices they wore strapped to their feet to make going in snow less clumsy were a marvel to beings more nimble than they.

Skyfire chewed thoughtfully on a strip of stag meat for a long while after the hunters had gone. Wary of her mood, and striving not to fidget for the first time in her young life,

Sapling waited while the woodland slowly darkened. The clouds thinned and parted, leaving the night all velvet and silver with moonlight.

At last Skyfire stirred. "We have no choice. We'll have to investigate the humans' camp by ourselves."

At once Sapling feared the Huntress would forbid her to go forward into danger; but Skyfire only tested the tautness of her bowstring and looked levelly at her young companion. "Can you move as quietly as a wolf?"

Sapling nodded. At Woodbiter's eager whine, she and Skyfire crept from the thicket and tracked the humans' strange footsteps. Moving swiftly, and in silence, the elves overtook the trappers before long; careful to remain out of sight, they followed closely as they dared.

Apparently the hunting had been poor, for the humans grumbled constantly as they shuffled over the drifts on their strange footgear. Skyfire and Sapling caught snatches of cursing between descriptions of traps raided by fierce wolves. In time, the first group of hunters was joined by a second party, which reported another snare tripped and tampered with by some woodland demon with three fingers. Wolf-sign had been seen at that site also, and when the first band of humans heard this, they made signs to Gotara, and looked often over their shoulders. Without comfort, the elves noted that curses shifted to threats. They ducked unobtrusively behind a fallen log while their enemies drew ahead, a huddle of knotty silhouettes against the moonlit ice of the swamp.

"What do you think they'll do?" whispered Sapling.

Skyfire silenced her with a gesture, listening intently as the loud-voiced leader of the humans shouted querulously to the others. "And I say this camp is ill-favored! We must continue south at daybreak, and seek the lands that our prophet has promised."

Skyfire and Sapling shared a glance of alarm. The threat presented by the humans now went from dangerous to sure disaster; for if they moved their camp as planned, no saving grace could prevent an encounter with Two-Spear and his war-minded comrades. Even sending was inadequate to describe the grief which would inevitably result if human and Wolfrider met openly in conflict.

"We have to find a way to stop them," Sapling whispered.

Skyfire said nothing, but grimly started for the swamp. Thwart the humans' migration they must, but no strategy could be plotted until elves had thoroughly scouted the enemy encampment.

The task took longer than expected, for the tents of the humans numbered beyond counting. "Thick as toads in a bog," griped Sapling. Tired, chilled, and scraped raw from crawling through briars and brush, she shook snow from her collar, packed there in a miserable wad since her dive into a drift to avoid a sentry. Her normally sunny nature had soured to despair. What could a skilled Huntress and a barely grown cub do against a band of humans big enough to overwhelm the forest? Skyfire could not offer a single idea; even Woodbiter walked with his tail down. In the valley below, between alleys of dirtied, trampled snow, the fires of the humans glittered like a multitude of fireflies during the green season.

Skyfire leaned on her bow, her frown plain in the moonlight. "I'm going down there," she said finally. "You must wait here until I get back."

Sapling offered no argument. What had begun as a merry prank, an adventure to make her young heart thrill with excitement, had now turned to nightmare. There seemed no end to danger and hardship imposed by the terrible cold, that untold numbers of humans should travel in search of new hunting grounds. Sapling huddled into her furs, uneasy and afraid, as the Huntress she admired above all else checked her weapons one last time, then vanished swiftly down the slope.

*   *   *

Accustomed to the clean scents of the forest, Skyfire found the human camp rank with the smells of burnt embers, rancid fat, and sweat mixed with poorly cured furs. She wrinkled her nose in distaste as she passed the first of the tents, but forced herself to continue. Moonlight transformed the terrain to a tapestry in black and silver, the tents like ink and shadow against snow. Embers glowed orange from the dark, where the occasional fire still smoldered. Skyfire crept forward, past the tenantless frames of snow-feet which lay stacked in pairs by the tent flaps. She ducked through racks of sticks bound with thongs that supported the long, flint-tipped spears of the humans. The design of the weapons proved that this tribe did more than hunt; they were warriors prepared for battle as well. Briefly, Skyfire entertained the idea of stealing the spears; even cutting the lashings and stealing away all the points. But the racks were too numerous to tackle by herself, and too likely, the humans stored other weapons inside their tents. Lightly as a Wolfrider could move, she could not raid on that scale without one enemy waking in alarm.

Dispirited, Skyfire ducked into the shadow of a tent. Never in her life had the tribe confronted such a threat; and her excursion into the camp yielded no inspiration. With little alternative left but to go back and attempt against hope to reason with Two-Spear, the Huntress faced the forest once more. Bitterly disappointed, she started off and failed to notice that her storm cloak had snagged upon a pile of kindling. A stick pulled loose, and the whole stack collapsed with a clatter.

In the tent, an infant human began to cry.

Skyfire froze. Barely daring to breathe, she hunkered down in the shadows. How Two-Spear would laugh if carelessness got her roasted by humans! Wishing the human cub would choke on its tongue, she waited, and heard a stirring of furs behind hide walls barely a scant finger's width from her elbow; at least one parent had wakened to the cries of the child. If the Huntress so much as twitched an eyelash, she could expect a pack of furious enemies on her trail. She forced herself to stillness while a man's irritable voice threaded through the young one's wailing. His curse was followed by a placating murmur from his wife.

Skyfire fingered her bow as something clumsy jostled the tent. Then she heard footsteps, and light bloomed inside. Described grotesquely in shadows upon hide walls, she saw the human mother bend to cradle her wailing cub. The woman crooned and rocked it, to no avail, while Skyfire weighed the risk of bolting for the forest under cover of the noise.

Angry shouts from the neighboring tents spoiled that idea. Galled by the need to stay motionless while the entire human camp came awake, Skyfire shivered with impatience. If she was caught, she hoped Sapling had the sense to stay hidden on the ridge.

The infant continued to wail. Even the mother grew irked by its screams, and her voice rose in reprimand. "Foolish child, be still! Or your noise will waken snowbeasts from the forest, and they will come and make a meal of your bones with long, sharp teeth."

The cub gasped, and sniffled, and quieted. In a frightened lisp it said, "Mama, no!"

"Don't count on that, boy." The light in the tent flickered, died into darkness, as the woman slipped back into her furs. "If I wake tomorrow and find nothing left of you but blood on your blankets, I'll know you didn't heed my warning."

Her threat mollified the cub to silence, and the woman's breathing evened out as she returned to sleep.

Outside, in the shadow, Huntress Skyfire lingered, still as a ravvit in grass. She waited, listening to the sniffles of a terrified human cub; her mind churned with thoughts of the fear inspired by the tracks of the humans' strange snow-feet, and the terror she sensed in the mother's voice.

Skyfire began to formulate an idea. By the time the little human had snuffled himself back to sleep, that idea became a plan to save the holt.

Cautious this time to stay clear of the kindling, the Huntress darted for the forest.

She arrived breathless on the ridge, and found Sapling and Woodbiter curled warmly in a hollow, asleep. "So much for undying admiration," she murmured, and laughed as Sapling awakened, sneezing as she inhaled a nose full of Woodbiter's tail fur.

"Up," said Skyfire briskly. "We have work enough for ten, and not much of the night left to finish it."

Sapling sat up with a grin. "You have a plan!"

The Huntress tilted her head, more rueful than serious. "I have a ruse," she confided. "Now waken your imagination, for before the humans awaken, we have to invent a nightmare."

So began the hardest task Sapling had known in all her young life. All night long they carved wood and trimmed the skins of their storm-furs and sewed them into the shape of a great beast, which they padded with cut branches. Woodbiter raided another trap, gaining a set of stag horns which they set in the jaws for teeth. Skyfire fashioned eight monster-sized imitations of a beast's clawed pads and, in the hour before dawn, announced that her "snowbeast" was ready for action.

"Strap these paws to your feet," she instructed Sapling. Then, saving two of the clawed appendages for her hands, she called Woodbiter to her side and tied the last four on him, while Sapling experimented by making fearsome trails of beast-prints in the surrounding drifts.

"That looks horrifying," Skyfire observed when she finished, and allowed one very disgruntled wolf to clamber upright. "But now I need you to help with the final touches."

The Huntress mounted the back of the wolf and placed the jaws of the snowbeast over her head. Muffled instructions emerged between the teeth, explaining that Sapling should place herself at Woodbiter's tail and lace the furs around them both, to flesh out the "body" of the beast. After an interval of laughter, and much tangling of elbows, the task was complete. A fearsome apparition snorted and pawed at the snow in the hollow.

"Now we make mischief on humans," the voice of Skyfire proposed from the gullet; and the snowbeast shambled off, with a wolfish whine from its second head, to do just that.

Once the two elves and the wolf coordinated with each other, they found they could run fairly fast; but the clumsy contraptions on their feet made silence impossible. Wherever the snowbeast passed, it made a fearful rattle, and the snapping of sticks and branches, added with the creak of its framework, carried clearly in the frosty air.

"If there *was* any game in this forest, it's on the run now," muttered Sapling. A giggle followed, half muffled by furs.

Quiet, now, sent Skyfire. **We've arrived at the first of the humans' traps.** Now began the dangerous portion of their night's work; for dawn was nigh, and the results of the snowbeast's frolic must not be discovered too soon.

Quiet reigned in the forest until shortly past daybreak, when the humans stirred blearily in their tents. The earliest risers crept out to light fires, and soon thereafter an outcry arose. Two supply tents on the camp perimeter were found ripped to shreds, and the culprit, whose tracks were pressed deeply in the snow, seemed to be a monstrous beast. No one had ever seen the like of such paw prints, but old tales told of a snowbeast which haunted the winter forests during seasons of extreme famine.

Fathers took no chances, but ordered their wives and children and grandfathers not to stray from the protection of the central fires. And the hunters sent to check the traps carried war spears, as well as knives and torches. They moved in bands of ten, for safety; but everywhere they encountered evidence of violence. The snowbeast had ravaged the traps, torn them to slivers, then trampled and clawed the surrounding snow to bare earth. Trees bore deep gashes, and near one trap the skull of a stag lay gnawed by powerful teeth, amid snow stained scarlet with gore. The band of hunters who found that trembled in their boots as they resumed their rounds of the trapline. The rattle of wind in the branches made them start, hands clenched and sweating upon the hafts of their weapons.

For all that, none were prepared for the apparition which lurked in the brush. Crouched like some nightmare forest cat, it fed in the shadows of a thicket, crunching the carcass of the stag with jaws that might have snapped a human in half at one bite.

"Gotara!" breathed the man in the lead. His snowshoe snagged on a twig, which cracked loudly, making him jump.

The snowbeast raised its head, spied the intruders, and raised an ear-splitting scream of rage. The humans saw then that the creature had two heads, the larger one eyeless and crammed with bloody fangs, and emitting a frightful, ululating wail. Below this, between clawed forelimbs, a second, wolflike head snarled and slavered and snapped. Six legs thrust powerfully beneath masses of brindled fur, gathered to bound to the attack.

The human in the lead screamed and cast his war spear. It struck the beast's flank and rebounded; and the beast leapt, plowing a shower of eddying snow.

The hunting party screamed and ran in stark terror. Tree branches whipped their faces. They dared not look back; the ravening snarls of the snowbeast sounded almost upon their heels. The breath burned in their chests, yet they did not slow until they reached the border of their camp. The snarls of the snowbeast sounded ominously through the wood as the men excitedly jabbered their tale. Howls echoed across the marshes, hastening the women who ran to wrap children in blankets and bundle up belongings and tents. Fear gripped the hearts of the humans like cold fingers as they banded together and departed, northward, where the lands were known, and safe.

By sunrise, no intruders remained to watch an elf back butt first from the bowels of the dreaded snowbeast. Tired, trembly, but able to contain herself no longer, she collapsed in a snowdrift, laughing.

Peering through the fangs of the snowbeast mask, Huntress Skyfire regarded her young companion with reproof. "Is that how you're going to greet Two-Spear, when he arrives here with his war party?"

Sapling sat up, snow dusting her eyebrows and her merry, upturned nose. "At least I look like an elf. If you keep standing there in that silly-looking mask, Graywolf will likely spear you for dinner."

At which point the jaws of the snowbeast clicked shut, and a tangle of wolf, and elf, and a mess of jury-rigged storm furs swooped and jumped Sapling in the snowdrift.

Longreach! Storyteller!

The summons came from nearby and with the visceral intensity that always marked the chief's bad moods. The old Wolfrider roused from his wolfnap, grabbed his warmest blanket as a cloak, and poked his head into the icy, winter night.

"Bearclaw?" Longreach asked, as if there had been any real doubt in his mind.

"I need your advice."

Longreach nodded and lifted the oiled-skin door of his bower a bare heartbeat before Bearclaw shoved past him. The bower, one of the oldest set into the Father Tree, was cluttered and scarcely large enough for one elf let alone two. That didn't bother Bearclaw; he just pushed his way over to the sleeping furs and thumped down on them. Whatever had inspired this visit did not bode well for Longreach's peace of mind.

The storyteller pinched a wick into his tallow-pot and lit it from the kindle-box. The tiny flame reflected blood-red from the chief's squinted eyes. It boded poorly, indeed. Longreach spread his fur across last autumn's dreamberry crop and settled in for a long night.

"Tell me about it," he urged the seething Bearclaw.

"Fire-stinking Cutter, that's it."

Longreach leaned closer, sincerely puzzled by the chief's

apparent rage; young Cloudchaser had never bothered anyone in his short life. "I'm sure the lad—"

"Wants to go hunting alone, he does. Middle of the worst winter we've had here in Timmorn knows how long, and the little shrike wants to go hunting."

"He means to help, I'm sure. The hunters have been ranging farther and bring back less—"

Bearclaw let out a liquid growl that contained every unhappy feeling a Wolfrider could have. "He means to get his soft-toothed self killed. As if I didn't have enough eating at my sleep with the tribe hungry and scrounging . . . and the man-pack doing the same . . . and now *he* wants to go hunting branch-horns in the frozen marsh."

The old elf scratched his beard and rubbed the sleepy-seeds from his eyes. "It's never easy to watch them grow up, is it?" he asked, cutting quickly to the heart of Bearclaw's concern.

Bearclaw tangled his fingers through his hair and looked away from the flame. "I'd forgotten the marsh. I shouldn't be watching my cub-son go there for his first hunt; I should be sending a hand of hunters and all the wolves—"

"Forgotten—well, my chief, we all forget. Why not blame me that I didn't use the dreamberries to help us remember? Or is the forgetting not what's really bothering you?"

"Puckernuts, Longreach, sour puckernuts—you know me too well for my own good. Cutter's solid—Timmorn knows he's more careful than I was on my first hunt. If he could only wait until spring. What's a few blinks of the moon when the rest of your life is waiting?"

"You have to let them go, my friend. They'll surprise you in ways you can't imagine—as I well remember—but you have to let them go—"

The Deer Hunters

by Allen L. Wold

It was a summer day at Halfhill. Four elves sat in the afternoon sun in the treeless space between the wide, nearly vertical cliff that gave Freefoot's holt its name, and the broad, gurgling, gravel-bottomed stream.

Suretrail, his back to the clay cliff—more than twice as high as an elf—was carefully weaving a plait of fibers and feathers with which to decorate his spear. The two javelins beside him had already been painted with red ochre and blue berry-juice. Rainbow, on Suretrail's left, showed him some tricks with the white, green, and black feathers. Her own spear was stained and carved with elaborate patterns.

On Suretrail's right was Graywing. She took off the raw-hide thongs that bound the flint point to her spear-shaft. It had become dull with use, and needed to be replaced. Fangslayer, across from Suretrail, was carving a new handle for his white quartz ax. From somewhere across the stream behind him came the occasional sounds of the four children laughing.

In the face of the cliff behind Suretrail were the dens of the elves, dug back into the hard clay among the supporting roots of the large, overhanging trees that grew above it and down its gently sloping back side. In the deep shadows at the top of the cliff sat five other elves in a line. Four of them were no longer children, but not yet adults in the eyes of their elders. Shadowflash, the fifth, as old as Suretrail, sat at one end.

Brightmist, beside him, was not thinking about Shadowflash at the moment, though for several seasons now they had been a little more than playmates, a little less than lovemates.

173

Rather, she was trying to figure out how to make Suretrail give in to their wishes.

Deerstorm, on Brightmist's other side, plucked a frond of fern and set it in her brown hair. Beyond her, Greentwig sat with crossed legs, staring down into his hands folded in his lap. At the far end of the line was Crystalmoss. She was quite a bit younger than the other three, but already showed tremendous promise.

Somewhere off to the north a wolf howled. Shadowflash left off his thoughts and turned toward the forest behind him. The cublings across the stream became silent. The four elders on the bank below him put down their work and looked up toward the sound. The howl came again.

"Freefoot's back," Shadowflash said. He started to rise but his companions did not move. After a moment's hesitation, he sat down again.

There were more wolf-howls. Fangslayer and Rainbow answered back. The hunting party had been gone for three days. A few moments later, Freefoot and Starflower, Fairheart and Moonblossom came through the trees from the upstream, western end of the cliff.

They and their wolves looked tired, and well they might be, for on the back of each of the wolves was an antelope, each nearly as big as an elf, caught out on the prairie to the north of the forest. The waiting elders greeted the hunters and helped take the carcasses down from the tired backs of the wolves. There would be feasting tonight.

"The antelope are doing well this year," Fairheart said. "Can you believe it, these are the weaklings."

Suretrail and Graywing began to butcher one of the antelopes while Fangslayer and Rainbow started on another. Then there was a crashing in the brush on the other side of the stream, and four very young elves came racing across the stones set in the water. Dreamsnake, who had been tending them, came a moment later.

The cublings—Dayshine, Warble, Starbright, and Feather—
hurried up to where the elders were carefully skinning the
antelopes, and begged for treats. Suretrail and Fangslayer
handed out bits of rich liver. It was all they could do to keep
the cublings from offering more "assistance" than was good
for them, or for the antelopes.

Freefoot spread out one of the skins, on which Fangslayer
and Rainbow placed the meat as they cut it from the bones.
Fairheart hacked off the horns and hooves and put them
aside. Graywing carefully split the leg bones, not only to
remove the marrow but also to save the bones themselves for
javelin points, awls, fine scrapers, and other tools.

Catcher was the first of the other elves to arrive. She
greeted the hunters cheerfully and displayed a brace of ravvits,
which she had taken from the traps that only she knew how
to make.

A moment later Glade and Fernhare came from downstream. Glade glanced up to the top of the cliff, where his
son Greentwig and his friends were still sitting with Shadowflash. They should have come down to help with the butchery. Instead they just sat, rather sullen and grumpy about
something. Not Shadowflash; he was his usual cheerful self.

Starflower and Moonblossom carefully separated the edible
organs from the intestines. These Freefoot and Catcher took
down to the stream to wash. Later they would be stretched
and dried for cord, bowstrings, and thread.

Two-Wolves and Grazer joined the group. Two-Wolves
took the job of prying the teeth from the antelopes' skulls.
Grazer, who was a full head taller than any other elf, helped
keep the children busy while the butchery was finished. Bluesky came last.

At last Shadowflash and the four young elves came down
from the top of the cliff. Antelope was not that common a
meal, and just enough different from deer to make it special.

Graywing, Bluesky, and Catcher passed around chunks of meat, choice pieces of liver, kidney, lungs, and brain.

Four antelopes proved to be just barely enough. It was fortunate that so many of the other members of the tribe had gone off on hunting expeditions of their own. All those present were able to eat their fill, and by the time Fairheart found it necessary to bring out fire for lights, there was nothing left of the antelope but belches, smiles, and some greasy faces.

By then the children were getting sleepy. Fairheart and Moonblossom collected their daughter Starbright and went off to their den at the downstream end of the cliff. Warble's father was one of those out hunting, so Dreamsnake took her to her place. Dayshine's parents, too, were away, so she went to sleep with her grandmother Bluesky. That left only Feather.

Freefoot reached down to pick up his cubling son and hold him for a moment, then handed him to Starflower.

"Aren't you coming?" his mate asked.

"In a bit." He pointed to where Brightmist, Crystalmoss, Deerstorm, and Greentwig were sitting by the stream, dangling their feet into the water. "There's something wrong and I want to find out what it is."

"They've been awfully quiet this evening," Starflower said.

"And they've been avoiding Suretrail," he told her. He nuzzled his son again, and then Starflower took Feather away.

Freefoot waited until all the others had gone off for the night before he went over to join the four young elves. "Why don't we take a little walk," he suggested.

They seemed pleased to see him, almost as if they had been hoping he would come to their rescue. They got to their feet and walked with him downstream, away from the cliff.

It was almost full dark, and the sounds of night had begun.

Beside them the stream gurgled pleasantly. Somewhere an owl hooted, in preparation for its night's hunt. Chirpers and other insects were calling stridently.

They walked without talking until they could no longer see the lights left out at the holt, then found a nice place where a rock shelved over the edge of the stream, mossy and soft and big enough for them all to sit on. They rested for a while, silent in the deepening night.

At last Brightmist spoke up. "We want to go on a hunt," she said.

"By ourselves," Deerstorm added.

"Well," Freefoot said, "I don't see why you couldn't do that."

"Suretrail said we couldn't," Greentwig said. "Fangslayer said it would be all right, but when we asked Suretrail, he said no."

"I see. Well, he must have had a reason."

"But now that you're back," Brightmist said, "maybe you can tell him it's all right."

"It's about time," Greentwig said. "We're not children anymore."

"We can take care of ourselves," Deerstorm insisted. "We've been on lots of hunts with the elders."

"But we always have to hunt what they want to hunt," Crystalmoss said, "and let them attack first, and sometimes we don't even get in on the kill until it's all over."

"Except for ravvits," Greentwig said, "and chuckers."

"Will you let us go?" Crystalmoss asked.

"I can't if Suretrail told you you couldn't," Freefoot said, "but maybe we can work something out. We saw tapirs at the clearing when we came by this afternoon."

"They're no fun," Brightmist said. "You can walk right up to them."

"How about the otters at the pool?"

"Yeah," Greentwig said with innocent enthusiasm. "They put up a good fight."

"No," Deerstorm insisted, "two of the bitches died this spring."

"Besides," Crystalmoss said, "Suretrail told us we couldn't."

"Hunt otters?" Freefoot asked.

The four were silent. They hadn't asked to hunt otters.

It was an old story. Children had to be protected while they learned to live and survive in the forest. But sooner or later they wanted a real challenge. The transition between childhood and adulthood was never easy. "All right," Freefoot said. "I'll see what I can do."

Suretrail and Bluesky were sitting in front of Bluesky's den when Freefoot got back to the cliff. In spite of the late hour they were both making arrowheads. Suretrail, who was putting thong-notches on the delicate flint points, seemed to know what Freefoot had come for. He put down the piece he had been working on and looked up at his chief. "Are you going to let them go?" he asked.

Freefoot sat down facing them. He watched as Bluesky took a large piece of nearly black flint and skillfully struck off a flake with a fist-sized rock. She turned the flake over and over, laid it down on her anvil stone and struck it again. It broke cleanly across. The two halves were somewhat overlarge but almost the right shape.

"I told them I'd talk with you about it," Freefoot said. "They want your permission."

"They're good cubs," Suretrail started to say as Fangslayer, then Catcher joined them.

"They're not cubs anymore," Fangslayer said.

"But did they tell you what kind of hunt they have in mind?" Suretrail went on. "They want to go to Tall-Trees for black-neck deer."

"Oh," Freefoot said. "I see."

"I think they ought to do it," Fangslayer said.

"They have to learn sometime," Catcher added.

"Of course they do," Suretrail said. "But you need at least four to hunt black-neck. If they wanted to go out with a couple of more experienced hunters, okay. I'm not worried about Brightmist or Deerstorm. It's Crystalmoss."

"She's the best thrower in the tribe," Fangslayer said.

"With stones and darts and javelins," Suretrail said. "That's not heavy enough for black-neck. And she's not even fully grown yet."

"It's Greentwig who's the real problem," Bluesky said. "He's just not ready."

"He's old enough," Fangslayer said.

"They don't have enough experience," Suretrail insisted. "None of them are ready for this kind of hunt yet. Black-necks are too tough, especially at this time of year."

"And Tall-Trees is too far away," Bluesky said. "It would take them half a day at least just to get there."

"And besides," Suretrail said, "I've already told them they couldn't."

"I still think they ought to have their chance," Fangslayer said.

"They'll never learn," Catcher said, "if they don't find out for themselves."

Glade, Grazer, and Dreamsnake came to join them. They already seemed to know what the discussion was about. Bluesky added wood to her fire so that they could be included in its light. The others made room for them.

"Talon and I," Glade said, "took Greentwig and Crystalmoss out hunting yesterday. Beaver, up by the marsh. Crystalmoss did all right. But Greentwig, I don't know. I don't predict a long life for him."

Bluesky brought out a pouch of dreamberries and passed it around.

"An elf his age should have an adult name," Fernhare said. "Crystalmoss has hers."

"I think Deerstorm has what it takes," Grazer said, "and not just because I'm her father. Brightmist, too."

"They want to do this for themselves," Fangslayer said.

"Of course they do," Glade said. "They want to prove themselves. But Greentwig is . . . just . . . the combination just won't work."

"He is something of a disappointment," Dreamsnake said gently. "But Glade, you and Fernhare can't take care of Greentwig all his life. He must learn—somehow—or die trying."

"I know," Glade said sadly.

"If Longreach were here," Bluesky said, "maybe they'd let him be a part of their hunt. He's not that much older than Greentwig. With five, that would be fine."

"If they could bring in a black-neck," Grazer said, "they would certainly prove themselves."

"They would indeed," Freefoot said. He chewed another dreamberry, then sat back to think.

"We can all remember," he said at last, "when we were first given the chance to hunt, not with our elders but on our own—not just for ravvits but for serious game." The others listened without comment. "We can all remember when we were first given full responsibility for our own hunt, whatever game and whatever place we chose. For some of us that's been a long time."

Suretrail looked away. His decision was being challenged. Fangslayer just stared into the fire.

"Suretrail," Freefoot said, "you did the right thing when you told them not to go."

Suretrail muttered an acknowledgment.

"But it's my responsibility now," Freefoot went on, "not yours. And Fangslayer," he turned to his older son, "you are right too. Those four are nearly of an age, and they must become adults. We cannot deny them their chance, as we all have had, even though they die. Even though.''

For a moment, all were silent. ''And it's not fair to Brightmist or Deerstorm,'' Freefoot went on, ''who will be full adults soon enough. Now is the time. Let us hope they all come back alive.''

The next morning Shadowflash went with Brightmist and the other young hunters when they left Halfhill. The weather was cool, and there was a slight mist in the forest. Shadowflash liked it when the forest was that way. Of course he liked the forest any way when he was with Brightmist. He wanted to go with her today, but he knew he would not be welcome this time. He was only going to see them off.

They went upstream a way and then the four young hunters paused to call their wolves. Answering howls came back from different parts of the forest.

The four youths were excited about the hunt, and now that they had finally gotten permission, a bit apprehensive as well. That was good.

After a moment Fog, Brightmist's gray bitch, came walking toward them. She was a big old wolf and seemed to know that something special was about to happen. Then Scarface and Mask appeared, bounding lightly through the brush. Scarface was Deerstorm's wolf, who bore the marks of a less than successful encounter with a forest pig. Mask was Greentwig's companion, black across the eyes and tawny brown elsewhere. Behind them came Dancer, long-legged and swift, bounding up to Crystalmoss's side. The elves greeted their animals, in the way of elves and wolves.

Then Brightmist turned to Shadowflash and put her hands on his chest. **We'll be all right,** she sent to him.

I know. Keep an eye on Greentwig. He did not look at the youth, tall for his age, handsome, sturdy, and somehow younger than Crystalmoss.

This could make a difference for him, Brightmist
sent.

It will, if he survives.

"Let's go," Deerstorm said. "You two can cuddle when
we get back."

The wolves were impatient too. They could sense their
companions' excitement and wanted to get on with it.
Shadowflash touched Brightmist's pale ruddy hair, then turned
and went back to Halfhill.

The hunting party went upstream to the west. The mist
dissipated before they got to the big south loop, which they
cut across instead of following, and by the time they got to
the marsh the day was warming. They had been too excited
to have breakfast so they caught a few of the marshrats that
lived there. The animals were so plentiful and slow that it
was hardly hunting.

The stream went on beyond the marsh, but they crossed the
water there and headed southwest. The ground rose. Bald
Hill was directly to the south, though its rocky top was not
visible from this far away. They passed its sloping shoulder,
moving quickly, ignoring the plentiful small game. It was an
easy walk, though the forest was dense with undergrowth.

Still, it was nearly noon by the time they got to the edge of
Tall-Trees. Brightmist had not been there before. She couldn't
help but pause as they left the denser forest and entered the
parklike area.

The trees were huge deciduous junipers, each one twenty
or thirty paces or more from its nearest neighbors. The
ground was covered with a ruddy-gray carpet of fallen foliage, scalelike and ankle-deep. The branches overhead completely covered the sky, so high that they got dizzy looking
up at them. The tree trunks were so big around that the four
of them together holding hands could not encircle one. The

bark was shaggy and loose, and gave no purchase when they tried to climb.

The forest floor was not completely bare. Here and there were a few small plants and shrubs that preferred deep shade, but they hardly obstructed the view. They could see for hundreds, maybe thousands of paces in every direction.

Some ways off was what, had it been in a clearing, they would have called a copse. It was a dense, rounded mass of brush and vines that grew where the trees were farther apart, and where the sun was able to come down from the canopy of branches overhead. It was maybe thirty paces across, its verge abrupt, and the taller trees within it were about four times as tall as an elf. Still, the lowest branches of Tall-Trees were many times higher than that. There were other similar copses farther off, some smaller, some larger.

They were all in awe of Tall-Trees. Even the wolves seemed to know that this was a special place, the last of an ancient forest left over from some previous age.

"Look," Greentwig said. He pointed. There, so far away they could not tell what kind it was, was a buck deer. It was walking alone, and they watched it as it went from one great tree to another and then disappeared into a copse.

"That's where we'll find the black-necks," Deerstorm said, "in the copses."

"Then let's go hunting," Brightmist suggested.

They went to the nearest place of brush, shrubs, and vines, several hundred paces from the edge of the forest. Except for the one deer, they had seen or heard no other life in the park. But there was plenty in the copse—birds, squirrels, insects, bats hanging asleep from the head-high branches. The copse was small, and there were no deer there, but they did startle a forest antelope, its head barely chest-high to an elf. They did not chase it as it went bounding off in search of a safer refuge.

They left the copse and went toward a larger one more

likely to shelter their chosen prey. It felt strange, walking in an openness that was still roofed by branches. They could see so far in all directions that for the first time they realized they were truly alone, truly on their own here. They felt rather small and young. The great clear spaces between the trees was not like a clearing, or the meadow, or the prairie; it was different.

As they went deeper into Tall-Trees, the copses became larger and farther apart. They quickly learned that while they could see great distances here, so could the other animals. They had to move carefully from one copse to another, to avoid being heard or seen before they got to the shelter of the brush. More than once they heard some unseen animal bounding away from the far side of a copse as they approached uncautiously.

Sometimes they saw white-tail deer, occasionally red deer, in the copses or crossing the park between them. The wolves wanted to hunt, and it was not easy to explain that that was the wrong game. They took an occasional ravvit or pouchrat, to fortify themselves, but avoided the prickle-spines and the badger they surprised out of its burrow. They found no traces of black-neck deer.

Black-neck were uncommon in the elves' hunting range. Most of the year they lived in the upland forests to the south and came here only during the month or so just before the mating season. They were far bigger than the white-tail or even smaller red deer, which lived here year round.

And at this time of year they were dangerous. The bucks, which would not eat much until the mating was over, were antsy with the upcoming rut, nervous, cautious, and prepared to fight with anything. The does, though not territorial, could also be deadly. Besides anticipating the mating, they would be protecting fawns and yearlings. White-tail or red deer would be far easier game.

But it was black-neck they wanted, and at last, in the

seventh and largest copse they had visited, they came upon traces of their quarry. The smell of the black-neck droppings was distinctive, and now that the wolves had the scent they could follow it.

The deer were not in that copse, but the trail was fresh and led them past several smaller copses toward another large overgrown area, some distance away. They hurried toward it, but cautiously.

The hunt was serious now. They entered the copse as quietly as they could, one step at a time, penetrating the dense growth of vines, bushes, tall grasses, and leafy herbs with as little noise as possible. The scent of the deer was strong, and fresh. They paused frequently to listen. There were squirrel sounds, bird calls, a ravvit dashed off through the brambles. But there was also the sound of a branch moving, and there was no wind, not even a breeze. They moved closer and could hear the sound of bark tearing. That was the deer grazing.

They kept in touch by sending as they closed in. They were excited when they saw the deer—two big bucks, five does, as many yearlings, and maybe four fawns. The wolves were naturally cautious.

The bucks were huge, over twice as high at the shoulder as an elf, their black manes thick, their antlers at full growth, broader than an elf could reach, with spear-sharp points. One of them would provide more meat than the four antelopes Freefoot and his hunting party had brought in. The more they watched, the more fascinated the elves became, and the more frightened.

Which one should we take? Greentwig asked. **There's a yearling.**

If we wanted that spindly thing, Deerstorm sent back, **we might as well have gone after red or white-tail.**

We don't dare try for a buck, Brightmist sent. Unless they dropped it on the first strike, they would be in danger of their lives. Later these two bucks would become deadly enemies; right now they would help defend each other and the rest of the herd.

How about that doe, Crystalmoss suggested, **the one on the far side.** It was the largest of the does, but also somewhat slower.

She won't have many more breeding seasons left, Deerstorm agreed. **The younger does could easily replace her.**

They circled into position, then Greentwig, who was farthest around, sent, **Wait!**

What is it? Brightmist asked, then she heard it too.

There was another animal nearby, in a thicker part of the copse, not that far from the doe. The wolves one by one caught the scent, and they, too, were distracted. The animal sounded large, and its scent was unfamiliar. Carefully, they moved to where they could see the creature.

At first they thought it was just a forest pig, but it was nearly half the height of the buck deer—taller at the shoulder than Crystalmoss—and fully as heavy. No forest pigs got that large. Its body was angular, its shoulders high and sharp, its face was knobbly and very long, its head huge, with a crest of dark reddish hair. And it had two tusks growing up from each side of its lower jaw instead of just one, each tusk longer than an elf's hand.

It rooted around the bases of certain bushes, digging up tubers and occasionally pulling plump fruits off the branches. And even as they watched they all got the same idea. What if they brought back this animal instead? The black-necks would be around for several eights-of-days yet, but this might be their only chance at a strange pig like this.

Pigs were, pound for pound, more dangerous than anything except badgers and wolverines. Even wolves and longteeth were cautious about taking one. They would have to be especially careful, not only because it was a pig, and so large, but also because it was unfamiliar and they didn't know its ways.

Quickly they planned their attack, then struck. Deerstorm's arrow bounced off the pig's boney face, Greentwig's lodged high in the shoulder, Brightmist's struck a rib, and Crystalmoss's javelin struck a flank.

The pig jerked up and squealed with surprise and pain as they readied for a second shot. The wolves closed in to keep the pig confused. The deer moved quickly away.

The three archers shot, but the pig's skin was tough. It squealed again and spun around. The wolves danced out of reach of its tusks. Crystalmoss threw her second javelin and hit the pig at the base of its neck, but the light weapon could not penetrate the bone and muscle. The pig crashed off, knocking Dancer aside.

They dashed through the brush in pursuit. The wolves raced ahead to try to turn it. Brightmist got her spear ready for a charge, but the pig zigged and zagged out of her way. Deerstorm and Greentwig couldn't get a clear shot with their bows through the dense undergrowth.

Crystalmoss threw a dart, which did little more than scratch along the pig's back. Then the pig turned abruptly south and burst out of the copse. The elves and wolves raced in pursuit. Crystalmoss recovered one of her javelins as it fell from the pig's neck.

The pig was running away fast. It seemed so very strong and tough. But there was blood on the ground, and as the pig ran it shook itself as if to dislodge the arrows still sticking into it.

They had committed themselves now. The pig was wounded, and they could not just let it go and eventually bleed to death. They had to kill it if they could.

Elves and wolves ran, just keeping up with the pig. They hoped it would wear itself out or come to a place where they could attack it more effectively. It led them southwest, in almost a straight line, and stayed away from the copses.

Once in a while one of the wolves closed in and snapped at it. Once in a while one of the archers drew up and tried a running shot. The pig almost ignored them.

One time Deerstorm and Crystalmoss raced up, one on either side, and both threw javelins. They hit the pig under its shoulders, but it just kept on running. Greentwig came up once and tried to hamstring the pig with his ax, but his blow went wrong and only cut the skin.

At least the pig was bleeding a lot and would eventually lose its strength. But when they finally killed it, how would they ever get such a heavy animal back to the holt?

They came to a part of Tall-Trees where there were many copses closer together, some of them only a dozen paces apart, and the pig had to swerve and turn frequently to stay on the clear ground. At one point the pig suddenly found itself confronted by a newly fallen tree, too big to jump over and too low to run under, and it was almost trapped. For a moment the pig was at bay, the wolves closed in and snapped at it. The pig swung its huge heavy head to one side, Mask tried to bite at its throat, the pig swung back and caught the wolf and tossed him into the brush.

Mask yelped, the other wolves hesitated, the pig charged through the elves and around the stump end of the fallen tree, and all but Greentwig turned in pursuit. He went to help Mask get to his feet. The wolf's side was badly cut, his ribs bruised, but he wanted to go on, so they did.

After that the wolves didn't try to get too close. Instead they ranged ahead, as if looking for another place to corner the pig. The pig, though bleeding even more, was running harder now, and the elves and wolves had to work just to keep up.

They came to the far side of Tall-Trees by the middle of the afternoon. On their left was the verge of the river, which formed the southern border of the park. The pig headed toward it, then veered more to the west again, toward the denser forest. While they could they got off a few more arrows into the pig's flanks. The elves hoped that the thicker brush of the forest would slow it down.

But the pig charged into the brush unhindered, and the elves and wolves, lighter in weight, had to work to get through the tangles of vines and creepers. The pig ran along the bank of the river, where the brush was thicker, and began to pull ahead of them.

As the chase continued through the thickest growth they lost sight of the pig now and then. It continued to gain until they could no longer hear the noise of its passage, and had to follow the trail the wounded animal had left. It was not difficult. The brush was broken, there were hoofprints in the ground, bloodspots and smears on the foliage. The scent of the pig was strong: fear and blood and sweat.

It seemed as though the pig was never going to tire, though the elves had. Even the wolves, especially Mask, were beginning to show strain. Most game, when chased through the forest, were as encumbered by the brush as the hunters.

The chase went on, into a broad valley. There was a subtle change of vegetation here, the undergrowth was more luxuriant, the trees were broadleaf red-twigs more often than not. The pig's trail still led along the bank of the river, too wide even here to cross.

They wanted to rest, but they dared not. Only the splattering of blood here and there assured them that the pig, though now far ahead, was worse off than they. At last the ground began to rise, the river rushed more rapidly as it came down into the valley from the uplands.

Even the gentle slope slowed them now. Their only consolation was that it had to be slowing the pig, too. The land continued to rise, the river beside them ran more swiftly. The water was broken by occasional rocks, and the forest on either side became somewhat clearer. Then they could hear noisy splashing up ahead. They knew they must be getting to the top of the valley, and, indeed, they soon came to a long expanse of rapids, between rocky banks. And there was the pig, still a good way ahead, running and stumbling along the bank, as if looking for a place to cross.

The river splashed through a thousand paces of jumbled rocks, a treacherous ford across the river. The pig was choosing its path carefully, but jumping strongly from one rock to another. The hunters fanned out and started to cross, in hopes of meeting the pig on the other bank, where they could attack it again.

But Mask was tired and whimpering. Greentwig paused to talk with his wolf and told him to rest there a moment and then go back to the holt. Mask was sorry to miss out on the kill, but knew his own strength. The wolf sat, and Greentwig hurried after the others, who were now partway across the river.

What a hunt! Greentwig nearly fell into the water as he hurried to rejoin the others. The pig had almost reached the other side, angling upstream, and the hunters were gaining on it.

They all reached the other side at the same time, though spread out up and down the rapids. The pig, instead of following the river upstream, where Brightmist and Crystalmoss were waiting, charged up the bank, leaving the river altogether. The elves pulled together to follow it into the forest.

This was more like the classical hunt. The forest was more open this high up, but the uphill work was strenuous. The pig chose a straight path, avoided gullies and brush, and the elves and wolves ran along beside and behind.

At last the land began to level. They had come to the uplands, and the pig was now running southeast. It was tiring, and they were able to keep up with it easily. The forest was different here, an older forest.

The pig occasionally stumbled as it ran. It was going to have to turn at bay sooner or later. And then it came to a break in the forest, a broad, semiopen glade. There were occasional trees spotted through the mostly waist-high brush and grasses. The ground was both soft and rocky, mud and moss between broken stones.

The pig was tiring rapidly now in the late afternoon. It struggled across the glade, thousands of paces across. The pig looked as though it was trying to get to the other side, so the elves and wolves put on speed and circled around. If they were going to finish it, it had to be here.

Luck was with them. Before the pig could get more than three-quarters of the way across the glade they were able to turn it into a shallow, rocky draw. Steep rocks formed the sides, and three huge oak trees grew at the far end, their roots a tangle that the pig couldn't pass. It turned and charged back, saw the elves and wolves, backed a step, then stood at bay.

The pig snorted angrily, kicked rocks and mud, smashed its face from side to side against roots and brush. The wolves ranged along the sides of the draw and snapped at the pig when it tried to climb out. Once the pig nearly made it but Scarface bit its nose, just out of reach of the tusks, and the pig squealed and dropped back.

They used their few remaining arrows carefully, aiming for the throat between the neck muscles and the shoulder bone. The pig thrashed around heavily with each hit. Crystalmoss and Deerstorm used the last of their javelins and hit the pig in the belly in front of the flanks. The pig snorted in rage.

It was bleeding copiously now, its movements were erratic, and it occasionally stumbled. Now was the time to go in for the kill. But Deerstorm had no more weapons, and Crystalmoss had only a few darts and a small ax. It would be up to Brightmist with her spear, and Greentwig with his heavy ax, to finish the matter.

Deerstorm went behind the pig and halfway down the rocky side to hit it with a rock. The pig turned toward her with a snort. Now Brightmist and Greentwig could enter the draw. Crystalmoss then distracted the pig from the other side. Greentwig and Brightmist got into position.

Brightmist planted the butt of her spear against the ground while Greentwig threw rocks until the pig charged. But Brightmist slipped on the muddy rocks and the pig, instead of impaling itself in its mouth or under its chin, ran onto the spear at its shoulder, all the way through the muscle to the bone.

Brightmist lurched to the side, out of the stopped pig's way. Greentwig stepped up and swung his ax at the back of the pig's skull, but the animal half turned and his blow, though strong and deep, only struck it in the shoulder.

The pig screamed. The spear was lodged in its shoulder, and it was crippled, but now Brightmist had no weapon. She backed off. The pig screamed again. Greentwig trembled. Then, when the pig turned toward him, he struck again. He hit it across the forehead, barely avoiding its tusks. There was lots of blood, but it was not a killing blow. The pig screamed again.

From all sides they heard the sudden response: heavy, deep grunts and bellows, squeals and snorts and moaning calls. The pig staggered back, panting and crying.

The elves stood paralyzed. There was crashing in the brush not far away, heavy hooves clattered on rocks, sucked at the mud, getting closer. Brightmist, Crystalmoss, and Greentwig clambered half up out of the draw. Deerstorm was already out, crouching on the edge.

From all sides more pigs were coming, from the forest, from other parts of the glade where they must have been concealed by brush or wallows. They came at a full run, responding the way all pigs do to the distress of one of their fellows, to the rescue.

The four young elves had just a moment to realize that the pig they had been hunting, as big as it was, was only a juvenile. These four boars, and eight or ten sows, were fully grown. Each was as tall as a black-neck deer, each weighed maybe three or four times as much. Their faces, long and bristly, were covered with callused knobs, their tusks were longer than an elf's arm.

The wounded pig screamed. The rest of the herd, with a dozen or so juveniles as big as the wounded pig in the draw, and even a number of piglets, came on from all sides, at full charge. The forest was a long way off. There was no place to run.

It was dusk at Halfhill. A few lamps were lit. Over by her den Bluesky was making arrowheads. Beside her for company, Catcher was making a trap from a springy stick, a piece of bone, and some fine cord woven from hair. Nearby, Dreamsnake was telling the cublings the story of how Freefoot had gotten his name.

Closer to the stream, Fairheart, his shirt off, was making a bow, shaping the wood with sharp flint. Beside him, Rainbow was repairing his shirt and trimming it with fancy feathers. Suretrail, Glade, and Two-Wolves looked on.

Downstream from them, Freefoot, Grazer, and Fernhare were working on the antelope skins under Starflower's direction. Graywing, Shadowflash, Moonblossom, and Fangslayer sat between them and the others, talking, digesting, calming down for the night.

"The kids ought to be back by now," Suretrail said.

"If they got a deer," Catcher said, "they'll have a hard time bringing it back."

"One of them could have come on ahead and asked for help," Rainbow muttered.

"No," Fangslayer said, "they've got to do that themselves too."

"After all," Moonblossom added, "Tall-Trees is a long way off; they might well have to stay the night."

"I don't think we should have let them go," Suretrail insisted.

Freefoot ignored the implied challenge. "It has to happen some time," he said softly. "They're of that age. If we hadn't given them our blessing, they'd have gone off anyway."

Suretrail knew that was true, but it didn't make him any happier. He tried to put his thoughts and worries out of his mind by watching Rainbow stitching on Fairheart's shirt.

One by one, as night fell, the elves finished their tasks and retired to their dens. At last only Suretrail, Rainbow, and Bluesky were left. The three just could not go to sleep. To keep busy they set about making arrows. Shafts, fletches, heads. They could always use more arrows.

Overhead the two moons were shining. They had been approaching each other during the last few nights. Would they kiss when they passed?

Just before dawn Freefoot, who was more concerned than he cared to admit, came out of his den with Starflower and little Feather. He saw Rainbow and Bluesky asleep, saw Suretrail coming back from the stream, and waited for him as Starflower, with a reassuring word, took Feather off for his morning bath.

"How much longer should we wait?" Suretrail asked him softly. Rainbow muttered in her sleep.

"Give them a chance," Freefoot said. "If they got a big buck, they'll have a hard job bringing it back."

Bluesky woke and looked up at them. "We made a lot of arrows last night," she said.

Now Rainbow roused too. "Are they back yet?" she asked.

"Not yet," Bluesky said, and went with her to wash up.

"And besides," Freefoot went on, "if it was a long hunt,

they'll have to sleep. Other hunts have turned out that way before.''

''I know that,'' Suretrail said, ''but not hunts half of whose members were too young or incompetent.'' And then he saw Glade and Fernhare, just coming out of their den. ''I'm sorry,'' he said, ''but it's true.''

''I know,'' Fernhare sighed.

Glade didn't say anything. On the one hand he agreed with Suretrail. On the other, he was the keeper of the Way, and knew better than anybody that Freefoot was right. He just went upstream, and after a moment Fernhare followed.

The conversation was rousing the other elves now, and one by one they came out of their dens. Freefoot went off to wash. Suretrail started to pick up all the arrows he and Bluesky had made. He was exhausted.

Shadowflash and Catcher came up from the stream. ''Were you up all night?'' Catcher asked.

''Made a lot of arrows,'' Suretrail said, showing them to her.

''They'll be all right,'' Shadowflash said as Bluesky and Rainbow came back with Fangslayer. ''Deerstorm has been there before, she's got good sense.''

''So has Brightmist,'' Fangslayer said. ''We had to give them the chance. We wouldn't worry about any other party of four.''

''That's just the problem,'' Rainbow said.

''I guess we can wait a while longer,'' Bluesky said.

The daily hunt was a minor affair, as the elves went after smaller game close to the holt. By noon, most had returned for a light meal. But Suretrail, Two-Wolves, and Rainbow couldn't stand it anymore. They went to sit with Freefoot, Starflower, Fangslayer, and Feather.

''I think we should go looking for them,'' Suretrail said.

''I have to agree,'' Starflower said.

"If they were all right," Two-Wolves said, "they'd not have kept Crystalmoss out this long."

"Then I guess somebody had better go after them," Freefoot said to Suretrail.

"I'm going too," Two-Wolves said.

"How about Shadowflash?" Starflower suggested.

"That's good," Freefoot said. "Grazer and Fernhare too. But it's getting on toward afternoon, you won't make it to Tall-Trees before dark."

"I know," Suretrail said, "but I think we should start out anyway. Tomorrow might be too late."

Mounted on their wolves, the five elders traveled as quickly as they could, following much the same route the four younger elves had taken two days before. It was indeed dusk by the time they came to Tall-Trees.

The area was too large to search, so they tracked first one way along the verge, then the other. At last Snaggletooth, Shadowflash's wolf, caught a trace where Brightmist had put her hand on a branch to move it aside.

They followed the faint trail from copse to copse, circling rather than going through. Always they found the trail on the other side. As they went they occasionally saw the distant shadowy forms of deer—white-tail, red, and even black-neck. But there was no smell of deer blood anywhere.

"I think it's time to shed some," Two-Wolves said. "It's late, I'm hungry, and Loper and Springer don't want to track elves with so much game nearby."

The others agreed, so when they saw a white-tail yearling they brought it down quickly and ate. By the time they finished it was full night. The dark did not slow them as they went on, but fatigue and full bellies did.

Some time later, in a large copse, they smelled pig blood. They entered the brush, smelled the spoor of black-neck, and saw the place where the pig had been struck.

"It wasn't a forest pig," Shadowflash said.

They followed the blood smell out of the copse and through the dark parkland. At one point the trail crossed bare ground, and they knelt to check for prints. It was a big pig, and had been running hard.

"If they just wanted supper," Grazer said, "why did they chose a pig that size?"

"Why a pig at all?" Suretrail wondered. "There were black-neck right there."

"More of a challenge?" Fernhare suggested.

"It looks like it must have led them quite a chase," Two-Wolves said.

"Foolish thing to do," Suretrail said.

"At least," Shadowflash said, "they decided to finish the job after wounding it."

Later they came to a place where they smelled wolf-blood and stopped, alarmed. Their wolves howled in distress. The elves howled too, and sent. There was no reply to their sending, but there was an answering howl.

They hurried toward the sound and found Mask. Greentwig's wolf was tired and sore and stiff, and the skin along one side was badly cut and it seemed that some ribs were cracked.

"He must have tangled with the wounded pig," Grazer said. The wolf was in no danger but needed rest and attention.

"He can't be the only survivor," Suretrail said.

Two-Wolves put his hands on Mask's head and stared into the wolf's eyes. But Mask was not his wolf, and the animal was tired, hungry, and thirsty, and not interested in wolf-talking. About the only thing Two-Wolves could learn was that Greentwig had sent Mask back from some place. After a bit Two-Wolves instructed Springer, the smaller of his two animals, to accompany Mask back to the holt where he could be tended.

The trail continued in almost a straight line through the park to the river, where they could see the trampled brush where the pig had gone. They followed, into the denser forest.

It was dawn by the time they came to the rapids high in the back of the valley. The sun, though still hidden by the forest across the river, was just coming up. The trail led to the rocks of the rapids, and was lost. Two-Wolves looked around. "Here's where Mask turned back," he said.

They were very tired now and had to rest a bit while they decided what to do next. They slaked their thirst, and Shadowflash and Grazer went to catch a few fish for breakfast. They came back with several large salmon.

When they had eaten and caught their breath they searched along the river, then forded the rapids where it was easiest and cast up and down the other side. At last they found wolf-prints in the mud, and followed the trail away from the river, upslope into the forest, and eventually to the uplands.

They pushed on as hard as they could until, by midmorning, they came to the semiopen glade. Here they could finally see the pig tracks clearly, of the wounded animal and of many others. The smell of pig was strong.

"Look," Fernhare said, pointing to the tracks. "The pig our deer hunters were after was just a juvenile."

"Are you sure?" Two-Wolves asked.

"See for yourself," she said. She pointed out other, much larger hoofprints. "Mountain-swine. I've seen their tracks before, way to the south."

They scouted cautiously. There could be other swine nearby. The pig smell was everywhere, bushes had been rooted up and small saplings knocked down.

"At least twenty animals," Suretrail said, "maybe more."

"Look at the size of those tracks," Grazer said. "Bigger than a deer, and heavier than a bear."

They didn't see any swine at the moment, but the ground was uneven, there were hollows, rocks, bushes, and the occasional tree where they could be concealed. The rescue party moved deeper into the glade. Some of the pig marks had been made recently. One pile of droppings was still warm. The wolves were quiet, slinking along. They didn't like this place at all.

Then they heard sounds to one side, distant snorting and grunting. They approached cautiously, well spread out and ready to run. And there they were, dozens of swine, of all sizes, the biggest truly huge, loosely gathered and moving around a place where three tall oaks stood, still some way off.

Two-Wolves looked up at the trees. Maybe . . . **Crystal-moss!** he sent.

Father! came the answer they all could hear.

Then the four young hunters yelled, and the swine thrashed around in the rocky-bottomed draw.

"They're up in the trees," Shadowflash said with obvious relief.

Are you all right? Suretrail sent.

The four young elves all answered at once, a jumble of thoughts and images. They were fine, but they were tired, cramped, and hungry. The pigs had stayed under their trees since the middle of the afternoon the day before yesterday, even during the night. Their prey had died last night, and they had hoped that, with its death, the other swine would leave, but they hadn't. The nearest other trees were too far away to jump to, and the forest was too far away to run to even if they could have gotten past the herd below them.

Even worse, Deerstorm's wolf had been killed shortly after they had gotten into the trees. Fog and Dancer had escaped, but Scarface had gotten cornered, tossed, gored, trampled, and later half eaten. Deerstorm was more distraught about that than her own predicament.

Hang on, Grazer sent. **We'll get you down.**

The elders tried to get closer, but the juvenile pigs and most of the piglets were out at the edge of the herd and could easily alert the adults. As they tried to decide what to do next, Dancer and Fog came slinking up from the forest. The other wolves whimpered softly, the elders hushed them up.

The forest, on the side of the draw from which the wolves had come, was not too far away, and the elders circled around to it.

"Let's see if we can make them chase us," Grazer suggested to Shadowflash. Shadowflash just grinned.

They left the others and walked toward the herd of swine. Then they started yelling and shouting and waving their spears. The piglets set up a commotion, some of the juveniles started to chase them, and they ran back to the forest. But most of the swine stayed at the draw, and those in chase gave up quickly.

The rest of the swine were now more upset than ever. Suretrail and Two-Wolves went around to the side and again taunted them by throwing stones at them. They, too, were chased back, by a sow and three juveniles.

But the other swine just got more upset. The elders could see the branches of the three oak trees shaking as the boars and sows shouldered against the trunks, as if they would knock the trees down.

"They're digging around the roots," Greentwig called to them.

"We've got to do something," Fernhare said.

Suretrail thought about it, then went toward one of the nearest juveniles and threw a javelin, which struck the pig square in the side. The pig screamed, the nearer adults turned and lunged, Suretrail ran.

Several swine gathered around the wounded pig, but Suretrail's shot had been too good. Even as other adults came to the rescue, the pig died. The swine jostled it, rolled it over, but didn't pay any attention to the elves. Instead they snorted and went back to the three trees.

"It was a good idea," Fernhare said.

"But not quite good enough," Shadowflash said. "Make some cord, as much as you can."

He took one of Suretrail's javelins, took off the bone head, whittled the end of the shaft to a point, then refastened the head backward, as a long barb. The others cut strips from their clothes and plaited a long and thin but strong cord which he tied to the butt of the javelin.

"I guess throwing it is my job," Grazer said. He was the strongest of the elves. He coiled the cord loosely over one arm and then went boldly out to pick a target.

The other elves followed at a short distance, to give him help if he needed it. Grazer moved carefully toward the herd of swine and picked out the piglet that was nearest the forest. Holding the end of the cord tightly with one hand, he took careful aim and launched the javelin in a high arc. It struck the piglet through the thick of the thigh, at nearly the full stretch of the cord.

He didn't pause but turned and ran back as hard as he could. The barb on the javelin held and the weight of the now screaming piglet nearly jerked the cord from his hand. The boars and sows bellowed in rage at the piglet's screams as he dragged it along behind him, and before he was halfway back to the trees the whole herd came running after him.

Two-Wolves and Shadowflash were waiting by a tree, and as Grazer came up they gave him a boost into the branches. As soon as he had a good hold he pulled in the cord and dragged the screaming piglet up after him. He was barely in time. A boar crashed hard into the trunk of his none-too-large tree, and it was all he could do to hold the tree and the piglet at the same time.

The swine trampled the undergrowth, snorting and grunting and shouldering the trees. Fernhare, Suretrail, and Shadowflash fanned out through the branches, making as much noise as they could to distract them. Though most of the swine trampled around under Grazer, others dashed back and forth following the three elders who squealed in imitation of the hurt piglet as they moved slowly away. It was enough to keep the swine from knocking down Grazer's none-too-large tree. Meanwhile he was holding the piglet, wishing he could put it out of its misery.

But Two-Wolves moved quietly off through the branches, away from the swine, and went back to the ground. He called all the wolves and hurried with them to where the youths were even now coming down from their refuge.

The four young elves, tired and cramped, mounted the borrowed wolves and raced with him back to the forest. Some of the swine came to investigate and started in pursuit, but the elves went up into the trees as soon as they could and the wolves scattered.

As soon as they were all safe, Grazer slit the piglet's throat. Now the other elders became quiet and slowly, one by one, moved off through the high branches. Grazer kept the piglet as he left the place. No sense letting good meat go to waste.

When they were a safe distance away they came down to the forest floor. The wolves rejoined them as they went back toward the river. When they could no longer hear the swine they paused to rest.

Shadowflash held Brightmist as they sank down to the ground. The other three young elves all sat, very subdued. The elders, too, were quiet. Even the wolves seemed relieved. Suretrail butchered the piglet, and let the kids eat it all.

"I thought you were going after black-neck," he said.

"We could have had one, too," Greentwig answered.

"At least that was something you could have handled," Suretrail told him.

"Would we have done any better," Fernhare asked, "if we had hunted that pig?"

"I guess not," Suretrail said reluctantly.

"Under the circumstances," Fangslayer said, "I think our

deer hunters are probably wise enough now to take care of themselves.''

''Sure,'' Grazer said, ''they didn't bring back a black-neck, but anybody can get in trouble.''

''It's not the kind of trouble we're likely to have in the future,'' Brightmist said from Shadowflash's arms. ''And besides, it was a good hunt before we got trapped.''

''I guess it was at that,'' Suretrail said. ''You did all the right things up until then.''

''And then, too,'' Crystalmoss said. ''We could have tried to run away.''

Then Suretrail reached out and hugged her. ''I'm so glad you're safe,'' he said.

Fernhare looked fondly at Greentwig, who still felt unappreciated. ''Nobody can argue about your hunting alone now,'' she said. ''You four seem to make a good team.''

''And as long as we have to go back through Tall-Trees anyway,'' Greentwig said, ''let's get us a black-neck.''

''That's a good idea,'' Suretrail said.

It was lopsided; one edge was so much higher than the other that the whole thing looked like it would slide right off the boulder Brownberry had set it on. Still, the little pottery bowl, with its wolf-print decorations, had survived an eight-of-day's bath in the brook without collapsing back to the mud from which it had been made.

"I think you're on to something," Longreach assured the scowling craftswoman.

"It doesn't look like the one in my mind."

She snatched it up and made to throw it far across the brook when the storyteller's fingers closed over hers.

"No need to be angry with it. See it for itself. As a bowl— well, perhaps it has a flaw or two; but as a tallow-lamp—see, the high edge will protect the light from the wind. . . ."

"It was supposed to be a *bowl*," Brownberry insisted, though she relaxed her grip and let her friend take the pottery into his own care. "They never come out the way my mind's eye sees them."

Longreach set the bowl, now a lamp, in the grass beside him. "At first they didn't come out at all. You'll get the knack of it yet. What's a few more tries?"

The chestnut-haired Wolfrider sat down with a sigh. "They laugh at me," she said without meeting his eyes. "Briar, Foxfur—even *Skywise*—they don't even try to hide it. Pike even asked if I was growing another finger."

There was no more potent insult in the Wolfrider's tongue than a five-fingered elf, yet the storyteller wasn't entirely surprised. Brownberry had pursued her notion of working with clay for many turns of the seasons now. The need to shape the red muds ate at her in ways she herself did not seem to understand. Perhaps it was some dormant aspect of her elfin heritage—a different shade of the magic that flowed through Rain and Goodtree—perhaps not. Either way, the need to shape something was not a need which erupted frequently in the Wolfriders.

His own thoughts found their ending, but Brownberry was still slump-shouldered. "What did you tell him?"

"I didn't tell him; I hit him one with my spear."

"That certainly got your point across—but there have been other ways, you know—"

Tanner's Dream

by Nancy Springer

"*Toad turds!*" Tanner exclaimed softly to himself. He had lived for over seven hundred years and been the chieftain of his tribe, the Wolfriders, for some four hundred of those, but the seasons had been quiet, spent mostly in wolf-time, the Always Now. Seldom had Tanner produced such an outburst or felt the need to. At this point, however, mere toad crap seemed inadequately disgusting. "Ripe, rotten toad turds!" he expanded in his soft, chirring, birdlike elfin tongue, staring downward through dense leaves. The man, the human, was standing directly under the oak tree, his crude fur skirt upraised, urinating.

Told you, came an amused sending from Tanner's side. On the broad oak branch beside him knelt Brook, his hunt leader. Though the human, and humans in general, took elfin speech for birdsong, Brook had a hunter's instinct for silence and preferred to send. **Every day, just like a dog wolf marking. It's a wonder he doesn't get down and sniff around.**

Timmorn's blood, the flood of it! Tanner exclaimed, sending also, lest in his dismay he should speak too loudly. **And the smell!**

Potent, Brook wryly agreed.

The human finished, shook the final drops off his member, let the stiff, smoke-cured leather of his skirt fall, and lumbered away toward a stand of hemlocks, leaving a yellow puddle slowly soaking into the loam at the roots of the oak. The man disappeared into dense forest. Stretched out full length along his supporting bough, Tanner let his head fall to the rough bark.

"My leathers," he groaned aloud. For under the tree, at the very spot the human had chosen to flood, Tanner had hidden a pit full of the finest hides Brook could bring him, layered with an exacting, laboriously gathered mixture of barks, acorn cups, leaves and berries, all bestowed with utmost care to undergo the silent, unseen process by which crude, flinty-hard, sun-dried hides would become—Tanner hoped—fine, supple leathers for his tribespeople to wear.

Brook reached over and gave his chief a light slap on the shoulder. **Lift-Leg we call him, even though he doesn't,** Brook teased, and then he went off, padding and leaping noiselessly through the treetops, bound for the hollow where he would drowse away the rest of the day while the human hunters blundered about below.

Tanner remained where he was, to brood.

"Humans," he muttered. "A stinking, muck-eating human."

This was rather strong language for him. Tanner was not

much in the habit of brooding or hating, but the matter of the urinating human had upset him deeply—the more so because no one in his tribe but him would care about it as he did.

He was a throwback, though he could not himself have explained it in that way. A throwback, not to the wild half-wolf urgings of Timmorn, but even beyond, to the gentle, beauty-loving nature of the high ones. Their blood stirring in him had taken a bent form, skewed his thoughts away from the thoughts of the other Wolfriders. He made a clumsy hunter, with no passion for the kill. He seldom rode on his wolf-friend, and there was no wanderlust in him. He had taken no lifemate, or lovemate either, in all his many seasons. But he had a dream, an artist's vision, of what leather could be.

Or rather, the dream had hold of him, as relentless as disease or infestation. Fine, supple, many-colored leathers, if he could just find the right mix of tanbarks and oddments . . . And now the human hunter had pissed on his pit. A year's labor, buried there, and another full four turnings of the seasons for it to steep, and Lift-Leg had taken it into his head to use that very place in all the vast Everwood as his customary spot to pee.

"Humans," Tanner moaned aloud again. Timmorn would have driven the man away. Two-Spear would have killed the human before looking at him twice. But Tanner had stayed in hiding.

Through the long summer afternoon he lay on the oak bough, his gray eyes thoughtful, restlessly stroking the hair of his short brown beard, until the fireflies came out at dusk. Then, as lithely as Brook (though the hunter was less than half his age) the Wolfrider chief made his way through the twilight treetops to the hurst, where his people were gathering for the nightly howl.

It was a hilltop, a bluff rather, overlooking the clear river that flowed northward into Muchcold Water. At its crest stood a grove of beeches, their bark nearly as smooth and pale as a Wolfrider's skin, gray of sheen, like Tanner's wolf-friend, Stagrunner. Spreading beech branches kept the forest floor beneath them nearly free of undergrowth. Around and between the gray gleaming trunks cubs were playing tag, they and some of their elders as well. As Tanner swung down to the ground he was met by smiles and a thump—a laughing, heedless Wolfrider, running into him, then darting past without a word, her long hair looking pale as moonlight in the night, tossing behind her. One of the cubs, Tanner recalled. A skinny youngster, half grown. Stormlight.

"Tanner!" It was Joygleam, one of the young hunters, smiling merrily along with Brightlance and Brook and others, her comrades. "I hear that luck is against you yet again!"

Without anger Tanner gave her his quiet half-smile. It was true that he had tried tanning leather again and again, seasons stretching back long before she was born, and there were always setbacks, and the stench sometimes was enough to drive a wild boar out of the woods—though never the lumpish humans—and never had he been wholly satisfied. But it did not matter. There was always the chance to try again. It was the reason why the tribe had stayed so long in one place, his tanning, his pits always being filled or waiting to be opened.

"Are you not glad you need not always wear stinking, rotting hides such as the humans do, Joygleam?" he asked her.

"Puckernuts!" cut in one of the elders before Joygleam could answer. It was old Fangslayer, one of the few Wolfriders who was older than the chieftain. Fangslayer had been grown when Tanner was yet a cub, and Fangslayer did not hesitate to speak his mind. "It's a waste, say I. Waste of time better spent, waste of shaper's labors setting the trees to rights after you're done taking the bark from them, Tanner, and now a waste of good skins, sitting in a hole in the ground for the humans to pass water on!"

Tanner said, "You would truly rather wear smoked hides rubbed with grease and brains?"

"It was good enough for me in your father's time," Fangslayer snapped.

"But that would truly be the waste," Tanner said, "when leather can be so much more. Don't you see, if I learn how I can make it thinner, softer, thin and soft as new leaves, and I can make it as many colors as the pelts of the wolf-pack. Or I can make it thick and hard, for protection in battle, should we ever have to battle the humans, or tough and supple for shelters, or I can make it stretch over a form as the humans stretch it for their drumheads. If I can learn to lace it tightly enough I will make pouches of it that will hold anything, even water. And—"

Caught up in his own fervor, it took Tanner a moment to notice that all the tribe had fallen silent and was gathering closer, listening to him. When he saw it, he stopped, lest they should hear promises where he had only dreams. He was reluctant to share such dreams; they were as nothing, he thought, before he made them true. To his tribe-mates he gave instead his shy, crooked smile. They smiled back, and some gently laughed. Fangslayer snorted and walked away. But the cub Starlight stood scowling earnestly at her chieftain, though he did not notice it. And Brook offered, "My chief, do you wish us to guard the pit from the human?"

The human tribe had come to their patch of the Everwood a mere hundred-some years before, and as yet knew nothing, or almost nothing, of the Wolfriders. Tanner and his people had learned new stealth; they had kept it so. Indeed, the rare human sightings of elves were hotly disputed around the tall ones' cooking fires in the evenings, and most of the humans scoffed more heartily than Fangslayer.

"No," said Tanner quietly to Brook, "thank you, but no. Let it go as it is." And he strode to the brow of the hurst to lead his tribe in the howl, to listen as tales were told of battles and migrations, of the days of Prey-Pacer, Two-Spear, and Huntress Skyfire, days so dangerous, so different from the safe and settled life of Tanner's time.

Night followed night, howl followed howl, and in the Now of wolf-time moons followed moons, scarcely noticed. Orange autumn moons, cold white winter moons, and through them all Lift-Leg remained faithful to his oak tree and relieved himself on Tanner's pit. Watery spring moons, and still Lift-Leg did not falter in his routine. And Brook, Joygleam, and the others gleefully brought their chief the news of it all the while, until, when the thaw finally came, Tanner had no heart to open the pit.

"I swear by Timmorn's bones," he said to Stagrunner one night as they sat atop the silent hurst, "I would like to just let it lie."

The wolf-friend sat stolidly under the starlight. Concerning things of this sort, Stagrunner was the only one Tanner could talk to. Brook was a loyal friend in the large things, but in the small things he could not be trusted not to laugh or bear tales; he too dearly loved a joke. Though to Tanner leather-making was no small thing.

"And if it were not for Fangslayer," said Tanner morosely, "I think I would do just that. Let it all lie and rot."

Stagrunner panted, his white teeth gleaming in a grin of wordless agreement.

"But he'd never let me hear the end of it." Tanner shrugged, suddenly putting on again the air of half-smiling bemusement that he wore like a cloak. "So open it I must. I believe I was born to be the laughingstock. Walk with me, my good friend?"

Side by side, they ambled off into the night together.

On another night not long after, a night of the full moons, Tanner led a troop of strong young elves down to the oak to help him open the pit. And though they were outwardly silent, many were the jests that were privately "sent," especially as they drew near enough to whiff the place's aroma.

But on the way back to the hurst there were no jokes at all.

"Well?" Fangslayer barked, meeting the group of elves with their bundles of heavy, still-wet leathers. And Tanner, in the lead, looked straight at him with a smile that was neither shy nor wry.

"They are nearly perfect," he declared.

The leathers were lovely, fine and supple, softer than they had ever been before.

A tanning agent without peer had been discovered.

For days Tanner luxuriated in heady victory. Eagerly he assembled the next year's batch of hides, already harvested by Brook and sun-dried atop the evergreens, where the humans would not see. Eagerly he fetched tanbark and dried leaves, expertly placing them with the hides as he set them in the ground.

The seasons went round the cycle of four, one more moment-year in the nearly-endless span of elfin life, and the next springtime, seemingly no more than a moment later, found Tanner once again in despair.

Lift-Leg, the human, had unaccountably changed his habits. Perhaps the smell had become too much for him. He had taken his bodily wastes elsewhere. Not even once had he vouchsafed to piss on the awaiting pit. Tanner had undertaken to service the site himself, but without much hope; instinct told him that elf urine was quite different from human. In desperation he had attempted to obtain wolf urine, without much success. And to add to his gloom, the struggle had caused the relationship between him and Stagrunner to become chill and strained. And the leathers, when they came out of the ground, were solidly second-rate.

All his tribesmates, even Fangslayer, tried to tell him otherwise. "They're fine," Fangslayer snapped. "Very serviceable."

The Wolfriders nodded, watching their chief with concern.

He had grown far too intent on his leathermaking to be laughed at.

"There's nothing wrong with this year's batch, Tanner," Brook told him. "Really."

Oddly, instead of comforting him, all this made him secretly furious, more furious than he had ever been when they had laughed. And oddly, it was one of the cubs, Stormlight, who was of better help to him.

She came to him where he was sitting alone for want of Stagrunner, sitting beneath the stars at the brow of the hurst. With no greeting or apology she sat beside him. "I know what you want," she said.

Still furious, all the more so since he could not shout at his well-meaning people, Tanner did not look at her or answer her. But Stormlight spoke steadily on.

"You want leathers as soft as flower petals, and colored all the hues of sky after sun goes down."

His head snapped around so that he looked at her.

"You want deerskins the color of honey, but softer than a newborn baby's hair. You want split pigskins as red as a robin's breast feathers, and purple as oak leaves in autumn, and gray as twilight, and deepwater blue. You want doeskins of milk white, able to be folded flat as a leaf and opened without a crease. You want the smaller skins, treewee, ringtail, even swamp rat, no less beautiful than the others."

She understood.

She, a cub, understood better than any of her tribe-mates. Tanner was astounded, for it was seldom that any of them, least of all the cubs, saw him as anything but a stodgy, eccentric elder with a sparrow-brown beard, an undistinguished body, and no skills at the hunt.

Anger gone as if it had never been, Tanner looked hard at Stormlight. He might as well have been seeing her for the first time. Indeed, she had only been in his long life for a mere eyeblink, fourteen years or so, a tiny span compared to his seven-hundred-some years. She had been a fair-haired flash darting past him in the night, no more. Now he saw a cub—yet not a cub. All slender quickness and lank lengths of growing bones, but something stirring in the fine, pale face, the huge, night-shadowed eyes faintly sparkling with star-light. She was a cub at the edge, the verge, of passage and adulthood. And she understood.

Tanner found his voice a trifle husky when he spoke. "I had not thought of the purple," he admitted.

"But I was right about the rest?" the cub demanded.

"More than right."

"So what are you going to do?" Her great eyes were intensely on him.

Tanner smiled with both sides of his mouth, finding his way suddenly made clear. "Is it not plain? I must obtain more human urine," he declared, and he got up and went off to call a council of the Wolfriders to set about it.

"My people," he told them, "I need your help."

It was a request that they could not lightly refuse, and they did not do so. But neither did they agree. And by the end of the night all the tribe was dark with doubt and grumbling about Tanner. No longer one to be pitied and protected, he. A danger, maybe even a madman, Two-Spear's worthy suc-cessor. Tanner found himself smiling, the only one smiling. He felt much more happy and comfortable as a danger than as a soft-spoken eccentric, a leader who seldom led, chief in name only and a disappointment to the tribe.

"There," he remarked to Brook after the others had scat-tered, muttering, to the tree hollows and hidden places where they spent their days. "Finally, I've given you some excitement."

Brook said unhappily, "What did you expect, after letting Fangslayer and Longreach and the other elders run everything for years?"

"You think I'm a fool, Brook? Why do you suppose I only

proposed that we watch the human camp until their habits become known to us? I plan to bring Fangslayer and his cronies around by degrees. What we really should do is dig a trap, make a net, and capture a human male to make urine for us.''

Brook stared and backed away. "You *are* crazy," he stammered. Then he bolted toward the safety of his daylight perch.

''And he's the one who always tells the tales of Two-Spear at the howl," Tanner remarked to himself. Shrugging, half smiling in the faint daybreak light, he took to the trees—but not to rest. Silently, by the hidden upper ways, he himself made his way toward the human camp.

Just as he reached the point where he could watch the human hunters setting out to run the deer toward the waiting spearmen at the river, he saw a flash of fair hair some distance below him.

Stormlight!

Her easy, swinging gait through the maze of lower branches slowed. Reluctantly she answered the sending. **I am here.**

I know you are! What are you doing?

Watching the human camp for you, my chief, since the others are too stupid to care.

He felt amused agreement, which he did not dare to share with her. Instead, he tried to sound stern. **Turn around. You know you should not be here. Go back to your family at once.**

I have none.

He had forgotten that she was an orphan, raised by the tribe, her parents killed in a hunting mishap years before. Childless and mateless as he was, and preoccupied with his leathermaking, Tanner had taken small part in the rearing of such cubs. He felt a jab of guilt, not only that he had forgotten, but that she could remind him so starkly, as if she should expect nothing more than forgetfulness from him.

Turn around, then, he sent more gently yet more firmly, **and go back to the place where you spend your days. I, your chief, command it.**

She went like a flash of birdflight, like a leaf on the wind, like cloud wisp, gone. From his higher, safer, more hidden vantage, Tanner looked on uneasily. For there was a human hunter standing on the ground beneath where she had been, staring upward with a puzzled scowl.

Tanner watched the humans. He did not come so recklessly near to them as Stormlight had done, for it was not in his nature to take unnecessary risks, but nevertheless, he lost rest and watched, and found ways to the nearer trees, day after day. At times the slow-witted human women, grubbing roots, would have needed only to look up from their toil to have seen him. Once a small child did see him leaping from oak to ash, but the women paid no heed to the child's babbling. Tanner spent the rest of that day in hiding and in compunction, for if he had been discovered so also would the tribe have been, and he felt it his duty as chief to protect them. Yet there was that in him which would have died, were it necessary, to fulfill his private quest.

That season there was unwonted silence and lack of merriment at the nightly howls. But one night when both moons were nearly at the full, as he sat alone afterward, Stormlight came to him and seated herself as abruptly as before, and said to him darkly, "I know where you spend your days."

He met her gaze, smiling. "It seems to me that you know everything about me."

She ignored that and went on. "You are watching the human village. I know it because I am watching, too, and watching you."

He was aghast. "Stormlight!"

"And you are going to get yourself caught if you are not more careful," she said to him sternly.

"You have disobeyed me!" Yet for some reason he found

that he could not be angry with her or impose a punishment on her, as a chief should do.

"You gave me no order but for the one day," she retorted with a defiant lift of her head.

"You know no cub is ever to venture near the humans!"

"I will not be a cub for much longer! Then I will come and go as I will, and where I will, climb up and touch the lightning if I like. Ride the gale down to the ground, if I can. Do as you do, if it pleases me."

Tanner stared at her. She was as wild as Timmorn had ever been, born to confront the storm, as wild as the wolves. There was that in her which could be as fierce as he was gentle and mild.

Her eyes met his, her eyes of deep indigo, darker than storm clouds, deep as midnight, and he felt the jolt shift his center, his bedrock of self, and felt the tremors run through the rest of him, and he knew her soulname, which she did not yet know herself. And sitting, stunned and quaking, he knew he had to live some small time yet at least, long enough to generate a cub with her.

The cub that always comes of Recognition, combining the best qualities of each parent, her daring, his . . . vision. . . . The cub that might someday be his heir.

Stormlight was trembling, edging away from him, her delicate face very frightened; she had felt it too. "What—what was that?" she stammered. "What have you done to me?"

She thought it was something he had imposed on her, a punishment for defying him. Quickly he reached out and laid a hand on her arm to keep her by him. "No!" he exclaimed. "No, it was not me."

"What, then?" she appealed.

"Far larger than either of us. It was Recognition."

"But I—but how can that be?" For all her proud talk, she was still very much the cub. "I—I am not yet—"

"I know, little one." He stroked her hair, shining like pale
water in the moonlight. "You are nowhere near ready, neither
your body nor your self. Let the high ones give me strength,
I will wait for you."

She stared at him. "But it is not fair!" she burst out.
"There should be lovemates for me, courtships, choosings!"
A wild light was growing in her eyes. A wolf, entrapped by
humans, Tanner had heard, would kill itself with fretting
against its bonds rather than submit. This daughter of the
wolves would take no more readily to the bonds of Recognition. "I have never wanted anything but to be free!"

Her cub, Tanner thought, might have those same wide,
midnight-blue, flashing eyes.

"It is horrible!" she cried. "Why should I be—be made a
prisoner to—to—"

Be bound to a dried-up old stick of an elf, she was
thinking, though she would not say it, not even in her frenzy
of shock and anger. But Tanner knew well enough.

You will be as free as I can make you, Stormlight. He
sent to her, trying to calm her. **The bond need not be for
life.**

She glared at him and sprang to her feet. "I'll see to my
own freedom, thank you!" she snapped. She strode away
from him, legs thin and gawky beneath her leather kirtle, and
he watched after her until she went out of sight in the night.

Then he lay back and sighed and dazedly looked up at the
stars. He was serene by nature, but Recognition had been at
least as much of a shock to him as it was to her.

"Tie me and skin me and cook me in a fire!" he muttered.

By dawn he was still dazed, and went and watched the
human village as he did every day, without really seeing
anything, and without finding out any more than he already
knew, which was that the humans were maddeningly random
as to where they put their urine and when they produced it.
When the sun was high he slept, right on a thick oak limb as

he was, for he felt exhausted. And when a great hubbub from the humans below awakened him, he felt yet so dizzied and weak that he did not at first understand what was happening.

Then he glimpsed a small head of fair hair, so fine it floated like flowerdown above pointed ears, and he knew.

The humans had Stormlight.

One of the tall ones' hunters was carrying her in his coarse hands, carrying her to the center of the camp at arm's length, gingerly, as if even in his triumph he was afraid of her. Other humans, women and striplings mostly, were crowding and swirling around, jostling each other for a chance to see, yet unwilling to come too near; a clear space always showed around the hunter and his captive. Even in his panic Tanner could see that Stormlight had not been hurt, at least not yet. And she might not be if she used her wits. The humans acted more than half frightened of her.

Stormlight! Be calm, be canny. I will bring help.

I—my chief, I am sorry. There is something wrong with me. I was clumsy and slow, he saw me—

Never mind that now. Keep your wits about you. Use their fear of you to fend them off. But do not make them so afraid they become enraged.

Please—come back quickly. . . .

At the distance, Tanner could not see the look on her face. Horror held him staring one moment more, and then he tore himself away and sped through the treetops toward the forest.

Ayooooah! Stagrunner! With all the sending strength that was in him he summoned his wolf-friend to more quickly carry him the remaining distance back to the camp. Within moments the wolf came leaping to his side, and for the first time in many seasons, and in high daylight, yet, Tanner rode, at speed.

Ayooah-yoh! Wolfriders, to me! Brook! Brightlance! Joygleam! Oakstrong! Scarp!

All those who were strong and fit for fighting he summoned by name, sending, and when Stagrunner stopped, panting, at the crest of the hurst, he heard slight, squirrellike rustlings in the beeches as they came to him. Hesitantly they came down to the ground, exposed to view in the blunt daylight, and stood around him with wary eyes.

They and many whom he had not summoned, Fangslayer among them.

"The humans have captured Stormlight," Tanner told them. "You cubs and nursing mothers, you elders, back to the trees, to hiding." His tone was curt, for only those he had summoned should have come to him; the others should have stayed in safety. "You who will follow me, bring weapons, send for your wolf-friends."

No one moved except to shift from one foot to the other and to shift eyes, glance at neighbors. None of them summoned their mounts.

"How did the cub come to be captured?" Fangslayer asked harshly, his voice sounding oddly loud, like the calling of the crow, in the forest hush. "How do you come to know of it?"

"There is no time now to talk of it!"

Brook said, softly, too softly, "You were spying on the humans, you and she, were you not? And you ventured too near. Is it not so?"

"And now the tribe is to pay the price of your folly," said Fangslayer. "Many lives might be lost, to try to save one."

Tanner felt his hands turn cold where they rested on the thick fur of Stagrunner's neck. He said, "Which of you wishes to challenge me for the chief's lock? Brook? Fangslayer?"

"I am too old," Fangslayer said stiffly.

"By the high ones, I think you have gone as mad as Two-Spear," Brook muttered. His hands balled into fists, and he shouted, "Yes! I will challenge you!"

He strode forward. His fists swung up as if that would help

him. But he faltered and slowed to a stop as his leaf-brown eyes locked with the wolf-gray ones of his chief in a battle of wills, a sending that only they two could hear. And while Stormlight in the human village down below wielded the thin blade of human fear and used it to hold her enemies off, Tanner wielded the fragile weapons of mind.

In a few moments Brook's fists fell, his face turned away. Tanner reached out and placed a hand on his sagging shoulder. But his gaze looked fiercely around at the others.

"I am your chief," he told them. "Does anyone dispute it?"

No one answered. The glances of some fell to the ground.

"Then hear me. Some of you have spoken truly. It is my duty as chief to see to the safety of the tribe. I have seen the faces of the humans, and I believe that they will be terrified of us if we strike now, in number, that they will flee, that no lives need be lost. But I have also seen your faces, and I will not require any of you to follow me. For my own part, I must go to the human village. I have no choice. Stormlight and I are Recognized."

A murmur of astonishment ran around the tribe. Even Brook's eyes snapped up. "When?" he demanded.

"Lately." Tanner smiled briefly, crookedly at him, then sobered. "I must go to her at once, alone if need be. I name you chief, Brook. I myself will tie the lock on your head, for I have seen your center, and it is good." He reached up to pull the leather thong from his hair.

"No!" Brook caught hold of his arm to stop his hand. "Keep it! May you keep it for eight hundred turns more. I will come with you to the human camp."

"And I," said Joygleam.

"And I," said Oakstrong.

And others. And others, and more, and they were all coming close to him, crowding around him with hands outstretched or upraised as if in triumph, and Tanner tilted back his head and shouted aloud, with no thought for caution any longer, "Ayooooah! Wolfriders!"

Before the sun had dipped low in the sky he had ridden Stagrunner to the laurel thickets at the edge of the forest, where he looked out at the human village, a score of strongly armed Wolfriders at his back.

Stormlight!

Lhu!

Tanner stiffened and swayed on Stagrunner's back, dizzied. It was his soulname.

Soulmate, he asked her, **have they harmed you?**

No. The tall ones are quarreling over what to do with me.

Be ready. We are coming.

His mind turned to the others, Brook at his one side, Joygleam at the other, the many at his back, and his sending embraced them all at once, and they all answered him. Out of the score of them, some frightened, most uneasy, sending made a unity, strong, steady, fierce.

No killing, my people, unless it is necessary. But if it is, smite hard.

We are ready, our chief.

"Ayooooah, Wolfriders! Attack!"

The human young relived it all of their brutish lives in nightmare.

Out of the shadows of the forest, the wolves, a storm-gray scud of them, streaming forward at the speed of birdflight, their gaping mouths showing their long, white teeth—and on each one, long hunting knife or sharp lance upraised, a—a creature, a demon, with fierce eyes that seemed to glow, upslanted and wild as the eyes of the wolves. And before there was time to do more than scream, the flood of them swept into the village.

Tanner, in the lead, sped straight to Stormlight, saw her squirming out of her bonds as if they were so much strangleweed. A few quick strokes of his sharp leather-cutting knife to help her, and she was free. **My eyes see with joy,** she greeted him.

He caught her up much as the shrieking human females were snatching up their children; he set her on Stagrunner before him. **My hands touch with joy,** he told her before he turned his eyes and mind back to the others.

The Wolfriders had needed to do no more than rush and threaten. The humans were fleeing, falling like storm-toppled trees in their frenzy to get away. Only a few, doughty Lift-Leg among them, stood their ground, and they all seemed too stunned to raise weapon. No bloodshed yet, Tanner saw.

"I have our sister, my people. Quickly, back to the hurst!"

Like one large, leaping wolf they wheeled to obey him. But a human hunter was in Tanner's way. The man who had captured Stormlight, he was not as frightened as the rest, for his slow mind was intent only on his prize, and he saw it escaping him. With a bellow of anger he raised his club to strike—

Tanner shouted and raised his knife, futile against so large a foe. Nearly helpless, Stormlight pressed against his chest . . . too late to send Stagrunner darting off to the side—the wolf snarled, longing to tear out the throat of this enemy, knowing he could not leap so high with the burden that was on his back. The club swept down—then dropped with a soft thud to earth as Brook drove his stone-tipped lance into the human's heart.

Tanner saw the quivering lance haft as the blow struck home, but he only heard the thump of the falling body, for he was forest bound, at speed, holding Stormlight in his arms, Brook riding at his side, and the others close at hand, and the wolves running hard, carrying them all out of danger.

Though never again would they be entirely out of danger. The humans knew their enemy now. A human warrior had been slain.

Brook said, "My chief, I had no choice."

"But you did! You could have let me be killed."

Brook stared uneasily, feeling once again as if his chief were going mad—until he saw the gray glint of mischief in Tanner's eyes. Then he laughed aloud.

"You have outjaped me," he declared, laughing, "after all these years."

"What, my chief, did you never tell him you have the soul of a scamp?" Stormlight twisted her thin body to look up at Tanner. But his face was somber, his fingertips stroking a storm-purple lump on her white-skinned temple.

You told me they had not hurt you.

Not but for that. It is where the tall one stunned me with a rock, capturing me.

He felt weak, as if starved by many days' hunger, touching her. Her soulname was pulsing in him like a heartbeat. He needed her as a parched forest needs rain.

"Set me down," she said, perhaps sensing some of this in him, perhaps feeling it in herself. "I will go take my passage at once."

"Come to the healer first, and to the howl, so that the tribe may see you are well," Tanner told her. "Then go."

It was a long howl. There was much to be discussed, for there was no telling what the humans might do. A heavy guard was set. More weapons were to be made, and breastplates of thick leather, to be worn even when hunting. Extra roots and forage of all sorts were to be gathered. No one was to leave the hurst alone. Tanner's people agreed to all this, and looked at him with a new light in their eyes. Theirs was again to be the life of legend, the life of the Wolfriders. Safety was perhaps, after all, not the only thing. Perhaps daring and courage were worth as much. Perhaps they might yet find a way to capture Lift-Leg's marvelous tanning agent for their chief.

To him, it no longer seemed so important. In time he

expected he would find something else that worked as well. Meanwhile, there was his Recognized to be thought of.

He took leave of her afterward, by moonlight, as she stood at the side of her wolf-friend who would bear her away and guard her during her vigil.

"As soon as I have found my soulname, I will be an adult, we can do the thing to make the cub?"

"Yes," he told her.

"I will come back as quickly as I can. I know you are suffering, you cannot eat. I feel the same."

"Yes."

"But I do not plan to stay with you," she told him bluntly, "after it is done."

"Of course not. I will not try to hold you." His hand lifted to stroke her cloud-wisp hair. "It would be like trying to hold the wind."

Lhu. I thank you.

He embraced her, held her pressed against his chest for a moment, then let her go, stood and watched as she rode her giant thunder-dark wolf off into the darkened forest.

When she was gone from sight he turned and went back to the hurst, thinking he would sit alone at the brow of the hill, as he had so many other nights. But he was mistaken. Not only his wolf-friend awaited him, but many of his tribe-mates were there waiting for him as well.

"It seemed to us," Brook explained awkwardly, "that we ought to be more together from now on."

"No more hunting alone?" Tanner teased him.

"No more letting you become a stranger to us. I, for one, was fool enough to think bad things of you, and I am ashamed."

Tanner said, "I let it happen, too. So much that is in me, I have never shared."

He sat at the brow of the hurst, looking up at the stars. They all sat with him.

"Together," Tanner echoed softly. "My people, often I have had a strange dream of a—a place I do not know, a sort of huge tree of many hollows, where all the Wolfriders could rest in one place."

"Show us," said Fangslayer gruffly.

So he shared with them the image in his mind with a sending that included them all. A generation later, when some of the younger ones of them, grown old, came at last to the holt, they would remember that night when Tanner shared with them that dream, and many others, and when they and their chief howled together of the Way and what the Wolfriders should be.

Longreach didn't join the long hunts anymore—he claimed too much wolf riding made his bones ache—but he joined the ones in easy range of the Father Tree. It was possible that his strength was less than it had once been or that his eyes were just a bit blurred, still what he had lost in sheer ability he had more than gained in cunning. He'd thrust his spear into the heart-flesh of a redbuck and felt the wolf-song within him trill as the warm blood touched his lips.

He was content, then, as they brought the carcass back to the hole to share with the others. His mind moved with the moment, so he was surprised when blond Treestump came up alongside.

"It's Moth, storyteller," the bearded Wolfrider said. "I'm worried for her. She's all set for her quest but there's something off-stride in her heart."

Longreach brought his mind to focus behind his eyes. There was no doubting the affection and concern in the hunter's face though Moth was no blood to him since Tanner's generation. The Wolfrider loved all the cubs—their own and each other's. If Treestump thought Moth needed a story or a shoulder, then Longreach would do his share.

"She's in the mist grove," Treestump said as he took the redbuck onto his own wolf's back.

The old Wolfrider put the gnarled trees with their dangling clumps of silver moss into Starwing's mind. The wolf melted

226

away from the others and carried him rise-ward to the grove. Moth was with her wolf-friend, looking very small and very frightened. Her face showed shock and then relief as Starwing cleared the shadows.

"I didn't hope—" she began, taking his hands before he'd even slid from Starwing's back.

He patted her straw-blond hair and tucked her face against his shoulder; he could feel her heart pounding and trembling. "You didn't need to hope, wolfling. One sent thought and I'd find you, you know that—"

What if I don't find it?

You'll find your soulname, don't fret about it.

She pulled away, leaving dark splotches on his tunic. "Why me?" she stammered through her sobs. "Why couldn't I find my name right here under the Father Tree like everyone else? Why wasn't I born knowing it like Cutter was?" Shamed by her cub-tears, Moth wiped her face on her sleeve— and left a long smudge across her cheek.

It made her look younger and even more forlorn. Longreach would have made up a name and given it to her right then if that would have made a difference. "You'll be seeking more than a name. Cutter was born knowing who he was and he'll know who he is all his life, I suspect. And the ones who find their names here, it's as if they're truly a part of the holt. But some of the Wolfriders have had to search to find their true selves."

And some of them never come back. Sent, not spoken, because the fear lay tight around the thought.

"Some," the storyteller honestly agreed, "but I can see by their eyes when they won't find a soulname, and I can see when they will. And what I see in your eyes, I've seen before—"

The Spirit Quest

—by Diana L. Paxson—

In the moist darkness of the soil, a point of life waited for its slow transition into form. Goodtree stilled, focusing her awareness upon it, trying to understand its essence, wondering if she could touch the power that would make it grow.

Goodtree—

Questing for the magic at the heart of things, consciousness registered the call, but noted no meaning. It was only sound-symbols, not a true name.

"Goodtree, where are you?"

Audible this time, the calling stirred memory, and awareness detached itself unwillingly from the essence of the flower. One pointed ear cupped instinctively to catch the whisper of skin-booted feet on grass.

Lionleaper?

Goodtree straightened, grimacing as stiffened muscles in slender limbs sent their own pained messages, and with a sigh remembered why she had wanted to be a tree. Her father, Tanner, chief of the Wolfriders, was gone.

The stiff foliage of the bearberry bushes that edged the clearing shivered, and a lithe figure, smooth-muscled and tawny as the beast from which he'd got his name, slipped past.

"Oh—this is pretty!" Lionleaper hunkered down beside her, patting the vivid moss beneath the trees.

Scent stimulated Goodtree's awareness of his physical nearness—the mixed smells of wolf on his tawny leggings, mint from the banks of the stream on his brown boots, and from the lightly tanned skin of his bare torso, the scent of his own pungent maleness. Instinctively she reached out to touch him, and he pulled her close and rubbed his cheek against hers.

"Nobody knew where you'd gone," Lionleaper said then, "but I thought I might find you here."

Abruptly Goodtree was separate again, green eyes widening in suspicion. "Did the others send you after me?"

"I don't take orders from anybody." His gaze went determinedly back to the moss. "But they're worried, Goodtree—they don't understand why you won't let them call you chieftain. I wish your mother was still alive—maybe she could talk sense into you!"

Goodtree shook her head, grinning crookedly. "You can't remember her very well if you think so! Considering how she fought against being chieftess to my father I don't think she would have dared to press the responsibility on me!"

"Are you trying to be like her?" asked Lionleaper. "Or are you still grieving for Tanner? We all loved him, but he's gone now—that's the Way—and it's no dishonor to his memory to tie up your hair in a chief's lock and carry on."

Defensively, Goodtree smoothed back her curls, golden as the sunlight that bathed the moss. The strand of ivy with which she had bound her hair came loose and she cast it angrily away.

"Is that what you want, Lionleaper?"

"You know what I want, my golden one!" he turned to her suddenly and she shrank from the glow in his amber eyes. Lovemates they had been, lifemates they might be, but she could not afford the closeness, could not take the chance that one night he might offer her his soulname and find out that she had none to give him in return.

"I say what I have said only for the good of the tribe," he added then. "Come back with me now. We have howled for your father; it's time to let him go."

For the good of the tribe! Goodtree thought as she followed Lionleaper back through the forest. *How can I lead the Wolfriders without knowing my true name? I wish it were not my father we were mourning, but me!*

It was the beginning of the green, growing time, and on the sandy slopes of the hurst the beech trees were already in delicate leaf against the somber dark green of the conifers. Soon the grass would be high on the plains that stretched between the forest and the southern mountains, and the great herds would move northward again. Time then for the elves to leave the protection of the Everwood for the good hunting of the grasslands, but for now it was enough to set the heavy furs of winter aside, and rejoice in the rebirth of the world.

When Goodtree and Lionleaper came into the clearing on the crest of the hill, those who had slept the day away were beginning to waken, wolves and elves emerging together from hollows beneath the great roots of the beech trees, or thickets where they had fashioned rough shelters. Goodtree staggered as a warm weight struck her from behind, and with a quick twist of her slender body, turned her fall into a grab for the brindled pelt of the great she-wolf who was pressing against her.

"Leafchaser! If you're too sleepy to walk straight, go back to your den!" Her words were harsh, but her arms were around the wolf's neck, her face buried in thick fur. From the wolf came a wordless amusement, and Goodtree had a momentary impression of herself as a cub to be knocked over in play until it had the wit to avoid or the strength to withstand it.

"Oh all right!" she answered, sitting back on her heels to stare into the wolf's yellow eyes. "I suppose it's my own fault for not sensing you were there." Leafchaser's eyes slanted as her jaws opened in an answering grin, then two pairs of pointed ears pricked at a long-drawn, distant howl.

Good hunt, much meat, came the wolf's images.

Hunters coming back. All around them wolves were answering in sweet harmony, and several of the elves had leaped to their friends' backs and sped down the slope to help the hunters bring home their kill. Goodtree could just remember a time when, for fear of the humans who roamed the plain, the elves had hunted only during the hours of darkness. But when the humans were not fighting elves, they fought each other, and for many seasons now their numbers had been too few for them to threaten the Wolfriders.

Goodtree stood up, tugging her close-fitting doeskin tunic back down over her leggings. She had eaten nothing since early that morning, and her belly was already rumbling in anticipation. Her anguish of the afternoon was forgotten. Joyously she cut a length of the clingsilver that twined up the trunk of the great beech tree and twisted it into a new wreath for her hair so that the little bell-shaped blossoms hung trembling over her cheeks and brow.

Soon new sounds heralded the hunters' arrival—Joygleam first, as befitted the senior huntress of the tribe, sitting her wolf-friend proudly despite her evident weariness, and then Brightlance and the others, each bearing a portion of what must have been a mighty beast indeed.

"The branch-horns are coming!" cried Brightlance. "Their forerunners are moving into the grasslands, and the main herd will be here soon. This bull was the first of them, but we were too clever for him. How I wish we could have brought his head too—his horns were like the limbs of this tree!" He gestured broadly, and the haunch he was carrying slipped to the grass.

Elves seized it eagerly and carried it into the clearing in the center of the hurst, and soon knives of flint and bone were stripping skin from flesh and carving the dripping muscle-meat into pieces so that everyone could share. They sat in a circle on the grass, and for a time the only sounds were of those strong jaws moving and an occasional growl as a wolf worried at a particularly resistant piece of flesh, followed by sighs of repletion as one by one, both wolves and elves were filled.

Goodtree leaned back against a friendly trunk, at peace with the world. The sun had sought its den and the first stars were pricking holes in the mantle that evening had drawn across the sky. Elfin eyes grew larger and more luminous as the darkness deepened. Then the child moon lifted above the trees, and one of the wolves lifted his pointed muzzle and sang out in greeting. One by one the others echoed him, and the elves joined them, their howling shifting imperceptibly into song.

> *"Two moons in the sky—*
> *High the way they go . . .*
> *To their hidden hall,*
> *Well the way they know . . ."*

The final vowel sounds were drawn out and held, providing a soft background as Acorn Songshaper continued. Goodtree could just glimpse his soft brown hair against the darker tree trunk, his thin body no broader than it was. He was gentle, as her father had been, and as she knew well, lying with him on the grass in the moonlight was like being part of a song.

> *"Wanderers are we,*
> *Free, we find our way*
> *Through forest, over hill,*
> *Still we cannot stay . . ."*

Goodtree felt her spirit shaken by a longing for something she could not name, and, opened to the emotions of the others by the sweetness of the music, knew that they felt it too.

> *"Forever must we roam,*
> *Homeless here below?*
> *Oh, are we all alone?*
> *Only the high ones know!"*

The Wolfriders had hunted through Everwood since before her birth, and yet, singing this song, Goodtree felt as if she had lost a place and a people that she had never known. For a moment she could almost see it, then the last echoes faded, and the image glimmered like a rainbow in the morning mist and was gone.

"Mold and mushrooms, Acorn, you'll dissolve us into puddles if you keep this on!" exclaimed Lionleaper, blinking rapidly. "Can't you find anything livelier to sing?"

"*Oh, Lionleaper is a hero—*" the Songshaper responded immediately. "*With him around what shall we fear-oh? Oh, oh, oh, aoow!*" Everyone began to laugh as the wolves provided the chorus, and as Acorn continued with verses describing Joygleam's success as a hunter, Chipper's expertise in working stone, and Freshet's ability to find dreamberries, someone began clicking out a rhythm on clapper stones. By the time they had surveyed the peculiarities of most of the tribe, someone else had added the twittering of a reed flute to the music, and Acorn was thrumming an accompaniment on the eight-stringed bow-harp he had made.

The music grew wilder, and elves sprang into the center of the ring to dance. The Mother moon trailed her offspring across the skyfields, and her leaf-filtered light dappled the soft grass. In that deceptive radiance the leaping figures of the dancers flickered in and out of vision. Goodtree rose to join them, then blinked, wondering if she had eaten too many dreamberries. But the music was headier than they. Forgetting everything, she danced, linked once more to the deep magic of the night.

Goodtree did not know how long it had been when she realized that the wordless song of the united tribe and pack had become a deep chanting—affirming their identity—

"From the frozen mountains to the pathless forest!"

"We are the Wolfriders, and the pack runs free!" came the full-throated reply.

"From the Muchcold Water to the Sea of Grass!" the chant went on, and the response was repeated.

"Blood of the high ones, Timmorn's children!"

"Led by chieftains' might and wisdom!" Unwilled, Goodtree was caught up in the litany.

"Rahnee the She-Wolf, Prey-Pacer, Two-Spear—"

"Huntress Skyfire, Freefoot, Tanner!" Goodtree jolted to a halt like a fleeing doe who senses the cliff-edge before her, but the tribe's response vibrated through her.

"We are the Wolfriders, and the pack runs free!"

"Goodtree, Goodtree, chiefs' blood, lead us!" They roared, and she stood trembling, mouthing denials that no one could hear. Exultant faces glimmered mockingly in the moonlight; her head was pounding and the meat she had eaten lay in her belly like a stone.

No! she sent finally, with a violence that flared like lightning through their ecstasy. **The tribe is safe here— what do you need a chief for? Choose someone else if you have to—but not me, not me!** Sobbing, Goodtree found the power of motion finally and dashed from the circle into the sheltering shadows of the trees.

Instinct urged her to run like a stampeded branch-horn. But the log that tripped her brought Goodtree partway to her senses—she sought escape, not death, and she must not go weaponless. Hastily she ducked into her shelter and slung bow and quiver across her back, wrapped the longtooth pelt that Lionleaper had given her around her shoulders, and picked up her bone-tipped lance. Then she was out again, a shadow among shadows, slipping silently through the trees.

She was halfway down the hill when the snap of a twig behind her startled her. She missed a step and her nostrils caught a familiar scent just as a gust of warm breath tickled her ear.

Leafchaser! Her sending held mingled relief and annoyance, but she knew that she could never have evaded her wolf-friend for long. But where Leafchaser could follow, others could trace her as well. What if the rest of the Wolfriders refused to let her leave?

Old friend, I don't know where I'm going. Are you sure you want to come along?

Whether or not the she-wolf had properly understood the sending, her determination to stay with Goodtree was clear, and the elf felt her heart imperceptibly lightened. It was not natural for either wolf or Wolfrider to hunt alone. She let the wolf find a way through the thick trees, but when they came to the river she forced the complaining animal to follow her upstream through the water. Even wolves would be thrown off the scent by that, at least for a little while.

But both the wolves and the Wolfriders had gorged to satiation, and bellies shrunken by winter's scarcities needed time to digest the considerable quantities of meat on which they had feasted. It was not until midmorning that they realized that Goodtree and Leafchaser were gone and began to search for them.

For two days Goodtree pressed onward, pausing only to hunt. Behind her was the deep forest and the ever deepening river that flowed downhill toward the Muchcold Water to the north. Before her the trees grew thinner, and at the end of the second day, she saw through the last outlying pines wind-ruffled grasses furring the long slope of plain that rose toward a blue etching of mountains, sharp against the sky.

They camped that night at the edge of the forest, listening to the incessant whispering of grasses in the wind. When morning came, Goodtree and Leafchaser shared the last of the meat. Then she sprang onto the wolf's narrow back, clutching at the thick neck fur and laughing joyously as Leafchaser leaped forward across the plain.

In the forest behind her, Lionleaper stilled as his wolf-friend Fang barked out the short call that told him that the animal had found the scent they were looking for. He tipped back his own head then and gave tongue, and heard the nearest elf echoing. From one to another the call carried back to the hurst where the fighting strength of the Wolfriders was waiting. They had been getting ready for the spring hunt in any case, and needed little preparation. Before another hour had passed, everyone who was fit for a long ride—a good two-thirds of the tribe—was mounted and ready to follow Goodtree's trail.

The first release of energy carried Goodtree and Leafchaser a half-day's journey across the plain. Leapers soared out of their way as they approached, but the little beasts sensed that they were not hunting, and would settle to cropping the rich grass again before they had quite passed. The first scattered bands of branch-horns did not even bother to do that much, knowing well that they were in no danger from a solitary hunter, whether it went on four legs or two. Goodtree stared admiringly at the play of muscle in their shaggy flanks and the immense sweep of horns that gave them the appearance of ambulant trees.

A walking forest . . . she thought then, wondering if elves could ever find the same sense of kinship with creatures like this as they did with the Everwood's trees. As the thought came to her she was aware of an odd sense of dislocation, as if she had lost something important. But she could not remember what it had been.

A few hours later they came over a rise, and Goodtree nearly fell off as Leafchaser halted suddenly. She felt the hair rising along the wolf's spine and sniffed at the wavering wind, questioning silently.

Longtooth hunting, came the wolf's answer.

The land fell away before them in a series of gentle ridges covered by a varicolored carpet of green and tawny grasses where the new growth was pushing through the old. The occasional small patches of brush made it hard to judge size or distance, and except for a rippling in the grass as the wind touched it, nothing moved.

Leafchaser started to circle around, but Goodtree stopped her, gripped by an unexpected sense of anticipation. The wolf snorted then and sat down, and Goodtree slid off her back and moved to the rim of the hill, where she squatted, becoming as still as the rest of the scene.

Then she felt a vibration in the earth beneath her. An outraged trumpeting split the air, and suddenly a hairy brown shape that even at this distance seemed the size of a moving mountain, heaved over the next rise. For something that big it moved astonishingly quickly, and Goodtree half rose, ready to run if it neared her, for one step of that flat-bottomed foot could have turned her into a stain on the soil. As it approached she saw the gleam of huge tusks and the sinuous upflung trunk and recognized a beast that she had half-believed a legend.

But the dun-colored shape that flashed after it was faster still, coiling and uncoiling in great bounds across the grass. And at the moment when the serpent-nose slowed and started to swing those murderous tusks toward its pursuer, a second longtooth exploded suddenly out of invisibility in the dead grasses, leaped to the great beast's shaggy shoulders, and clung, snarling furiously as it sought for a killing grip on the spine.

The first cat leaped for the huge haunches and fell back again as the serpent-nose spun. But now two more lions magically appeared, leaping and slashing with claws sharper than the Wolfriders' knives. But this prey was not to be taken easily. The serpent-nose bucked and stamped, flexible trunk seeking to capture one of its tormentors.

As Goodtree forced herself to take a breath, one of the lions missed its leap, and as it rebounded the huge head swung and caught the cat on its tusks, lifted and flung it in a squalling arc to land with a sick thud a good distance away. But the movement had opened the way to the first longtooth's savaging jaws, and in that moment the sword teeth pierced through muscle and sinew and snapped the spine.

The serpent-nose reared upward, blasting its agony, looming against the sky. For a moment it seemed impossible that something that big could ever fall. And then, with the ponderous inevitably of some great tree uprooted by a winter storm, the giant beast swayed and toppled to the ground.

Goodtree felt the ground shake beneath her as it fell. Dying, the serpent-nose continued to struggle, but with its spinal cord cut, its movements were purposeless. Ignoring them, the big cats pounced upon the twitching carcass and began to feed. She sensed from Leafchaser a rather wistful approval, for even the full wolf-pack with riders would have hesitated to tackle something that size.

Goodtree herself was admiring the perfect teamwork and discipline with which the longtooth pride had caught enough meat to feed them all for several days. Her stomach rumbled as the hot blood smell came to her on the shifting wind. She only wished the tribe could do so well. The wolves' way was to run down their prey, but she wondered if perhaps the Wolfriders could learn something from the big cats she had just seen. Riderless, the wolves could chase their chosen prey until it was exhausted, then herd it into the elves' ambush where a well-placed arrow or lucky cast of a spear might reach a vulnerable throat or eye. She would have to ask Joygleam if that had ever been tried—

—And at the thought, Goodtree remembered why she was here, alone. Tasting bitterness, she stood up. The longtooth male lifted his head from the kill to look at her, decided that something so puny was no competition, and returned to his meal.

He was probably right, Goodtree thought unhappily.

Lionleaper had fought one once, an old cat weakened by the winter snows, and taken one of its great fangs for a hunting knife. But he had been badly wounded in the battle, and roundly scolded by Tanner as well. Foolish feats of individual valor were not the Wolfriders' Way—elf lives were too valuable to be wasted. Elves did not kill each other, but far too many died defending the tribe from other enemies.

Only together did they have the strength to survive, and as a result the Wolfriders were rarely out of sensing range of other members of the tribe. No wonder she felt incomplete, alone out here beneath the empty sky. If she had not had the comfort of Leafchaser's calm presence, Goodtree thought she would have sat down again right where she was and howled.

As it was, she felt a suspicious ache in her throat as she climbed onto the wolf's bony back and directed her to continue her steady trot toward the distant hills.

Together, the Wolfriders wound through the Everwood more slowly than a single rider, but they were still following Goodtree's trail. Lionleaper led them, but Acorn was close behind.

The warrior had never had much use for the song maker, especially when he saw how Goodtree favored him, but there would have been no honor in challenging someone who was obviously so much weaker. Even to himself he did not admit that what he won with blows he might have lost with words.

Now, however, Lionleaper found the other elf's presence oddly comforting. The rest of the tribe loved Goodtree too, because she was Tanner's daughter, because she was part of them, their chosen chieftain. But the warrior sensed that of them all, perhaps only he and Acorn loved her because she was herself, sometimes merry as the morning sun, warming all she smiled on, and sometimes distant as some glittering star, lost in some inner realm to which neither of them could follow her. But at least she had still been there, and they had known that eventually she would come back to them.

But where was she now, and why? There had always been something unfathomable in Goodtree, even in the moments of greatest intimacy. Joy and sorrow he could understand, but not flight, if that was what it was, for her trail was not the erratic wandering of a lost cub, but a purposeful movement toward some goal that only Goodtree knew.

If she was killed, or she never returned to them, what would they do? Timmorn's blood flowed in all the Wolfriders, but additional generations of leadership had given the chiefly line a special quality that made it impossible for Lionleaper to imagine anyone else as head of the tribe, even—despite the times he had chafed at Tanner's caution—himself.

We will find her—we *have* to— he thought, and only realized that in his intensity he had been sending when he sensed Acorn answering him.

She's still all right. I had an impression of her a little while ago, as if she wished she could tell us about something she had seen.

"Where?" Lionleaper said aloud. "Where is she now?"

"On the plains somewhere—there was a feeling of space around her," Acorn replied, urging his wolf alongside Fang.

Lionleaper nodded. "That's where we're headed. Another day's travel and we'll be there."

But will Goodtree be waiting for us? anxiety added, *and will she be happy to see us when we catch up with her?*

The plain rose almost imperceptibly, but steadily, and that night Goodtree and Leafchaser slept curled together in the grass at the base of the foothills. The mountains that had been an irregular gray wall when she fell asleep were revealed in luminous precision in the clear light of dawn, tree-clad folds and ridges rising to jagged peaks sharp against the translucent sky. But the light showed also a glacier carven cleft as if the mountains themselves were welcoming her. Eagerly they began to climb.

As is the way of mountains, the path that had looked so easy from a distance proved less open than it had seemed. Very soon Goodtree dismounted so that she could use all four limbs to climb, and there were times when Leafchaser's paws could find no purchase and she had to help haul the wolf up the scree. But although the climb was in places difficult, it was nowhere impossible.

Gradually the stands of budding hardwoods and the rocky moraine of the lower slopes were left behind, and they came to groves of conifers and little mountain meadows where scatterings of purple and white flowers jeweled the new grass. By this time the sun was sinking once more, and Goodtree saw the peaks suffused with mauve and rose. Too tired to hunt, elf and wolf-friend found a sheltered place at the edge of a meadow and were asleep almost before the last light was gone.

A cold poke in the armpit brought Goodtree suddenly awake when the mists of morning still hung heavy in the trees. Pulse pounding, she struggled to unwind herself from the furry folds of the lion pelt and sit up, sending a frantic query to Leafchaser.

No danger, came the silent reply. **Deer in meadow . . . hungry!**

Goodtree grimaced, realizing, now that she was upright, that she ached in every limb. All her senses counseled a return to sleep's oblivion, but Leafchaser's steady amber stare would not release her.

Oh all right, I'll try, she agreed finally, **but if you think I'm going to hit anything you're in worse shape than I feel!**

Hungry . . . repeated Leafchaser, and Goodtree realized that she was hungry too. The wolf was right. They were only going to feel worse if they went much longer without food.

The deer were in the meadow, dappled as the forest floor

with legs so slender they almost seemed to float above the grass. The wolf scent made them uneasy, so Goodtree sent Leafchaser to circle around upwind. But even when a shift in the breeze carried her own scent directly toward them they did no more than lift their delicate heads, long ears swiveling in curiosity. They had never encountered elf before, she decided, and had no way of knowing that this new scent they were ignoring heralded a predator more dangerous than the wolves they rightly feared.

For several minutes she watched them, forgetting her sore muscles as she identified two does with their new fawns, and the guardian stag. Then another deer moved out onto the meadow—a split-horn buck, his red hide ragged where his winter coat was coming away. She lifted her bow and nocked an arrow, holding it half-drawn, waiting. The young buck moved this way and that, as if he was trying to hide behind the other deer.

Move downwind for just an instant, then away, she sent to Leafchaser. In a few moments she saw all four dainty heads lift questioningly and caught a hint of wolf-scent on the breeze. The does nudged their fawns nervously toward the edge of the wood as the stag started forward. But the young buck stood with one foreleg half-lifted, poised on the edge of flight.

And in his moment of indecision, Goodtree's own choice was made. With a single smooth motion she drew the bowstring back and released it, and the arrow flew flawlessly toward the paler fur behind the buck's elbow; flew, and struck, boring between the fragile ribs to penetrate the pumping heart behind them.

The buck gave one convulsive leap and fell, dead before he hit the grass. The other deer, finally realizing their danger, disappeared into the trees in a few frantic bounds. Now that the hunt was over, Goodtree felt her aching muscles once more. Stiffly she moved toward her kill, leaving a wavering trail across the dew-pearled grass.

The deer's eyes were already dulling as she knelt beside it, but she could sense the startled spirit near.

"Thy spirit for my spirit, thy blood for my body, brother—as mine shall feed others, a circle of life without end!" she said softly, and stretching the neck taut, drew her knife carefully across the buck's throat to release its blood into the soil.

She felt Leafchaser's familiar presence at her shoulder. Her nostrils flared at the sharp tang of blood and her stomach grumbled sharply. Cutting carefully down from the gash in the throat, she tugged slippery hide away from the red flesh it had protected, and together, elf and wolf began to feed.

Sustained by that nourishment, the pair made good time during the morning's climbing, and just as the sun reached the summit of the sky, Goodtree found herself suddenly looking downward. Rocky slopes fell away before her, less steeply but otherwise much the same as the ones she had climbed. But beyond them stretched a green plain to which spring had come sooner than her own, and at the edge of sight the misty blur of a forest.

With an odd throb almost like Recognition she identified it, seeing in her mind's eye green, leafy spaces friendlier than the woods of home. She took a deep breath, scenting the sweetness of sun-warmed grasses mingled with the crisp mountain wind.

I will go there—someday I will go see, she promised herself, but memory of the Wolfriders tethered her. Whether she had been running toward something, or only running away, she understood now that she *could not* leave them behind. For the first time it occurred to her to wonder what the tribe was doing now.

With a sigh Goodtree turned away from the tantalizing vista ahead and looked around her. She was standing in a cleft in the hills. To one side gray stone sheered upward to a jagged crown barely softened by a straggle of stunted pines. In the other direction, two ridges met and plunged downward in a jumble of rock and trees cut by the silver ribbon of a mountain stream. As it neared the pass, the canyon opened out into a small meadow, but the stream turned southward, toward the distant forest she had seen.

It was an omen, thought Goodtree as she considered the canyon once more. Getting up that would be difficult, but not much harder than parts of the climb she had already made. And she felt a growing curiosity about the source of that little stream.

Carefully Goodtree began to climb, but as the summit grew nearer, she scrambled more quickly, caution fading so gradually she never knew when it disappeared.

Acorn clapped his hands to his head with a cry.

Fang stopped short as Lionleaper turned. Another stride brought the songshaper's wolf up to them and Lionleaper slid from Fang's back to catch the other elf as he fell.

"What is it? Did something hit you?" The warrior looked wildly about. Behind him he saw the rest of the tribe, stretched out in an irregular line across the rolling plain. The plain! What could drop on Acorn here? Swiftly he scanned the shivering grasses, searching for any sign of an enemy. But he saw nothing, and the sensitive noses of the wolves found no trace of any foe.

Joygleam jogged up beside them, her lean features creasing in concern. "Is he ill?"

"No—" said Lionleaper. "I don't know, but I'm afraid—" He could not voice the words. Acorn moaned and stirred against him, then relaxed once more.

"Afraid, warrior, because sickness can't be faced with a sword?"

"No!" Lionleaper glared at her over the singer's head. "Acorn thinks he's been sensing Goodtree. He said she was all right, traveling straight across the plain ahead of us, except when she stopped to look at the longtooth kill, and your trackers say the same. I'm afraid something's happened to her, and he is picking it up somehow."

The hunter sobered abruptly. "Dead?"

"I don't think so." Lionleaper swallowed, not liking to think about what might happen to Acorn if Goodtree died while they were mentally connected this way.

He looked down at the limp form he held. Once he had despised the song maker, frustrated because he and Goodtree shared something which the warrior could not understand. It would have been easy to hate Acorn now, linked to her in a way that none of them understood. He had thought at first that this bond somehow meant Recognition, that he had lost any hope of Goodtree's love—but he had never heard of such a connection even between the most devoted of mates. And now his anxiety for Goodtree had swallowed up all lesser emotions; as he felt the other elf shudder in his arms his heart was wrenched by an odd mixture of pity and envy for his pain.

"He can't ride—what do you want us to do?" Joygleam asked practically.

Lionleaper stared at her. He knew that she had had to perform the final mercy for comrades more than once when they were wounded beyond bearing on hunting expeditions far from home. They had had no healer in the tribe since Willow had died.

I don't know! You're older than I am—why are you asking me? he wanted to shout at her. He was perfectly sure now that he would not have taken the chieftainship if they offered it to him on a white wolfskin. But for now he had to pretend he could do it—he had to hold together long enough to find Goodtree—alive. . . . And he was suddenly determined that when that happened Acorn would be alive too.

"Let's make camp now. We can tend Acorn here and let the weaker ones rest while the hunters go after meat."

Joygleam nodded, and presently they settled Acorn on a

soft bed of furs where a hillock curved around and provided a little protection from the wind. And Lionleaper stayed by him, smoothing the damp hair back from his brow and giving him water when he began to stir. But it was dawn of the following day before he came back to consciousness fully and told them that Goodtree had hit her head, probably in a fall, but she was on her feet and on her way once more.

Her vision still blurred if she turned her head too quickly, but Goodtree kept moving. She had come to herself just as the sun was lifting above the eastern peaks, to find Leafchaser licking her face anxiously. She hurt everywhere there was a where, but she was lucky to be alive and intact, and she knew it. There was no excuse for the carelessness that had made her miss her footing and fall. She told herself that whatever she was seeking would still be there when she arrived, but even now she found herself hurrying.

The way had grown easier, but the pines through which she was moving now had been forced to grow at an angle by the pressure of the wind, so that the evidence of inner ear and eye conflicted; she found herself inadvertently leaning so that they would seem upright. Finally she closed her eyes, and gripping Leafchaser's thick ruff let the wolf lead her through the wood.

The wind deformed those trees, but they changed, and survived. . . . She wondered then, *Have we elves also changed to survive this world, and if we have, what were we like when we began?*

Only the wind answered her, and she could not understand what it was whispering. The brisk touch lifted the damp tangles of pale hair from her brow and tingled on her skin. It sang in her blood, stimulating her circulation until the throbbing in her head faded finally away. The wolf stopped then, and Goodtree let go of her and opened her eyes.

Below her lay a circular valley—no, a cup, a crater in the

heart of the mountain with a round lake in its center that blazed back the brilliant blue of the sky. There was meadowland around it, and groves of trees like none in the Everwood, all in exquisite miniature.

Goodtree gave a great sigh. There was a feeling here that set an odd tremor rippling through her belly—the same shiver that came to her sometimes when Acorn told his tales. There was power here; she could feel it, and she would seek it even if it proved too great for an elf-woman to bear.

She folded the lionskin and laid it down, slipped bow and quiver off her shoulder and set them atop it, and the long-bladed spear after. She would not need them where she was going. She must pursue this path fasting now. She pulled off her doeskin tunic then, and leggings and boots as well, scarcely noticing as the wind pebbled her pale skin. The Wolfriders went to their soul quest naked as they were born.

Leafchaser, I am going down there. You must guard these things for me and let none come after until I return. Do you understand?

Amber eyes stared into hers for a moment, then the wolf pushed her cold nose into Goodtree's hand. **Come too . . . hunt for you. . . .**

No! No hunting! I have to go alone! Please stay here and guard!

The great wolf sat down, head slightly averted, tongue lolling as she panted in the thin air. She could not remember when Goodtree had tried to find her name before, and failed, but she recognized the finality in her elf-friend's sending. With a gusty sigh, she sank the rest of the way down and looked up at Goodtree.

Will guard. . . . Come soon. . . .

Three days later, Acorn and Lionleaper stood where Goodtree had stood, and looked down into the valley where she had gone. The sun still shone brightly, but far to the west cumulus clouds were capping the peaks with white towers. Leafchaser sat beside the pitiful pile of possessions that had been too much weight for Goodtree's spirit, but when the two elves began to seek a way down the slope after her, the wolf rose, snarling, to block their way.

Lionleaper looked at his companion helplessly. "She told Leafchaser to stop us!" He supposed they could ask their own wolf-friends to get the she-wolf out of the way, but he was not sure they would obey.

"Goodtree doesn't want us to follow her!" exclaimed Acorn in sudden anger. "We've hounded her for almost an eight-of-days, but we have to stop now—"

"Why?" Lionleaper began. "We don't even know if she's still living!"

"Even if she were dying, we wouldn't have the right. This was her choice. And there's magic in that place. We can't go down there. Don't you yet understand?"

"No. . . ." Lionleaper hunkered down beside the pile of abandoned clothing with a sigh. "All I understand is that I had to follow her."

Acorn's sudden smile transformed his angular face. "So did I. . . ." He lowered himself to the stone.

"The others are safe enough in the little vale at the top of the pass. I'll send Fang with a message for them," said the warrior. "Do you know enough stories to fill the time until she returns?"

Acorn laughed. "Long ago, in the time of legends, the high ones came to the world of two moons . . ." he began.

By the end of the first day, Goodtree's belly was cramping with hunger until she wanted to scream. It had been that way when she tried this before, she remembered, and tried to distract herself by focusing on her surroundings.

For her vigil she had chosen a grove of what she called sun trees, for they were new to her, rising like columns covered with smooth bark that had a golden sheen. Their leaves were a translucent pale green edged with sunlight, and the radiance that shone through them filled the grove with a gold-green glow. If she concentrated on it, perhaps she could feel the luminous warmth penetrating her body. Her heart shook with longing to understand the secrets of those trees.

Fill me! Transform me! she prayed, opening her awareness to the sensation as if she were trying to contact a cub who was just learning to send. And for a moment she did feel it. Then the demands of her belly distracted her. She swore, and settled herself to try again.

Sometime during the third day the hunger pangs left her. Goodtree looked down at her naked body with a curious detachment. Her breasts were still pointed and firm, but her hipbones jutted painfully and she could count her ribs. It occurred to her that several days of hard travel after a lean winter had not been the best preparation for fasting, but the thought had no power to disturb her now.

What was disturbing her was memory.

Living with the wolves made it too easy to see life as they did—a succession of events whose connections were rarely remembered or recognized. The moons and the seasons flowed by; cubs were born and the old were killed or died. But one cycle of the seasons was much like another, and those who died nourished the unborn so that nothing was really lost, only transformed.

It was a good way to live, a way that had enabled the Wolfriders to deepen their bonds to the beasts with whom they shared their lives so that both survived. But there were times when understanding cause and effect required a linear view of reality. Perhaps, once she had done this, Goodtree would never have to think this way again. But to understand who she was now, it was essential for her to remember who she had been.

With the same discipline with which she would have backtracked an animal to its den, Goodtree began to move backward along the paths of memory. The death of her father was a recent sorrow; the death of her mother more distant but in its way more painful, for Stormlight had died as violently as she had lived.

But how Goodtree's parents had ended did not matter. What was important was that with each death she had felt as if she had failed them, and there was too much that she could never say to them now. And yet somehow it still needed to be said.

They were so different! she thought in wonder. *How could they have Recognized, and produced me?* In theory, the offspring of such a union should have the best characteristics of both parents, or at best, something new. *But I can't do anything unusual,* thought Goodtree, the easy tears spilling from beneath her eyelids. *Until I find my soulname, I don't even understand what every other grown Wolfrider knows!* She shifted position on the grass beneath the sun tree as if she were in physical agony.

Mother! Why couldn't I have your courage?

The image of Stormlight came vividly to mind: midnight eyes bright and pale hair sparking wildly, preparing for the hunt as if she was going to war. Goodtree remembered sitting behind her mother on the wolf's back, clinging for dear life as they charged into a herd of branch-horns. She heard once more her mother's yell of triumph as the sharp spear bit, and relived her own terror when the murderous horns grazed her as the beast fell. She had sobbed hysterically all the way back to the hurst, and her parents had argued over it for hours— that was a painful memory too.

O my father, why couldn't I have inherited your calm patience?

She remembered the gentle abstraction in Tanner's face, already weathered by the years when she had been born. A lock of brown hair would fall over his eyes when he was

working—and he usually *was* working, always trying to re-
fine the process he had invented to tan the leather the Wolfriders
wore. She had wanted to help him, she remembered, so that
he would be pleased with her, but the acrid preparations he
used had blistered her hands, and the fumes had stung her
eyes until she ran away, weeping. He and Stormlight had
argued about that, too.

I cried a lot in my cub days, Goodtree thought distaste-
fully, *but maybe I had reason. When did I stop being so
sensitive, and why?*

A chieftain's cub was adopted by everyone in the tribe,
and she had certainly never lacked for food or care. But
apparently it had not been enough to make up for the sense of
separation she felt from the two beings she loved most in the
world. She did not know what would have become of her if
she had not had Leafchaser.

When Goodtree was small she had been sure that her
father was the wisest elf in the tribe, just as her mother was
the bravest and the most beautiful. But as she grew older, she
had fought with her mother, refusing to hunt with her or learn
the craft of the warrior and Stormlight's skills with the
stabbing spear. Instead, she had spent long hours alone,
practicing with the bow. Her father had tried to talk to her
about the craft of the chieftain. Tanner had been old when
Goodtree was born, and she understood now that he had
suspected how young she would still be when she succeeded
him. But she had refused to hear.

*But they are both gone now, and I cannot turn back the
seasons to seek them!* Once more she wept as if her parents
lay newly dead before her, but it was the loss of all they
should have shared that she was weeping for. They had tried
their best to help her, just as she had tried to please them.
There was no blame for either them or Goodtree—all they
had needed for understanding was time.

But they had not been given it. Where had those bright

spirits gone when the flesh failed them? Was the soul extinguished, or did it dissipate like mist before the sun? Or did Tanner and Stormlight live still in some realm where even wolf-senses could not discover them?

Darkness had fallen while she was still retracing the tangled paths of memory. Exhausted, Goodtree fell into a fitful sleep in which her unconscious replayed all the incidents of her cubhood with implacable clarity. Only when the rising sun illuminated the grove with a glow that was almost silvery, as if it were being filtered through clouds, did she awaken, or rather, shift consciousness, for she could scarcely feel her body now.

That was the solution! It was the flesh she wore that prevented her from communicating with Stormlight and Tanner—she wondered why she had not understood that before. If she could leave the clumsy thing behind her, perhaps she could catch up with them.

Breathing slowed and grew shallower; sight fixed on the flutter of golden leaves and then lost focus; senses shut down until Goodtree was only a point of awareness hovering in a haze of light. But it was not enough for her to lose herself, however pleasant it might be. What she was seeking lay elsewhere. Her spirit strained like a pup struggling against the birth-caul, and suddenly she felt warmth like the she-wolf's tongue dissolving the last constrictions, and she was free.

Mother? Father? Familiar presences flowed comfortingly around her. **Myr . . . Lhu . . .** Goodtree recognized the two she had known as Tanner and Stormlight.

We are here . . . we have always been with you . . . could you not feel our love?

With that answer, Goodtree received from them a totality of acceptance that healed wounds that had festered in her spirit for far too long. Freed, she sank deeper into the magic, awareness expanding to encompass it. Myr and Lhu were only part of something larger, a multiplicity of glories which she gradually recognized as the essence of the world around her, as real as the physical appearances she had known.

And as she perceived them, Goodtree named them, understanding with that act the inner truth of tree and flower and stone. She knew how the rootlets of the grasses spread through the rich soil, sensed the absorption of nutrients from the earth and the transformation of sunlight into energy, and more deeply, the cell-deep changes that made the plant grow.

But the grasses were only marginally aware. It was far more rewarding to touch the deep enduring life of a tree, its spirit encircled with rings of memory. Now, the tree's upper branches rustled and swayed in the wind, but its trunk recorded its biography. One year had been dry and hard, another so cold that heartwood cracked; lightning had scored a shapely trunk, and the tree was still slowly curling bark over the scar; floods had bared roots and torn branches away. All these things Goodtree remembered, and with them understood the internal patterning that enabled the tree to adjust to trauma and still continue to grow.

Some emptiness within her that no bond with elf or wolf had been able to fill accepted union with the trees and was satisfied. And in that knowledge she understood her own essence at last and named it.

Neme! I am Neme! And this is my true home!

Neme perceived the minimal life-processes of her own body, and understood how its elements would nourish the trees around her when the last tenuous connection between flesh and spirit faded away. Then she would be part of the grove forever. She would never again have to deal with failure or loneliness or fear.

Seeking that union, Neme's spirit quested outward. Beyond the Golden Grove, oak and beech woods whispered the same response to the rising wind. She felt their movement as if she herself were moving, sensed their leaves' adjustment as clouds dimmed the light, knew the strength that rooted them, understood even the layering of soils and the structure of underlying stone.

Ever more widely her spirit expanded. Now she perceived the roots of the mountains, where hidden earth-fires burned still. Awareness identified Acorn and Lionleaper, keeping their patient vigil beside the wolves, and felt them flinch beneath the first stinging drops of rain. Neme sensed how the land folded downward to the pass and without surprise she perceived the Wolfriders camped beside the stream.

The rain fell with a sudden fury, and the elves and wolves scurried for the dubious shelter of the bank. Neme's body was wet now as well, but that did not concern her. She was too fascinated by the way the leaves gave to the pressure of the rain, and the soil absorbed the water that fell.

Here at the top of the world, the soil was stretched as thin across the stone as the skin of a starved beast over its bones. Water soaked swiftly into what earth there was, and when the soil could contain no more, began to pool in hollows and sheet across bare stone. She rejoiced as thunderclaps shook the heavens, rock trembled, and more rain poured down.

The little stream was becoming a torrent. Water leaped from every outcropping, scoured every crevice, funneled through every fold in the stone, tugging loose pebbles, leaves, and fallen branches free and carrying them onward, at first sluggishly, and then with gathering power.

The flood grew quickly. In the time it would have taken an elf to shoot a quiverful of arrows and gather them up again, the stream had changed from trickle to torrent. Now the upper canyon roared with the rush of swirling waters. Small branches gouged at the banks and tangled in larger ones to form temporary dams until the growing force of the waters blasted both free. Collecting and bursting in stages the river rushed downward, scouring all that lay in its path, and Neme's spirit shared the explosion of raw energy.

When the waters reach the pass, the Wolfriders will be swept away. . . . came the thought of her mother. The statement held neither accusation nor sorrow. It was simply an observation, leaving her own response free. Neme felt a tremor shake her spirit as emotions she thought she had left behind her with her body stirred. Why should the plight of bodied creatures move her?

If the flood takes them they will only be transformed, and become as we are now. . . . she protested.

Those who were left behind cannot survive without them, came her father's reply. **The Wolfriders will be no more.**

In the canyon, the waters roared like a longtooth balked of prey. The communication of the elves was timeless, but the flood was growing fast.

Isn't it better to be like this, without the anxiety of the search for food and shelter, the body's pain at wounds and the spirit's pain at loss? Was she arguing with her parents or with herself, now?

Or without the pleasure of tasting fresh meat, feeling the warm caress of the sun or the cool kiss of rain, without the delight of a lover's touch and the warm weight of a cub in your arms? Emotion throbbed in her mother's thought now.

We chose the adventure of living as physical creatures! Without that, we could not be what we are now! her father added passionately. **If the tribe dies, all that we have suffered and learned will have been in vain!**

But it was her mother's words that struck home, as truly as one of Stormlight's spears. Memory was like a fire exploding through Goodtree's being. Vividly she remembered Lionleaper's strength and Acorn's sensitivity. Joygleam's dour fortitude and Freshet's unflagging humor; from the oldest beard to the smallest tousle-headed cub she remembered them, and as a mother loves her cub she loved them, knowing all their faults and virtues, and all at once her own fears were forgotten in a greater agony.

As if a bowstring drawn to the breaking point had been suddenly released, Goodtree's spirit snapped back to her body again. She convulsed and moaned, soaked and shaking with cold, so confused by the abruptness of her transition that for precious moments she was not sure where she was or why.

Then a fresh gust of wind sent needles of rain against her, and she pushed herself upright with a cry. The grove was a maelstrom of thrashing branches, and the wind howled louder than any wolves. She strove to focus her will, sending with all her strength to Joygleam, Chipper—any of the elves in the pass.

But they were too far, or perhaps too distracted by the storm, to hear. Gathering her strength once more, she reached outward to the peak above the valley, and was rewarded by an incredulous response from Acorn.

Flash flood's coming down the canyon! Can't reach the others—*send*—they have to climb out of the way!

Yes! I'll try—

More faintly, she heard Lionleaper vowing to go with Fang to warn them. But could they be in time? Sobbing, she collapsed back to the muddy grass, letting her spirit expand once more into the elemental chaos around her. Again she rode on the wings of the wind and felt the force of the waters that were hurtling down the canyon.

She could see, also, the tiny figures of the elves and their wolf companions, huddled sodden and terrified. But the chaos rushing down upon them filled the canyon well above the rocks where they had taken refuge. If Acorn's message had reached them, they had not understood it, and Lionleaper could never get to them in time.

NO! Goodtree did not know to whom she was sending, but she *could not* lose them, not now, when she had just understood how much she loved them all!

Mother! Father! Help me!

We have no power in your world—use what you have learned!

Learned? But what did she know except that those she loved were going to die, and she was helpless to prevent it? And what had she learned in her vision besides her name?

And at the thought, as if she was Recognizing herself, the syllable that was her soulname resounded once more in her awareness. *Neme* . . . a sound which held the essence of all that she had experienced, the totality of living strength and green, growing things . . . and trees. . . .

And trees! She understood their slow transformations, but if she could somehow accelerate those processes—

—With no more time for thinking, Goodtree thrust her awareness toward the canyon, finding roots deep in the walls just ahead of the waters. A sharp nudge set a loosened rock-face clattering toward the streambed; diverted waters sluiced earth after it, but she knew that would not hold for long. There, where the earth had fallen, tangled masses of brambles now swung free. Pouring all her concentration into them, she stimulated growth and sent them reaching greedily for the rocks that had fallen into the stream.

Nothing could get through a bramble patch—she knew that from painful experience—but a sufficient force of water might wash the whole mass away.

Above the brambles grew some twisted pines. With a frantic apology, she wrenched the roots free, launched two of the bigger trees downward to strengthen the dam, slid several saplings after them in a shower of earth, and stimulated them to lace powerful roots through all the rest.

And then there was no more time to do anything. With a roar like the world ending, the flood funneled down through the canyon, struck the logjam, and burst upward in a fountain of muddy spray.

Goodtree thrust her consciousness into the heart of the dam, reaching out to each vine and tree and tendril like a warchief sending to her fighters, rallying, compelling, holding them to their places through sheer force of will. She shuddered to the buffeting as storms of water strove against her; held on while the pressure crushed her, and then clung still harder until she knew no more. . . .

Like a longtooth balked of its prey the snarling waters tore at the unexpected barrier. Streams spouted between rocks and poured over the top of the dam in a hundred waterfalls. Gradually, the level behind it fell, but by the time the water reached the shallow streambed above the pass, the Wolfriders had all scrambled to safety on higher ground.

As if the flood had been no more than a cub's tantrum, the clouds were brightening, separating, and letting the spring sunlight through. Light glittered on wet rock surfaces, and glowed in the steam from soaked soil.

Clinging to one of the pine trees that had remained on the rim of the canyon, Lionleaper stared down at the disorganized tangle below in wonder. Floodwaters could do strange things, he knew, but it was hard to believe that a construction of such complexity could have been achieved by chance. And yet, if it had not been chance, what power had saved them?

"It feels like magic—" said Acorn, leaning nervously over the edge. "Timmorn's blood! What a song this is going to make one day!"

"Let's not start talking about stories until we know the ending—" Lionleaper answered grimly. "We still don't know what happened to Goodtree!"

"There will be a song, perhaps my greatest, whatever the outcome. I know the power that drives me. . . ." Acorn straightened with a sigh. "But there will be no joy for me in the making of it if the ending is tragedy." He met Lionleaper's eyes soberly. His face was smudged, and damp brown hair clung close to his skull; scarcely a sight to charm a maiden. But Lionleaper supposed he looked no better. He could scarcely bear to wonder what condition Goodtree was in now.

"Have you felt—" The warrior could not finish his question, but Acorn understood him.

"Nothing—not death, not life. I get no sense of Goodtree at all. . . ."

"Well let's go find her then!" said Lionleaper explosively. "And if that cursed she-wolf of hers tries to stop us I'll strangle her!"

Goodtree swam up out of endless depths of darkness to awareness of pain that almost sent her back again. But someone was calling her, not by her soulname, but with a depth of anguish that compelled her attention. She took a deep, aching breath, letting awareness extend to limbs that felt as if they had been beaten with sticks. Exhalation became a moan, and abruptly she was shivering.

High ones! Her skin is like ice! We've got to get her warm somehow!

The sending had a familiar flavor, but she was too tired to identify it. She felt motion; her body was turned, and another naked body pressed against her back. She tried to curl up to protect her belly, but someone else was there, holding her close, and her feet touched the familiar rough warmth of wolf-fur.

Leafchaser? After an unmeasurable time Goodtree summoned her wits sufficiently to grope for the touch of her old friend's mind. She felt a kind of anxious amusement in return.

Silly cub! Don't leave me behind again!

Well perhaps she was a cub at that. Certainly she was curled up like a cub with its litter-mates, all tangled together. Returning circulation was gradually ceasing to be painful; she sighed and pressed closer to whoever was holding her, wondering where she was.

"Goodtree?" came a whisper in her ear. "Are you awake?"

Scent identified Lionleaper, but then who was behind her? Goodtree forced open her eyes and met his anxious smile. She blinked in confusion, shifted in his arms to look around and met Acorn's brown gaze, deep as a forest pool. It was their body heat that was warming her, and a warmth of the spirit came to her from them as well that welcomed her back to consciousness. She gazed from one to the other in wonder. Back at the hurst they had been unacknowledged rivals, but now she sensed only harmony.

The faces of the two elves had a radiance that came only partly from joy. The light was golden; Goodtree looked beyond them and saw sunlight filtered through fluttering green-gold leaves.

The Golden Grove! Abruptly she remembered her journey, and the storm, and her name. She stiffened in their arms.

''The tribe—'' Talking was painful, and she switched to the speech of the mind. **Are the Wolfriders safe? Did the dam stop the flood in time?**

That was your work then! Yes, they're all safe, and thanking the high ones for a miracle! sent Lionleaper, but from Acorn came another question, **Goodtree, why did you come here? What have you become?**

She closed her eyes in relief, wondering how to answer them. She seemed to be a treeshaper, she thought, remembering how the vines and pine trees had obeyed her, and perhaps in time she would discover other masteries. But that was not what she needed to say.

Goodtree turned over so that she could slip an arm about the songshaper and the warrior as well and hold them as they had held her. She swallowed, meeting their eyes, and made her voice obey her will.

''I'm the chieftain of the Wolfriders now. . . .''

"Must we always fight with the humans?" Woodlock asked as he braided flower stems together for Rainsong's hair.

"It's fight or run, isn't it? And we've done enough of both since the high ones came here," Rainsong replied sadly.

They were the quietest and gentlest of the Wolfriders. It was fortunate they'd been born near the same time and found each other. It would have been more fortunate, Longreach considered, if they'd been born when Prey-Pacer was chief or Freefoot or one of the other rare times when Wolfriders and humans did not intrude on each other's hunting grounds.

"I wish they'd just tie their bundles on their backs and go someplace else. We were here first." Her voice held both the hopes and the angers of the innocent. "The Father Tree is the Wolfriders' home—why can't they understand that?"

And wasn't that the problem? Never before had the Wolfriders stayed in one place so long, but since Goodtree had worked her magics on this grove it had been home to the tribe and none of them could imagine leaving it. The humans had changed too, put down their own sort of roots and made their own Father Tree, not with living magic but with piles of stone and little bowers where everything grew in straight, unnatural lines.

"Wouldn't they ask the same of us?" Longreach asked softly. "They have been by the caves a long time themselves."

Woodlock shook his head, his eyes growing uncommonly

fierce. "It's ours—everything we can see from the highest branches of the Father Tree. It belongs to our wolves and it belongs to us."

Longreach shook his head. Such belligerence, such a sense of possessing—was this truly Goodtree's legacy through the Father Tree?

Rainsong took the finished flower-wreath and placed in on her hair, but the hard look did not fade from her eyes. "Someday," she whispered, forcing the thought deep into her mind where she'd find it no matter how wildly the wolf-song sang. "Someday we'll frighten them away."

The storyteller gathered his legs under him and pushed himself to his feet. There were stories—sad stories—that had an answer for her bitterness. But Bearclaw's Wolfriders could no longer hear them or learn from them. Strange—because they were almost all about Bearclaw's father—

Lessons in Passing
by Robert Lynn Asprin

The child was not far from the village center, playing in the sun as his mother worked in front of their hut. Suddenly, a movement as small as a butterfly's wing turning on a flower caught his eye. One of the forest demons was standing at the edge of the woods watching him with a half-bemused smile.

He had heard of them, of course, and even glimpsed one once when the tribe had surprised a few of them at the river. His parents warned him of them when they said they loved him, and threatened him with them when he was bad. Once, when he was still a baby, he had dared to tell his mother he thought they were beautiful and had been thrashed for his honesty: once by his mother, and again by his father after his mother told him of the indiscretion. Now he knew better and kept his thoughts to himself.

Child and forest demon examined each other with open curiosity.

The demon didn't look dangerous. If anything, being closer to the child's size, he seemed less threatening than the adults who ruled his existence. True, his hair was wild and unkempt, but that made him seem even less like an adult and added to his mysterious allure.

The forest demon smiled fully now and beckoned to the child before disappearing into the brush.

The child started to follow reflexively, then hesitated. If he was caught playing with a forest demon . . .

He shot a guilty glance at his mother, but she was engrossed in her work, oblivious to her son's temptation.

Maybe just for a little while. She would never know. . . .

The forest demon appeared again; this time his summoning gesture was a bit more impatient. His grin expanded to show mischievous eyes and teeth before he vanished.

The lure was too great. The child headed into the brush after his new playmate, unmindful of the brief stretch of almost-dry mud which lay, as if by accident, across his path.

The mother finished her task of preparing the ingredients for their evening meal and glanced around for her son. As was her practice, she had saved something for him—a small handful of berries this time—as a reward for not bothering her while she worked.

The fact he was not immediately in sight did not alarm her, as he was inclined to wander. When a casual search in and around their hut failed to disclose him, however, her concern grew.

Her husband had a notoriously poor temper, and she was reluctant to call attention to her negligence if, indeed, the child had simply wandered. On the other hand, if their only son was truly endangered . . .

Caught in indecision, she wandered closer to the edge of the woods, peering anxiously into the shadows, hoping to find her youngster curled up asleep in the shade. Almost by chance, her eyes fell on the stretch of mud, and her heart faltered in her chest.

A moment later she was running back into the village, shrieking her panic as she went. She had no thoughts for the berries still clenched in her fist, their juice streaking her arm as her tears streaked her face. Also gone were any worries about her husband's temper. Such fears now meant no more to her than the berries.

There were two sets of tracks in the mud: one the barefoot trail of her child, and the other . . .

The forest demons had their son—and only swift action from her husband and the other hunters could save him!

The forest demon smiled at the child as he led him deeper into the forest. His name was Mantricker, and he had earned it many times over through his antics with the humans.

Through his early life, he had lived with the rest of the Wolfriders in blissful ignorance of the tall, five-fingered hunters and their ways—save what was recounted by the story-tellers. The tribe's move to the holt had removed the humans to the realm of legend; their importance grew or diminished depending on the story.

Then the humans arrived again, drawn to the area by the same plentiful game and water that had first attracted the elves. As soon as their appearance was noted, all the old arguments among the Wolfriders of how to deal with the humans erupted again, as if they had never stopped. With the death of his mother, Goodtree, the chieftainship had fallen to Mantricker, and with it the arguments.

Some of the tribe favored moving again rather than having to deal with the intruders. Others were ready to take arms and drive the humans from the area. The territoriality of their wolf-blood boiled at the idea of surrendering their hunting ground to another group, particularly a group as inept in the woods as the humans. The majority of the elves, however, listened to the arguments in confusion, then turned to their chief for leadership.

Mantricker himself could see no clear path in the matter. On the one hand, he strongly resisted the idea of leaving the holt Goodtree had labored so long to build. It was the tribe's home and to be defended at all costs. Unfortunately, he was equally repelled by the idea of open combat with the humans. Even if the tribe could win, they would lose. That is to say, they would lose their way of life; the idyllic existence that made them different from the humans. He argued hotly with the advocates of war saying that to fight the humans, they would have to become like the humans: killing what was feared or could not be understood.

So the arguments continued. Though they might lie dormant for turns on end, eventually some comment or incident would spark the debates anew. In the meantime, the situation remained unchanged, with humans and elves dwelling in dangerous proximity.

Finally, Mantricker had hit on a solution that was uniquely his own. Since open combat wouldn't work for a variety of reasons, the humans would have to be convinced that this area was not desirable for them. Mantricker, along with the rest of the elves, believed that humans were always at war with their environment. All he would have to do was convince the human tribes that their wars were going badly.

So began the campaign that confirmed Mantricker's name many times over. He became a self-appointed nemesis of the five-fingered invaders. He spooked game away from the human hunters and sprang their traps so that often their village went hungry. He spent two eights-of-days building a hidden dam that dried the humans water creek overnight. Spying on their village, he heard them whispering about angry forest demons. Rather than anger their invisible tormentors the humans hauled their water from a different, distant creek, but they stayed in their village and continued their blundering ways in the forest.

Mantricker adopted new strategies: slipping into their village at night, stealing weapons or food, openly confounding their efforts to live a comfortable or secure life. In response, the humans began leaving stacks of weapons and food outside their village, trying to appease the forest devils who sought their treasures invisibly by night—but still they stayed.

Throughout his efforts, Mantricker had to deal with growing resistance within his own tribe. While most agreed that his solution was worth trying, without exception they protested his decision to take all the risks himself. It was too dangerous, they argued. More than that, it was the tribe's right to share the risk, and the fun, of the campaign.

Mantricker stood firm. Surprising many who had seen weakness in the young chief's earlier indecision, he gave precise orders and demanded strict obedience so long as he was their acknowledged chief. True, the task was dangerous, but bringing all the Wolfriders to the human village would multiply rather than reduce the risk. He had decided on this action to preserve the elfin way of life and shield the tribe from danger . . . not increase the contacts between humans and elves. The idea was his, and so too would be the danger.

Unwilling to challenge their chief, the tribe respected his orders though they didn't like what was happening. They liked even less the next tactic their chief tried after his earlier efforts proved fruitless.

Frustrated by the humans' dogged determination to stay,

Mantricker tried an even bolder approach. He now showed himself to an occasional hunting party, warning them to leave the lands. If they pursued, he would lead them far afield, then double back, obscuring their tracks and signs so that they became lost in the forest. After a few terrifying rounds of this, the humans learned to signal to each other by beating on hollow logs, but they ignored the meaning behind his warnings and stayed.

Today, Mantricker was embarked on yet another attempt to convince the humans to leave. This trick was one that the chief did not like himself, but he was growing desperate. If the humans would not leave to save themselves, perhaps they would move to protect their children.

Studying the child anew, he hoped the humans cared as much for their cubs as the elves did for their own. Everything he had seen so far while watching the village seemed to indicate that they did. If not, today's lesson on vulnerability would fall once again on deaf ears.

The young human was fearless as he blundered along in playful pursuit. More than once the chief found himself laughing at the child's antics as he would at cubs of his own tribe. If only humans could be frozen at this age, like wildcat kittens, then maybe elves and humans could live together in peace. Unfortunately kittens became wildcats, and little humans became big humans all too fast. In the adult form, both were deadly and unpredictable.

In midlaugh, Mantricker's thoughts leaped unbidden to his own cub, and his smile faded.

He was worried about his cub. . . . No, his son really couldn't be called a cub anymore. Bearclaw had already gained his physical maturity, and his performance in the hunt that won him his name left no doubt as to his ability to take his place beside the other hunters of the tribe. Still, Mantricker had difficulty thinking of him as an adult.

The chief had told his lifemate and his son of his new plan, though he had not confided in the tribe as a whole. His lifemate had been fearful, but supportive, as she was in all his plans. Whether she took this position because she believed in his thinking or because she knew she could not dissuade him he didn't know, nor did he want to. The unpopularity of his scheme was already making him feel isolated and alone, and he was afraid of losing one of his few remaining confidants.

Bearclaw, on the other hand, crowed enthusiastic over the plot and renewed his pleas to be included in his father's activities. His eagerness to pursue a plan Mantricker himself judged dangerous distressed him both as a father and as the Wolfriders' chief. His son had a wild streak in him, a recklessness he did not recall from his own youth. Tales of Rahnee and Two-Spear flashed across his mind, and he found himself wondering, not for the first time, if Bearclaw was one of those throwbacks that occurred from time to time in the tribe: one who was more wolf than elf. The youth's enthusiasm over his father's schemes always seemed more centered on the thrill and glory of the moment than on any adherence to a goal or long-term plan. Still, Mantricker loved his son deeply and hoped he would have time to complete his growth before the burdens of chiefhood were thrust upon him.

Unbidden, a new thought thrust itself into Mantricker's head. How similar were the feelings of humans and elves toward their offspring? A threat to the Wolfriders' cubs wouldn't scare them away, but rather kindle a flame of anger and resentment that would never die.

For a moment, the elf faltered in his resolve, but then the calls of the pursuers reached the child's ears. Mantricker had been listening for some time, but now the child had heard and was looking around, confused, there was little choice but to see the plan through.

"Call to them," he said, smiling at the child. "Your hunters need all the help they can get."

The child hesitated.

"Don't worry. They'll blame me, not you. Call to them."

As the child raised its voice in answer to the hunters, Mantricker tried unsuccessfully to convince himself that there was no need for bloodletting. No. His verbal warnings had always been ignored. He had decided at the conception of this plan that blood would be necessary to drive the lesson home.

The hunting party was noisier than usual, and the child's father was painfully aware of that fact. By including nearly every man of the village who could carry a weapon, he had also brought along many whose inability to keep quiet had long since barred them from the better hunting groups. Even the skilled hunters were making a racket, complaining loudly that they were being led into trouble. Never before had a forest demon left such an obvious trail. There was no doubt in their mind that they were being tricked again, baited into doing exactly what the forest demon wanted.

The child's father was aware of the danger, but he didn't care as he pressed the party for even greater speed. Whatever threats the hunters might be exposed to were nothing compared to those same threats directed toward his son, alone and unarmed. His only fear was that the noise of their passage might scare the forest demon into disappearing and taking his child with it.

Finally, abandoning all hope of silence, the father raised his voice and called to his son, hoping against hope that speed would do what stealth could not. The other hunters took up the cry and soon the father had a new fear: that their adult voices would drown out any response his child might make. He was about to command them into silence once more when he heard the plaintive warble. His son's voice . . . or at least the voice of a young human child and there could only be one this far out in the woods. The call came again, prodding the father into swift action as he called back to the hunters then plunged recklessly in the direction of the sound. The boy didn't sound scared. Perhaps he had somehow escaped the clutches of the forest demon and was now wandering free. If so, they had to reach him before the forest demon found him again by following the same call.

Bursting through the brush into a clearing, the father froze at the sight before him. He barely had the presence of mind to throw his arms wide, restraining the hunters behind him from a headlong rush into the catastrophe.

His son was there at the far side of the clearing, but so was the forest demon, standing just behind the boy with one hand resting lightly on the child's shoulder.

"Leave our forest!" the demon called. "Go back where you came from. The forest is ours and we don't want you! I've warned you before, you don't belong here! Even if you fight us, which you can't, there are your children! Now go!"

There was a sudden flash of light. The father saw, too late, that it was a knife, and blood sprang from the boy's cheek.

The hunters charged into the clearing with an animal cry, but the forest demon had already darted out of sight into the brush. Without knowing how he got there, the father was kneeling by his son.

"Are you hurt? Is it deep?"

Without waiting for a response he seized the boy's head roughly and turned it to find the answers for himself. The wound was not deep, but it ran from the point of the jaw to the hairline, narrowly missing the eye. The eyes themselves held more shock than pain, and the tears were beginning to well as the child began to sort out the confusion of the flurry of activity. It wasn't a life-threatening wound but they should get his son back to the village without delay.

"Let's go!" the father called to the men who were hurling their spears into the brush without aim or target. "Stop that! You're only throwing away your weapons! The demon's long gone now."

With that, he gathered the child in his arms and set out for the village, neither looking nor caring if anyone followed.

Bloodsinger was roused from a deep slumber by a sending so strong he flinched from it as if it were a physical blow. Instantly alert, he rolled to his feet and stood quivering as his wet nose tested the air. There was nothing in the immediate area to pose a threat, but still his gray-black fur rose in fear and warning.

The sending was from his elf-friend. Strange. Their hunts together had become so infrequent that his rider had sunk from the wolf's Now-dominated thinking into vague memory. Still the bond of loyalty remained strong, and Bloodsinger would no more think of ignoring the sending than he could conceive of not hearing the call of the pack.

The summons came again, weaker this time, as if the sender had exhausted himself with his first desperate plea. The wolf was in motion at once, going from statue stillness to a full run in the space of a few steps. His rider's second sending had established direction, if not actual location, and that was all the information Bloodsinger needed to spring into action.

Forest animals are never completely oblivious to their surroundings, however, and as he ran Bloodsinger caught the scent of the man-pack. His elf-friend's call, which had been distress as much as it had been a summons, came from the center of the scent. Ivory fangs showed long and sharp as a low growl escaped his throat, but he did not break stride.

This growl, which continued to rumble in his throat, was his trademark, the trait which had given him his name. Unlike his packmates, who hunted in silence, Bloodsinger's eagerness while on the scent expressed itself in growls or small yips of anticipation. Needless to say this tended to spook the game prematurely, but his strength and speed allowed him to make the kill even after giving his prey a warning. It was dangerous to warn the man-pack, or so his elf-friend had told him when they stopped hunting together. An involuntary growl might be annoying on a hunt, but it would be disastrous on a mission of stealth. Bloodsinger did not object or even follow his rider at a hidden distance; he didn't hunt the man-pack. Normally he shunned their range, as did most of the wolf-pack; it was easy enough as the man-pack never tried to hide their stench.

Now, however, he was being called and called desperately into the man-pack's territory. While the wolf never sought out a fight, he would not swerve from protecting what he considered to be his, and that included not only the wolf-pack but his elf-friend and Wolfriders as well. If the humans wanted trouble, he'd make it for them.

Another sending came, and the wolf altered his course slightly. Even though this call was even weaker than the second, the beast sensed he was nearing his objective and slowed to a trot. Loyalty was fine, but his natural cunning told him to investigate the situation before rushing in blindly.

At last he saw his rider and drew to a halt, his ears cocked forward in query. Something was wrong. The elf was on his feet, but holding onto a tree limb with both hands for support. Following the instinct which lets predators avoid sick animals, the wolf circled to study his elf-friend more closely.

Midway around, Bloodsinger saw and understood the problem. One of the man-pack's throwing fangs protruded from his elf-friend's back. It was as long as the elf was tall, and heavy, too, as it sagged to the ground. Reassured that it was not sickness or madness which made his elf-friend tremble, yet concerned by the blood-on-metal smell of the glade, the wolf whined and drew closer.

"Bloodsinger . . . you're here. . . . Good. . . . I was afraid you . . ."

The beast didn't understand the words, but felt the emotion of relief behind them. While the joy of meeting was shared,

Bloodsinger was still perturbed by the throwing fang. A throwing fang meant dead-meat, but his elf-friend wasn't—couldn't be—dead-meat.

Seizing the throwing fang in his mouth, Bloodsinger tried to remedy the paradox the only way he could: jerking his head from side to side until the two were no longer connected. It worked and the throwing fang wrenched free, but his satisfaction was overridden by a sudden dark sending from his rider who arched in pain-tension for a moment, then hung weakly from the tree branch.

Dropping the stick, the wolf tried to lick the wound, but the elf threw a groping arm across him and drew him into eye contact.

"Bloodsinger . . ."

The wolf waited as the familiar weight shifted into his back with uncharacteristic slowness, but instead of feeling the balanced poise of his rider, the burden suddenly went limp and still. After a few moments, the strangeness of the situation began to vex the animal.

No orders. No low conversation. Not even a guiding pressure from the knees. What did his elf-friend want?

Bloodsinger was already aware that something was seriously wrong with his elf-friend, but was unsure of what to do about it. When a wolf feels unwell, he usually pulls apart from the pack to heal or die. His rider, however, had specifically summoned him. Did he want company? Companionship?

Partly in an effort to comply with his rider's probable wishes, and partly in an effort to get help in a puzzling situation, the wolf decided to carry his rider back to the Father Tree, where the other elves made their lairs. Yes. That was a good plan. Did they not pull painful thorns and such from between toe-pads?

Bloodsinger turned toward his decided destination, but was forced to halt almost immediately as his burden lurched sideways across his back. There was a moment of cold predator appraisal, but then the decision was reached that the distance was too great to drag his rider in his jaws. With a whine, the wolf started on his journey once more, walking slowly this time and choosing his path carefully so as not to dislodge his delicate load.

Beehunter was the first at the holt to realize anything was wrong. Picking his way along one of the upper branches of the Great Tree, his eye was suddenly drawn by a movement along the creek-bed. It was a wolf, and in a moment he identified it as Bloodsinger. That in itself was unusual, for their wayward chief's wolf-friend was seldom seen these days, much less near the holt. And what was he doing? The beast was moving unnaturally slow. He wasn't tracking or hunting for his head was held high, so what— Then Beehunter saw the figure on Bloodsinger's back.

Before Beehunter reached the ground, his sending had alerted the holt, and the elves gathered around the wolf and their chief. Even as they eased Mantricker to the ground, dark glances were exchanged, for the terrible wound was all too apparent, and the tribe's healer was off with the hunt, as was the chief's lifemate. Though the spark of life still flickered, there was not a one of the assemblage who doubted it would soon fade, though none cared to state it out loud. The Wolfriders never died a peaceful death; when death came it was invariably a sudden and unexpected guest.

"Father!"

The small crowd gave way as Bearclaw dashed to the chief's side. He assessed the situation with a glance and grabbed the shoulder of the nearest Wolfrider.

"Quick. Get the hunters. Take Bloodsinger and—"

"No."

Mantricker's voice was almost too weak to be heard, but it still carried the firmness of authority.

"But Father . . ."

It's too late, my son. Besides, the tribe needs meat now more than they need a chief . . . at least, this chief.

Bearclaw sucked in his breath sharply, but signaled for the others to stay where they were.

Mantricker tried to raise his arm, but tensed at the agony of the movement and it sank back to his side.

"Someone . . . untie my topknot."

Bearclaw started to do his father's bidding, but his hands halted as if they had encountered a wall. He raised pleading eyes to the others, and Beehunter stepped forward to remove the chief's sign of office.

"Bearclaw shall . . . be your new chief. He . . . will be a better leader . . . than I was for . . . he is closer to the tribe."

With tremendous effort, Mantricker raised his head and looked around the group. Seeing no objections, he closed his eyes and let his head drop.

Learn from my mistakes, young chief. Do not let your duty set you apart from the tribe. Be with them, share with them. And the humans . . . do not underestimate them. They are not so different as we think. They love their cubs. I was wrong to attack them unprovoked, even alone. There may even be a chance—

Then there was silence. The total silence which can only be final. Mantricker was gone, his final thoughts as closed to the tribe as his life had become.

Bloodsinger rose and whined, his ears alert. He had also noted the passing spark. His elf-friend had become dead-meat, and that he knew how to deal with.

Silently, solemnly, the elves draped their dead chief's body across the back of his wolf, and watched as the beast bore it away into the shadows of the forest.

Bearclaw was the last to turn from the sight. When he did, he found the eyes of the group upon him, and tasted for the first time the pressures of leadership.

"There will be a howl tonight," he said. "Let the talking be done there when we are all assembled."

With that, he turned his back on the tribe and, like a wolf, went off by himself to nurse his pain.

The night was chilly, but few felt it as the last echoes of the assembly howling died away. All were eager to hear what their new chief had to say, for his appointment had been confirmed as soon as the hunting party had returned, his own mother tying the topknot on his head. Even the wolves who had joined their elf-friends sat with their ears forward as if waiting for words they could not understand.

Bearclaw stood up then, and if his new topknot was unsteady, he was not.

"The path of the Wolfriders has always been decided by their chief," he began abruptly. "It is therefore your right to know the mind of your new chief as it affects your lives . . . to know of any changes I will make in the Way.

"I am young, younger than many of you, but old enough to know the ignorance of my youth. For that reason, I will continue to follow the ways of my father unless events prove those ways must be changed."

A low murmur started, but he held up his hand for silence.

"One thing I will change immediately, however, for in his dying moments Mantricker taught me a lesson. No longer will your chief leave the tribe to harass the humans, nor will any Wolfrider strike at them unless attacked or provoked. We will try to share our range with them, to live in peace if possible."

Growls rather than murmurs met this announcement, but Bearclaw silenced them with a snarl.

"Do you think *I* like this decision? This day the humans have killed your chief, but he was my father. A part of me cries for vengeance, but a greater part speaks with the heaviness of a chief. Mantricker knew the risks of his actions, and they finally caught up with him as we all knew it would one day. His last words were an admission that he was wrong, that the humans are not so different as we think. Am I then to ignore this lesson and attack the humans? Shall I provoke them because they struck back at an elf who now admits he was wrong? As your chief, I am now responsible for the entire tribe, and if there is a chance we can live at peace with the humans, it must be done!''

As the young chief supported his decision, Brightwater, the tribe's storyteller, popped another dreamberry into her mouth. Soon it would be her turn, and she had never spoken at a howl prompted by a chief's death before. Nervousness made her overindulge in the berries as she prepared to delve into her memory, and images were beginning to wash over her, overlaying the moonlit howl.

What to do about the humans? It seemed the Wolfriders' history revolved around that question. Make war against them with Two-Spear's reckless abandon? Try to avoid them as Tanner had done? Chief after chief paraded in her head, yet none had had a truly workable or enduring answer. Not Mantricker, and, she feared, not Bearclaw.

"Timmorn Yellow-Eyes, Rahnee the She-Wolf . . ."

The chief-saying had begun. What was she to say when it was over?

". . . Prey-Pacer, Two-Spear . . ."

What tale of the past could she summon that would not cast aspersions on their new chief's decision? It would be totally inappropriate to say that she thought that not only Mantricker, but Bearclaw as well, was wrong . . . that disaster loomed in the chosen path.

". . . Huntress Skyfire, Freefoot . . ."

In desperation she leaned forward and rested her head in her arms, feigning sleep. Let the tribe laugh at the storyteller who had too many dreamberries and fell asleep during a howl. Better that than admit the lessons her memory was summoning up.

*   *   *

Not far away, another gathering was being held. The human hunters pressed closer to the warmth of their fire and tried to pool their knowledge. How many of the forest demons were there? How were they armed? Could the hunters hold their village if attacked?

At length, one rose to address the assemblage. It was the father of the boy who had been taken that day.

"Why do we babble like frightened women?" he demanded. "We have no choice. If nothing else, today has taught us that the forest demons are evil and cannot be trusted. We have tried to live in peace with them, to appease their thieving with gifts, and they show their gratitude by taking our children.

"Now they tell us that if we go, they will leave us alone. I ask you, can we believe them? My son trusted one, and now he lies in our hut with a wound on his face. I say whether it's here or at another camp we must take a stand against these demons, so why not here? We must guard ourselves and our families, and if that means attacking first, then so be it. That is the lesson I've learned this day, as has my son. We will never forget it. Tell your sons, and your sons' sons, that they will not have to learn it as painfully as we did!"

The group rose to their feet shouting their approval and spears were shaken at the surrounding woods.

Thus it was that two groups raised their voices that night, one in howls, the other in shouts, commemorating the lessons they had learned, lessons on which they would base their futures.

Pike sat cross-legged on the rock, his lower lip stuck out as far as his unruly thatch of bangs. **I don't want to,** he sent unnecessarily.

"You agreed when I showed you where the dreamberry bushes were and when I showed you how to dry them so they wouldn't lose their flavor or their power."

"That was then, this is *now*."

Longreach drew his brows together, giving a hint that he hadn't always been everybody's friend; that he had, in Freefoot's day, run as wild and stubborn as any Wolfrider could imagine; that he had not been the dreamberry guardian until after Bearclaw brewed up his first batch of dreamberry wine and scared poor Brightwater out of her wits.

"*Now* is what I'm talking about. *Now* is when you learn to do something beside *eating* the dreamberries. I'm not going to do this forever and I've chosen you to take my place."

"What about Skywise?" The lower lip didn't stick out quite as far now.

"A dreamkeeper is like a chief and Skywise—" Longreach hesitated as images of the deep-thinking young hunter played through his mind. "Skywise doesn't *go* where the other Wolfriders go. No one but he, himself, can follow the dreams he keeps."

"They could follow mine?" The young elf sat straight, eyes wide and eager for *now*.

Anyone could have followed Pike's dreams. Pike—the most ordinary of the Wolfriders—a rarity among Bearclaw's tribe, as he had been born to lovemates, not lifemates—Rain's son outside of Recognition. His eyes he'd gotten from his mother but the rest—well, they all saw a bit of themselves in Pike.

"They'll follow once you learn to lead them."

Pike gave a tug at his cheek-tuft, pulling it back from his face. The hair came untamed as soon as he nodded his head. "I can always try, I guess, for *now*."

"Think of it as another reason for the dreamberries," Longreach said, hiding a smile as Pike's face turned red as the berries themselves. "Now it's always best to start with a tale that you know."

The lower lip flared out for a heartbeat, then retreated. "Bearclaw, then," Pike said, grabbing a heaping handful of berries. "And . . . and . . . Joyleaf's favorite necklace."

"You're learning fast. Don't give anything away."

Night Hunt

―――――――*by Diane Carey*―――――――

The beast moved nearer to the cave mouth. Even the fires crackling softly could not dissuade the tug of a stronger instinct. The smell of blood made feral nostrils flare, and the beast's eyes narrowed in anticipation. Only the sky was angrier.

But this was not the anger born from having been threatened, nor fear of any kind; rather, it was born of indignation and the boiling struggle between thought and instinct. The beast knew in her intelligent mind that death waited here, but not the natural death to which she would someday submit in a cuff of sleep. Death in this place, because of its violence, would make her fight and bring to the surface every reflex of survival. The suffering, then, would last much longer. She would feel these creatures' claws, feel her flesh rip between their teeth, and even though she knew death was coming, she would fight all the harder. Nothing like going to sleep in the coolness of her own den.

She smelled the object of her quest. Her heart thumped rapidly inside the rough, gray coat. Through the dark cave mouth she homed in on the blood—not the scent of butchery. This was the scent of need and she meant to answer it.

She moved forward, more like a cat than her own kind, only her lower legs and shoulder blades moving. As though to scoop up the scent, her head hung low. The aroma became succulent and drove her mad. She hardly blinked at all now. Behind her, the yellow glow from the campfires ended abruptly at a line of large rocks, which kept the breezes from moving inside the den. It was here . . . here, and very close.

Pausing as her eyes adjusted to the blackness, the beast picked out shapes on the cave floor—long rolls of animal skin, wooden receptacles full of fruit, a stone-lined cavity that had recently held fire but now was cool and ashy.

The beast moved in. Her own gray fur remained flat against her back instead of ruffled up in a crest as it might have been were she not the intruder here; this danger was of her own making. She hesitated only once, crouching back as one of the bundles on the floor groaned, rolled over, and settled down again. Still crouching, she crept forward and reached a wooden tub with a small roll of ravvit fur inside. She trembled violently now, in waves brought on both by tension and by the insurmountable drive she felt. Here was the source of the blood-scent—a pool of desires and needs and warmth.

She pulsed within herself. Her kind did not fully understand possession, but she had to have the bundle of ravvit fur.

So she took it. Suddenly. Quickly. Before the fear closed in. And she dragged it toward the cave mouth. When the long bundle behind the rocks stirred, the beast took the ravvit fur in her teeth and lifted it awkwardly, expecting it to fall apart. When it remained intact, she got a better grip and scrambled out of the cave, her paws scratching at the hard ground. Behind her the noises of panic arose to chase her out of the cave. They were awake. And they were shouting with their strange, cutting voices. The night was her friend and it hid her well. Soon she was gone.

The cave dwellers were all awake within seconds. When they pieced together the tragic bits of evidence, they came out of the caves and hunted along the ground until they found the beast's paw prints.

Then they began to light the torches.

Night over the holt felt wrong.

Upon low-hanging clouds flickered an unexpected patchy glow. The undersides of the clouds went orange, then gray-black, then orange again where the trees were thin. There was very little noise. A footfall . . . the rustle of hands pushing aside boughs and branches . . . quiet voices, very rare, worried.

Worried or *something*. Bearclaw tried to decide. The words could not be understood from this high up, this far away, but he heard the voices and their tremors and tones. He stayed hidden. It was his art.

Beside him, Strongbow's silence felt different tonight too. Not even the mild sensation of question crossed between him and Bearclaw, and Bearclaw felt stiff in that isolation. Both tall for elves—and Bearclaw even a bit taller than the archer— Bearclaw and Strongbow had to dip down slightly to see through the separation in the leaves before them.

The torches continued to move, slowly, across the forest floor. Tall hunters moved beneath them, each bearing a torch. They moved randomly, their only pattern being to spread outward, step by step, expanding the scope of their—

"What are they doing?" Woodlock crowded in beside Bearclaw in the privacy of their heavily-vined vantage point, unable to bear the tension.

Hunting, Strongbow decided, but only because it comforted him.

Bearclaw immediately said, "They're not hunting."

"Then what?" Woodlock asked, quietly moving a stray branch from his thick gold hair.

"I don't know," Bearclaw grumbled. "But I don't like it."

They've got to be hunting, Strongbow sent. **There's no other reason for it.**

"Humans don't hunt at night." Bearclaw watched only a few more seconds. "Those walking hairballs are afraid of the dark. Both of you stay here. Tell me if anything changes. I'm going back to the holt. I want to talk to Rain."

He traveled back to the Father Tree overground. The forest floor was unsafe tonight and Bearclaw had to have answers. The five-fingered hunters were predictable, and he disliked it when they decided not to be.

Tonight Bearclaw saw none of the holt's mythic beauty as he approached, saw nothing of the flickering fireflies against the dark tree shapes or the indigo patches of paler blue where moonbeams slanted through the canopy of leaves overhead. He missed entirely the prettiness of the holt's skirt of wildflowers and the brush of common weeds that added a cushiony comfort to the ancient trees. The great trunks flared out into tangles of roots as thick as Bearclaw's whole body, but tonight he used them as stepping-stones, without a thought of how important they were. He hopped over the thin brook that trickled through the center of the holt, and headed for the central tree.

Both above and below him twisted the snarl of timber and

leafage that was home for the Wolfriders. Treeshapers had made other trees grow into the Father Tree ages ago, creating a great knot of branches and trunks and tunnels and hollows. Thus, the holt had its own underground and overground systems, each tunnel or hollow carved out and weathered to smoothness by time and use. Bearclaw could hardly remember anymore which of the hollows had been created by tree-shapers he had known personally and which had been made by Goodtree herself. All he knew as he approached the embracing clutch of huge trees, nestled as they were in their cool evening cloak with its milky belts of moonlight, was that the holt looked particularly vulnerable to the bite of flames.

The Father Tree's usual mossy coolness closed around his shoulders as he slipped into the big opening that led to all the hollows. To his left was a stepway of chunks of wood carved out of the inner trunk. It led to the thick hollow branches where young Skywise lived, high up in the next tree, in a place where the stars could be watched. Bearclaw ignored it and headed down a packed slope, deep into the ground, to the hollows between the ancient root system there. Rain's hollow was the deepest in the holt. Here, in the earth's cool belly, Rain's healing herbs could be stored, and his lichens and mosses and mushrooms grew freely.

The walls were lined with animal skins, trapping in the warmth from a small fire glowing in a pit at the hollow's center. Few of the Wolfriders were comfortable with fire other than the little chunks of tallow Rain prepared for them, which they used to light their hollows, but Rain kept the small flame glowing both for warmth and for melting ingredients for the remedies he used. Tonight Bearclaw approached the opening to Rain's hollow as a cat approaches the water, seeing the fire more than anything else. For a long time he stood in the shadow of the opening, while Rain obliviously plucked seeds from a collection of nightbloomers he'd gathered. Rain's bushy sideburns and short chipmonkish features gave Bearclaw less comfort than usual. The coneshaped leather headpiece with its long tails made Rain's ears seem extra large, and his orange hair glowed unnaturally in the firelight. He went about his grinding, humming sweetly. He was always happiest while tending his herbs.

Bearclaw stood in the shadows, listening.

Rain reached for a jar of murrawort with one hand and popped a dreamberry into his mouth with the other, then went on humming. But when he brought down the jar, his eyes caught a shadow in the opening of his hollow—and he flinched.

"Oh . . . Bearclaw, are you hurt?" He buried his surprise in concern. Though they had already spent a long life together, he would never get used to the chief's blade-boned, blade-eyed face any more than he would get used to dealing with Bearclaw's imperishable will.

That face, bracketed by a triangle of whiskers, moved slowly into the hollow. Rain gathered in Bearclaw's rough, lean appearance, noting once again how the chief's eyes were nearly hidden by thick bangs. The fawn-brown hair was poorly cut and climbed down around his features like vines around a jutting of rocks. With the bound-up lock that marked him chief mounted high and shaggy, Bearclaw's wild mane seemed patterned after the turbulent mind it sheathed. Rain absorbed all that with some difficulty, as always.

"Why should I be hurt?" Bearclaw asked. His words were blunt as the thoughts of the wolves he ran with.

Rain shook off the effects of the ungracious entrance and moved toward him, proving to himself that Bearclaw had some other reason to be here. "I've never known you to come in from a night hunt without the others."

Bearclaw came fully out of the shadows. "Have you ever known the tall ones to hunt at night?"

Rain's narrow eyes grew narrower still. "A strange question." His voice was barely a whisper. He spoke so softly, the other Wolfriders sometimes wondered why he didn't just send all the time, like Strongbow.

"It's a strange night," Bearclaw said. The firelight played on his features, but it didn't like him and avoided his eyes.

Rain continued, "Are you telling me the humans are moving in the forest and hunting?"

"They're moving," came the chief's verbal shrug, "with fire. But they're not hunting. They're not beating the bushes or tracking or anything."

"Hmm . . ." Rain clasped his hands together as he did when there was nothing to do with them. "Are you sure they aren't just doing one of their night things? Rituals, I mean. After all, Crest just . . . just left the pack—"

"You can say she died. My wolf-friend is dead," Bearclaw snarled. "You don't have to pretend."

"Died . . . maybe they found her."

"When a wolf dies, there's nothing left to find," Bearclaw grumbled. "The pack took care of Crest. Those oversized greengrubs couldn't find her any more than we could."

"Well, then," Rain said, "to answer your question—no."

Bearclaw spat out a few choice expletives—something about the mating preferences of humans—then turned and angled back into the shadows.

Once more alone, Rain simply sighed.

Bearclaw slipped through the maze of hollows, once again embraced by comforting coolness. **Joyleaf.**

Here, beloved, the immediate answer came.

As he slipped into his own hollow, Bearclaw steadied himself with the firm courage in his lifemate's sending. There he found her, a glorious opposite of himself. Her hair was as sunny as his was muddy, as curly as his was shaggy. She was female, entirely. Her blue eyes made his seem hardly eyes at all, but sharp stone lances shooting toward whomever he looked at. And where his was the pale skin of a night creature, Joyleaf's cheeks always held the memory of flowers. He found her in the light of a single lamp, nursing a tiny infant at her breast. He strode up, almost as though to pretend nothing was wrong.

How's our little cubling?

Together they gazed at their newborn son, a thing so tiny that Bearclaw hesitated even to touch him sometimes. The baby was asleep, his tiny mouth working against Joyleaf's breast, a crown of wheat-pale hair already hiding his eyes. His little fists were barely the size of acorns as they pressed his mother's fountain of life.

Joyleaf turned her curled smile up at her lifemate. **What've you done?** she sent. **Have you stolen another human cub and given it to the wolves?**

Her plan worked. Bearclaw hunched slightly and said, "You know I don't really do that anymore. I just like to say I did."

"Then what frightens you?"

He wasn't entirely surprised that she already knew something was amiss. That was part of being thoroughly Recognized. "I don't know yet. The humans are in the forest tonight and I don't know why. Until I do, I want you to go deep into the Father Tree. Go into the rear hollows with Clearbrook so you can get out the back way if you have to."

"It's that bad?" she asked, her mouth straightening into a pink ribbon.

Bearclaw gazed down and felt he could fall into her huge blue eyes, rounder than was usual for elves. He *had* fallen into them once, and never climbed out. "I don't like to take chances. Not with that herd of belches. And they're acting strange as mad bats tonight."

Joyleaf nodded. "All right." She slipped her forefinger between her infant cub's tiny mouth and the skin of her breast, breaking the suction and releasing the cub into Bearclaw's arms. The baby slurped discontentedly, then settled immediately into deeper sleep, smelling the distinct scent

of his father against him. Bearclaw held the impossibly small
bundle between his shoulder and his neck, soaking in the
vibrance of new life, wishing he could continue holding their
cub for the rest of the night. Usually he didn't like to hold
cubs so young, but tonight felt . . . different.

Joyleaf rearranged her clothing, gathered what she needed,
and took the cub back into her own arms. "You should tell
the others," she mentioned as they left their hollow and parted
in two different directions.

"When I know more," he said.

Joyleaf paused at the top of the rise. "Tell them now,
beloved. It's their right to know."

He knew she had him cornered with his own conscience.
He shook his shaggy head and muttered, "Hairballs . . . all
right. I promise."

His lifemate smiled. Finally they parted.

Bearclaw went to the core of the great Father Tree and
filled the holt with his thoughts in a single clarion alarm.

**Wolfriders, hear me! The humans are in the forest to-
night, carrying fire. Stay near the holt. Be prepared for
whatever comes.**

From all over the holt came incorporeal answers—Rain . . .
his daughter Rainsong . . . Treestump . . . Rillfisher . . . Foxfur . . . Clearbrook . . . One-Eye . . . Moonshade . . .
Briar . . . Redmark . . . Amber . . . River . . . Brownberry . . . Longreach . . . and others he didn't wait for.
They'd heard him; that was all that mattered right now. From
all over the vast snarl of trees, above and below, from out in
the forest and down by the pond, members of his band sent
their answers upon the winds of thought and he knew, at least
so far, that they were all safe. Satisfied, he moved up the
root-slope toward the open forest.

And ran headlong into Woodlock, who was panting from
the long run. "Bearclaw," he gasped, "they've changed
direction. They're heading toward the holt."

*   *   *

The beast hunkered down, covering the small bundle of ravvit fur with her warm body, guarding her catch with instinctive slyness. She hid in a thicket now, deep within layer upon layer of viney overgrowth. Twice the fire-claws passed by her, near enough that she smelled the crackling wood and the sweaty bodies carrying them. They were good at silence, these enemies of hers, better than she expected them to be. But then, they were hunter-creatures like herself, and had learned to be silent, lest they miss their kills.

Tonight she would be the kill, unless she lay very . . . very still.

They passed by and moved on, searching for her. She felt her mate in her mind—nearby, but unable to move through the fronds and brushwood lest the enemy notice him. She hunkered even lower, gathering the ravvit bundle close to her silver coat.

When the enemy passed by and was gone, and before more came, her mate slipped through the coppices to join her in the thicket. Around them was a perfect wall of glossy dark-green vines that had grown up around the dead branches of a fallen tree. To one side, the great trunk still lay, decaying and bare, but massive enough to hide them. It was almost hidden itself in the natural predation of other plant life. Its morbid branches curved around them, bent by their own collapse, and created a hideaway. But it was also a prison.

The male beast floated between the vines to his mate's side. His body was blacker than the shadows from which he emerged, bigger than the female's by half. And he was enraged.

From deep in his throat a long growl drew out. When his mate sought him with her snout, he responded with a vicious snap. She recoiled, her head dipping to the moist ground. Only her gray eyes dared approach him.

The male stalked her as if she were prey, coming around to

the side where the chunk of ravvit fur lay half-covered by silver coat. This time it was the female who growled. The two beasts locked eyes in mutual threat. The male's spine arched and gave rise to sharp shoulder blades. His sable fur rose into a crest.

The female backed down with a tiny whimper, but only after her mate moved to her other side, away from the bundle of ravvit skin. They smelled more fire . . . more smoke. Images of fear and threat cluttered their animal minds, and finally the male lowered his thick body down beside his mate's. Their heads dipped down until the ground brushed the undersides of their jaws. Daring not even a quiver, they waited for the fire to pass.

Ever since memory, the Wolfriders had been responsible for every misfortune to befall the humans who shared their forest. Fear and misunderstanding remained the cleft between the two tribes. Somehow Bearclaw knew that, but he was as guilty as the humans. There were times when Joyleaf made him see that. Tonight he saw nothing but the threat. Resentment clawed deeply into his chest as he watched from the treetops while humans and their torches searched for the hidden holt. They knew it was in this direction, but so far they hadn't discovered exactly where. He resented his tribe's having to be accountable for the humans' faulty god, who so poorly cared for his charges, so much so that the humans had come to believe that anything not directly complementing or worshipping him must be demonic.

So the Wolfriders were demons. Bad weather, accidents, ill magic, crop failure, poor hunting—it was all the elves' fault. Born of fear, the danger swelled as he watched.

"Bearclaw, I don't understand. . . ." Woodlock's voice trembled now. He gripped the branch beside Bearclaw and actually had to hold on to steady himself.

We've got to fight them, came Strongbow's opinion,

thoughts so direct they were barely words at all. The archer held his bow over his shoulder like a spear and glared out from beneath the band around his forehead. Over it his russet hair hung untended, some of it reaching lower than his shoulders. Strongbow's philosophy—get things done. **If they find the holt—**

Bearclaw heard the archer's thoughts and gazed hungrily down at the fluttering torches with their amber hazes cast upon the forest's leaves. Who among the Wolfriders had not dreamed of killing the humans once and for all and having the forest to themselves? He couldn't count the times he'd come within a spitfall of declaring war on the tall ones. If Joyleaf hadn't been there to talk him out of it—

Kill the humans, Strongbow wanted. Bearclaw crawled inside that idea and swam around for a while. Felt pretty good, too.

All at once he grumbled out a second truth lying dormant beneath the first. "They don't want the holt. They want something else. And they think we've got it."

"What makes you say that?" Woodlock asked.

"They always think we've got it."

"Got what?"

Bearclaw started to explain, then changed his mind. "Be quiet."

"What are we going to do?" Woodlock persisted, atypically.

Bearclaw opened his mouth to speak, not sure what he was going to say, but never got the chance. Strongbow's sending stopped him.

Fight. What else?

Bearclaw closed his mouth, tipped his head, and gave the archer an annoyed sneer.

Woodlock shifted uncomfortably.

Strongbow twisted his leather wristguards to tighten them, then adjusted the quiver strap across his chest; he would kill to defend the holt. Bearclaw would assemble the elves into a single force, bringing out their best fighters. Moonshade. Treestump. Pike. Longreach. Clearbrook. Foxfur. River. **I'm ready.**

His clear thoughts vanished as Bearclaw uttered words the archer never expected to hear:

"Well, I'm not."

Strongbow stared at his chief.

But Bearclaw wasn't explaining. He simply watched through the night-blackened foliage while fireglow puckered the night. Beneath them, spreading wider and thinner across the depths of the forest, the torches continued their slow search, moving ever nearer to the holt.

After a disturbingly long time, the chief moved down the long branch on which they stood together, peering through the leaves, and said, "Woodlock, I want you to count the humans. I want to know how many—"

Kill smell

Bearclaw wavered suddenly. He caught himself on Strongbow's shoulder and endured a tremor passing through his mind. For an instant he felt himself on the forest floor, hidden in thick overgrowth, wrapped in distress. He put his hand to his head.

Woodlock doubled back to him, coming along the same branch. "Bearclaw?"

Without turning more than his head, Strongbow leaned slightly toward Bearclaw. **You all right?**

Bearclaw closed his eyes. "I think s—"

Blood hunt.

He squeezed his palm against his eyes and pushed his way out of the invasion. He groaned with the effort—but won.

It was over.

He shook himself. With some strain he pulled his hand away from his face and forced his eyes open. "Do you hear anything strange?" he asked.

An eerie shiver went down Woodlock's spine, judging by the way his shoulders hunched slightly. "No . . . do you?"

"Strongbow?"

Nothing. The archer still looked at him, but now his expression was different.

"You didn't send?" Bearclaw asked. This disturbed his friends. Bearclaw didn't ask things twice.

Just told you.

"Someone from the holt?" Woodlock hoped.

Bearclaw struck him with a reproving look and barked, "I know all of you."

Woodlock almost apologized, but frowned instead and moved a few steps down the branch, away from his chief. "We should get out of the tree. If it happens again, you might fall."

"Yes . . ." Bearclaw fought to clear his mind. "Out of the tree."

They didn't have to help him down. He had recovered quite enough to drop steadily into the ferns below by himself, but they did watch him. By the time they were all standing at the base of the tree together, Woodlock was muttering again; it gave him comfort to think things out aloud, even as Strongbow found solace in his perpetual silence. "It could be a trick," the gentle elf suggested. "Maybe the humans have found out how to send and are trying to draw us out."

Bearclaw shook his head. "Those five-fingered stench piles have all the cunning of dry moss. Humans sending— that doesn't make sense."

Who needs sense? Strongbow argued. **We know what they're doing. It's time to respond, Bearclaw.**

"No. Not yet."

Are you saying we're not going to fight? Not going to kill them?

"We'll fight. But killing humans might not be like killing deer. I don't want to go in blind."

I'd go in hacking.

"You would. But you don't have the whole tribe to worry about, and I do."

Woodlock's mouth curled upward on one side. "Good for you," he said. He didn't care what Strongbow thought.

The archer gripped his bow tighter and brandished it threateningly before Bearclaw. **But it's the Way.**

Bearclaw struck him with a look. "Maybe the Way doesn't work all the time. I have to find out *why* they're coming toward the holt."

We're easy prey if we wait. They'll find the Father Tree—

Sharp knuckles crashed across Strongbow's jawline, reeling him backward. Somehow he managed to stay on his feet and brought a trembling hand to his mouth.

"I know that, stinkhole!" Bearclaw hissed. "Think past Now for once! There's something different about this." He paced away, his body taut and twitching, bare arms strung like bowstrings. He spun on Strongbow, his words striking out in a personal attack. "Use your head for something other than a place to put your nose. We can't kill them all, no matter how well we fight. And we'll have to kill every last human once we start. If we don't, they'll come back on us like bad meat and we'll never be done with it. Don't forget how easily they can have more whelps."

They're vulnerable at night, Strongbow shot back. **And they're stupid. They spread themselves too thin. We can kill them now!**

We can't!

Strongbow had to lean forward slightly to brace against the abrupt shock of Bearclaw's sending.

The chief spun around and blasted with molten thought. **This is more than just an attack on the holt, fool!**

"We have to use more than our instincts, Strongbow," Woodlock echoed.

Strongbow lashed out instantly. His nail-hard sending made Woodlock flinch. **Stay out of this!**

Suddenly the archer was wrenched back around by a force more physical than sending could ever be. He found himself face to face with ferocity. Bearclaw's eyes speared at him, looking ultimately wolfen tonight—nothing elfin here anymore. "Leave him alone."

The two elves locked glares and did not look away.

Without blinking, Bearclaw rumbled, "I gave you something to do, Woodlock. Do it."

Woodlock knew he lacked the strength to stand between these two if they were truly determined to challenge each other. With a despondent sigh, he set his lips and melted into the forest.

Bearclaw gritted his teeth at Strongbow. "Are you challenging my authority?"

What if I am? Who says your line must be the only chiefs of the Wolfriders? The rest of us have something to say about it too.

"Oh? Do you? And who would be chief? You? Treestump? Maybe Rain or Woodlock."

Or my lifemate. She's got all your experience and four times your judgment. I spit on your chief-blood.

Bearclaw circled the archer now, prowling around him with a disgusted expression curdling his features. "You do and I'll make you lick it up. You're the one who always wants to follow the Way. Well, the Way says from parent to cub—*my* parent to *my* cub—straight back to Timmorn's blood."

Too bad you don't have Timmorn's brain.

Bearclaw's teeth showed as his lips quivered back in rage. Veins bulged in his arms. Too furious to speak, he sent his feelings directly to Strongbow's mind. **I should kill you for that.**

Strongbow's head snapped sideways, his gaze landing on the mossy ground beside him. **Tonight might mean the deaths of many Wolfriders. Including you.**

They leered at each other with a mutual bitterness so spiny it nearly drew blood. Finally, Bearclaw broke the spell. "Then you can howl over my carcass."

He stalked off the way Woodlock had gone. Behind him, torchlight flickered between the trees.

He was still stalking when Woodlock popped out of the branches, breathing heavily, and gasped, "I counted twice eight of them. And there are more coming from the camp. I'm sure they outnumber us."

Bearclaw thought about it. What Strongbow said made sense. If a chief had said those things, there might never be a chance to think about it; it would already be done. But because the ideas came from a source outside himself, Bearclaw automatically resisted. Yet Strongbow's logic was good. Certainly the humans would spare nothing and no one if they found the holt, no matter what caused the anger. Sixteen or more humans . . .

In his mind, Bearclaw carefully considered his Wolfriders. They could all hunt, of course, but fighting was different. Redmark was the best tracker and he loved the chase, but he usually left the actual kill to someone else, unless he was alone. Clearbrook could fight as well as Bearclaw himself, but she thought she might be with cub and he didn't want to take any chances. Amber was fair with a knife, but she had an infant even younger than Bearclaw's tiny son—the little she-cub called Nightfall. Skywise . . . no. Too young for this kind of thing. Eager, but too young. One-Eye—yes. Now, there was a fighter. Steady, but willing to give in to the killer's instinct at the appropriate second. Strongbow—went without saying. The archer's lifemate, Moonshade, was always dependable, especially if she and Strongbow could fight near each other. Rain . . . no. Rain never participated in the hunt, coming along with the hunting party only to ease the death-pain of an animal who had not died quickly. He would put the thrashing, agonized prey at ease, calming it so that its last moments would not be moments of terror, until the Wolfriders could dispatch it with a single thrust to the brain. Then there was Longreach, as good at amusing the tribe as he was with—

Blood guilt.

Bearclaw staggered. His hands clamped the sides of his head. He plunged sideways into Strongbow, who had followed him through the forest at a slight distance.

"Bearclaw!" Woodlock caught the chief's elbow.

Something was in his mind. Bearclaw knew that for certain now. "Stay back," he choked, wrenching away from the others and stumbling to the center of the clearing.

Dangerous.

Grimacing, his teeth bared again, he forced his hands down and willed himself to relax. Something was trying to overpower him—or contact him. There on the mossy mound in the clearing, he stood still.

Strongbow and Woodlock shared an uncomfortable glance—almost an embarrassed awareness of each other—and immediately looked once again at Bearclaw's back. He turned away from them. They couldn't see his face at all.

Bearclaw no longer fought the invasion. He gave himself to the impassioned sending as it overwhelmed his thoughts and replaced them. He felt nauseated, disoriented. Pictures of carnage flooded his mind—images of mutilation, of blades or teeth chiseling through bone while on the run—panic—splattering flesh—blood.

Were they images of madness? Or intent? —And which was worse?

"There's something out there."

The others stiffened behind him.

Humans?

"Not humans. Something else."

Woodlock unconsciously moved closer to Strongbow. "And it's sending? What could do that?"

Animal?

"One of our wolves?" Woodlock offered.

Bearclaw frowned. "Our wolves don't send like . . . like what I'm getting."

"What are you getting?"

"Images . . . no—feelings. Like the hunt and the kill."

"Something out there means to kill?"

"Or has already," Bearclaw concluded.

Woodlock scanned the forestscape with new apprehension. "And the humans are blaming us . . . Bearclaw, what can we do? Reason with them?"

Invite them home for a game of stones, Strongbow sent on a sting of bitterness.

Woodlock's anxiety made him face the archer boldly now. "But I don't want to die fighting a cause that's not ours! The Wolfriders shouldn't pay for something we didn't do."

Insulted, Strongbow pushed past him and confronted Bearclaw. **What is it? Can you tell?**

The night became a bodiless enemy, its silence like an animal's throaty growl. The three Wolfriders stood alone in its midst. Even Woodlock and Strongbow imagined they felt something—perhaps only because Bearclaw did.

"A bear," the chief murmured, "or a big cat . . . a longtooth—maggots! I don't know. Maybe something we've never seen before. It's out there, hiding or waiting. . . ."

"But how can it be sending?" The tremor came out in Woodlock's words no matter how hard he tried to steady it. He forced himself to unclench his fists, loathing the images of Rainsong's beautiful face crumpled in fear when she learned of this. He longed to have the problem solved and finished before he had to go back to the holt and tell her what was going on. Bearclaw would surely order him home when things got bad—he always did. Woodlock knew he was nothing with a blade and only fair with a bow, but he shuddered at the idea of waiting at the holt to see if death was coming tonight. "If it killed humans, how can we defeat it? And if it hurt them, why would they head toward our trees?"

"Maybe they don't know what it is either," Bearclaw said. "If you were human and you didn't know what animal hurt you, what would you think?"

Woodlock stared at him and tried to put it together. Bearclaw waited, hardly even breathing, forcing his tribe-mate to piece out the problem. It was hard for a Wolfrider to think like a human, to imagine life among the animals and trees while not really a part of them. The humans hid from the night— usually—and they either hunted or feared all the creatures of the forest. Woodlock's task was a strain. Bearclaw continued to wait.

"No . . ." Woodlock's eyes drifted closed. "Our wolves!"

Our wolves? Strongbow hadn't put it together yet, either. **What do you mean? What do the humans want with our—** He stopped suddenly, and nearly choked on his own sending. His eyes glazed with sudden knowledge.

Bearclaw looked at him. "Now you know. And Woodlock's right. We shouldn't pay for another beast's kill. And neither should our wolves. We've got to get the humans off our trail. Woodlock, go back to the holt and tell our pack to move into the hills and stay away for a few days."

"But if we have to fight—"

We can't fight the humans without our wolves!

"Swallow it, Strongbow! We'll fight them on squirrel-back if I say we will. Get going, Woodlock."

"All right . . . Bearclaw?"

"What?"

This time Woodlock's message was sent rather than spoken, excluding Strongbow as he gazed at his chief. **We'll follow you, no matter what happens.**

Touched to calmness, Bearclaw breathed deeply and squeezed Woodlock's shoulder. Then he gestured him off into the woods toward the holt.

He and his archer stood in the core of their home forest, between their holt and the encroaching humans, whose torchfire they could now smell strongly as it wafted through the trees.

"We've got to find the longtooth," Bearclaw said.

First sensible thing you've said all night.

Bearclaw hovered a moment before leading the way in the direction the poignant sending had come from. "Let's hope it's not the last."

The images of fear and hurt and flesh flayed to the bone led Bearclaw unerringly to the area of forest where the beasts lay together in their thicket. As he came nearer, he moved more slowly, trying to piece together more and more of the images as they came to him. They no longer caused him pain, but something was touching the deepmost parts of his being—even his soulname fluttered toward the surface now.

And that frightened him.

Could he be so much beast himself that a longtooth or a demon-beast or something with thoughts so horrible could actually reach his soulname? Joyleaf knew his soulname, as a Recognized lifemate must. And Crest had known it before she died. She had been his wolf for moons uncounted, and when she saved his life during an attack by enraged waterbirds in the far lakes, Bearclaw had given her his soulname in gratitude. It was part of the Way, as Strongbow would have insisted, but it was also a matter of choice.

Now, though, he had no choice. His soulname floated near the beast's sending star at the top of his mind, swimming in and out of the kill-thoughts, ready to jump into one of them and be taken freely by the invader. All at once he had something else to guard besides his holt and his tribe. The barriers to his personal self were being clawed down. Only constantly reminding himself that he was chief and had responsibilities kept him from fleeing in the opposite direction, farther and farther from the distressing thought waves gushing over him now. Behind him, Strongbow was still apparently unaffected. This sending came only to Bearclaw. So close now, he ached to know what beast this was who stirred his soulname and almost caught it.

Before them, still many paces away, lay a giant fallen tree, sheathed in vines. Its plate of roots rose high out of the ground. Evidently some cataclysm of the earth had pushed it out, and it had collapsed, sacrificing itself to the nourishment of other life. Now it hid the source of Bearclaw's shredded perceptions. He stopped. Behind him, Strongbow stopped too.

"There," the chief said quietly. "It's there."

Will it attack?

"If it has to," Bearclaw whispered.

In his mind he saw a blackness that had life—a creature more dark than a bottomless pit, blacker than the starless sky, driven by instinct and yet—more than instinct. It knew the difference between sense and impulse. It had *chosen* to send; he felt that clearly.

We'll have to kill it. Strongbow drew an arrow. **I'll do it.**

"Stay where you are. I haven't decided yet."

What needs deciding? It's the only way we can prove to the humans that we didn't hurt them.

"I'm getting tired of you. Now stay here."

You're not going alone.

"I'll go as I please," the chief snapped, teeth showing. Moment by moment he became more like the images he saw.

He started forward, slowly, but a hand in the crook of his elbow pulled him back. Astonished, he looked to his side and saw the face of embodied determination.

You are not, Strongbow sent, **going alone.**

Mellowed by the disorientation in his mind, Bearclaw let

himself be overcome by Strongbow's willingness to face the unknown at his side. Others would not be so willing, he knew. It was a gift. He would accept it. ''Then, follow.''

He moved once again toward the wall of vines.

The two elves moved carefully, one step at a time, around the huge plate of torn roots, around to the other side where hedgy overgrowth concealed their quarry. Strongbow kept his bow nocked and ready to fire. A longtooth or a bear would attack instantly, without warning. He couldn't be sure of Bearclaw's condition, with all this sending and confusion, but he was sure of himself and kept the arrow leveled over Bearclaw's shoulder.

''I feel pain,'' Bearclaw said, hushed, ''but not body-pain.''

What, then?

''Heart-pain.''

Strongbow resisted the cold shiver that ran down his arms. **Didn't know you had a heart.**

Even in the midst of ''heart-pain,'' Bearclaw smiled his wicked smile.

They stopped abruptly as a faint glow of torch flame washed across the vines before them. The humans were coming closer. Time was sifting away.

The elves froze still and remained still until the torch glow passed. Each of them felt the new urgency—having passed them, the humans were now between them and the holt. If anything was to be done, it must be done soon.

Too soon for Strongbow.

He nudged Bearclaw out of the way and approached the vine hedge quickly, before Bearclaw could shake off the numbness of the beast's sending.

The chief blinked, his concentration broken. To his horror, Bearclaw watched his archer shove through the vines and take aim at a looming shape that rose before them there. He heard the *twang* of the bowstring and a distinct *thud* as the arrow struck not flesh, but the hard ground. Incredible! Strongbow had missed—

Sounds of struggle flashed at him, both into his ears and into his mind through sending. Strongbow was sucked into the vines. The leaves closed up.

"Strongbow!" Bearclaw rushed forward, eyes so wide they burned. He grated to a stop at the vine hedge, gripped by a notion no Wolfrider had had before; the beast sent whole-thought into his mind!

Reversing the course, he sent, **Don't hurt! We can help!**

He barely understood why he would send such a message. Only now did he realize that the rabid sendings had been messages of desperation, not of intention. Help what? Why had he told the beast they would help it? What could Wolfriders. do for a longtooth?

The vines rustled violently, and there was a great gush of breath as Strongbow's form catapulted over the root plate and crashed through dense foliage. Bearclaw drew back his sending star instantly. "Hairballs—!" he swore, and rushed through the leaves, thrashing around until he found Strongbow crumpled beside a stump. Bearclaw shuddered as he lifted the archer to his feet. If Strongbow had fallen a pace farther, the stump's jagged spires would have impaled him.

Strongbow's eyes were squeezed shut in pain. His arms coiled around his ribs. Bearclaw got a good hold of him and dragged him deeper into the woods, away from the fallen tree. He leaned Strongbow against an outcropping of rock and checked for bleeding.

"Look at me," the chief demanded when he could find no cuts—only red tooth marks scoring the archer's rib cage. Bearclaw tore a leaf from a nearby frond and pressed it to Strongbow's ribs. "You all right?"

Strongbow struggled through a brief nod. He leaned heavily against the rock wall and wiped his mouth with the back of his hand, still breathing heavily.

"That was stupid," Bearclaw said.

No stupider . . . than doing nothing. . . .

"You don't know what you're talking about," Bearclaw

told him. "The longtooth doesn't want to kill us *or* the humans. I thought it was sending me dreams of killing, but it wasn't."

They were dreams of flowers, then.

"They were dreams," the chief said firmly, "of fear. There's a difference. They're images of what it thinks the humans will do to it."

Strongbow straightened up with effort, still holding his sore ribs. **And what the humans will do when they reach the holt. Don't forget that. We have to kill the longtooth and put it in front of the humans. They'll find it and leave us alone. It's the only way.**

"There's more than one way!" Bearclaw bellowed. "If the longtooth has killed, then it's entitled to its kill."

Then, what do we do, *great chief*? Offer them *our* home, wolves, and cubs instead?

"Idiot! You're impossible to talk to!"

And you're perfect proof that the blood of chiefs carries no chief's wisdom. You'll never be half the chief your father was.

Bearclaw prepared to rip away Strongbow's thoughts, lips peeling back from white teeth; but something stopped the flood of accusations and tirades that gurgled in his throat. He looked at Strongbow's battered form, saw the concern as well as the challenge in the archer's half-hidden eyes beneath the headband, and shook with the effort of pulling the anger back within himself. He raged so in his mind that even the beast's sending was crowded out.

In a low kind of firmness, he intoned, "You'll say the same thing to my son some day." With a gesture that ended the argument, he stomped a cake of mud from the bottom of his boot and scraped the sole with the long metal knife he called New Moon. He hadn't even realized the blade was drawn. Drawn . . . on Strongbow?

"Come on," he said, and turned back toward the fallen

tree, already thinking about how he would deal with the beast within it.

He was halfway back to the fallen tree before he realized Strongbow was not following. Bearclaw turned to look.

A different being stood there against the rocks. The harshness was gone from the angular face. The archer's arm hung limp at his side now. His eyes were fastened unseeing on the ground.

Bearclaw came slowly back to him. Strongbow didn't move, not even when Bearclaw's eyes, squinting with suspicious concern, peeked into the corner of his vision. The silent question was neither spoken or sent. Bearclaw waited for it to be answered.

Like a brush leaving delicate swipes on a cave wall, the mild sending came—very unlike the usual terse snaps of Strongbow's mind.

I hope I die before I must see your son become chief.

He might as well have shot an arrow into Bearclaw's chest. Bearclaw hated new territory, especially inner ground. He shifted his weight and licked his lips. "What kind of talk is that?"

A tinge of sarcasm mellowed the words.

Strongbow's mouth twitched. No other response.

Bearclaw reached out uncomfortably and took hold of the muscular bow arm, welding the bond. "Come on, soul brother. Let's get back to business before I give you my soulname and embarrass us both."

You know, you could lose your hand.

"I know."

Bearclaw stood flush against the vine hedge. His arm sank deep into the leaves. True—he expected to feel the keen cut of fangs in his flesh, but he steadied himself to the bond between his mind and the beast's, and endured the chance of dismemberment.

Strongbow stood close beside him now, cooperating. The way of violence hadn't worked. He had seen new facets in his chief this night. He would deal with them cleanly and head-on, for he knew nothing else. Bearclaw was still chief.

Strongbow flinched when Bearclaw did—something had rustled deep within the leaves.

Something?

Yes . . . fur. Moist flesh. He's sniffing me.

He?

Definitely.

They waited.

Bearclaw vowed he would allow the hand to be bitten off before he withdrew it from this test. Hot breath puffed against his hand. He closed his eyes, bracing for—

The sending came again. More violence, but this time the violence of the victim. In his mind Bearclaw saw four tiny bundles of fur, torn and bleeding. He had to steady himself against the image of flapping wings and the sickening picture of talons—a predator bird's weapons spread wide and dangled with bits of flesh. He felt the heart-pain once again, as though it was suddenly new. The pictures became clearer and clearer in his mind. The beast had left its den in despair. Now it lurked behind the vine hedge, calling out to what it thought was a kindred spirit.

Teeth closed around his fingers. Knuckle by knuckle, his hand was encased within a huge, wet maw. The jaws closed to press his hand, but never broke the skin. His palm lay against a sopping tongue. The teeth held tightly, testing him. Sweating, he awaited the verdict.

The jaws tightened around his hand, pressing sharp fangs into his skin, separating the tendons between his knuckles. Bearclaw gritted his teeth, determined to tolerate the pain. If this was a challenge he would endure it. Sweat poured down his forehead beneath the shag of bangs and a grunt was forced from his lips as the fangs pressed deeper into his hand.

He waited to feel them pop through the skin and flood the
beast's maw with elf-blood. Then—the pressure eased off.
Bearclaw panted away the pain as his hand started throbbing,
but still refused to retreat. He waited.

It came. A firm tugging. He was being pulled into the
thicket. He resisted only slightly before allowing the vines to
engulf him.

Bearclaw . . .

Don't interfere. I'm all right. Stay there.

The leaves brushed his face, grew thinner, and opened
before him. Though he expected to see a bear or a longtooth,
he really wasn't as surprised as he thought he should be.

A wolf.

Not from the home pack. This one must have come from
very far away indeed to be so unknown here. The wide head
and jaws into which Bearclaw's hand disappeared were black
as obsidian. But the wolf's hide did not shine like obsidian.
The beast was more like a great hole in the night, cut out of
the forest fabric and left empty. Except for its eyes. Bearclaw
almost backed away from the yellow slashes through which
the wolf peered at him. Like two crescents of torchlight, the
eyes looked as though they might be blind. But Bearclaw
knew the wolf could see him—quite clearly.

The animal was massive, hunched over until his head
snaked along the ground, more like a bear than a wolf. He
moved in slow, effective motions, not the quick jolts of a
cornered animal.

Not like the twitching of his mate, who Bearclaw saw with
some surprise as he was drawn into the thicket's core. A
she-wolf lay before him, shivering from nervousness. Evidently she did not trust him as her ghostlike mate did. She
coiled her silver body around a lump of fur. But the fur was
moving. There was something inside. Bearclaw squinted at
it, wishing there was more moonlight.

Something nudged the back of his thigh. The huge male.

Cautiously Bearclaw approached the female and slowly knelt beside her, keeping an eye on those tense jaws. He reached for the lump of fur—

And tumbled backward when the she-wolf snapped at him.

Instantly the big male corralled his mate in a jaw-lock around her throat. He held her down, growling a clear threat if she interfered again. She rolled onto her back in the subservient position, and no longer challenged Bearclaw's right to look at her bundle.

He folded back the layers of ravvit fur.

Bearclaw?

"Strongbow, come here."

The archer pushed his way through the vines, took in the odd sight with a shocked expression and his typical silence, then moved around the edge of the thicket toward Bearclaw. He gave the nearly invisible black wolf an especially wide berth.

Bearclaw was crouching down, looking at something. Strongbow leaned over his shoulder, and inhaled sharply.

What in eight storms is that?

Bearclaw looked up at him. "What do you think it is? She stole it from the humans. Her own cubs were killed by eagles in the mountains. She just wanted to suckle it like Timmain did."

What are we going to do? Will she give it up?

"Would you? She took it. She thinks it's hers." He looked up rather cagily at his archer and added, "It's the Way, you know."

Strongbow inclined his head slightly to his chief. **All right, I know.**

Bearclaw's wily smile twisted his lips. "Get out of the thicket. I'm going to try something. Maybe I can make the shadow-wolf understand."

He stood up, waiting until Strongbow was out of the thicket entirely. Then he moved to stand before the great black beast and concentrated upon a sending star of now-thought.

Minutes passed. The scent of fire drifted ominously back upon them, a constant reminder. Outside the thicket, Strongbow peered through the blood-dark trees to the yellow flashes of firelight moving across the forestland. **Bearclaw, they're getting closer.**

"I know that. Come back in."

Exasperated, Strongbow shoved through the vines again. **Now what?**

He stopped, rocked by what he saw—the shadow-wolf lay across his mate's shivering form. The she-wolf lay complacently beneath him, helpless, almost despondent.

"Get your bow," Bearclaw said. He was standing over the tiny fur bundle which had caused such trouble. He gathered the ravvit fur up carefully and collected the squirming newborn baby into his arms. So much bigger than an elf cub— but still helpless. Bearclaw offhandedly wondered if he would have felt this much for the infant before his own cub was born. Probably not. His cubling's birth had changed him, he grudgingly admitted. He didn't like to have Strongbow see him act so protective of the human whelp, and stood up quickly. "She's giving it back. Let's put it where it belongs before the humans get to the holt. From the direction of the fire-smell, they're almost there."

We're going to the humans' camp?

"One of us is. You do whatever you want."

Bearclaw wrestled the five-fingered baby into a better position against his chest. The infant gurgled and yawned, but its belly was full of warm milk from the she-wolf's aching and swollen teats and it made no complaints as he carried it out of the thicket.

Strongbow—very, *very* cautiously—retrieved his bow from where it had landed jammed between two branches of the fallen tree, and followed his chief through the forest.

The human camp was desolate. Only a single fire burned in a pit at the camp's center, the fire they had used to light the torches. Bearclaw and Strongbow would ordinarily never venture to such a place, but tonight was far from ordinary. Several times Bearclaw stopped short and listened. Strongbow had no idea what he was listening for until the halting sound of sobbing filtered out of one of the caves.

Stay here, Bearclaw sent firmly.

Strongbow didn't have any arguments this time. He dipped into a shadow, watching nervously as Bearclaw took a deep breath, clutched the human infant to his chest, and disappeared into the cave's wide mouth.

Agonizing minutes slogged by. Strongbow dared not even twitch. Bearclaw would have his hide if he interfered. The sobbing inside the cave stopped, then changed pitch—a different message altogether.

Bearclaw slipped out the corner of the cave mouth. Strongbow started breathing again. Bearclaw joined him in his shadow.

She was hardly old enough to *be* a child, much less have one, the chief sent.

Humans multiply like flies, Strongbow responded.

Bearclaw gripped the archer's wrist and turned him toward the woods. **Move along, reckless one.**

The elves were barely within the comforting cloak of trees before a clanging signal rang out through the forest. It was the ringing song of stone against stone, a song the elves heard sometimes in their sleep, when they knew the humans were calling each other, and the Wolfriders would curl up against each other and be glad they roamed at night rather than in the daylight.

Deep within the woodlands, within a few trees of the holt itself, the torchbearers turned suddenly, stared for a moment in disbelief, then ran with their crackling fires back through the forest to their own camp.

The newborn elf cub suckled greedily at the nipple in his tiny mouth, his tongue pressed up around the source of nourishment. It was a peculiar kind of ecstasy, but every infant born to every kind of fur-bearer understood it.

Bearclaw put his arm around Joyleaf's shoulders and together they watched their precious chief-son suckle to his heart's content.

"Are you sure about this?" Bearclaw asked her. "It's you I'm worried about."

Joyleaf's lashes dropped and rose again over her sky-blue eyes and she gazed placidly at her newborn cub. "I learned to share you," she said. "I can learn to share him."

She reached down and scratched the short, pricked-up ears of the she-wolf. The animal lay on her side in the middle of their hollow, nearly entranced with the joy of the tiny mouth at her teat. The warmth within her flowed easily from her heart to the heart of the elfin female.

Bearclaw sensed the invasion of his presence in this feminine art. He touched Joyleaf's face, unable to word his feelings, and slipped out of the hollow, and out of the holt altogether.

It was nearly dawn. The sky glowed with shades of pink from the horizon. A new day. The forest was still dark, and an eternity had passed since sun-goes-down, when the humans first lit their torches. Now the forest snoozed peacefully. The torches had been guttered hours ago.

Bearclaw wandered into the forest. He told himself he was just wandering. But when he stopped wandering, he was at the fallen tree. He moved through the vines, but the thicket was empty. Only the blackness of pre-dawn fell here now.

Immediately he left, and wandered—perhaps foolishly—near the human camp. Something drove him to seal in his own mind the end of the terror. He had to be sure the humans had forgotten their rage.

He watched for a while as gossamer shapes moved about in the pre-dawn haze, gathering kindling for a new campfire, preparing the day's fruits and meats, stretching after the little

bit of sleep they'd managed to get last night. Humans . . .
just acting like humans instead of avengers.

Bearclaw stiffened when he saw something vaguely
familiar—the same woman-shape he'd perceived in the darkness: the girl with the baby. She emerged from the cave,
holding and hugging her newborn child, kissing the rosebud
face and playing with the tiny fingers that gripped her thumb.
After a moment, she handed her child to another woman,
who seemed to love it almost as much.

Bearclaw drew his shoulders in. The girl had held her baby
as Joyleaf held their own cub—a special holding. By the
dawn light, these tall ones were no longer his nightmare, and
with that came a touch of regret.

His eyes narrowed suddenly, acute to movement. His
thoughts dissolved into wolf-time, and he sank back into the
leafy brush.

The girl was walking toward him, toward the woods, her
safe cave-porch left behind. With a piece of soft leather she
was buffing something cradled in one hand.

He drifted deeper into the bushes, and became still.

The leaves and branches around him rustled gently. Her
leather skirt brushed by, near enough to touch. She paused,
less than an arm's length away. Seen through the leaves in
the dimness of new-dawn, she was only a faint outline as she
tugged at young branches and placed something in them.
There was a faint clink of stones, but no other clue. Satisfied,
the girl paused for a moment to gaze thoughtfully at what she
had done, almost as though a decision was not yet completely
made. But then she turned and, without a backward glance,
returned to her encampment.

Bearclaw waited until his heart stopped pounding.

The smell of humans clung to the tree. For the first time in
his long life, Bearclaw was drawn to it.

There, hanging on a stubby branch, was a bit of dawn.
Red-gold amber and green water-polished pebbles reflected

his wry smile. "Toad turds," he muttered. Too bad—he had always enjoyed hating the humans.

His whiskered face twisted into a grin as he tossed a glance toward the retreating human girl. He slipped the necklace over his head. The amber was warm against his skin, the pebbles cool. He would give it to Joyleaf. It would gleam against her neck like the glow of her hair and the shine in her eyes. Yes, Joyleaf should have this gift. Sometimes it is harder to share than to give, and Joyleaf had given the greatest sharing, after all.

Dawn. Time to retreat to the holt.

This time he didn't bother with his usual morning sending that would rouse the tribe from their activities and tell them to retire to the safety of the holt. If they didn't know by now, then too bad. He sauntered along with his private thoughts, rather self-satisfied.

Relief.

He stopped.

Before him, the darkness moved. With his mind, Bearclaw listened.

The ebony wolf lowered its head, and sent.

Renn.

Astonishment tingled through Bearclaw's body. The night beast knew—he *knew*!

The Wolfrider chief's faint trembling suddenly ceased as a glimmer appeared in his own mind and he also knew. The rightness of it overwhelmed him with a deep and intriguing calm.

His eyes grew slim. **Blackfell.**

This time the wolf came to him. As though nodding, its massive head glided close to the ground at the end of the thick arched spine. Crescent eyes glowed, unaffected by dawn light. Bearclaw put his hand out slowly.

Yellow eyes closed as the black beast's muzzle slid under Bearclaw's fingers. The bond was made and it was true, truer than either wolf or elf could yet know. As twin moons faded into the lightening sky, two night creatures melted like shadows into the forest's deep and silent embrace.

Afterword

It occurs to us (the four of us occupying the editor's seat) that an observation may be made by the readers of this volume, to wit: This world is one grim place! The elves seem always to be scrambling for bare existence, Recognition is a pain, and they don't have a lot of fun. In reply, I offer a possible explanation and a ray of hope.

I think that whenever you collect a tribe of very creative people together and turn them loose in a universe not of their own making, they will make their first forays into the territory cautious ones. It's the "don't want to step on any toes" syndrome. There's an awareness on everyone's part that, not only do the characters have to be introduced and fleshed out, there are also conventions to be followed if the internal logic of the land is to be maintained. This doesn't lend itself easily to wild abandon. At first.

However, as I mentioned earlier, I'm getting signs that a certain feisty attitude is beginning to manifest itself among all concerned. The "I'm going to do things with your character that *you* never dreamed of!" gambit. Personally, I can't wait for all the writers to read all the stories, to see what sparks are struck off into the tinder of volume two. This volume deals in large part with the struggle for survival. The next one, I'm going to suggest, ought to concern itself with the other side of the coin: the many and varied pleasures to be found out of life. The discussions promise to be . . . interesting.